Beneath the Palisade

Reliance

Joel Skelton

Dreamspinner Press

Published by
Dreamspinner Press
382 NE 191st Street #88329
Miami, FL 33179-3899, USA
http://www.dreamspinnerpress.com/

Beneath the Palisade: Reliance

Cover Art by Catt Ford

ISBN: 978-1-61372-403-3

Printed in the United States of America
First Edition
March 2012

eBook edition available
eBook ISBN: 978-1-61372-404-0

This book is dedicated to young Martin Andrews, who somehow found the courage to ask the love of his life, handsome Calvin Medford, to his senior prom. This book is also dedicated to Martin's parents, Joyce and Ken, who thought nothing of it.

I WOULD like to thank Willie Larson and the helpful staff of Hennepin County Medical Center for the wonderful input and advice I received. HCMC rocks!

Thanks to Kristopher Krentz (aka Str8 Cat) for his insightful scene input and character embellishment.

Mucho thanks to my eagle-eyed beta readers: Ann Hinnenkamp, James (aka Pearle) Gunderson, and Jennifer Hutchins—their helpful notes and suggestions were invaluable.

A special thank you to Jennifer Hutchins, who tackled the bulk of the research for this book. It was a collaboration I will cherish forever.

A hug to my partner, Patrick (aka "P") for extending the leash. You are and always will be the sparkle in my life.

CHAPTER

One

"ACTION!"

Why the hell did I ever let myself get talked into this?

Looking into the warm spring morning sunlight, Ian Burke sucked in a deep breath and pushed the flatbed cart down the narrow asphalt path toward his mark, a small square of silver duct tape.

"Cut!"

"Are you kiddin' me? Whattaya mean, cut? I was just startin' out." Frustrated, he looked over to Andy, his director, for an explanation. "I mean, come on, give me a break."

"You have to be aware of your body language at all times, Ian." Andy took his directing responsibility seriously. "You look like you're just going through the motions. Smile, look enthused, and don't be afraid to shake your booty as you head toward your mark. Remember, women and gay dudes are your audience. They garden."

Andy, his best friend dating back to grade school, owned the South Minneapolis garden center Jungle Gems providing the backdrop for the commercial they were shooting. Ian was, for all practical purposes, Andy's business partner. While Andy concentrated on the day-to-day operations, Ian focused on the landscaping end of the business. Over the last few years, Ian's workload had steadily grown, to the point where it was now possible for him to branch out and form his own company, Burke Landscaping.

"You want to generate business, right?" Andy paused, forcing Ian to cough up his "you're right" look. "Trust me, the perfect arborvitae ain't gonna do it. You have a hot ass, so use it. Doesn't he have a hot ass, Spencer?"

"Your ass is so hot it makes me want to be gay, dude. I mean, if I could go there, your ass would be the reason. Totally, I wouldn't just say it if it wasn't the truth. Allison commented on your ass the other day when she was helping me pick out jeans. 'I think these make your butt look hot like Ian's.' That's exactly what she said to me."

Ian rolled his eyes and shook his head. Spencer, a friend he and Andy had both known for years playing baseball together, was their official, highly enthusiastic straight ambassador for all things related to, as Spencer loved to refer to gays, "your people." An ex-film school student, Spencer eagerly offered his retired camera skills.

What a couple of tools.

Joking aside, he felt blessed. Andy and Spencer wanted nothing more than for his newly launched landscaping business to succeed.

"Action!" Andy shouted after he had returned to his mark. "Lookin' good. Good… good… don't rush. Remember you're looking for the perfect one," he instructed. "Hey, I caught that little butt wiggle. Sweet. Did you catch that, Spencer?"

"Took my breath away, dude. Seriously."

Ian glanced to the right as he inched forward, shaking his head, careful to show what he hoped would be the right amount of disappointment on his face.

Oh no, that one won't do at all. Nope.

"That's perfect, Ian. Yes! Look forward now, you're almost there. There it is! You see it, the perfect one. Show us you see the perfect one."

Well looky there, it's the perfect one.

This was a good take. He felt confident and in control. An element of frustration along with a strong desire to get this whole thing over with fueled his need to nail this. As he approached his mark, he looked to the left, pushed the cart slightly past the mark, and stopped.

"Perfect. Remember, hands on hips and then flash that smile," Andy encouraged.

As instructed, he planted his hands on his hips, smiled, reached down, and hauled up a flawless three-foot spiral arborvitae, placing it on the center of the cart. Displaying the required look of satisfaction he'd struggled with in earlier takes, he pushed his prize shrub past the mark to the end of the row.

"Cut! That's a keeper," Andy chimed.

SEATED in a plush embroidered club chair, Harper Callahan, fresh from his workout at the Y, looked over the low cocktail table and listened. Careful not to display any sign of distaste, he reached for his wineglass and sipped. Confident his face displayed both interest and approval and certain it would be some time before he'd be required to respond, he allowed himself to step out of the conversation.

He was being set up. Before he'd ever sat down in the bar of this ridiculously expensive steakhouse, he had seen the writing on the wall. Along with named partners Duncan Price and Arthur Wabash of McPherson, Price & Wabash, he had worked diligently over the last year to defend Jasper Flynn, the mastermind of one of the most extensive and ugly Ponzi schemes to ever rock the state. Despite their efforts, Jasper had been convicted, and due to the severity of his crime, he was refused bail and jailed on the spot. *We did what we could for you, Jasper.*

With plenty of loose ends to clean up on the case, including an appeal likely to go nowhere, he surveyed the room while he waited for Arthur and Duncan to get around to the point of today's impromptu meeting.

A few tables down, he recognized a guy he'd gone to law school with. The man was surrounded by other men his age. They were laughing and enjoying themselves. He needed to start enjoying himself. How effortlessly he'd cast aside one of his grandfather's most important lessons—there's more to life than work. With his thirtieth birthday now history, it was time to reevaluate his priorities.

He had to admit, for the most part, he enjoyed his work. He found the Jasper case fascinating in its scope. The son of a soda distributer had parlayed a business degree from a small local college into arguably the region's most prestigious brokerage. Caught in the make-it-up-as-you-go investment environment of the last couple of years that had almost brought the entire nation to its knees, fearless in his desire to both please his clients and pad his wealth, Jasper had falsified his investment prowess to a level that garnered national attention. He admitted that during a period of roughly two years, he'd schemed to defraud people by purportedly selling investments in a foreign currency trading program.

Harper glanced back to the table where his classmate sat. The guy's name escaped him. He was handsome. The years had been kind. Harper looked over long enough to spot the wedding ring on his hand. *You've found the balance, my friend, haven't you?* He probably worked at a vibrant, progressive firm where he felt appreciated and, at the end of the day, came home to a loving spouse and maybe a few adoring kids to keep life lively.

Love—the concept of loving and being loved—had inched up the ladder of priorities recently. He vowed then and there to start hunting for his own special someone.

"Let's cut to the chase, Harp, my boy."

He was brought back to the moment upon hearing his name. He hated that both Duncan and Arthur had gotten in the habit of calling him "Harp." He took it as a sign of disrespect, which it probably was.

"Neither Arthur nor I are ones to beat around the bush." Duncan leaned forward in his chair. "If you've learned one thing in the six years you've been with us, it has to be that."

"What's on your mind, Duncan?" He could see the bus a mile away.

"We put up a strong fight on Jasper's behalf. Despite the outcome, we should be proud of our efforts. But unfortunately, we're not done with this mess. I promised Jasper, and I'm a man of my word, that we would do everything in our power to make sure Phyllis stays on the good side of the law."

We'd like you to stay focused on Phyllis. Come on, say it. I'm waiting.

"We'd like you to stay focused on Phyllis. Arthur and I will continue to work up the appeal. Harp, she's going to be a handful no matter how she's approached, but we think someone with your talent would stand the best chance of keeping her in check. She's walking a fine line, and I have absolutely no confidence we're going to be able to keep her out of prison. And that's fine as long as we can demonstrate to Jasper that we tried. You tried," Duncan corrected himself, shifting in his chair.

"It's what we think is best." Arthur had a habit of adding an unnecessary comment to, if nothing else, prove to the group he was paying attention.

Well, if it's best for you, then as the rule goes, it's gotta suck for me. It's gotta suck for me because you creeps have me by the balls with my partnership so close. I'll make partner, and when I do, I won't be doing this dog and pony shit anymore.

Harper sipped his wine and smiled. "Gentlemen, don't you think I already knew what you were going to tell me? Come on now, what kind of lawyer would I be if I was blindsided by my own teammates?"

Arthur and Duncan reached for their wine at the same time, nodding their heads and chuckling at his frankness.

"I get the situation you're in. I got it from the start. I'm surprised it's taken you this long to bring it up." He held his gaze on the partners, forcing them to look away. "Of course I'll do it. I'll be the face of the firm, take a hit for the team."

Arthur and Duncan laughed with relief, winking back and forth to acknowledge the fact that they'd hired on a winner. They'd signed on a star, a yes man, a dutiful slave to the partnership who would wipe their asses if called upon, or so they thought.

It took every ounce of concentration he had not to laugh. Keeping the ball in their court, he took another sip of the seventy-five-buck chuck they served up in this stuffy monument to corporate excess, and smiled.

"Harp, you make this so easy for us." Arthur nodded with relief.

"Arthur, look. I can't imagine the partners publically going to bat for this... bitch." Jasper was bad enough, but his wife had a zero balance in the old sympathy bank. "I'm young, I have, knock on wood, a long career ahead of me. It only makes sense that I go in there and fight a losing battle. Did you honestly think I would have a problem with that? Arthur, I mean come on. Duncan, my God, you didn't think that, did you?"

"Well...." Duncan visibly struggled to find the right response.

"Well…," Arthur echoed, finding himself in a similar situation. "I… we… knew you were the best man for this job. We've always been able to rely on you."

"Arthur, you know I love you both. You took a babe here and turned him into a lawyer. Wait, not just any lawyer, but a pretty good lawyer, eh?"

The partners were giddy with relief.

"This is a temporary speed bump in your career, Harp." Duncan raised his glass for emphasis. "A year from now or sooner, it will all be forgotten, and poor Phyllis…"

Arthur and Duncan both shook their heads in unison.

"…will be pushing the library cart down the prison cell block." There was no soft spot in Duncan's heart for Phyllis Flynn.

"Oh for Christ's sake, Harp, I wish I'd had your intuition and drive when I was your age." Arthur came to life now that he and Duncan had achieved their goal. "We were impressed with your work from day one. Listen, there's something else we need to talk about here."

Harper smiled, sipped his wine, and leaned back in his chair.

You're smiling and happy because you've pulled the strings and made your puppet dance. Here comes that faux-father face you probably perfected on your own kids.

"Harp, to show our appreciation for… well, for being a team player, Duncan and I would like you to know that we've begun the process to make you a partner. Once Jasper is sentenced and we're free and clear of Phyllis, the three of us will regroup and carry on. There's plenty of profitable law out there for the taking."

"ALLISON, you want another chardonnay, sugar?" Ian asked, racing around his tiny kitchen.

"Yes, please."

"How's everyone else doin' in there? The popcorn is almost ready."

"We're good. Get in here, Ian. Three minutes and counting," Andy shouted.

He hustled, emptying the popcorn maker into a large purple plastic bowl. He grabbed the half-empty bottle of chardonnay from the fridge and snagged a bottle of beer for himself.

"Okay." He plopped down on the couch between Andy and Allison. "This is so exciting. I can't believe we get to see the commercial in prime time. I thought the only time slots I could afford on my budget would be in the middle of the night."

"My friend Stewart at the station pulled a few strings. You probably won't get too many of these, but I know he's doing what he can." Spencer, who elected to sit on the floor inches from the television, was obviously proud he could make something happen for Ian. Spencer and his wife, Allison, were the kind of friends that, over time, became family. Ian felt blessed to have such a caring and fun inner circle to call his own.

"Back to Mobile Home Makeovers after a word from our sponsors."

"What?" Spencer asked defensively to a room full of giggles before scooping a mountain of popcorn into his hand. "I never said we had a spot on *60 Minutes*."

"It's cool." Ian leaned back, using Andy as a pillow.

"It's show time!" Andy shoved him back to the center of the sofa.

"Shut up and listen!" Allison ordered.

The group gathered in his small living room sat glued to the thirty-six-inch flatscreen, barely able to breathe in anticipation. The television blinked, blinked again, and then the lofty strains of Copland's "Appalachian Spring" filled the room.

"Spring is just around the corner. Now's the time to make those plans to finally have the backyard paradise you've been dreaming about. Burke Landscaping can make all of your lawn and garden dreams come true."

"Oh my God!" Ian squealed. "I love it. It's me. It's me. It's—"

Andy silenced him with a slap on the head.

Ian, along with his posse, watched with silly grins as he pushed his cart toward that perfect shrub.

"Cute butt, hon."

"Thanks, Allison."

"Here's my favorite part." Andy struggled to suppress giggles. "Look at Ian's face when he sets that frickin' shrub down on the cart. The satisfaction, it kills me every time I see it."

"You're vile," Ian said, unable to mask his delight at being ribbed for something that really was funny.

"Buddy, I'm sorry. It's just so funny to see—"

"*Shut up!*" Spencer inched even closer to the screen.

"*Here at Burke Landscaping, we treat each project, each yard as if it were our own. Burke Landscaping—Professionals who care.*"

"Woohoo! That was awesome!" Spencer jumped to his feet and went right into his self-proclaimed happy dance, a strange mix of agitated body movements he did whenever he was feeling happy.

"Yeehaw!" Ian leaped to his feet, clapping wildly. "That was totally awesome! Wow! I can't thank you guys enough for making this happen for me."

High fives were exchanged all around.

"Allison, the voiceover text, it was perfect. Classy and professional." He planted a kiss on her cheek.

"You're welcome, honey."

"Andy, and this is serious, that's the first time I've heard your voice and didn't think to myself, who's the broad with the stuffy nose?"

"Shut up, you bitch!" Andy pulled him down on the couch and smothered him with tickles and sloppy smooches. When he was able to free himself, he scurried over to Spencer, giving him a hug. "If this ends up making me serious money, I'm sending you back to film school. Thank you!"

"Ian, have you mentioned to Spencer what we were talking about?" Andy raised an eyebrow for emphasis.

"Ummm… not yet."

"What? What are you two homos up to?" Spencer displayed genuine concern. "It's never good. I can't believe you're both so mean to me, and after all the good I do for your people."

"It's nothing bad, Straight Cat," Ian said, patting Spencer on the shoulder to reassure him they were on the level. "Andy and I think you should be the team captain this season. I know you'll have the support if you throw your hat into the ring. Dude, before you say no, consider another entire season of having to listen to Snotty Scotty."

"Oh man, I don't know. Allison, what do you think?"

Ian held his breath. Spencer wouldn't dream of making this decision without consulting his wife.

"I'm Switzerland, honey. I'm not getting involved in this one. Besides, captain or not, I'll still lose you two nights a week."

"Dude, I had no idea your wife was so bitter about baseball," Andy whispered, with no intention of keeping his comment a secret.

"Careful, you never want to come between a bitch and her man." Allison showed her claws.

"I know that's the truth." Andy batted away a French-manicured claw.

"Come on, dude," Ian pleaded. "Andy and I will help you with the paperwork and the organizing. We can't go another season of ball with Snotty Scotty bitching at us. Free blow jobs for a year… huh… huh? Whattaya say?"

"Hey, I like that offer," Allison said with an exaggerated sigh of relief. "My jaw gets really tired, and if push comes to shove, I'd have to admit it's not my favorite thing in the world."

"Thanks for sharing that little tidbit, honey." The forlorn look on Spencer's face sent everyone into hysterics. "Listen up, you two… I'll do it."

"Yes!" Andy shouted.

"I'll do it because I can't listen to Snotty Scotty for another season either. But the blow job offer—thanks but no thanks. Neither of your lips are getting anywhere close to Elvis, got it?" Spencer took a step behind Allison for protection.

"Got it!" Ian and Andy cheered, bumping knuckles.

"My jaw gets tired too." Andy looked over to Allison.

"Not mine," Ian said proudly. "I could go all night."

"On that note—" Spencer chugged down the last of his beer. "—time to hit the road, my dear. We have twenty minutes to get home before blow job time. You can limber up in the car."

HARPER stared down at his notes. He'd spent the better part of the evening reviewing the law surrounding the court order freezing all of Jasper's assets. Specifically, he needed to become very familiar with the role of the court-appointed receiver in order to head off any potential violations Phyllis might be entertaining.

Maybe I should just cut off my dick. It would be so much easier than baby-sitting Phyllis.

Phyllis was a nutjob. And because he'd agreed to it, she was his nutjob. Lately she'd been showing up at the firm unannounced, demanding either Arthur or Duncan—or both—detail for her how she was going to maintain the lavish lifestyle that obviously meant more to her than her husband, Jasper. Phyllis had good reason to be concerned. No matter what he did to try and prevent it, she would likely lose every penny she'd ever set an eye on and millions of dollars' worth of possessions, including homes, jewelry, and most damaging, her exalted position as one of the grand dames in the city's cutthroat society game. From champagne to the food pantry. He was unable to muster up even the smallest amount of compassion for Phyllis.

You're a bitch, and you deserve what you have coming. Oh God, what time is it?

Looking down at his watch, he was surprised to see it was already past one in the morning. He'd been at this long enough. Hungry, he walked into the kitchen and poured out a bowl of cereal. After sprinkling it with sugar and adding milk, he headed into the living room, snapped on the television, and sat on the sofa. As he was about to enjoy his first bite, his cell phone rang.

Who could be calling me at this hour?

Setting his bowl down, he sprinted into the dining room.

"Harper Callahan."

"This is Phyllis Flynn."

You've got to be kidding me. How scary is this?

He leaned on the dining room table, more than a little freaked out at Phyllis's timing.

This woman has to be whacked. How did she get my cell phone number? Oh, that's an easy one. Arthur. Of course, you prick.

"Phyllis, it's very late. Is everything okay?"

"Of course it's not okay. Do you honestly think I'd go around calling people at one in the morning if life was okay?"

The bitch has a point.

"No… no… of course not. What can I do for you?"

"You can make goddamn sure I stay in this house. That's what you can do for me."

He wasn't sure how to respond. Hadn't Arthur and Duncan set some expectations for her? Did she honestly believe there was a chance of that happening?

"Phyllis… of course… I'll do the best job I can for you. Please believe that."

"Don't think I don't know what Arthur and Duncan are doing. I'm not stupid, you know."

"Excuse me? I'm not sure I know what you're talking about."

It was true. He didn't have a clue what she was talking about.

"How old are you?"

"Thirty."

"Exactly. You're a pup. My future is in the hands of a goddamned kid. You don't think there's anything about that upsetting to me?"

"Phyllis, please be assured—"

"It's Mrs. Flynn to you, and don't you *ever* forget it."

Oh God. I don't think I can do this. I don't think I can—

"You there?"

"I'm here… Mrs. Flynn."

"Know one thing, you… you little bastard. If I end up losing this house, you're going to have to answer to me. Trust me, you don't ever want to find yourself in that position."

"Mrs. Flynn, are you threatening me?"

He had had enough. There was a difference between finessing a difficult client and dealing with a wing nut. Phyllis Flynn was out of control. If he got anything through to her tonight, it had to be that he was not, and never would be, frightened of or threatened by her.

She'll be cleaning toilets this time next year, if she's lucky.

"I keep my house and my bank account, Mr. Callahan. That's the only option you'd better be entertaining. Sleep well. I'm sure you're busy."

Click.

"Good night, Phyllis."

Well, that was two tons of fun.

He padded into the living room a wreck. His head was pounding. He gulped down a spoonful of cereal. It was mushy. He couldn't eat mushy cereal. Returning the dish to the kitchen, he dumped it into the sink and ran the disposal. Phyllis Flynn had robbed him of his appetite. And despite her gracious blessing of sleep, he knew right now it would be impossible. Pouring a glass of milk, he headed back to the sofa. Why bother with the bed at this point?

He was ready to take one for the firm, but this Phyllis crap was inexcusable. Partnership or not, he was going to have some words with Arthur and Duncan when he got to the office. Glancing at his watch, he wiped the perspiration off his forehead and realized he was due at the firm for a meeting in six hours. Studying during law school had taught him not only the fundamentals of being a lawyer, but how to function on little to no sleep—a valuable component to being a successful lawyer curiously absent from the curriculum.

Are you looking for sexy single guys and girls like these? Pick up the phone and call the number on the screen. Real single women and men waiting to speak to you, so what are you waiting for?

Harper stared at the television in despair. This piece of crap ad was directed at losers like him. *This isn't working out so good, is it, Harp?* Alone and tired, he couldn't escape the hopelessness of it all.

Watching this deplorable commercial made him sink into the depths of depression.

It's live, one on one, and discrrrreeeeet! So what are ya waiting for? Pick up the phone and call—now!

Harper downed his milk and laid his head on the sofa pillow. There wasn't much about his life right now he liked. Socially, he was dead. Friends he'd made in law school had long since given up on him. You can't continually ignore invitations and expect people to keep including you. For the last several years, the firm had been his friend. *What a fucking mistake I've made.* A feeling of emptiness nagged him as he stretched his long legs over the arm of the sofa. Chancing a glance back to the television, he watched a handsome dude push a cart down a pathway lined with shrubs.

A landscaping commercial. Really? At this hour? Damn! There's another thing that's fallen through the cracks since I got chained to the Flynn case—my crappy yard. I can't go through another summer with a crappy backyard.

He had lived in his house for three years. It had taken him two years for him to come up with an idea for the small inner-city yard that he liked. He knew he wanted a water feature. The bigger the better. He wanted a nice grilling area, and plants. Plants that looked great all the time with little to no effort.

You've just discovered your reward for having to deal with Phyllis. Do the backyard.

If he was going to start entertaining people—well, dating, if he was honest with himself, he wanted a nice yard to bring someone back to.

"... here at Burke Landscaping, we treat each project, each yard as if it were our own. Burke Landscaping—Professionals who care!"

Cute butt. Ah, don't kid yourself, Harp. He's probably some model who hasn't seen a spade in his life.

Still, all it took was a phone call to get the ball in motion. Harper got up from the couch and went back to the dining room. Packing up for the office, he scribbled "Burke Landscaping" on his notepad and went back to the couch for a few hours of sleep.

CHAPTER

TWO

"… SO IF you could bring in two dozen of those globe yews from Fredrickson's, that should just about do it for the Highland Park job."

Ian, seated in Andy's cluttered back office, looked over his list. He had just completed the week's "product review." He loved to call it product review because it sounded important. It had become a Monday morning ritual for the two friends.

"Just a second," Andy grumbled, annoyed by something he spotted through the one-way mirror he'd recently had installed. A self-proclaimed control freak, Andy needed a way to monitor what was going on in the front of the store while he sat in the cramped little office doing paperwork.

Ian glanced over his shoulder and followed Andy out of the office into an adjacent break room.

"Emmett, what the hell are you doing?" Andy scolded. "There's a woman standing by the counter waiting patiently for someone to help her. If I'm not mistaken, that someone she's waiting for would be you. So get off the frickin' phone and get your butt out there. Pronto!"

"Sorry, Andy! I'm on my way," a mousy voice replied. "Trevor, I have to run. Oh… I love you way, way more. I'll call you in a few minutes."

"*No he won't, Trevor!*" Andy bellowed. "He'll be dropping by because he doesn't have a frickin' job any longer." Andy plopped down in his desk chair. "Dammit! Combine young love with lazy and you've got yourself a whole pile of trouble. Sorry, Ian, where were we? Oh… right, the globe yews. Twenty-four, did you say?"

"Yep. And that... should do it. Want me to pick you up for practice?" Ian asked.

"Sure. Speaking of, Straight Cat called me this morning in a tizzy. He's having second thoughts about being captain."

"I knew that was going to happen." He thought for a moment. "I'll tell you what, I'll call and offer to pick him up too. We can work him over on the way to the field. He'll do it. Spencer has his drama requirements like anyone—"

Ian was interrupted by Lady Gaga blaring from his pocket. "Hang on, this is probably him." He spoke into the phone. "Burke Landscaping, this is Ian." He and Andy locked eyes as he listened to the caller.

"Well, the best thing would be for me to come over and take a look. We can discuss your ideas, and I can throw out some figures. Ballpark it, you know." Ian winked at Andy and then covered the phone and mouthed with excitement, "It's a new client."

"Ask him how they found you?"

"Huh?" He didn't have a clue what Andy was talking about.

"Are they calling you because they saw your television spot? Hello!" Andy shook his head and rolled his eyes in frustration.

"I need a piece of paper... and a pen. Hurry," Ian hissed out the side of his mouth while he dashed around the desk.

"Here," Andy said, producing both. "Ask them!"

"Yes, 5204 Benton. I know right where it is." He scribbled down the address. "Well, how about later this evening? I have baseball practice. How about seven thirty? There should still be enough light to get a good look around."

Ian nodded while he listened. "Great! Thanks so much." He was interrupted by a sharp punch to his shoulder.

"Oh, if you don't mind, may I ask how you found me?" He looked over to Andy, crossed his eyes, and then wagged his tongue in hopes of getting his friend to lighten up.

"Thanks. Thanks, the commercial is new. The television," he whispered over to Andy, jumping up and down.

"Right! See you tonight." He stared at his phone. "Incredible! He caught the commercial last night."

"I would never have guessed. Hey, what did I tell you? And you didn't think this was going to work." Andy was never shy about taking credit where credit was due.

Up until producing the commercial, all of his jobs had come through Andy. Customers would come into the garden center looking for product and oftentimes lament they didn't have the time or the knowhow to tackle a landscaping project. At that point Andy would suggest Ian, and they'd be set. It was a good working relationship, but unfortunately it didn't happen enough. It appeared the commercial was going to be his solution to that.

Bring it on!

"ONE in the morning?" Duncan appeared surprised. He walked over and poured a glass of water from a pitcher placed by his thoughtful secretary Gladys prior to the beginning of their meeting.

"And not only was it one in the morning, Duncan." Harper followed the partner around the table to make sure he emphasized that Phyllis Flynn calling him wasn't part of the "under the bus" deal he'd agreed to. "She threatened me. Her tone was threatening."

"Phyllis is a pushy old broad, and she's probably crazy on some level," Duncan offered, sitting down at the head of the long conference table, the leather chair conforming to his huge, familiar ass like they were the best of friends. "But she's harmless. I've known her for decades. Harp, she's losing her money machine. Can you imagine? She's desperate. For her sake, I hope something's been stashed away so she doesn't end up selling magazine subscriptions over the phone. Lord knows she hasn't an ounce of talent or skill to do anything else. Prison might be her best bet." Duncan sipped his water. "You're going to charm the knickers right off her, Harp. She's not going to know what hit her."

Duncan, you have no idea how much I want to kick your patronizing, fat ass.

"I've got a lot to think about here, Duncan. I'm not complaining about the work involved with the case. That I can handle. I can't handle some lunatic wife calling me at all hours and treating me like crap."

"Harp, honestly, is Phyllis really *that* difficult?"

"Duncan…." Harper sat in the chair next to him. The leather was neither familiar nor welcoming. "Glad to know I can contribute, but this bitch is out of control."

"If she continues this bothersome behavior, you and I will work together to get her in line."

This wasn't the response he'd been hoping for. After all, he was doing them a favor by agreeing to baby-sit this wretched woman, so the least Duncan could do was bat her back down. "I'm going to hold you to that, Duncan."

"You have my word. Now shall we get on with the meeting?"

Why don't I just walk out the door and never look back. I mean, really, what do I have to lose?

Understanding their Phyllis discussion had come to an end, he got up and opened the door. Gladys Crumley, Duncan's secretary, and Brent Burns, Harper's assistant, were waiting outside for the meeting to start. They shuffled in and took their seats.

"Okay! Thirteen days and counting," Duncan proclaimed, clapping his hands together. "Harper, why don't you bring us up to date."

Sure! I'll call you at the country club if we need your help.

Reading off his notes, he went over the events and loose ends needing attention before Jasper's sentencing. Jasper had been convicted on one count of tax evasion and one count of mail fraud. Combined, he was facing up to twenty-five years in prison. During plea negotiations, Jasper had agreed to help the government locate and return assets to the victims. Had he refused to cooperate, the sentencing guidelines would have called for a sentence of between twenty-seven and thirty-three years. Having already celebrated his seventy-third birthday in the clink, there was no doubt in anyone's mind he would spend the rest of his life incarcerated. Less fascinating but more problematic to the partners as they had begun to prepare Jasper's appeal dangled his ruthless and conniving wife, Phyllis.

"Brent, while Gladys will be helping Duncan and Arthur put together an appeal, unfortunately—" He glanced over to Duncan to make sure it was fully understood. He was doing him and Arthur a hell of a favor by taking Phyllis off of their hands. "—you and I will be focusing on Phyllis Flynn. However, I'll be representing Jasper at the sentencing, and I'd like you to be there with me in case anything unexpected comes up."

"Sure thing, Harper." Brent was unable to hide his enthusiasm at the prospect of having a front row seat to one of the most anticipated legal events the area had seen in a long time.

Harper enjoyed working with Brent. His assistant was bright and efficient. When possible, he did whatever he could to make Brent's job more meaningful and interesting.

"Duncan, I know you and Arthur will be making periodic visits to hold Jasper's hand. As part of my strategy to manage Phyllis, I might use Jasper as an instrument of communication back to his wife. At the very least, it will show him we are doing what we can for her. So let's keep each other abreast of our visitation plans."

"Arthur and I have discussed involving Jasper in the appeal process as a method of providing what we think will be some much-needed distraction to his upcoming sentencing, but an appeal is technical—he wouldn't be of much help to us. I like your idea of including him in your efforts to corral Phyllis." Duncan looked down at his watch.

Are we keeping you from something, Dunc?

"I'll put together a schedule, run it past Arthur, and have Gladys communicate it to Brent," Duncan added with a slight hint of impatience.

"That would be helpful," Harper said, looking around the room. "Anyone else have anything?" His inquiry was met with silence. "Okay, that's it for now. Thank you."

Gladys and Brent filed out of the conference room. "Can you think of anything I'm forgetting?" He looked to the partner for a response.

"Not a thing! You're on top of it as always, Harp."

If you only knew how little that means to me.

"I THINK Snotty Scotty was relieved Spencer volunteered to take over for him. Didn't he look relieved?" Ian squinted to make out the house numbers as he navigated his truck down the quiet suburban street. "Hey, I have to go. I'm here. Wish me luck on my first television gig."

"Luck!" Andy said before adding, "Call me tomorrow and let me know how it went. Or stop by the garden center, and maybe we can grab a burger or something over lunch."

"Will do. Later, dude."

He pulled his truck over to the curb and parked in front of a handsome Tudor on the corner of the block. *The corner is a plus,* he thought as he hopped out of the truck with a clipboard in his hand.

The yard looks well maintained. Those old pines framing the door should go. There's no way they can be pruned back to a decent shape after so many years of neglect. Too leggy. He mentioned the backyard. I wonder if the client is up for making some changes to the front? Sell him on the idea. It's cheaper to do it all at the same time.

He stepped up and rang the doorbell. A small side window ran the length of the door. Ian snuck a quick glance, but it was too dark inside for him to see anything.

It's probably unprofessional of me to show up in my uniform. But hey, I'm accommodating the client here. He waited patiently. A kid on a bicycle went whizzing past. *Wish I could afford to own something this close to the parkway.*

Growing impatient, he rang the bell again. Seconds later he heard footsteps approaching and the door being unlocked.

"Burke Landscaping, right?" asked a masculine voice.

Ian couldn't be sure, but it was entirely possible he gasped when the handsome face appeared from around the door. Deep, dark eyes, short black hair, the chiseled chin—he stood only a few feet from one of the most attractive men he'd ever come in contact with.

"You're the guy from Burke Landscaping, right?"

"Ah… yeah, I'm Ian Burke."

"I thought so. You said you'd be coming from practice, so… well, the uniform, I just figured you were the guy. I'm Harper, Harper Callahan." The handsome man stepped further onto the stoop, extending his hand, letting the screen door shut behind him. "Thanks for stopping by tonight."

Ian shook hands. "Right. I mentioned I'd be coming over from baseball." Ian was careful not to give any visible sign the man's firm grip had left him weak. *Landing on my knees right now would so send the wrong message.*

"Why don't you follow the walk around to the back. I'll throw some shoes on and meet you there."

"Great!" Ian knew it was best to let the goofy smile on his face blossom and fade away on its own. Any attempt to harness it would only risk an unexpected resurfacing.

This guy is gorgeous!

He fought off an urge to give Andy a quick call to share his good fortune.

Wait, I know. I'll find the right moment and snap a shot of him with my phone.

He walked along the side of the house to the backyard. He was stopped by a closed gate. Pushing the latch up, he was careful to close it once he had entered. Not bad, he thought as he glanced around the yard. The dated chain-link fence could either be removed or hidden with shrubs, depending on what Harper—*Awesome name!*—had in mind. He stepped further into the yard. It was a nice big space with very little existing landscaping. He and Andy called these spaces "clean slates" because they required very little to remove before planting. Some of the homes in this area had jungles that had to be yanked out first. They were a real pain in the ass.

"Sorry to keep you waiting," Harper said, stepping out of the back door. Dressed in loose-fitting sweatpants and sweatshirt, the handsome prospective client bounded down the steps to join him.

"Hey, that was you in your commercial. Nice job! Have you gotten much business from it?" Harper sounded impressed.

"Well, it's only been running for a few weeks. I've had some calls. Hopefully as the season progresses, I'll have more." He still couldn't believe he had his very own commercial.

"Terrific! Ian… Ian, now you have to be honest with me when we talk about the landscaping design. I've got some ideas, but I don't know squat about this stuff. Promise you'll pipe up and steer me clear of a disaster?" Harper led the tour around the yard.

This is off to a good start. He wants to know what I think.

"Sure. You're lucky. You have a clean slate to work with back here. Why don't you let me know what you've been thinking about." Ian reached down into his pocket to make sure he had his phone. If nothing else came of tonight's meeting, he was leaving with a picture. A keepsake.

"Well, I've lived here for three years now. The people before me had a large dog they kept back here, and as you can see, the grass has never recovered." Harper stood in the center of an area of compacted dirt. "I'd like to start with a patio. Maybe a patio with an arbor or some type of structure over it? Vines, would that work?" Harper placed his hands on his hips, drawing Ian's attention to the ample bulge in his sweats.

"You mean vines covering an arbor?" Ian needed to be sure he was tracking.

"Stupid idea?" Harper winced.

"Not at all. There're several varieties that are fast growing. I can contract out for the arbor construction, that's no problem. Before we get too far along, did you have a budget in mind?" He wanted to make sure the client didn't get worked up over an idea he wouldn't be able to afford. It happened all the time, and to backtrack away from it was never easy.

"You mean I have to pay for this?" Harper feigned amazement, wiping an imaginary band of sweat from his forehead.

I'm sure we could work something out. Positive, in fact.

"Sucks, doesn't it?" Ian fought off a brief urge to jump his devastatingly handsome new client.

Did you just say sucks, doesn't it? Sucks? Sucks, Ian? Get a grip. This is business.

"I hadn't thought about a budget, to be honest. Can we just shoot for the moon, and then if I have to, scale the design down if it gets to be too costly?" Harper returned his hands to his hips and strolled over to the side of the yard facing the street, treating Ian to a marvelous butt shot.

"You bet!" Ian gave the yard another once-over.

"What team do you play for?" Harper turned suddenly to face him.

"Excuse me?" *Don't go there, Ian. Oh, buddy, you don't want to do that!* He fought for control. "I play for the Hornets... in a city league." When he felt it was safe, he glanced up at Harper to make sure he'd interpreted his question correctly. *Never give up hope!* He had. "Do you play?"

"Not since Little League, and I don't see it happening anytime soon. I love watching baseball. I have it on in the background a lot when I'm working." Harper reached down and plucked out an early weed.

"Well, if you're ever interested in watching, we play at Beecher Fields. They're just south of the lakes. Regular games are on Wednesday nights. Usually we start about six thirty." *Or we can play catch back here. You know, just you and I.*

"Hey, thanks, I might have to check you guys out." Harper tossed the weed over his shoulder.

Okay, that's enough of the chitchat. Back to business.

"What else did you have in mind back here?"

"I was thinking...." Harper strolled across the yard to the far corner.

Get the phone out. This is the perfect time to take a shot.

"Can we talk water feature?" Harper turned to face him.

Snap!

"WHAT the hell is this?" Andy asked, staring at the phone. "Is it part of a shoe?"

"I know. I'm so bummed. I thought I was holding it at the perfect angle, but it turns out I wasn't. You won't believe this guy, Andy. I wanted you to see for yourself. He's serious hot. A little taller than I am, say five eleven and maybe 175 pounds. He's our age, late twenties, thirty tops. Great shape. Well, he had on sweats so I couldn't tell for sure." Ian was surprised he was getting so carried away, but he was talking to Andy, who was used to it. "But his face, man, his face is so incredible. Chiseled chin, nice five o'clock shadow going on, deep black eyes and jet black hair. I'm not kidding you! The man is hot!"

"Maybe you should contract this job out." Andy could suck the fun right out of one of his moments of unbridled lust faster than anyone.

"Shut up! He's some kind of professional, I think. Doctor or lawyer, maybe. You know the type, they screw you if it's convenient for them but can't be seen in public with you because we're from the wrong side of the tracks. We're beneath them, but not in a good way. And besides, I'm pretty sure he's straight. I didn't pick up on any of the typical vibes." He exhaled and forced himself to slow down, realizing he was borderline out of control.

"You mean his doorbell didn't have a 'Hello Dolly' ring tone?" Andy asked dryly.

"You're jealous or something," Ian barked back.

"Whatever. Any idea what product you'll use?" Andy attempted to right the ship.

Reluctant to get down to business, Ian went over the notes he'd thrown together at Denny's earlier that morning while wolfing down a Grand Slam. "I'm going over later to have another look around and—" He couldn't suppress a giggle. "—take some more pictures. I should know more after today."

"Bring a camera this time, Spanky." Andy slapped him on the back.

Spanky—Ian wished he could wipe away history and be done with that awful memory once and for all. Neither Andy nor Spencer would let it die. Spanky was a nickname that surfaced from time to time, usually in connection with a stupid move he'd made. The name dated back to the first year he and Andy had been living in the city. It was his twenty-third birthday, and to celebrate, Andy and a few buddies took him out for a night of bar hopping. *How could I have been so stupid?* Toward the end of the evening, he found himself in the arms of a hot leather daddy. Kisses led to serious fondling, which in turn led to him being tied to a bed at daddy's house, scared out of his wits while daddy spanked his bare ass with a riding crop. He'd been branded with "Spanky" from that day forward.

"What are you going to do first? I'm thinking you'd be better off getting the digging done for the patio and the arbor up before you start planting. What product I don't already have, I can special order to arrive by the end of next week. When are you starting?" Andy looked over at the nude fireman posed seductively on the charity calendar he'd received as a birthday gift.

"I told him I'd be over in the morning to kick things off. Once I have a good idea of what will work, I'll do a plan for Harper. I love that name. Isn't it cool? Harper?"

"Beats the hell out of Walt." It was obvious by the way he lingered at the wall that Andy hadn't taken time out of his busy schedule to enjoy this month's hottie.

"I called Arlan Stemple. He's agreed to take care of the excavation part. I found a design on the web for an arbor I think Harper will like, and if approved, I'll have Prairie Planks throw it together. I talked to Earl earlier in the week, and he said they were still slow."

He was proud of himself. This was one of the bigger jobs he'd landed, and it all seemed to be lining up nicely. Since the commercial had run, he'd gotten two other calls. One from some drunk lady who had more than landscaping on her mind, and the other a retired couple who wanted help planting a perennial garden. He jotted down a note to call the couple. The world didn't revolve around Harper Callahan, he reminded himself. He needed to give all of his clients the red carpet treatment. Word of mouth from a successful job was, as Andy had put it, wagging a mud-stained finger in his face, "the cheapest and the most effective advertising there is."

HARPER stepped from the shower into his bedroom. The suit he had planned to wear along with a shirt and tie was hanging on a hook in back of the closet door. He'd gotten into a habit of picking out his clothes the night before to shorten up his morning ritual. If you were coming off a night of very little sleep, having your clothes ready to roll was a huge benefit. Throwing his towel on the bed, he stepped into black boxer briefs. A white T-shirt came next. He'd been taught never to wear a dress shirt without a T-shirt underneath. The T-shirt always made the shirt look so much better, even in the middle of summer when the days were scorchers. Pants, belt, socks, and shoes followed before he threw on his suit coat and headed down the stairs. A noise outside the kitchen window startled him. Looking out, he spotted Ian from Burke Landscaping marking off areas in the yard with twine.

Pouring a cup of coffee, he leaned over the counter and watched Ian march up and down the yard. *We have to be about the same age. God, I love that crazy mop of hair. It looks like a rooster's.* He was dressed in khaki shorts, a hooded sweatshirt, and work boots, a look he had always envied, on some guys that is. Very few could pull it off, but Ian of Burke Landscaping was a man who could—and then some. As natural as a suit felt on Harper, the khaki shorts and sweatshirt looked to be the right choice for Ian. And those legs, those hot, hot legs. Strong, bulging calves curved up to a nice tight butt. His waist was slender but not skinny. Shoulders were well developed, and although he hadn't had the opportunity to see his arms in a T-shirt yet, he was sure they were muscled, finishing off the hot workman look he seemed to own. The images he'd already collected of Ian in his baseball uniform brought about a familiar tingle, his body's way of communicating approval.

Glancing at his watch, he knew he had to shut down his spy mission, but not before he stepped into the backyard to say hello.

"Ian, you're at it early," he greeted, stepping out into a gorgeous spring morning.

"Hey! Good morning. Wow, suit and tie. Looks good!" Ian flashed a thumbs-up.

Not as good as you look in those shorts. Damn! Oh, and by the way, has anyone ever mentioned to you that you own the word adorable too?

"Thanks! So, what's happening today?" Harper forced himself to survey the yard.

The landscaper detailed what he had planned, but Harper hardly heard a word. Everything about this guy standing in his yard fascinated him. The slow, relaxed lilt to his voice and how it contrasted with his abundant energy. The purposeful, athletic way in which he moved. His warm, engaging smile. Harper tried to focus but couldn't to save his soul. *Am I getting hard? Seriously?* "I am!" he cried out.

"What?" Ian asked, taking a few steps forward.

"Oh… I am… I am thinking this backyard is going to turn out great!" He felt his face flush.

"You have a perfect yard to work with. I should have sketches over to you in the next day or two." Ian looked over to see if he approved.

"Terrific! I can't wait, and when it's all said and done, you'll have to join me out here for beers to celebrate." He needed to retreat so he could regain his composure. He couldn't recall ever being this rattled by anyone.

Beers to celebrate? Oh, Harp, my boy, your opening statement needs more work than you thought. That was soooo lame.

"Sounds great! I should mention, some nights we might work a little later than others. I'm not sure I'll be here, but one or two of my helpers could be. I wanted to let you know if you come home and there're strangers in your yard. I've worked with these guys plenty of times, and you have no worries." Ian tossed the ball of twine in his hand.

"Oh, thanks! Do what you have to do. So, you have everything you need, then?" *Retreat now before you really screw this up.*

"Yeah! We're in good shape. Thanks!"

Ian, you don't have any idea what you're doing to me, do you? I'm going to have to figure out a way to tell you.

FOR most of the drive over to the ball field, Ian listened to Andy bitch about a local vendor who had one more chance before he told him to take his frickin' pachysandra starters and shove them up his ass.

"I have people stopping in expecting these things to be in stock. I'm tired of covering for that lazy sack of shit. Sorry, I just had to vent." Andy sighed and crossed his arms.

"I'm sure if you do have to send him packing, he'll have deserved it." He was only half listening as he pulled into the parking lot.

"How did it go today over at Dreamboat's?" Andy stepped out of the truck.

"It went fine. Harper came out and talked to me this morning. Dressed in a suit. Why can't I find guys to date who wear suits?" he whined. "I always get the jeans and stained T-shirt dudes. You should have seen how hot he looked."

"You meet the suit types in college. You and I bypassed that route. Let's go over and check Spencer's batting order." Andy made a beeline for their pal.

"Look what the cat dragged in—Tweedle Dee and Tweedle Dumb." Spencer looked up from his clipboard.

"Hey Tweedle Dick, got a batting lineup we can look at?" Andy asked.

"Sure enough do. Damn, I play ball for nights like this. Think about the poor saps who are stuck inside watching *Wheel of Fortune* or some other shit like that."

Baseball for Spencer was like church to some people. Ian loved this about his friend. The whole experience was sacred. A part of his life he couldn't live without.

"Is Allison coming?" Unable to muster up any interest in the batting lineup, he settled on some small talk.

"Naw, her mother is over. They're going through garden books. Andy, I'll probably have an order for you in the next day or two," Spencer warned.

"No sweat. Let me know and I'll put it together." Andy buried his nose in Spencer's clipboard. "I sure hope Allison doesn't get on that crazed heirloom tomato thing this year," he added, looking up for a second. "I didn't want to say anything, but I took a real hit in the wallet rustling up a few of the varieties she'd set her sights on."

Ian looked around at the stands. A few stragglers. Nothing like later in the season when the team had gelled and everyone was in the groove. Then the stands would be full. It was a little too early yet. For the next few weeks, the Hornets would practice on both Tuesday and Wednesday nights. When the actual season started, they would practice on Tuesday and play a team on Wednesday. The weekends were kept free up until the tournaments.

"Well, let's get practice rolling." Spencer blew on the shiny new whistle Allison had picked up for him the day before.

Playing centerfield bored Ian, but tonight, it was just what he needed. He struggled to keep his mind on the game. Meeting Harper had unleashed a desire, a need that begged for attention. *Maybe it's time to go on the hunt again.* He was surprised. For the first time in as long as he could remember, he didn't slam the door on the idea of seriously pursuing a relationship. But he would need to be more cautious this time around and look for warning signs no matter how good the sex was. Kevin, the last man in his life, had been great in bed and worthless at anything else. Kevin's laziness and lack of responsibility had crept up, suffocating and choking Ian's existence. Life with Kevin had ended poorly with friends caught in the middle. It was embarrassing to admit to being manipulated by a large dick. It wouldn't happen again. This time around would be different. He wanted a guy who would challenge him, give him a run for his money in and out of bed. Ian chuckled. It was curious how meeting someone like his new client could trigger these thoughts. Oh well, a handsome man, a warm spring night... he'd leave it at that, he decided, when he realized he'd been sniffing his glove for the last several minutes.

Concentrate!

The team looked good. There were decent hits and lively base play right out of the gate. Striking out his first at bat, he popped a fly out to left field on his second time up, which was promptly caught by Snotty Scotty to end the inning.

A series of hot pitches kept the outfield quiet in the next inning. He couldn't stay focused. The image of Harper in his suit had occupied a good portion of his thoughts all day. It was one of those strange attractions. Almost like having a crush on a movie star. You fantasized about them with the understanding you would never actually get to do anything with them or, in this case, to them. He had plenty of ideas about what he'd like to do with a Harper Callahan. Plenty of ideas.

He was brought back to reality by the loud crack of a bat. He watched the ball sail high into the air, hang there long enough for him to sneak a quick glance at home plate—*Is it?*—and then descend rapidly right—*Holy shit! He's here. Harper's sitting in the stands!*—past his open glove.

"Hey," Ian called up to Harper in the stands when the game had ended. "Thanks for stopping by."

"Thank you. I really enjoyed watching you play." Harper stepped down the bleacher seats until he'd reached the bottom. "I've driven by these fields a million times and never thought to stop and watch. Thanks for reminding me they were here."

"We love it when people come to watch." Ian wasn't sure what else to say. *What's he doing here? He's not some kind of nutjob, is he?* Judging by Harper's appearance and his home on the popular parkway, this guy had some bucks. Why wasn't he sitting in some expensive seats watching the Twins play if he enjoyed baseball so much? *Really? You got off on watching us practice?*

Although Harper begged off on joining him and his teammates for a beer after practice, he did linger around long enough to be introduced to both Andy and Spencer, who, despite Ian's fears, managed to be on their best behavior.

"I think he might be sweet on you, Spanky," Andy mentioned when they had gotten to the bar. "I wish he was sweet on me. He's a certified bone-in hottie."

They were seated at "their" table in the corner of Merl's Liquor Lounge.

"Listen, cheek-splitters, you both need to give the dude a break," Spencer challenged, guzzling the last of his beer and pouring another from the second pitcher of the night.

"Cheek-splitters?" Ian looked over to Andy and, without a word exchanged, agreed not to acknowledge Spencer's lame cut, even though this was one they hadn't heard before. Spencer was good for at least one offensive name a night. He and Andy kept a list.

"It would be a hell of a thing to read at his funeral," Andy had speculated with pride.

"And he'd like that," Ian had confirmed.

"You lost us on that one, Breeder Bob." Ian was reminded he needed to spend some time on the Internet searching for straight dude slang. "Give him a break because…?"

"From what I've heard so far, you're grasping at pubes with this one," Spencer argued. "You have no concrete proof he's one of your people, that's number one. Number two: Ian, the dude told you he loved baseball... so... is it crazy that you reminded him of how easy it would be to hop in his car, drive a few blocks, and get his baseball fix on?"

Spencer could only play man-crush with them for so long before he tired of the game.

"Yeah, you're probably right," Ian agreed, downing his beer. Even if his new client had ulterior motives for showing up, it wasn't anything he felt like pursuing. Finding sex when he needed it had never been a struggle. Messing around with a client was a path he knew he'd be better off not going down. Even if the client did top the charts in the looks department. *It's not worth it, Ian. It never is.*

CHAPTER

Three

IAN sat on the grass and cracked open his soda. It amazed him how somebody else's yard could start to feel like his own in such a short period of time. Not always, but the feeling happened more often than not. This was his third visit to Harper's, and already it felt like home.

Does it feel like home, or do I want it to be home?

All afternoon his thoughts darted back and forth from his designs to Harper and his unexpected visit to the field. *Spencer's right. The dude just wanted to get out of the house and watch baseball.*

Setting his sketches out, he sipped his soda and reviewed his work.

It's maybe more than he's expecting, but I think it makes the best use of the space. It's a starting point.

The designs were ready to scan and e-mail. He had provided two water feature options. One called for a buildup of rock near the patio as the source of a gentle brook which would cascade down to a pool located off to one side of the seating area. If he went with this approach, he'd have to be careful to keep the feature small—relaxing and not distracting or overbearing. The other idea, the one he seemed to be gravitating back to more often, was to build up the far left-hand corner of the yard in a series of terraces and from there cascade the water along the side of the yard all the way down to the patio. Because this feature began at a distance, it could be bigger and more dramatic. He'd present the two options to Harper and let him decide.

Swigging down the last of his soda, he gathered up his sketches and shoved them into his shoulder bag. Standing, he discovered his leg had fallen asleep. Limping around in a circle, he froze when a bright blue Smart Car pulled into the driveway.

No way! It can't be! He hadn't considered still being around long enough to run into Harper.

Now what am I going to do? I can't even walk!

"Hey, Ian, what a pleasant surprise." Harper opened the back gate and entered the yard. "How's it going?"

Feeling trapped and ridiculous, he chanced a step forward, a big mistake. His leg buckled, and he landed on his knees.

"Wow, you okay?" Harper scurried over to him and offered a hand.

"My foot fell asleep," he admitted, accepting Harper's hand as he stood back up.

"I hate it when that happens." Harper laughed. "I wasn't sure what was going on with you."

He wasn't sure what was going on with him either. Having Harper stand so close was electrifying. If he'd felt like this before, he couldn't remember when.

Is it warming up? I feel hot!

On his feet again with Harper's help, he shifted his weight back and forth until he was certain his drowsy leg could support him.

"It turned out to be such a nice day, I decided to work on your yard design here. I'll scan this stuff when I get home tonight and send it over to you in an e-mail."

"You could do that, or if you're not in a rush, I could grab us a few beers and we could go over them now. You in a hurry to get out of here?"

He was excited to show off his designs. He liked what he'd done, which in the past had been a clear indication his work was solid. And he didn't have anywhere else he needed to be.

This is against my better judgment, but what the hell. Maybe I can figure out what this dude is up to.

"Well, if you're not busy with something else,"—he was careful to keep the excitement out of his voice—"let's take a look at what I've worked up for you. I can answer any questions or concerns you have now."

"Cool! I'm excited to see what you've done. How's the leg? Can you make it from here into the house okay?" Harper gave him some space to test his walking abilities.

"Oh yeah, it's back to normal." *Maybe I can wet my pants for an encore!*

"Follow me." Harper headed toward the back door. "We can spread your designs out on the dining room table."

He followed Harper into the house. The back door opened into a small, updated kitchen. He came close to letting out a squeal when he spotted a pasta faucet over the stove.

Someday I'll have one of those.

Harper opened the stainless steel refrigerator and pulled out two beers. "I've been on an ale kick lately. Will this be okay?"

"Sure," Ian said, taking the beer. "I'll drink anything."

"I'm not fussy either. I also have wine, so let me know. And Jameson. With a name like Callahan, you're almost expected to have it on hand. Through here's the dining room."

He followed Harper through an arched opening into a cozy dining area anchored by a huge, dark buffet. "I'm going to get out of this suit. Make yourself at home. Mind if I turn on some music?"

"Not at all." For the second time in a matter of minutes, he felt hot.

Harper walked over and grabbed a remote off the buffet. Lady Gaga filled the room, the origins of the sound undetectable. "Okay, see you in a minute."

Cool! He likes Gaga.

Setting his bag on a chair, he pulled his designs out, arranging them in the right order for his presentation. He contemplated what chair to take and eventually chose one on the side. He'd save the head of the table for his client. Taking his seat, he looked around the room for some "Harper" clues.

To his right, he could see into the living room. There was a fireplace. *Sweet!* It smelled really good in here. Was it Harper's cologne? The few pictures he could see from where he was sitting were contemporary, bold colors that warmed up the stark white walls. The hardwood floors were covered with deep, rich area rugs. The rooms looked both tasteful and masculine.

He tried to suppress a grin as he imagined Harper undressing on the second floor. The stairs must be located somewhere in the living room. And they were wooden, he deduced when he heard Harper going up.

Is he standing up there in his underwear? Boxers or briefs... or boxer briefs. Hmmm, I vote boxers.

He was about to scold himself when he heard footsteps coming down. Reaching for his beer, he took a sip and came close to spitting it out, a reaction to Harper, who swept into the room dressed in running shorts and a T-shirt.

"How's the ale? Are you enjoying it?" Harper examined the label of his own bottle, waiting for a response.

"Yes," he managed to eke out, trying desperately not to choke.

Like his head, Harper's legs and arms were shaded with black hair. He loved men with black hair. He loved how sexy black hair looked when it was wet and matted to the skin.

This dude is incredible. He's got it all going on.

"Let's see what you've got." Harper plopped down in the side chair directly across from him. "I'm really excited."

"Ah... okay." He reached for his designs and flipped through them one more time to make sure they were in order before starting. "Here's a sketch of how I envision your patio to look. I'd like to suggest you use some old street pavers. They're not the cheapest route to go, but I think they would work great. The pavers I have in mind are well worn, with an occasional spot of street paint here and there. Lots of character."

"I love the herringbone pattern you have shown. I'm sold! Can you get enough to do the pathways to the garage and around to the front of the house?" Harper seemed to genuinely like what he was looking at.

"Sure. You're a step ahead of me. I was hoping you'd go for keeping the pathways and the patio consistent."

"That was easy. What's next?" Harper sipped his beer and smiled.

There was the slightest hint of playfulness, a challenge in his voice when he posed his question. When he looked up from his sketches and saw the goofy grin on Harper's face, he felt his face flush for the second time, or maybe the third.

He showed Harper the design he had in mind for the arbor and described for him a few aggressive vines to cover the frame.

"You know how you're not sure what you want until you see it? This is exactly the look I was going for. Nice work!" Harper leaned in, examining the designs.

This was going well. Ian paused for a minute and took a sip of his beer. Harper seemed impressed with his choices and easy to please. Several times as he explained the differences between this vine choice or that type of wood, their eyes locked. Those deep, dark, wonderful eyes. And he had a dazzling smile. Beautiful, bright white teeth, perfect in every way. Ian struggled to stay focused. This guy was giving his resolve a real run for its money. His self-imposed "hands off the clients" rule faced its most challenging test yet.

"You have no idea how much I've wanted to have the yard done over." Harper sat back and smiled. "To know that it's finally going to happen is really awesome. I feel so lucky to have seen your commercial." Harper raised his bottle and sipped, never taking his eyes off Ian.

Can we talk about lucky?

"I'm glad. It's fun to work with someone who gets into it," he shared, because it *was* fun. *It's hot fun!*

Many of his past clients were only interested in going the cheapest route. Even though he was good at it, he hated designing around a skimpy budget. It sucked the fun right out of the process. "For the outline around the yard, I'd suggest you keep the existing fence," he announced confidently.

"Really? It's so ugly."

This was the first time since they had sat down that Harper had questioned his concept. Ian was ready with his response. "Well, it won't be when we get done hiding it with clusters of shrubs."

Ian opened a magazine and pointed out several specimens he had in mind. "I like to do clusters of several different varieties as opposed to a straight line of one variety like you often see. Also there should be several openings in the border where you can see to the street. This design will show you where I propose to put the openings. By putting the openings here…"

Ian turned his design around so Harper could view it from his angle, and in the process, their hands touched. He reached for his beer.

I wonder if this guy has any idea at all what he's doing to me. This is nuts. I'm so not in control.

"…by putting the openings here," he continued after making sure his beer was headed down his throat, "your seating area, the arbor area will be hidden from the street, giving you privacy. People would have to leave the sidewalk and walk up the incline to peer over in your direction. You, on the other hand, can walk over to the openings and see down the street if you want. Is this enough privacy?"

Again their eyes locked. Harper grinned.

"What?" He chuckled out of nervousness.

"It's perfect. I'm very happy." Harper leaned across the table and asked, "Can I talk you into another beer?"

Can I make it through another beer? I'm turning into putty.

"Come on, one more?" Harper leaned in even closer.

The combination of his twinkling eyes and megawatt smile was impossible for Ian to resist. "Sure!" He tried to identify the vibe coming from Harper. "There're a few more things we should cover."

Ian sat mesmerized as Harper collected their bottles and sauntered past on the way to the kitchen. He was becoming aroused, and there wasn't a thing he could do about it. He forced himself to try and stay on track. Shifting through his notes, he reviewed the aspects of the backyard design he'd yet to cover.

"Did you have time yet to think about a water feature?" Harper asked, this time sitting at the head of the table, close enough that his bare leg brushed for a brief second up against Ian's.

Ian belted back a healthy swig from his new beer. Unless he was mistaken, and by this time he was pretty sure he wasn't, Harper was coming on to him. And if it wasn't that, it sure as hell was something.

"I've got two water options for you to consider." He slid his sketches over.

Hang in there, you're almost done.

Ian went into detail regarding the pros and cons of each feature. At one point, Harper leaned in to compare sketches and reduced the distance between them by half. Using every ounce of concentration available, Ian managed to forge ahead.

"Would you like some time to think about these? You don't have to decide tonight." In his haste to get through his presentation, he feared he might have rushed this last part, which seemed to be so important to his client.

"Ian, which one do you like best?" Harper sat back, folding his arms across his chest.

Those eyes, that smile. "I like... I like...." He had to clear his throat. "I like the one that originates in the far corner. It can be bigger, and bigger is usually the route to go."

Milliseconds after his "bigger" comment, he lost his battle with composure and started to laugh. "I'm sorry—"

"No.... No problem." Harper chuckled. "I hear ya, big is always better." Harper held up his bottle in a toast.

"Something like that." They clinked bottles.

"I love this. I'm on board a hundred percent with what you're proposing. You really have a talent."

Ian's palms had begun to sweat. Harper moved closer to him and once again reduced the distance between them to inches. "Oh, well, thank you." Ian felt embarrassed. He'd never learned the trick to feeling comfortable accepting a compliment. Because he was so physically attracted to Harper, he couldn't trust what he said or how he reacted. *This isn't good.*

"I'm starving. Can you hang around for dinner? I can grill burgers or we can call for a pizza... anything works for me."

This is your business, he reminded himself. He couldn't chance losing control any more than he already had. As much as he wanted to stay, in an instant he decided it was best if he didn't. "I'd love to, but I have to pass. A friend of mine is expecting me."

HARPER waited for the jailer to slide open the door. He couldn't say goodbye to the gunmetal grey cell block fast enough. The drab yellow visitation area felt warm and comforting in comparison. He signed out on the clipboard, stepped outside, and welcomed the sunshine.

The man he had just left was broken. So much so, it was hard for him to imagine the kind of vibrant personality Jasper Flynn had had prior to being convicted. Where was the charisma, the passion this man had once had that allowed so many smart people to have the wool pulled over their eyes? Whatever Jasper had going for him before, being incarcerated had drained it. Harper felt sad for him. Jasper was despicable, which he fully understood. But from a basic human perspective, to see a life like his destroyed was humbling.

Enough Jasper for now, he thought as he got into his car. He had a more pressing issue to contemplate. One Ian Burke, to be specific.

I bet he has a boyfriend. How could he not? A catch like that, he has to have guys after him all the time.

He pointed the car in the direction of his office while his mind raced toward Ian. Had it been a twist of fate that when he'd finally made a conscious decision to pursue a relationship, Ian had popped into the picture? He had almost forgotten what it was he found physically appealing in a man. Ian, in an instant, had brought it all back for him. From the floppy mop of brown hair on top of his boyishly handsome face to his bulging calves, he was perfection. And he came across as such a nice guy. A kind, genuine soul.

There was a tension, something in the air they seemed to share as they were going over the landscape plans. He was sure he recognized something. More than once while together, he sensed Ian was sending out an "I'm interested" vibe. And their initial meeting couldn't be overlooked either. Setting ego aside, he knew he was considered handsome. Well, very handsome if he was being true to himself. And over the years, he had come to understand how his looks affected others. He had the ability to make those who found him appealing act nervous and flustered. It happened all the time. He'd gotten so used it, he rarely ever noticed anymore, unless, like in the case of Ian, it mattered. Ian had been very flustered on their first meeting, and that, in turn, offered him hope.

Harper parked and headed into the building. Depending on the amount of e-mails and calls he'd be required to return, he hoped to find time to revisit his research on potential clawback litigation. He was convinced if he knew the rules well enough and he could establish an element of trust, he might be able to ward off, at least for the time being, the attack that would surely be directed toward Phyllis Flynn. He found it necessary to treat this as an exercise rather than personalize it. This wasn't about Phyllis. It was about his skills as a lawyer. He welcomed the challenge. It was unfortunate he had to waste this effort on the likes of Phyllis Flynn.

He'd only been at his desk for a few minutes when he heard a commotion in the hallway.

"For Christ's sake, Duncan, I paid for these goddamn offices, and don't you ever forget that. Oh, this must be the… the boy."

Framed in his door stood Phyllis Flynn with Duncan Price panting behind her.

"May I help you?" He didn't need to be introduced. He'd observed her uppity pouts in the courtroom during her husband's trial and found her to be a revolting individual. Up until now, he'd been able to avoid a face-to-face meeting. Today his luck had run out.

"Callahan, how did a nice Irish boy get mixed up with these clowns? I'm Phyllis Flynn."

"Of course you are," he said, rising from his chair. "We spoke… very early the other morning. Duncan, how nice of you to bring Mrs. Flynn around to meet me."

"Duncan had nothing to do with anything. I'm calling the shots here, junior."

"In that case, please have a seat." He gestured to one of two chairs opposite his desk. "What can I do for you?"

"Listen, you little snot," she hissed. "Take this advice if you're as smart as you are pretty." Phyllis advanced a few steps forward.

He felt his right eyebrow rise in anticipation.

"If you know what's good for you, you'd better eat, shit, and breathe my fucking finances. This is no longer about Jasper. We know how successful you were with *him*. You clowns call yourselves lawyers? You're scum. Goddamned scum!"

"That's enough, Phyllis. I know you're upset, but that's quite enough." Duncan reached for her arm to lead her out of the office.

"Touch me like that again and I'll flatten you." Phyllis held her ground. Duncan retreated to the hall.

"Is there anything else, Mrs. Flynn?" Harper asked without emotion. "As I mentioned to you on the phone, I'll do the best I can for you. I can't imagine doing anything less. Now, you can insult me to your heart's content if you'd like, but frankly, I'm not sure how that will benefit either of us."

He stepped forward, understanding his body language would indicate he wasn't at all fearful of her threats.

Phyllis seemed to defuse. Reaching into her clutch, she pulled out a hanky and wiped who knew what from her cheek.

"You protect me, you hear?" She froze her gaze on him, making his skin crawl.

"Loud and clear. Oh, and Mrs. Flynn, provided it isn't the middle of the night, feel free to call anytime."

"Out of my way, Duncan, you asshole!" Phyllis shoved Duncan up against the rich mahogany wall, replaced her hanky, and stormed down the hall. Several seconds passed before Duncan stepped back into his office.

"She's a powder keg," he said, failing miserably at a smile. "I'm sorry you had to go through that."

"Hey, Duncan, it's me, Harper. Skin as thick as an elephant. I'm good. Now I'd better get back to work before the day gets away from me." He stood his ground, forcing Duncan to leave without saying another word. Behind the safety of his desk, he buried his head in his hands. *Tell me something, Harp. Is this really worth it?*

WHEN Ian arrived at Harper's Saturday morning, Arlan Stemple was already waiting. Typically, he avoided working Saturdays for several reasons. First and foremost, the clients were usually around, and it never failed, they almost always forced a question-and-answer session about gardening that added hours to his day. In this case, it wasn't the client, it was Arlan. It was Arlan's only free day in the next couple of weeks, so he was thankful he could have the digging completed so the rest of his design could unfold as planned.

"Just makes it!" Arlan re-coiled his tape measure with a loud snap.

"What just makes it?" Ian asked, walking up to the excavator, who was standing outside the driveway measuring the gate leading into the backyard.

"I thought we'd have to take down part of the fence to get the digger in, but it just makes it."

"That's great. The client is keeping the fence." Ian stepped into the yard.

"So how's this one going to go?" Arlan asked, following close behind.

"I've got the areas marked off for you." He looked over to make sure his lines were still in place. "Why don't you get yourself ready to go and we'll talk about depth. Any boulders you run into, try to separate out. I'll use them in the areas I have to build up over in that corner. I want to see what we end up with today before I order any rock brought in."

He checked his watch. It was almost nine. *Harper should be awake by now.* Ian had left a message with his assistant the day before informing him they'd be working today. Harper had told him to come by whenever he wanted.

Now that he'd had a few days to recover from their last meeting, he felt more in control of himself. He felt like a player. If Harper had an interest in him, bring it on. He was game. And it wasn't that he didn't want something to happen. The thought of romping around in the sack with someone as handsome as Harper certainly got the old juices flowing. Being taken advantage of was a different story altogether. Whatever was going on with Harper, Ian felt confident it'd happen again. If he allowed something to develop between them, fine, but it was going to be on his terms.

Arlan was a master with a digger, twirling it around in the confined space like a toy. By midafternoon, his work was complete, and the digger was loaded back onto its small flatbed trailer.

"Thanks, Arlan." Ian slapped the door of his friend's truck. "Send an invoice and I'll work it into mine."

"My pleasure. Send me more easy jobs like this. I love 'em!"

With Arlan out of the yard, Ian could start moving wheelbarrow loads of dirt and rock over to the corner where the water feature was planned. It was best to get as much in place as possible before the fill was made heavier by the seasonal rains, which were right around the corner.

He had another reason for wanting to hang around. Although it was possible Harper had gone out of town, knowing work was being done in his backyard over the weekend, Ian held out hope he'd return so they could have the opportunity to spend some time together. It had been the wrong move, not accepting Harper's offer to stay for dinner the other night. Refusing had prolonged the inevitable. He had to get a handle on his feelings so he could move on. Nothing good could come from this man-crush he was developing. *Why am I having such a struggle with this?* He'd come across guys like Harper before. They played you right into bed, and when the attraction wore off, they threw you out on your ass without as much as a wave goodbye. Handsome guys with money were always shallow. Harper, though he seemed like a regular dude, was probably no different, Ian figured, except maybe better-looking than most. If he looked hard enough, he'd find a crack in the plaster. *What if I don't find a crack?*

His stomach rumbled. *It's candy bar time!*

He drove the few blocks to the convenience store and bought a Snickers bar. When he got back, he was surprised to find Harper surveying the progress.

"Hey," Harper greeted. "You don't waste any time, do you? Wow! This is so exciting."

"Hi there. Yep, we're moving right along. I thought you may have gone away for the weekend."

"I wish. I went into the office early this morning to get a jump on next week. Did I mention to you I'm a lawyer?"

You didn't have to. "I had you pegged for either that or a doctor."

"Doctor, I wish. I can't do blood. I spent most of *Sweeney Todd* staring at my popcorn box."

Harper's admission cracked Ian up. "I do okay with blood. Snakes scare the crap out of me, which is a definite disadvantage when you're in landscaping." He sensed an opportunity and, in a split second, decided to take it. "Sorry I wasn't able to stay for dinner the other night. Any chance you're free tonight? Maybe we could grab a bite somewhere or—"

"Ian, are you a mind reader? I was just trying to get up the nerve to ask you the same thing, but I wasn't sure I could handle another rejection."

"Oh, well, I'm not usually one to refuse a meal. Hey, I've gotta run home and shower. Do you want to meet somewhere? Can I pick you up?"

"Let's see, it's closing in on four. What part of town do you live in?" Harper adjusted his watch.

"I live in Hopkins. Not that far." He hoped Harper wouldn't offer to pick him up. His shabby little apartment was an embarrassment.

"Okay. Hey, I got an idea, why don't we meet up at Leona's. They have great steaks. It's my treat. With all the extra time I'm putting in lately, the firm owes me… and my guest,"—Harper gestured over to him—"a decent dinner. You okay with that?"

"Leona's? Ah… yeah. Who wouldn't be? That's one of those *special occasion* places. Are you sure?" He loved Leona's and had only been there a few times because it was so pricey. As long as dinner wasn't coming directly out of Harper's pocket, how could he refuse?

"Yes, very sure. Let's meet there around seven. Does that give you enough time at home?"

"That's perfect! See you then." He fought off the urge to skip to his truck and then hated himself for it.

"HELLO, may I help you?"

Before answering the guy dressed in a suit at least one size too small, Ian squinted in the low light to see if he could spot Harper. Coming up short, he stepped up to the host stand. "I'm meeting another guy. He has black hair—"

"Ah yes, I think we have a match." The host pivoted in a precise move reminiscent of the military. It didn't surprise him one bit this twit knew who he was referring to. He caught a strong sense of envy as he was led into the dining room.

"Ian, welcome!"

He was surprised when Harper rose from his chair and embraced him.

That was *your cologne I smelled in your dining room. Mmmm.*

"I just got here." Harper gestured for him to sit. "Haven't had a chance to order a drink yet. What do you feel like?"

Ian took a seat across from his gorgeous dinner partner. *You get better-looking each time I see you. What's up with that?* Harper was dressed in a black turtleneck and grey pants. In a word, he was stunning. Giving Leona's his best shot, Ian had chosen a deep burgundy dress shirt and the nicest pair of khaki slacks he owned.

"You look great!" Harper said, displaying a devilish grin.

Oh yeah? Then why do I feel like an unwanted stepchild at the rich kid's birthday party?

"Thanks! So do you." *Was that weird? We just complimented each other on our outfits.* "What are you drinking tonight?" It was best to get this moving along. He needed a drink to calm his nerves in the worst way.

"I'm tempted to have a martini, but I think I'd better pass. They make me crazy. You mentioned the other night you enjoyed wine. Should we order a bottle? They have an incredible red here I love."

"Perfect!"

Harper signaled for the waiter, who stood only a few feet away. "We'll enjoy our wine for a while before ordering."

"Of course, sir," the waiter responded.

"If you're starving,"—Harper brought his focus back to Ian—"let me know."

An entire bottle of wine was consumed before the subject of ordering food surfaced. At Harper's suggestion and much to his surprise, Ian ordered the bone-in rib eye without a single giggle.

"How's the steak?" Harper asked, ignoring the waiter hovering over their table and refilling their wineglasses.

"It's incredible. This is so nice. Thank you." He resisted the temptation to pick up the bone with his hands and gnaw on it. Harper, who had sat back in his chair, held his wineglass to his chest and looked over with an alluring smirk. Ian held his gaze for as long as he could and then retreated back to his plate.

"May I ask you a personal question?"

He looked back up. Harper hadn't moved. "Yeah, sure," he replied with a nervous chuckle. *Whatever this is, let it happen, Ian.*

"Are you seeing anybody right now? Are you in a relationship?" Harper swirled the wine in his glass.

Harper's frankness made him sit up in his chair.

Here you go. Hang on! "Not at the moment. How about you?" He held his breath.

"Not at the moment. Are you *open* to seeing anyone?" Harper asked with another expert swirl.

"Dating, you're talking about dating?" He wanted to make sure he understood the question.

Harper smiled and nodded.

"Honestly, I hadn't thought about it. I guess so, if the right—" He stopped himself just in time. He didn't have to finish. He knew what Harper meant. And the answer was yes. "Yes."

He couldn't prevent the blush he knew colored his cheeks. A chronic condition he could count on at moments like this. Whatever was happening to him on the outside, it delighted Harper, who chuckled.

"You don't have to answer. You can nod if it's easier. Do you want to start seeing *me*?" Harper leaned forward, his gorgeous eyes focused on Ian, awaiting his answer.

Ian felt his trouser leg lift slowly off his shoe until it reached midcalf. "Is your foot rubbing my leg?" he asked, both aroused and astounded.

"Oh for gosh sakes, is that where it went?" Harper blurted with mock despair. "I was starting to panic. I didn't know how the hell I was going to get out of here."

Ian laughed. He'd caught small glimpses of silly in Harper a few times during the evening and loved it.

"Harper, I have to be honest. I'm not looking for a one-night stand. I know that wasn't what you asked, but I need to make sure you understand that." It was his turn to sit back. *Listen carefully to how he answers this. It could be the crack in the plaster.*

"I'm not looking for that either. I'm at a point in my life where I need someone to be there with me," Harper confessed with an entire year's supply of sincerity. "I'm hoping that someone will be you."

Ian took a minute to let this one settle in. In his wildest dreams, he would have never thought the evening would go in this direction. It was time to step up to the plate and trust. "I'm thinking it's worth a damn good try." He was amazed at what had so nonchalantly wandered out of his mouth. Several seconds passed by without a word said between them.

You're one handsome man, Mr. Callahan. And the best part is, I'm having a hard time believing you're full of shit. You might just be the real deal.

"What are you doing for the rest of the evening?" Harper asked.

"I have no plans," he answered evenly. *Drop the sword and surrender, Galahad.*

"How about a fire, a movie, and...."

"See where it goes from there?" Ian smirked, guessing he'd finished Harper's question for him correctly.

"Check please!"

THE toilet flushing woke Harper. How odd to hear his own toilet flush while he remained in bed. *Ian!* He turned to face the door in time to see his handsome, naked new boyfriend saunter through the door.

"If it's possible, you look even better in the morning. Get back in here!" He pulled back the covers.

Ian picked up the small empty wrapper on the bedside table and flashed an evil grin.

"You made me beg for it," Harper teased.

Ian slid in between the sheets, taking Harper into his arms. "You're pretty amazing, Mr. Harper Callahan."

I don't know what I love more about being with you. The sex or you just holding me like this. "Does this still feel like a good idea, starting… us?"

"Oh yeah." Ian kissed his head.

Cupping Ian's neck, he slid up closer until their lips touched, brushed back and forth, and then parted for a long, lazy kiss.

"Have you had many relationships?" Ian asked, smooching Harper's eyelid and nose.

"Let me think… there was my scout leader, the pastor at church, my high school guidance counselor, my uncle Nick, and I briefly dated the milkman the summer I spent studying for the bar. And you?" He had only a second to savor how wittily he had responded before Ian pounced on top of him, pinning his arms over his head.

"You're in big trouble now," Ian warned, biting down on his nipple.

"Ouch! I'm sorry. I'm sorry, please," he giggled and begged in unison.

"Not as sorry as you're gonna be." Ian bit down on the other nipple.

"Okay, okay, I give. I'll tell the truth, I promise," he pleaded, even though on another level he welcomed Ian's nibbles.

"You get one more chance," Ian cautioned, easing himself onto his side.

"I've only dated. No relationships. I came out my freshman year in college and never allowed myself the time to pursue anything more. I'm new to this, Ian. I hope that doesn't scare you." He hated how virginal he sounded.

"It doesn't scare me. We'll take us one step at a time. Everything will be fine, you'll see." Ian planted more kisses, this time on his chest. "By the way, I love black hair. It's soooo sexy."

"How about you? Have you had many relationships?" Harper thought about stopping himself, but the impulse was too great. Reaching down, he took Ian into his hand and gently squeezed, waiting for a response.

"Careful, that's not a toy, you know. But don't be too careful." Ian snuggled closer. "A few relationships. The longest lasted for almost two years, and it's been over with now for a year. It was a nightmare. My problem, and I hope this doesn't scare *you*, is trying to find a guy that's willing to *work* at a relationship. What we're starting here…. Harper, unless you're not who you appear to be… well, I'm in it for the long haul. The little kinks, if there are any, we can work on along the way. Nobody's perfect. You'll discover things about me you won't like. I'll discover you're perfect." Ian tweaked his nose. "You can't just turn and run at the first sign of trouble. Most guys don't get that. Did that make any sense?"

He couldn't believe how much sense Ian made. He'd had this very discussion with himself before. How people are so fickle. How the grass always looks greener on the other side. People chasing after the perfect relationship, which, in his mind, probably didn't exist. "Where do I sign?"

"Well, you already have the pen in your hand." He felt Ian's cock pulsate.

"That was a good one." Harper chuckled.

"That was pretty good, wasn't it?" Ian worked his nipple between his fingers until it was rock hard. "How are you this morning? I hope I wasn't too hard on you? I wanted you. I couldn't control myself. You're the handsomest man I've ever been with."

"Back at you. I'm fine. A little sore, but in a good way. That's an awfully large pen you have."

Ian laughed. "Do you want more? No begging this time, I promise. Unless you like begging, and if you do, we can explore that route. I'm game."

He thought about answering but instead rolled over onto his side.

"Where do I find another…?" Ian propped himself up on his elbow.

"The top drawer. There's a small tube there too." He couldn't wait to have more of Ian.

Ian rolled over and found what he'd been looking for. Moments later, Harper felt Ian's slick finger begin to massage him. "Let's try this nice and slow, okay?"

A buzzing on the table startled him. "It's my cell. I might have to take this. Sorry."

"I'm not going anywhere."

"It's my grandmother, one minute." He sat up and took the call.

"Hello, Gram! How are you?" Harper reached over and ran his hand through Ian's hair. "I'm doing great! Are you home from church already?"

He smiled to Ian while he listened. *Ah, Gram, I can't wait to tell you the good news. I have a man in my life. You're going to love him.* "I'm sorry to hear that. He'd been sick for a while, hadn't he? Well, she's lucky she has you for a friend." He whispered to Ian, "Best friend's husband died," then spoke into the phone again. "I'm going to do some grocery shopping. Get the car washed. I've got a whole list of chores I should do." *Like enjoy sex with my new boyfriend.*

He felt Ian's hand brushing the hair on his chest.

"Work is going well, which reminds me—Gram, I'm still working very hard on the Jasper Flynn case. I'm not going to be able to get home for a while."—"I'll tell you about it too," he whispered to Ian once more—"You sound good, Gram. I miss you so much." *I need to be a much better grandson to you.* "When this whole thing is over, I'll come and visit, okay? I'm good. I have plenty of money. Thanks, though." He covered the phone to giggle. It felt even sillier being asked about his money situation in front of Ian. "Love you too. I'll get a card off to Eloise. Bye!" Harper gave the phone a kiss and placed it on the night table. "That was my grandmother down in Iowa. She's all I have for family that I know of. She and my grandfather raised me. We lost Gramps two years ago to the big C. It was awful."

"I'm sorry." Ian kissed his shoulder.

Realizing he'd just unleashed a boatful of information, Harper gave Ian a moment to digest it. This was the discovery phase of his relationship. He was thankful nothing had to be filed with the court.

"Can I ask what happened to Mom and Dad?" Ian stopped petting him to listen.

"Plane crash. I was very young. I have some memory of them, but it's limited."

"Wow." Ian resumed combing Harper's chest hair with his fingers. "I'd love to meet your grandmother sometime."

"She's going to adore you." It felt so good to have another man touch him. "How about you, Ian? As long as we're talking about family."

"My parents are still around and both doing well. They live in Buchannan, a very small town near the Minnesota-Canadian border. That's where Andy and I grew up. Andy, who you met the other night at the field, is my best friend. I have a sister who lives with her family in California. She's two years older. I have a younger brother who is still single. He's a realtor in Chicago. Pretty boring stuff. We all get along. No drama."

"I hope to meet them one day." Playful jabs from behind demonstrated to him Ian's eagerness to make love. He turned and kissed Ian, who returned the kiss. "I can't seem to get enough of you," he gushed.

"That's a very good thing," Ian said with a wink.

"Why's that?" he asked.

"Seems I'm all dressed up with no place to go."

He thought about this for a minute, and then he got it. "Oh." He laughed as he rolled back onto his side.

"Nice and slow," Ian whispered into his ear at the same time he was visited again by a warm, curious finger.

I'm starved. Ian's the first real nourishment I've had in years. I hope I don't scare him away.

"I like nice and slow." He reached behind and pulled Ian's arm across his chest.

"Let's do it another way this time. I want to see that handsome face of yours." Ian stood and gestured for him to move to the end of the bed. When his butt had reached the edge, Ian lifted his legs and rested his feet on his shoulders. "Are you comfortable like this?" Ian's eyes were filled with kindness as he smiled down and caressed Harper's inner thighs with his warm, strong hands.

Ian's not selfish. He's making love to me.

"I'm great." Harper reached up and stroked Ian's muscled arms. "Are you enjoying this?"

"What do you think?" Ian chuckled, leaning forward until he was poised to enter.

"I've never done this when it hasn't been rushed. I...."

Ian entered him and paused. "Something this good should never be rushed. Am I hurting you? I want you to enjoy every minute."

"You're not hurting me. No matter what or how we do this, I can't get close enough to you," he confessed as Ian pushed further in.

"Does this help?" Ian bent down until their chests met, resting his elbows on each side of Harper.

Harper reached up and stroked Ian's hair. "You're the man I've always fantasized about."

"You fantasized about having a poor landscaper make love to you? Really?" Ian slid all the way in and stopped.

"Yes, but I have to admit, the landscaping part of the fantasy is a bonus. It's everything else you are, Ian. You're a kind person, I can tell. You're a giver and not a taker. I want to prove to you I'm the same. Tell me what you need from me and I'm there."

Ian cupped his hand behind Harper's head and brought it up for a kiss. Their tongues brushed and danced together until Harper relented, allowing Ian to kiss him deeply. He reached around and hugged his lover around the waist. Seconds later Ian began to slowly thrust in and out. Harper trembled, hugging Ian tighter to his body.

"I don't need a lot, Harper. Honesty, that tops the list," Ian whispered after he'd broken off the kiss. "Are you sure I'm not hurting you?"

"I never thought this could feel so good," Harper purred. "I'd be lying if I told you honesty wasn't big on my list too."

"What?" Ian laughed. "Was that supposed to be a joke?"

"No. I say stupid things like that all the time. I was serious."

Ian reached under with both arms, bringing Harper up tight against his chest. At the same time, he intensified his effort below. Harper moved his arms up around Ian's neck. He could feel Ian's hefty thighs slap against his butt.

"Oh man," Ian moaned. "I'm not going to last long. This is just too... amazing." Easing Harper back onto the bed, Ian paused, moving a hand up to Harper's lips and parting them.

Harper took first one finger, then two into his mouth. Ian twisted his fingers until they were wet and slippery. Removing them, he smiled and took Harper into his hand and stroked. "You have a beautiful cock. It's perfectly shaped."

"Just lucky, I guess." Harper laughed. He didn't know what else to say. *You can't imagine how lucky I am.*

Ian milked him until he slid effortlessly up and down inside Ian's large palm. "Ahhhh, I'm not going to last long either."

Ian slowed his pace, working his fingers around Harper's swollen head. "You're sensitive here like I am." Ian teased and squeezed, the whole time looking down with a smile.

"You're driving me crazy." Harper pounded the bed in response to Ian's touch. Just when he thought he couldn't take it anymore, Ian gripped Harper's entire shaft in his hand and began to pump him hard.

"That feels so good. Please don't stop," Harper begged.

"I couldn't stop now if I wanted to." Ian began thrusting his hips with purpose.

Harper reached up to take over for Ian's hand, but it was shoved away. "Oh, Ian...."

"Lay back. Oh God," Ian roared. "I'm there. Let it go, Harper. Cum for me."

"Oh yes," Harper moaned seconds before he sprayed jets of warm sap all over Ian's chest.

Ian collapsed on top of him, panting and dripping wet. "Feel like trying this again sometime?"

"Ian...." Unable to communicate how wonderful he felt, Harper clamped his arms and legs around his handsome landscaper and squeezed. *I'm never going to let you go.*

CHAPTER
Four

"IAN, this is insane. He gave you a key? You know this is insane, right?" Andy leaned across his desk to emphasize his point.

Yes, he knew this was insane. He and Andy were merciless on other couples who rushed into relationships when they hardly knew one another. *This is different.*

"What do you want me to say? Did I plan for this to happen? No. It… well, it feels like the right move. I can't explain it, it just does." He hated himself for not having the nerve to make eye contact with his best friend. It was hard to justify an instinct, and that was about all he had. After spending yesterday in bed with Harper, he was convinced the man didn't have any cracks. He was worth pursuing; there was no question about it.

Andy shook his head in disbelief. "I'm not trying to tell you what to do, but I hope you're using your brain here and not your… damn it all, Ian, you need to go at this with some thought. That's all I'm saying."

Andy, give me a break here. I'm in the right place at the right time.

Ian looked around the office, not sure what more he could say to his friend. He hadn't expected this strong a reaction. Despite the fact that Andy thought him careless to move so quickly into a relationship, he felt confident he was making the right decision. He could be very tough on himself. To save his soul, he was unable to come up with a reason not to take the Harper leap. Where were the warning signs? Sure, you could argue that in such a short time, do you really know very much about a person? Even after being put on the spot like he was now, he was convinced this one was worth the risk. But he knew there was no defense he could call upon that would wipe away Andy's concern.

Wow! It's clean and organized in here! He'd been so nervous earlier he'd failed to notice the change. "When did you find the time to overhaul the office? Looks great!" He hoped his observation would, at least for the time being, cause Andy to lighten up.

"It wasn't me. I gave Emmett a raise last week with a list of conditions. Little adjustments I felt he could make. I came in the next morning, and voila! Of course it took me three hours to locate stuff, but hey, we're talkin' baby steps here."

He'd recently sensed a paternal pitch in his friend's voice when discussing his young employee. "Emmett's lucky to have you for a boss. He'd have his ass booted by now working anywhere else."

"He doesn't know it, but he's an experiment," Andy whispered, gesturing for him to turn around to see if the subject of their conversation might be lurking in the break room.

Ian stretched around and found it empty. "We're cool."

"I'm working on Emmett in subtle ways to make him more responsible and successful." Andy took a sip from his water bottle. "It's tough when you come into a job without a work ethic. I'd like to kick his parents' butts for sending him out in the world with so little to work with."

He had no doubt in his mind that if Andy were to ever come in contact with Emmett's parents, God help them, they'd definitely get a piece of his mind. "We come from good stock, you and I, Andy."

"Okay, I'm over it." Andy slapped his desk.

"Over what?" Ian cocked an eyebrow, waiting for another round of "careless Ian" to ramp up.

"I'm over the fact you fell to your knees at the mere sound of a zipper." Andy folded his arms across his sturdy chest and grinned.

He had his friend's blessing. It had been a tough battle, but it was worth it. "He's from good stock too." Ian winked.

He shared all he knew about Harper Callahan, which, sadly, wasn't much.

"There's more," he teased when Andy failed to keep the conversation flowing.

"No doubt." Andy had lost interest in his "my new boyfriend" story.

"Jasper Flynn, the guy in the news lately for swindling all the money from his investors? Harper is defending him."

"The guy's been found guilty," Andy fired back.

"I don't know the specifics, but I think that's what he was expecting." He surprised himself at how defensive he sounded.

"Wow, I'd sure hate to be in that dude's shoes." Andy reached for his phone to scan for messages.

"Well, when Harper told me about the trial, he didn't seem very bummed out. It was no big deal, all in a day's work kinda thing. He was more concerned about Flynn's wife, who I guess is a real piece of work." Ian embarrassed himself, realizing he was putting some serious wear on Harper's welcome mat. *Shut up already.*

"Now and then there are pictures of her in the newspaper. I've always thought she looked mean, even when she was smiling." Andy shuffled a stack of product catalogues on his desk.

"Like Mrs. Babbett, our third-grade teacher?" Ian was happy to change the focus of their conversation. "Remember how wicked her smile was? It scared the crap out of me. I think she wanted to beat us but couldn't." He slid a catalogue he'd been looking at across the desk to Andy.

"I wanted to beat her, I know that. Well, I have to get out on the lot and start filling an order. Somebody is supposed to be here at three to pick it up."

"Andy," Ian said, getting up from his chair, "thanks for being the bad cop."

"No problem, Spanky." Andy strolled over and took him into his arms. "We've looked after each other for so long it comes naturally. I'm on board. You deserve someone special, and it sounds like you might've found him."

"THAT was a good practice, don't ya think?" Spencer asked. He and Andy gave Spencer a hand lugging the equipment back to his car.

"Yeah, we're starting to gel, I can feel it." Andy waited for Spencer to open his trunk.

"Why does Mitch want to move into the outfield? He's too responsive to waste out there." Ian was disappointed he wouldn't have his trustworthy second baseman to throw to. Trapping runners between first and second had been a specialty they'd developed over the last couple of seasons.

"I think he's concerned about the baby. Donna is due in a few weeks, and he wants to make sure he has all the free time he can to enjoy playing daddy. Anyway, that's the gist of what I got from our telephone call last week," Spencer explained.

With Ian's encouragement, Spencer had assigned Larry Pelter to replace Mitch. It would take some time, but they'd click soon enough. Larry was wasted in the outfield. He was smart and quick. A necessity for playing second base.

"Thanks for the help, knob-gobblers. See you at Merl's."

"Not me." Ian looked away.

"It's starting." Andy glanced over to Spencer to see if he caught on.

"What's starting? Is there a bodybuilding competition on tonight? Wait, are you broke?" Spencer looked up from the trunk of his car.

"No, I'm not broke. I'm busy. I have plans." He needed to hold his ground here. Although he couldn't rely on Andy to help him out, he hoped his buddy would refrain from adding another log to the fire.

"Oh, I get it." Spencer shook his head sadly. "It's new boyfriend disease, isn't it? 'Forget all about your other friends' disease. I've seen it a million times."

"Call it whatever the hell you want, but yeah, I guess it is."

"You're going to let him get away with this?" Spencer wasn't giving up without a fight.

"I'll cut Spanky some slack for now. He'll be begging us to hang around for another beer before we know it."

"So, which one of you is the girl?" Spencer grinned, knowing he'd stepped across the imaginary line of acceptable insults with such aplomb.

"Interesting you should ask me that, Straight Cat. Andy and I have been asking ourselves the same question about you and Allison for years."

Spencer, unable to mask his delight in Ian's sassy comeback, blew his whistle while the three friends exchanged high fives.

Because of their schedules, Ian had planned to meet Harper after practice. It was agreed he would pick up Chinese on the way over. Unsure of what Harper preferred, he chose three different entrees from Peking Palace. He was surprised when he arrived to find the house dark. *Maybe he's watching television with the lights off?* He pressed the doorbell and chuckled, recalling Andy's line about a "Hello, Dolly!" ringtone. *What an idiot.* He pressed it again and waited. Turning to head back to his truck, he remembered Harper had given him a key. Entering the kitchen, he fumbled around in the dark until he found the light switch.

"Harper, you here?"

Setting the food on the counter, he went through the house, turning on lights. A quick visit to the upstairs confirmed what he had suspected: his boyfriend had been detained at work. It was strange being here without Harper. Strange, too, because it felt good to be here. The place had a welcoming feel to it. He turned on the oven and, after opening many wrong drawers and cupboards, found what he needed to have dinner organized and waiting. Helping himself to a beer, he sat down on the couch and turned on the television. To his delight, the Twins were playing the White Sox.

ANGRY at himself for not calling Ian, Harper pulled into the driveway. *Thank God!* The lights were on, a good sign Ian was inside waiting. He couldn't imagine another night without Ian. Grabbing his briefcase, he got out of the car and locked it. *Whoops!* He unlocked the car and reached into the backseat for the small box. *Can't forget this!*

Something smells delicious! In the kitchen, he spied the empty plates and glasses arranged on the counter. The television was on in the next room. He dropped his briefcase off on the dining room table and carried the small package behind his back into the living room. Ian, still dressed in his uniform, was fast asleep on the couch.

Harper stood beside the sofa and looked down at his hunky boyfriend. *Do you have any idea how happy I am now that you've entered my life? I'm going to love you like you've never been loved. I'm going to work so hard at making sure you're happy, and if you're ever not happy, I'm going to do whatever it takes to make you happy. What do you need to do in return?*

He smiled. This was a no-brainer if there ever was one. *You need to trust my love for you. I require no other changes.*

"Hey, sleepyhead." He bent down and kissed Ian's neck.

"Harper." Ian opened his eyes and smiled. "Wow, I can't believe I fell asleep."

"Sorry I'm so late. I should have called." He knew he had plenty of changes to make after being on his own for so long. "I guess that's something I'd better get used to remembering if I have any chance of keeping you happy during this Flynn mess."

"It's cool. I figured that's where you were. Have you eaten? Dinner's warming in the oven." Ian rubbed his eyes and sat up.

"I'm starved." He decided to change his plan. Dinner first and then gift. Gift required an explanation and possibly a discussion. It would be better to approach both with a full stomach.

"Here, this is for you,"—he presented the small box—"but let's grab some food first, okay?"

"Sure!" Ian took the box from Harper and shook it next to his ear before setting it on the table. "I wonder what it could be."

"It's nothing. Well, that's not exactly right." *Ian, it's the beginning of everything.* "Come on, slugger, let's eat."

Ian pulled the containers from the oven and opened them up. "This is shrimp in garlic sauce. This is kung pao chicken, and this is chicken chow mein. There's white and fried rice. Oh, and egg rolls. How'd I do?"

"I'm going to have some of everything. They all look good." Harper grabbed a plate and handed it to Ian. "You want another beer?"

"Actually, I'd like a glass of milk."

Harper chuckled, opening the refrigerator. "Of course, what else does a growing twenty-eight-year-old boy drink?" He poured a glass for Ian and grabbed a beer for himself. "Let's watch the rest of the game while we eat, okay?"

"Perfect!" Ian led the way into the living room.

"Wow!" Harper placed his plate down on the coffee table after wolfing down a healthy portion of each entree. "Did that ever hit the spot."

"What was your favorite? I wasn't sure what you'd like." Ian sat back.

"Garlic shrimp. Okay, it's gift time." He handed the box to Ian. *Relax. There's only two ways this can go.*

"What's this all about, anyway?" Ian seemed genuinely excited to be the recipient of a gift.

"Well, I've been thinking…. Go ahead, open it."

He had been thinking. For most of the day, he'd weighed the pros and cons of what this was all about. Trusting his instincts, he'd decided to go for broke and had sent his assistant, Brent, on a shopping trip when he'd decided on the appropriate gift.

Ian removed the metallic paper, exposing a long, narrow box. "I hope you didn't go overboard. I love presents, but really…." Ian giggled.

"Trust me, you're worth every cent and so much more. Now open it." Despite coaching himself over and over in the car, he was surprised at how nervous he was.

Ian opened the small box and, after a second or two, looked up, bemused.

"Is the color okay?" *Follow the script, Harp!*

"All right, what the heck is this about?" Ian chuckled, removing a bright blue toothbrush from the elaborate box.

"Ian, last night was painful, not being with you after our incredible weekend together."

"So you bought me a gift? Let's see, if I stay away, I get gifts? I'll have to remember that."

"That's right." Harper laughed. "And you get gifts for summer solstice, double coupon day, and whenever there's been a blackout. You've hit the jackpot." He brushed Ian's chin with his thumb. "This Flynn case, it's going to continue to suck the fun out of everything. My only saving grace is to have you to come home to. For the next couple of weeks, could you, would you consider…."

"Moving in with you?" Ian tested the bristles on his new toothbrush. "Great, it's a medium, just like at home."

Harper held his breath.

"Sure. It only makes sense. I have a ton of work to do around here, and—" Ian placed the box and the toothbrush on the table and put his arm around Harper's shoulder. "—last night was no picnic for me either. I was awake half the night trying to come up with a way for us to spend time together. I knew this was the best solution but didn't know if I should ask. I didn't want to come off as pushy."

Harper burst out laughing. "As you can see, I do pushy really well."

"But you're right about the phone call. You need to work on that."

"I promise! Anything else? I'm a quick study, and not to brag, but I'm used to getting all A's."

"Just this." Ian leaned forward and kissed him.

"When this Phyllis thing settles down,"—he buried his head in the crook of Ian's neck—"we'll spend a whole bunch of time at your place."

"Well, let's cross that bridge when we get to it. I love your house. When I was here alone, I still felt comfortable. I mean, it feels a whole lot better now that you're here." It was Ian's turn to have a nervous laugh.

"Nothing you could have said could have made me feel happier." He rubbed Ian's knee, his body sending unmistakable signals at the thought of rubbing much more once they'd gotten into bed. "It's been a long day for us both. Let's leave this mess and head upstairs. I'll take care of it in the morning, okay?"

"Thank you, Harper." Ian stroked Harper's face with his warm hand.

Harper removed the hand and kissed it. "Thank you for what?"

"For the toothbrush. I thought at first it might be some tacky piece of jewelry." Ian's eyes twinkled.

"Like this?" Harper pulled from his pocket a handsome black onyx and leather bracelet.

HIS large suitcase in one hand and an armful of shirts still on their hangers in another, Ian trudged up the narrow stairs of Harper's to the small empty room across from the bathroom. Harper had mentioned a small dresser and the closet if he needed it until they could figure out a permanent solution. He hung his clothes in the closet and walked over to the dresser. On the top was an envelope with his name on it. He picked it up, noticing that the otherwise very neat and orderly Mr. Callahan had atrocious handwriting. In it he found a note wrapped around a check for $10,000.

> Ian,
>
> Welcome! Please consider this your home now too. I'm smiling as I write, because I can't remember a time in my life when I've felt this happy. It's like I've stepped out of the storm and into the sun when thinking about you... us. If you need to get a hold of me for any reason, call my assistant Brent (553-9887), and he'll track me down. The check is an advance for your work and supplies. Hugs and kisses, Harp.
>
> PS: I emptied the drawers and ran a damp towel inside to make sure there weren't any dust bunnies.

It does feel like home, Harper. You feel like home too.

Ian plugged Brent's number into his cell phone and emptied his suitcase into the dresser. By the time he was back in the yard, Earl from Prairie Planks had pulled up with the arbor.

The two men unloaded the pieces and carried them into the yard. They placed the four posts into the holes Ian had pre-dug. Next, using two ladders, they began piecing together the four sections of the top, an ornate grid that would eventually support the vine Harper had requested.

"Looks great, Earl. Thanks for getting this done so quickly."

"No prob. We were just standing around twiddling our fingers. Orders are starting to come in, so I expect from here through the rest of the season we'll have plenty to keep us busy. Geeze, Ian, I'm impressed. Looks like you had the holes right on the money. This thing is as straight as it can get."

Kinda like you, Earl.

"Well, after the fiasco we had out in Maple Plain last year, I learned my lesson. You were a trouper to stick with me on that one," he reminded Earl with a guilty shake of the head.

"Oh hell, I'd forgotten all about that." Earl chuckled. "We had a hell of a time out there, that's for sure."

Ian thanked Earl and sat down with his clipboard on one of the lawn chairs Harper had dug out of the garage, to go over his notes. Now that the arbor was in place, things could really start rolling along. Dirk, a friend who had helped with paving jobs in the past, needed money and was happy to help out. Dirk had agreed to come over later that morning to start. Ian still needed to call a plumber to have a line run from the house out to the corner of the yard where the water feature was planned. This needed to happen today. Andy had the list of product, much of it already in stock, and it could be delivered anytime.

Reminded of one more thing, he scrolled through his contacts until he found what he was looking for and pressed Call.

"Bright Spot, this is Nathan."

"Hey, Nate, it's Ian Burke." *Awesome, he's in.*

"Oh hi, Ian. What's up?"

"Can you or one of your guys come out to a house in South Minneapolis today? I'm working on a job that requires lighting." He had his fingers crossed that this would work out.

"Sure, I can come. When were you thinking? I'm alone in the shop right now, but I'll have someone else in here after lunch."

"How about one thirty?"

"I can make that work. What's the address?"

Hanging up with Nate, he surveyed the yard. There was still so much to do. He wasn't under any deadline Harper had given him. It was his own. It was odd working for someone you were dating. It felt too much like Harper was supporting him, and he couldn't tolerate that feeling.

HARPER was seated on the top row of the bleachers with his briefcase open next to him and his laptop on his knees. Earlier there had been rumblings of thunder, but for the time being, the storm appeared to be staying to the south. The Hornets had already started practice. Ian was playing first base. Harper watched, fascinated, as the pitcher wound up and threw the ball. Like a leopard waiting to pounce on his unsuspecting prey, Ian waited to see if the batter would bite on the pitch. With a loud crack, the bat connected with the ball, sending a line drive rocketing toward second. The ball bounced off the ground and was caught by Larry Pelter. Larry pivoted and whipped it to Ian, who snagged it out of the air with ease and tagged the batter a split second before he charged across the base.

God, that was hot to watch. And he's all yours, Harp! He reluctantly fought off an image of Ian in his baseball outfit taking him over a log in the woods—a marvelous combination of two of his most beloved fantasies: guys in baseball uniforms and outdoor sex.

He returned to his work until he felt the vibration of footsteps coming toward him. Looking up, he assigned them to an attractive woman with short blond hair. She smiled as she approached.

"Harper?" the woman asked, continuing her advance.

Startled she knew his name, he answered tentatively, "Could be...."

"I'm Allison. I'm a friend of Ian's."

She had a warm smile. He did a quick inventory of names Ian had mentioned in the short time they'd been seeing each other. Allison was familiar, but he just couldn't link it to save his soul.

"Hello, Allison. Guilty as charged. I'm Harper Callahan."

"I don't mean to disturb you if you're working."

"No… no you're not disturbing me. I should have left this at home." He closed his laptop and slid it into his computer bag.

"Do you mind if I watch practice with you? I have wine coolers if you're interested. Berry and peach." Allison gestured to the green eco-bag slung over her shoulder.

"Please, please have a seat." He had plenty of work to do, but it was time to call it a day. "Wine cooler. I'm not sure I've had one before."

"The berry flavor isn't as sweet as the peach."

"In that case, I'll try the berry."

Allison reached into her bag and pulled out a colorful bottle and snapped off the top. "There you go."

"Thank you." He waited to sip until she had one too.

"So… Ian… he's had nothing but wonderful things to say about you." She sipped.

"Allison, I'm sorry, but I have to ask, how do you know Ian?" He sensed it might be in his best interest to start this one off on the right track.

"Oh, no problem. I'm married to the guy down there that… that… ah shoot—that just struck out. That would be Spencer. Spencer met Ian when he joined the Hornets a few years ago. Ian's a sweetheart. His friendship means a lot to us."

"Right! I met Spencer last week along with Andy. I don't recall seeing you here, though."

"I stay away early in the season. Once things get into full swing, you'll see me around all the time. I came tonight in hopes of meeting you." Allison sat, leaving what he judged to be the appropriate amount of space for two individuals who didn't know each other.

He sipped his cooler, thankful he hadn't offended her.

"So tell me a little about yourself, Harper."

He complied with Allison's request, covering the basics. Turned out she had worked in a law office for a short time while in college, and that prompted more questions and discussion. Soon the conversation made its way back to her intended subject.

"Ian is without a doubt the kindest, most giving person I've ever met. I can't even say that about my husband. We love him like family."

He sipped his cooler, letting Allison's last comment drift for a minute before he responded. Sure, this was a friendly visit, but there was an agenda here that only a dimwit could miss. It was time to be assertive and step up to the challenge.

"I'm a lawyer, Allison. I'm not the best lawyer in the world, but I'm pretty sure I'm not the worst. Part of being a lawyer is to assess the situation and adjust the game plan accordingly. Unless I'm missing something here, you've come bearing gifts."

"The wine coolers?"

"Oh, nice try."

"Thank you." Allison chuckled. It was clear she was on to him too.

"The gift you bear is a gentle little message, a gift-wrapped piece of advice that I think goes something like this: harm our dear friend Ian in any way and prepare to die. Did I get close?"

"Actually, you were spot on." Allison offered her bottle to his for a toast. They clicked and sipped. "Harper, Ian's not stupid. He's a good judge of character. We're all just a little surprised at how fast you guys are moving. Well, that and we're selfish as hell about the time we spend with him. Will you promise me you'll be honest with him? We can deal with the rest if we know he's not being screwed over."

"I love it that you feel this way. When I first met Ian, besides the fact that he's about as cute as any person deserves to be, I sensed a kind soul, a gentle man. Characteristics I'd always hoped the man I fell for would possess. Your frankness confirms what I'd hoped. I promise to be honest with him. I promise to treat him better than anyone, including you. I mean that in the best way possible. However, I wouldn't put any money on us *not* working out."

"I like you, Harper Callahan."

"And I like you, Allison…?"

"Hardpecker."

Caught off guard, he sprayed berry cooler out in all directions.

"Gotcha!" Allison proclaimed proudly. "It's Benson, Spencer and Allison Benson."

IAN could not have been happier. He'd had this night planned for several days, but because of Harper's schedule, he wasn't sure if he'd be able to pull it off. Pouring wine into their glasses, he heard the welcome sound of Harper coming down the stairs.

"Oh man, that shower felt good." Harper strolled into the kitchen smiling.

"Come here, counselor." Ian beckoned with his finger. "Yum, you smell so good." He rubbed his face into Harper's T-shirt.

"Counselor. How Della Street of you. Hey, are there times when I smell bad?" Harper lifted Ian's head off his chest.

"Haven't come across one yet. I loved Perry Mason. I bet Della was great after you got a few drinks in her. Here." He handed a glass to Harper. "Cheers!"

"Cheers! Wow, those steaks, they look great. Are you going to cook them in the oven?"

"Nope!"

"Hmm… not the oven." Harper surveyed the kitchen. "Are you going to pan-fry them?"

"Nope!"

"I'm running out of options. Are you going to boil them in chocolate milk?"

"Go put on your flips. We're heading out to the backyard."

Harper did as he was told and followed him out the door.

"Ian, this looks great. I love the pavers. And the arbor, it's all coming together so well. Oh look, you scored a grill. A grilled steak at home, what a treat!" Harper sounded like a little kid, his reaction to the yard so honest and genuine.

Ian knew in his heart the time was right to make his move. Harper, without coming right out and asking for it, begged for a sign of commitment from him. To prove to himself he was approaching this relationship responsibly, he'd waited so long to express his true feelings it seemed almost cruel. He wanted Harper to know what he was feeling inside. Harper needed to know this so they could begin to grow their relationship.

"Harper, I've been holding back on you, but I can't any longer."

"Oh God, are you pulling the rug out from under me?" Harper leaned against an arbor post for support.

"No. I'm standing here, next to you, because I want to tell you that I love you. I love you, Harper Callahan."

He watched Harper process what he'd just heard. He blinked, and then his lower lip quivered. "Ian...."

"I just wanted to say it." He cupped Harper's round, pert butt in both hands. "I wanted to get it out of the way so it wasn't strange or awkward. I love you. I'm certain of it. I love saying it."

Wiping his eyes with his sleeve, Harper wrapped an arm around his waist. "Ian, I love you too. This is the honest truth. I could have said I love you the night we had dinner at Leona's."

He welcomed his man's kiss. They took turns nibbling and pecking each other until their tongues got involved and the kiss turned passionate.

"Hey! I have a surprise for you. Ready?" Ian broke away, unable to wait a second longer.

"I'm ready for anything you can throw at me, you handsome devil." Harper planted a smooch on his cheek.

"Drumroll please!" Ian gave the cue and then laughed as Harper did his best to imitate a drumroll. Walking over to one of the arbor posts, he flipped a switch. At first, nothing seemed to be happening, and then the sound of rushing water tumbling over rock filled the backyard.

"The water feature!" Harper shrieked.

"Yep, but hang on." He flipped another switch, and the backyard was magically transformed into a garden paradise. The water feature, the patio—he had worked with Bright Spot to create pools of accent light that seemed to shine out of nowhere. "Is this kind of what you had in mind?"

Harper walked around the yard in wonderment. "I'm cry-happy. This is amazing, Ian. It's spectacular."

"Enjoy, Mr. Callahan. I have to grill."

The air had chilled considerably by the time the steaks were ready. Ian insisted they eat inside. He would have loved to celebrate the backyard coming together into the wee hours, but Harper needed to be in the office early the next morning.

They chatted up a storm all through dinner. Harper confessed he'd lost track of so many friends over the years, and now that he felt good about his yard, how nice it would be to throw a great big bash so their friends could meet when it was finished. "I love that idea," Ian assured. "I can't wait to meet your friends."

"Thank you. Tonight was so special." Harper rubbed Ian's back after they'd brought their dishes from the dining room into the kitchen.

"Hon, you go upstairs and get ready for bed. I'll finish down here." Harper looked exhausted. Even though he talked very little about work, Ian knew his boyfriend's days were challenging in a very different way than his own, which could be physically exhausting. Harper's work required intensive thought and strategy, leaving him empty and distant by the end of the day.

Stepping away from the sink, he took Harper into his arms. After a few long, lovely kisses, they swayed together for several minutes without saying a word. It felt so good to hold him. It was anyone's guess what the next few weeks would be like. He was confident they were, as a couple, heading into it in the best way possible—two men in love.

"Okay, I'm off to bed. See you upstairs."

Ian finished picking up, and when he was certain he'd collected everything, he started the dishwasher and headed toward the stairs. Halfway up, he heard Harper's voice.

"What did I tell you? You will not talk to me in that tone of voice, do you understand?"

As Ian entered the bedroom, Harper shot him a distressed look. "Yes, but you haven't been honest with yourself, Phyllis. And you know this."

Harper rolled his eyes as he paced back and forth, holding his phone away from his ear.

"Phyllis… oh, I will call you Phyllis or anything else I want to, you got that? So, Phyllis, are you sitting down? I got some news for you."

Ian was amazed to see a side of Harper he'd never imagined. His voice, his posture, had been transformed from the soft-spoken, loving, wonderful man he'd just sent upstairs to bed into a caged lion.

"Whether you accept it or not, Phyllis, your husband will be going to prison for a very long time. That's the reality. I'm going to try and salvage as much of your money as I can for you, and hear me when I say this—I'm going to do that for you not because I want to, or like you, or want the best for you. I'm doing it because I'm being paid to do it. And here's another thing we need to clear up—I'm a fucking damned good lawyer, Phyllis Flynn. You and your husband are extremely lucky to have me. Did you hear that? You are fucking lucky to have Harper Callahan on your side. So go have a good cry, and after you've done that, prepare yourself for the worst. He's going to jail, and you… run the risk of losing everything."

Ian stood frozen in the doorway. Harper's chest heaved up and down. His eyes were on fire. Seconds passed, and then Harper placed his phone on the table. "Can you believe this shit? The woman's a lunatic. I swear to God, I'm this close to throwing in the—" He was interrupted by the doorbell.

"You expecting anyone?" Ian backed out of the room.

"No."

"Relax, and get ready for bed. I'll get it." Reaching the bottom of the stairs, he peered out the side window. A woman paced back and forth on the sidewalk.

"Hello, can I help you?" Ian asked when he'd opened the door.

"Who the hell are you?"

The second she opened her mouth, Ian knew he'd come face to face with Harper's nemesis, Phyllis Flynn. Standing at the bottom of the steps, she resembled a wealthy coolie. Dressed in dark capri pants and a satin blouse accented with narrow jewel-tone stripes, she completed the look with sparkly gold slippers, giving the multitude of jewelry around her neck and wrists a good run for its money.

"I'm Ian."

"Where's Callahan? I know this is his... house."

"He's...." He didn't have a clue how to handle this situation. Turning, he hollered up the stairs, "Harper? Please come down."

"Who are you? The boyfriend?" Phyllis shook her head in disgust. "This just keeps getting better and better."

Ian was spared having to respond when Harper stepped through the door, positioning himself between them. He moved to the side so he could watch from the window.

"Phyllis, you showing up here, at my home, is absolutely unacceptable."

"You think I give a shit what you think, faggot?"

Ian, fearful Harper might do something he would later regret, reached out and put a hand on his shoulder.

"I'll tell *you* what's unacceptable. It's your goddamn disrespect." Phyllis moved up a step, but Harper held his ground. "I won't have it. You work for me. Me! What about that can't you understand?"

"Apparently about as much as you understood from our conversation a few minutes ago. By being here, you're not doing a thing to help your situation. I hope you know that."

"That's my point, you idiot. I don't have a situation. You have a situation. And your situation is about to get a fuck of a lot worse. I will make your life so goddamned miserable if you don't start shaping up, you'll wish you were never born. Never born, understand me?"

"It's been a lovely little visit, Phyllis. I can't thank you enough for stopping by. Now if you'll please excuse us—"

"Keep it up, Callahan." Ian watched from Harper's side as Phyllis stepped down. "I'll wipe that smug little smirk off your face, you can count on it. You work for me. Got it?" Taking a few steps down the walk, she turned back. "Impressive little shit shack you have."

Phyllis stomped down the walk, climbed into the car she had left running in the middle of the street, slammed it into gear, and in her attempt to make a hasty retreat, drove up over the curb as she rounded the corner.

"Wow." Ian wasn't sure what he'd just witnessed. "She's insane."

Harper started to laugh.

"What's so funny?" Ian asked, unable to find any humor in Phyllis's visit.

Harper pointed to the end of the sidewalk where it met the curb. "I saw it earlier but forgot to go out and pick it up." He was laughing so hard, he had to lean into the side of the house for support.

Ian walked down the steps in hopes of spotting what had triggered Harper's funny bone. It didn't take him long. The streetlight captured it beautifully. Right where Harper had pointed sat a Marmaduke pile of dog crap with a petite footprint planted right in the middle of it.

"Shit shack," Harper roared.

"HARPER, wake up. You're having a bad dream. Harper, wake up." Ian grabbed Harper's shoulder and gently shook it.

Since having it out with Phyllis Flynn the other night, Harper hadn't been sleeping well. He'd been tormented by a series of violent dreams. This was by far the worst.

"Harper, Harper, it's me, Ian."

"What? Oh God, oh…." Harper propped himself up with one arm and blinked to get his bearings. Droplets of sweat trickled down from his hairline. "I'm sorry. I was having another one of those awful dreams."

"I know, sweetie, I know. Stay right here, I'll be back in a minute." He got up and walked to the bathroom, returning with a large bath towel. "You're soaking wet. Here." He dried Harper's face and chest. "Lift your arms."

When he'd finished toweling him off, he stood and walked around to Harper's side of the bed, straightening out the sheets and the coverlet. "Do you remember any of your dream?"

"I was coming out of the courthouse,"—Harper snuggled up to him when he had returned to his side of the bed—"and no matter where I turned, people were lashing out and chasing me. Reporters, Phyllis, everyone. It was like they were hunting me. I couldn't get away. I want this case to be over with so badly."

"Oh, baby." He invited Harper, still breathing heavily, into his arms. Ian gently petted and stroked his man. "It will all be over soon."

"I had no idea the Flynns would take such a toll on me," Harper confessed. "I don't know what I would've done if you hadn't been here. As crappy as things are right now, having you in my life has meant so much. Knowing you'll be here when I get home at night, no matter when that is, is so comforting. I hope one day I can repay you for all you're doing."

Ian rested his head on Harper's shoulder. "You make it sound like work. I've been waiting for years to play house with the right man. Hey, you got home too late to see, but most of the planting is done in the backyard. I had to do it in the rain, but that's a good time to plant. It's easier on the product."

"I can't wait to see." Harper yawned, pulling Ian's arm tighter across his chest.

"When you think about it, all this time you've been wrapped up in this case, you sure haven't missed any nice spring days." Ian wasn't sure what would be comforting at this point.

"This summer is going to be so much fun. I can't wait to be at your opening game." Harper seemed to melt into him.

"Do you have any idea how proud I will feel knowing you're there?" He kissed the top of Harper's head, still moist from the bad dream. "Listen, I know how much pressure you're under now." He wanted to make sure Harper understood this. "I'm here for you. Let me help you if I can."

"Right now, being held by you is exactly what I need." Harper snuggled closer.

"I know I could never do it," Ian admitted with another kiss.

"It's a job. Nothing more, nothing less." Harper turned onto his side and backed into him. "But I have to tell you, and this is just between you and I, Phyllis Flynn hasn't done her husband any favors. The judge is going to throw the book at her, not Jasper. Poor guy. He's going to be one of those people who, after a year or so in prison, gets sick and dies. He'll gradually shut down."

Ian looked over at the clock on Harper's side of the bed. It read three thirty. "Try and fall back to sleep. I'm here to watch out for you. I won't go anywhere. And"—he gently nibbled at Harper's ear—"I love you."

"Mmm…." Harper yawned large. "I love you too."

HARPER woke the morning of the sentencing to one of Minnesota's perennial spring insults, snow showers. He showered and dressed, and when he got downstairs, Ian had an egg, toast, and coffee waiting.

"What's it like the morning of a sentencing?" Ian handed him a steaming mug.

"It's fine. The press will be all over the place. That puts a different spin on things. Look at this weather, dreary and cold." He glanced out the window at the backyard. All of Ian's hard work was blanketed with a light dusting of snow.

I'd give anything to spend today with Ian.

Harper was surprised at how relaxed he felt. The writing was on the wall. Jasper Flynn was sure to be awarded one of the harshest sentences possible despite his pleas for leniency. All anyone could do at this point was let the process run its course. And that's what made it so hard to leave this morning. Whether he was at the sentencing or not, the outcome would be the same.

"What do you do on days like this?" Harper sipped his piping hot coffee cautiously.

"Further into the season, I can use rain days to catch up on invoicing, ordering, maybe some sketching and planning. But business isn't there yet for me to have anything to catch up on. I think I'll go over to my apartment and pick up a few more things. Then I'll stop by Andy's and see if I can help him out. If you get a chance, give me a call and let me know how things are going." Ian walked over and wrapped his arms around Harper. "I wish you didn't have to go in this morning. I can think of more than one thing I could do to you on a day like today."

"You stop!" Harper begged, accepting a smooch on the lips. "I'm already dreading the rest of the day. Oh man, I lost track of the time. I have to run. I'll call you, I promise."

Harper spent much of the day reviewing a new pro bono case involving a woman who had voluntarily surrendered her three children because she was unable to control her methamphetamine addiction. Now that she was clean, she was having second thoughts and had hired an attorney to help get them back. The guardian ad litem, a county employee who monitored the situation, advised the mother was still a risk. Harper had been asked to defend the county's opinion. An hour before he was scheduled to leave for the courthouse, he reviewed his sentencing notes and, for the first time all day, felt the familiar pangs of nervousness. Minutes before they were to leave, his assistant, Brent, showed up at his office door.

"Hey, Harper. Ready to head out?"

"I can't find my phone. Have you seen my phone?" Frustrated for being such a scatterbrain, Harper searched his desk and bookshelves.

Brent joined the search, finding the phone buried underneath a pile of case notes.

"Sorry, I thought I looked there." He tucked it in his coat pocket.

"Do you want me to call Mrs. Flynn?" Brent had a history of winning over difficult clients and most likely viewed Phyllis Flynn as a prime test of his considerable people skills.

"Thanks, but no. I wouldn't wish that on anyone. I'll call her when we get in the car. I wouldn't be surprised at all if she was a no-show. She doesn't care about Jasper and probably has a nail appointment she can't miss."

"Duncan and Arthur are already on their way over." Brent glanced down at his notes.

"Great! You ready for this?" He stepped out of the office.

"I know it's not going to be under the best circumstances, but I'm looking forward to being in court with you." Brent trailed Harper out the door.

He knew Brent was excited. Harper was glad he'd thought to include him. On the way to the car, he called Ian.

"Burke Landscaping."

"Ian." He'd fallen in love with Ian's voice too. *Love... it's everything they said it would be and more!*

"Oh hey, Harper."

"I'm off to the sentencing. If you have access to a television, there might be some local coverage after four. I'll try not to be in tears." He opened the car door and hopped in.

"I'm at Jungle Gems helping Andy out. I'll run into his office and check it out. I love you. See you at the house later."

"I love you too. Bye!" Glancing over at Brent, he figured now was as good a time as any for an Ian update.

"I have a new man in my life, as you might have already guessed from the favor you did for me the other day. His name is Ian Burke, and he's a landscaper. I thought you should know, as you'll probably at some point be talking to him." He looked over to Brent for a reaction.

"I'm happy to hear that. Have you guys been seeing each other long?" Brent adjusted his seat belt.

"No." He chuckled. "But it feels like we have. I mean that in a good way."

"Sure. I understand. I'd love to meet him."

It might have been because he was looking for it that he detected a slight hint of jealousy in his assistant's response. Harper suspected a crush had developed. Little signs here and there were hard to ignore. Although Brent was a fair catch, Harper wasn't inclined to dip his pen in the firm's ink.

He punched in Phyllis's number. To his relief, the phone went right into voice mail. Either she was on another call or she had it turned off. "Phyllis, this is Harper Callahan. If I'm going to be of any service to you, I need you to return my calls. I'm on my way over to Jasper's sentencing. I'll look for you when I get there. I'll keep my line clear if you need to get in touch with me."

At the top of the courthouse steps, he was surprised to see so much press already gathered. With Brent right on his heels, he ignored their questions and charged past onto the elevator leading up to Judge Morrison's courtroom, 2C, where the trial had taken place. Inside the double door, he was relieved the judge had maintained his stance, limiting the number of media permitted inside. A quick glance around the room confirmed Phyllis, at least for now, was a no-show. He looked at his phone to make sure he hadn't missed a call or a text before silencing it. He and Brent took their seats next to Arthur and Duncan, leaving an open chair in the middle for their client.

"Any word from Phyllis? I left a voice mail, but she hasn't returned my call," Harper looked to the partners for a response.

"Nothing on this end." Duncan glanced over at Arthur, who shook his head.

Jasper Flynn, dressed in a charcoal suit and a black tie, was led into the courtroom. Brent stood and escorted him over to his chair.

"Even though the decision is made," Duncan whispered in Jasper's ear, "do your best to show your human side. Just make sure not to overreact. Show some confidence, and above all, be respectful."

"Relax as best you can," Harper said, squeezing Jasper's arm. "Today's sentencing is not much more than a formality—"

"The appeal is almost ready to be filed, and you may see this judge again," Duncan interrupted.

Ah Dunc, God forbid our client come away from this massacre without knowing how courageously you fought for his freedom.

Jasper nodded with unmistakable fear in his eyes.

In a matter of minutes, the courtroom was packed from floor to ceiling with the people Jasper had screwed. The court reporter sat down in his "cubby" to the left of the judge's throne while the administrative clerk sat behind her big computer screen to the right. Harper gave her and the court reporter a business card to ensure they had the proper spelling of his name. He enjoyed interacting with the court staff. He'd take every opportunity he could get to convince them he was really a good guy despite his role in Jasper's defense.

Back in his seat, he watched the judicial law clerk quietly slip into a chair on the sidelines. The admin clerk picked up the phone to let the judge know the room was ready. The bailiff stood and, in his best monotone voice, demanded, "All rise."

Harper felt at peace while people around him announced who they were for the court reporter so it went on the record.

Nothing I say today is going to change your mind, is it, Judge?

He knew regardless of how well he pleaded for leniency, the decision had already been made. Based on the judge's reactions and comments during the trial, he held out little hope their client would be given a break.

The judge asked the prosecution for their final thoughts, and the courtroom fell silent.

As expected, Naomi Hendricks, the dowdy and incredibly plain lead prosecutor, whined about her disgust for Jasper and the financial plague he'd inflicted on the good folks who just happened to be voting members of the constituency that elected her boss.

This is a big flash in a very small career, Naomi. Enjoy!

He was brought back to the moment when the prosecution, in the hopes of squashing any notion the judge may have had for not imposing the maximum sentence, produced for the court a handful of Jasper's victims.

"You robbed us of our retirement," a man said, trembling with emotion. "Instead of spending our final years enjoying…."

Harper was forced to stare down at the table while the man speaking struggled to gain control.

"… the wife and I are working full time. We have nothing left."

Spectators in the courtroom reacted noisily as the man walked back to his seat. The next victim was called up, and Harper winced when he saw her rise and walk to the podium using a walker. *Oh God, this is going to be a bad one.*

"Twenty-five years ago—" The woman stopped and pulled a hankie out from the sleeve of her lavender sweater. "I'm sorry. Twenty-five years ago my husband invested with Jasper Flynn, only months before—" She stopped to blow her nose. "Months before he passed away from lung cancer. When he died, Flynn…"

Like the previous victim, this woman was debilitated by emotion and anger. *Oh please make this end.*

"…he placed his arm around me and promised me everything was safe with him. And it wasn't. It's all gone! I hope you never see the light of day," the woman shouted over to Flynn before a deputy helped her back to her seat.

"Mr. Callahan, is there anything you'd like to say on behalf of your client?" the judge asked, raising an eyebrow as if to say "proceed at your own risk."

Harper sucked in a deep breath, adjusted his tie, and stood. Taking a minute to collect his thoughts after the drama he had just witnessed, he began, "Your honor, Jasper Flynn comes before you today understanding the crimes he was convicted of committing require punishment. Mr. Flynn's intentions have always been to help his clients, his friends, financially prosper."

He was forced to pause while the courtroom exploded with a wave of angry response. The judge, after a few moments, silenced the boos and hisses with his gavel.

"Mr. Flynn did not act out of malice," he continued when he thought it safe. "His actions were those of a desperate man in fear of failing those closest to him. We respectfully request your honor to keep Mr. Flynn's intentions in mind when imposing sentence."

He gulped as he paused to weather an even stronger tone of dissatisfaction that swept over the courtroom, a reaction to his portrayal of Jasper as anything other a monster. He made eye contact with Jasper's detractors before turning to face his client directly. He wanted to remind the judge of the human side of this man, not the convict.

"This is a husband," Harper forged on, undeterred by the mood of the spectators, "a father, a loyal friend who acted with the best interests of his loved ones in mind. The economy was crashing, and Jasper panicked—not for himself but for his clients, his friends."

He stared down at his notes. At least for his part, he was making some ground. The reaction to his last few statements was mere grumblings. He paused for a few more beats to emphasize his point. "It's likely difficult for those who lost money to remember Jasper is more than just a financial advisor whose choices cost them dearly. I ask those people to consider how far they would go to protect their loved ones from the catastrophes relating to the financial meltdown the rest of the country battled."

He squeezed Jasper's arm in a sign of solidarity before sitting back down.

"Nicely done," Duncan whispered.

I don't know what more I could have said. We're definitely not the home team. Taking a deep breath, he waited for the finale to begin.

"Mr. Flynn, will you please rise," the judge commanded when the courtroom had calmed.

Harper, along with the entire defense team, rose alongside Jasper, acting as literal and figurative supports for their client.

"Is there anything you'd like to say before I sentence you?" The judge sat with his arms folded in front of him.

Jasper cleared his throat and addressed the court. "I understand the anger in this room. I truly hope someday these fine people will know why I did what I did."

His opening statement triggered a flood of rage. Again, the judge was forced to use his gavel to silence the many who cried out in anger.

"Nothing I can say will change anything," he continued, his voice burdened with emotion. "I know the people in this courtroom won't believe it when I tell them how deeply sorry I am this has—"

"Why should they believe you?" the judge snapped back. "All you've done to them is lie and spend their money."

The judge's terse response caught Harper by surprise. It appeared to shake Jasper to his core, but somehow he found the courage to continue.

"I just wanted to apologize, your honor."

"Why?" Judge Morrison shot back, this time with even more conviction.

Jasper began to weave back and forth. Harper closed the gap between them in the event he started to go down.

"Why should anyone believe anything you have to say? You cheated people out of millions and you spent their money, and I think you've taken up enough of our time today."

Harper stared forward in astonishment as Judge Morrison swiftly sentenced Jasper to twenty-five years for his crimes. The judge went on to encourage the victims to consider seeking remuneration via civil action.

Bye-bye, Jasper!

Out of the corner of his eye, Harper saw his client crumble.

"I'm sorry." He took hold of Jasper's arm and held him up until the court officers could take over. Flynn was devastated. His worst fears had been realized.

This is your fault, Phyllis. Your greed drove your husband off the deep end. And the worst thing, you can't even find it in your heart to be here for him. You're the lowest of low.

Once Jasper was out of the courtroom, Harper led the defense team over to shake hands with the prosecution and exchanged pleasantries like "you did what you could" and "nice work, counselors."

That was a special kind of awful! Get me the hell out of here!

Picking up his briefcase, he left the courtroom and was immediately inundated with questions from the press. He did his best to hide his lack of empathy for his client while addressing the numerous inquiries about Jasper's sentence. Brent kept him moving through the crowd. Duncan and Arthur were nowhere in sight.

Out on the steps of the courthouse, he ran into a virtual roadblock of reporters.

"How do you feel about the sentence?"

"Do you plan on appealing?"

"As you can imagine, I'm very disappointed in the outcome." He thought carefully about his next choice of words. "Jasper is a victim of the economy, and I would have hoped…."

Distracted by a flurry of activity to his left, he scanned the crowd for its source. He first spotted Phyllis charging up the steps, shoving people out of her way, and then, to his horror, the gun pointed directly at him.

Putting his hand up as if it would somehow protect him, he hollered out, "No, Phyllis! No—"

CHAPTER
Five

EMPTYING the mop bucket into the drain under the dishwasher, Alex returned it to the little room off the kitchen that housed a beat-up washer, dryer, and cleaning supplies. Until the weather turned warmer and stayed warm, the Lip Smacker, a café located just outside of Castle Danger on Highway 62, would open for breakfast and lunch only. The weekday hours available to work while he completed his senior year of high school were from two thirty to four each day. Audrey Pakenpooch, the owner, did whatever she could to work around his school schedule. When the season hit, he worked around her schedule. Audrey felt, and at times acted, like his mother. It was special to him that she had known his mom while she was still alive.

Before punching out, he hauled the garbage he'd bagged earlier and left lined up along the wall to the dumpster behind the diner. Business was slow, making garbage detail a snap.

Outside, he noticed the warm afternoon air was starting to chill. Winter was reluctant to leave the North Shore. This year, winter had been stubborn as hell.

Grabbing his letter jacket from the tiny break room, he punched out, locked the back door, and climbed into Zits, his beat-up orange Jetta. Colin, his best friend, had christened the car Zits because of the little brown hail dents covering it. Old Zits was reliable, about the only good thing anyone could say about his ride.

Okay, Zits, what are we gonna do now?

The last thing he wanted to do was go home. *Anything but that!* At some point he knew he'd have to, but the longer he waited, the better the chances his dad would be passed out on the couch in front of the television. These last several weeks had been rough. Dad had been laid off from the taconite processing plant in Silver Bay, and when he wasn't working, he was drinking. Alex had to be careful during these drinking binges or risk pissing Dad off. When Dad was pissed, his belt came off. *Bastard!* His old man seemed to resent him more and more as he got older.

Make it through graduation, and then... I'll have options. Hey, I know what I can do. I'll head over to Norbert's.

He parked Zits in the busy parking lot of the convenience store and strolled in, waving at Norbert, who never ventured far from the cash register.

"Hey there, young fella," Norbert greeted him with a wave back.

"Hi, Norbert. I'm going to check out your magazines."

"Be my guest. I put out a few new ones yesterday. I'll sell you the girlie one you've been hiding behind if you promise not to tell your dad."

"Thanks, but I'm good."

He was grateful Norbert had put the reading section in the back corner by the fishing lures. He could spend a good deal of time here unnoticed. Glancing up and down the rows of magazines and paperbacks, he quickly spotted what he had been looking for, and he was in luck—one of the new ones Norbert had mentioned happened to be his favorite: *Men's Physique*.

He'd discovered it last year when he was desperate to add some much-needed fuel to his fantasy pool. *Men's Physique* was filled to the brim with pictures of handsome guys in various stages of undress. One past issue featured a picture of a naked dude stepping into the shower. His muscled butt had captivated Alex for hours and hours. So much so that that page of the display magazine was showing wear.

This month's edition didn't disappoint. A feature on rodeo stars and what they do to stay in shape caused his jeans to tighten.

I'm going to have a man like this someday if it kills me.

Engrossed by a picture of a blond cowboy smiling down from the saddle, he was startled when he discovered someone standing next to him. *Where the hell did you come from?* Unsure of what to do, he placed the magazine back in its spot and took out, only because it was close by, the latest *Birds and Blooms*. The stranger snapped up his copy of *Men's Physique*. When it became obvious the man was not going anywhere soon, Alex stuffed the stupid nature magazine back in the rack and headed for the door, frustrated to have his fantasy time halted.

"You leaving already, Alex?" Norbert asked as he handed change over to Mrs. Crawford, Bud Crawford's widow.

"Catch ya later, Norbert."

Stepping into the parking lot, he contemplated driving over to the Pamida in Two Harbors but, with gas prices on the rise, thought better of it. He walked over to his car, but before he had a chance to get in, he was surprised to see the same man who had stood so close to him at the magazine rack, headed in his direction. Although he hadn't had the courage to look at the man's face, he recognized the burgundy jacket he was wearing. The guy smiled at him as he crossed in front of Zits and walked over to a dark blue Range Rover.

I wonder how old he is? Maybe thirty-five, tops? He's still in pretty good shape.

He climbed into his car and chanced another glance in the direction of the Rover. The man seated behind the wheel smiled. Alex could feel his face flush. Nothing like this had ever happened to him before. Curious and faced with going home as his only other option, he pretended to organize some papers lying on the seat next to him to buy some time to figure out what was up. When he thought enough time had passed, he looked up. The guy was still there, still smiling. He smiled back. The man rolled down his window and motioned for Alex to do the same.

Okay, I'll play along.

"Hey, what's going on?" the guy called out after he had rolled down his window.

"Nothin' much." Every nerve in his body was on high alert.

"Same here. Are you up for anything?" The man poked his head out of the window.

He was up for plenty but wasn't sure how to respond. Alex liked what he saw. The guy was good-looking. His hair, how it was cut short like a Marine, was a plus. Alex had a thing for that Marine look. "Depends. What did you have in mind?" Alex tried to sound calm even though his body was beginning to vibrate with anticipation. His face and neck were hot.

"We could drive around for a bit. Get to know each other." The man smiled and winked.

"I'm kinda short on gas." *If this guy is so eager, let him pay for the gas.*

"No problem. I just filled up. Come on over and hop in."

Even though he knew what he was about to do was very wrong, he couldn't stop himself. He got out of the car, turned in a three sixty to make sure he wasn't being watched, then walked in the direction of the Rover. When he arrived at the passenger side, the man reached over and opened the door for him.

"I'm Mike, by the way." The man's eyes were kind.

"I'm Alex." He closed the door and reached for the seat belt. *Dummy! Why did you tell him your real name?*

"I never venture off the highway. Maybe you know some cool side roads or a spot we can drive to and talk… talk with some privacy. There's probably a good hour of light left before the sun sets."

He buckled up. Mike's car was clean. And he smelled good too. *Where could we go to… talk?*

"Got any ideas?" Mike adjusted a dial on the dashboard. A gentle, steady flow of air began to blow out of the vents.

Alex thought for a second, and then he had it. "Yeah, I think I know of a place. Turn left onto the highway, and we'll head back toward the palisade." Mike followed his directions, and after they were about a mile or so away from Norbert's, he signaled to turn off the highway onto a dirt road leading down toward the lake.

"This might not work, but it looks okay for now," Alex cautioned, not having been down to the abandoned cabins since last fall. He wasn't sure what condition the road would be in.

"As long as we aren't plowing through deep snow, we should be all right. This buggy has really good traction. Where're we goin'?" Mike slapped the steering wheel, obviously fired up.

"The old Palisade Beach Cabins." He looked over to see if it met with Mike's approval. "They've been abandoned for years. Went under when they were redoing the highway and putting in the tunnels. Tourists stopped coming for a while until the road work was completed. The owners couldn't hold on."

"Sounds perfect. Hey, I'm curious. How old are you?"

"I was eighteen in January," Alex lied. He knew why the dude was asking and wondered if the guy would've asked him to leave if he'd said seventeen. *Probably not.*

"Really? That's what I was hoping you'd say. I was thirty-two in January. January thirteenth."

"January fifteenth." Alex tried as hard as he could to own his lie.

"Capricorns. Put it there, fellow Cappy!"

He accepted Mike's hand and shook it. It was a strong, warm hand. He felt the butterflies reappear.

"I don't know what it is about the spring air,"—Mike's casual adjustment of his crotch wasn't lost on Alex—"but it makes me crazy, if you know what I mean. I'm on the road most of the week, and I get really starved for some… company."

He felt the tightness in his jeans reappear. It didn't take a rocket scientist to understand Mike was admitting he was horny. Something was going to happen if Alex agreed to play along.

Colin's got Sarah. Why shouldn't I have some fun too? Nobody's gonna find out, parked way the hell back here.

"When you get up to this hill, veer over to the left. If the snow isn't too deep, there's a place to park behind the office with a view of the palisade and the lake."

Mike followed his directions and parked when they had reached their destination. "Wow, that's a big chunk of rock, isn't it?"

Alex never tired of the view from here. The palisade, an immense lava formation, was one of the largest on the North Shore. The huge rock loomed over them, making him feel like an ant. From its top, you could look out and, on a clear day, see the south shore of Superior along with a few of the Apostle Islands.

"You're very good-looking. I bet you hear that all the time. Those green eyes of yours are killer." Mike turned in the wide seat to face him.

He blushed. He wondered how this was going to play out. "Thanks! So are you." He began to wonder if he'd stumbled upon his cowboy.

"What sports are you in?" Mike asked, inching over.

"Wrestling."

"I played football, and for a couple of seasons I was on the golf team. I enjoy sports. You look like you take good care of yourself."

Alex didn't know how to respond, so he waited to see if Mike had any more questions.

"I'm doing all the talking here." Mike's hand brushed against Alex's knee. "What do you like to do?"

I wish I knew.

"What do *you* like to do?" he countered, thinking it best to let this guy take the lead.

"Well." Mike's hand slid past his knee and inched slowly up his thigh. "It looks like you've got some action going on in there."

He felt a tremor of anticipation rocket through his body when Mike's hand brushed over the bulge in his jeans. "I can help you out with this if you want me to."

He closed his eyes as the man's hand gently petted his crotch. "Okay." He gulped.

"Sit back and relax. We're in no rush," Mike whispered.

He pushed back into the seat. Looking down, he watched Mike's hand inch its way to the zipper of his jeans.

IAN flew into the office. Andy was seated behind his desk. "Where's your remote?"

"Excuse me? Oh I'm sorry, I thought this was my office. I get so confused some days."

"Where's your remote? Jasper Flynn is being sentenced as I speak." He was at Andy's mercy after conducting his own search.

"I haven't seen you this worked up since your Bowflex video arrived. Here!" Andy unearthed the remote, which had been hidden under a pile of paperwork. "You'll have to explain to me why this would be on television."

"Harper thought the press might be looking for a comment from him after the sentencing." Ian scurried out from behind the desk.

"Very well, then." Andy returned to his paperwork.

Ian powered up the little television his best friend kept on a shelf in the corner. They had passed many a slow summer afternoon watching the Twins and sipping beers.

"What channel do you think it might be on?" He began a frantic search in hopes of locking on to live coverage from the courthouse.

"That's a good question. You'll have to bounce back and forth until you find the right one. I'm going to grab a soda. You want one?" Andy got up from his chair.

"Yes, please." He did as Andy suggested. *Ah, come on... Harper, where are you?*

"Here." Andy handed him a can and plopped back down in his desk chair.

"It's after four. I'm not having any luck. Any other ideas? The judge was supposed to sentence him at four." He refused to give up.

"Not really. Keep trying. Maybe they'll cut to it once it's all said and done." Andy reached behind his chair and grabbed more paperwork.

"Yeah, you're probably right." Ian started at the beginning of the channel lineup. "Not on two, not on three, not on four, he's not on five…. They should have a channel dedicated just to local news."

"They do. Try channel eight." Andy looked up from his work.

He landed on channel eight just in time to see the screen go from a car dealership commercial to a young blonde chick standing on the steps of the courthouse.

"Sources inside tell us Jasper Flynn has received the maximum sentence. If this is in fact accurate, there's one thing we know for sure, Ted. Jasper Flynn is going to be behind bars for a very long time. Potentially the rest of his life."

Back in the studio, Ted said, *"Gina, we just confirmed Jasper Flynn has in fact been sentenced to twenty-five years in prison for masterminding one of the most despicable Ponzi schemes this area has ever seen,"* Ted piped in enthusiastically.

Ian watched as the camera panned away from Gina to the doors of the courthouse as a steady stream of people exited and started down the steps.

"As we mentioned at the beginning of our broadcast," Gina said, smiling into the camera, *"we hope to have a few words from the attorneys involved as they leave the courthouse."*

As if choreographed, the second Gina finished speaking, Ian spotted Harper coming out the large expanse of doors.

"He doesn't look very happy," Andy said, taking a sip of his soda.

"Mr. Callahan! Mr. Callahan, could we get your reaction to today's sentencing?"

Ian was bursting with pride. Harper looked movie-star handsome in the navy suit Ian had picked out for him to wear the night before.

"Harper let me pick out his suit and tie for today. Doesn't he look hot?"

"When doesn't that man look hot?" Andy leaned over his desk and pointed. "Hey, what's with the bracelet? Did you leave your handbag out in the truck? Wait, let me see your shoes."

"So not funny. It was a gift from my *man*. Oh look, Harper stopped in front of Gina." Ian moved closer to the television.

"Did you expect this harsh of a sentence?" Gina stuck the microphone up to Harper's lips. Ian licked his.

"As you can imagine, I'm very disappointed in the outcome. Jasper is a victim of the economy, and I would have hoped—"

"What happened to the sound?" Ian pressed the volume on the remote, but nothing happened.

"He just stopped talking. I still hear background." Andy gestured for the remote.

"No, Phyllis! No—"

"Why is he holding his hand up like that?" He handed the remote back to Andy.

A loud pop rang out of the little television with surprising clarity.

"What was that?" Andy sat up in his chair.

Harper, displaying a surprised look on his face, staggered back a few steps, clutching his arm as others behind and around him scattered up the steps and out of view. Ian watched with growing horror as Harper, cradling his arm, glanced downward before dropping out of the camera frame entirely.

"I'll drive." Andy lunged for his keys.

I CAN'T believe this is happening. Please don't let him be hurt too bad. Please don't let him die.

Ian was stunned by what he'd witnessed on the television. The thought of Harper being injured, shot, propelled his mind in a million unwanted directions. "I've heard about this happening to other people." Battling waves of anxiety and nausea, he looked out the window of Andy's pickup as they pulled into the hospital's parking ramp. "There was a wedding in Mankato a few summers back. The bride was killed in a car accident on the way over to the church. It was over before it started for them." He turned to Andy, horrified by a thought that had just surfaced. "It was her. Phyllis Flynn. I bet she shot Harper."

"We don't know any details." Andy reached over and patted him on the knee. Earlier, the radio in the truck had confirmed their worst fears—an attorney had been shot coming out of the courthouse and had been rushed to Hennepin County Medical Center. "*Stay tuned to KLOY for the latest updates as this tragic story develops,*" the announcer had encouraged.

"He's lucky he was only a few blocks from HCMC." Ian knew Andy was trying his best to remain positive.

Stepping out of the car, he discovered his legs were trembling so much he could hardly walk. Andy grabbed him by the arm, and they followed signs directing them to the emergency room entrance. Already news organizations were setting up remotes across the street.

"May I help you?" a guard asked as they entered through the automatic doors.

"We're friends of Harper Callahan," Andy told the man.

"The emergency area is a secured area. Please check in at the desk. They will direct you from there."

"Hello, are you a patient or a visitor?" A woman looked up from her computer screen.

"We're here to see Harper Callahan." Andy assumed the role of spokesperson and stepped up to the desk. Ian had never felt this lost and helpless in his life.

"Yes, here he is. There's a waiting area down this hall on the right. Either the charge nurse or the chaplain will update you on Mr. Callahan as soon as they are available."

The chaplain? Oh God....

"Andy," he whispered as they walked toward the banks of chairs outlining the waiting area, "she said the chaplain. You don't think...." He thought he was going to throw up.

"I don't know what to think, Ian. Let's try and stay calm until we get more information."

The waiting area was over half full of people from all walks of life. He tried not to stare, but a mother with an adorable little girl caught his attention and kept it. Maybe it was his mind's way of providing a diversion to keep his nervous system from overloading. The little girl's innocence paired with the stoicism of the mother fascinated him. He knew from the expression on Mom's face something tragic was occurring outside of her control.

I don't want to be here either. I'm so scared.

"It's been about twenty-five minutes since...." Andy paused.

What had halted his friend's comment? Always the strong one, the tremor of fear in his voice was uncharacteristic. "Twenty-five minutes since we left the shop," Andy continued. "I wonder how long we'll have to wait until someone updates us."

"Part of me doesn't want an update." Ian reached for Andy's hand and held it tight.

The emergency area was surprisingly calm. Nothing like you'd expect to see on television, he observed. There were a few people who looked distraught, but a few were actually smiling and happy. Occasionally there were messages over the intercom directed to the staff. They were all spoken in a controlled, even voice that neither soothed nor caused additional distress.

"Ian Burke?"

He looked up to see a gentleman with a kind face standing at the edge of the waiting area. Both Ian and Andy stood. "I'm Ian."

"Hello, Ian. I'm Willie Larkin, one of the chaplains here at the hospital."

Chaplain, oh please, no. Please don't say it. He had a brief vision of last rites being said over Harper's body. He struggled to stay standing.

"Why don't you and your friend follow me, and I'll update you on Mr. Callahan's condition."

Condition. He's still alive. "He's still alive," he whispered to Andy as they followed the chaplain out of the main reception area across the hall to a small private room.

Once they were seated and the door was closed, the chaplain leaned forward. "I know you're Ian,"—Willie pointed at Ian with his pen—"but I haven't had the pleasure." He pointed to Andy.

"I'm Andy Ashton, Ian's friend." Andy shot Ian a look that comforted him in ways words could not.

"Nice to meet you. Andy, my father's name was Andy. Okay, I need to ask. Ian, what is your relationship to Mr. Callahan?"

Ian looked over to Andy for a clue on how to answer. He and Harper were so new. Should he say boyfriend?

"Ian is Harper's partner," Andy said without hesitation. "And they live together," he added.

"Very good." The chaplain made note on the document he'd brought with him. "Do you know if any family has been notified?"

"Harper only has his grandmother. She lives in Iowa." Ian thought for a second before continuing. "I can call her when I know more. She's elderly, I believe, and hasn't met me yet."

"If that's the case, then I'll leave the decision when and how to communicate with her up to you. I know what you must be going through, Ian… and Andy,"—the chaplain made a point to include them both—"so I don't want to waste time before we talk about Mr. Callahan."

Ian was relieved he didn't have to spend any more time validating his relationship. He'd heard horror stories circulating about other men whose relationships had been ignored in situations like this.

"Mr. Callahan is in our trauma bay right now. We can go there if you'd like, but I have to caution you, it can be a very dramatic experience if you're not prepared for it. Your partner was wounded both in the arm and in the chest. There will most likely be evidence of blood loss. I suspect they are in the process of stabilizing him and doing a surgical evaluation. That's as much as I can tell you."

Ian thought about what had been proposed. "I'd like to see him." He looked over to Andy for his approval.

"Are you sure you can handle it?" Andy rubbed his shoulder. "I don't think I can, Ian. I'm sorry, but I don't do well in situations like that."

"I know." Ian brought his hand up to his mouth in an attempt to stop the intense wave of emotion resulting from the mention of Harper wounded and bleeding. "You don't do well around blood." He reached for Andy's hand.

"I'll go into the trauma bay with you and remain there for as long as needed," the chaplain offered. "There are vending machines right around the corner if you need anything while we are away," he informed Andy. "Let's go find out how your friend is doing. You'll need to wear this." The chaplain handed him a clip-on badge, stood, and held open the door.

Ian gave Andy's hand a squeeze and got up from his chair. "It's okay. I'll be fine." He wiped his eyes on his sleeve and then clipped the badge to his shirt pocket.

Chaplain Willie led the way past the Emergency Room entrance, through double doors to an area which resembled more of what he had expected. Medical personnel moved about them with purpose as they stopped before another set of doors.

"This is what we call the trauma bay or the stabilization area. Unless something has changed very recently, your partner is the only patient being treated. There are four bays in the room. It would be my guess he will be over to the left when we enter. I will try to find out more for you when we are inside. Please do not approach your friend unless I or one of the doctors gives permission. They are focused on his care, and the last thing we want to do is get in their way." Willie paused, forcing Ian to acknowledge he understood what he was being told.

"I understand." He braced himself.

Chaplain Willie opened the door, and as he had speculated, a team of medical people were huddled over someone in a bay directly to their left. Willie quickly guided him over to the other side of the room, out of the way of the activity. Ian could not have imagined what he was now witnessing. There was blood, *Harper's blood,* pooled on the floor directly below the table where he was being worked on. Ian felt his knees begin to shake as he came to grips with the scene unfolding before him.

"The small screen they are looking at is the sonogram. I would guess they are trying to assess the damage caused by the bullet and are now determining whether or not the bullet can be removed or left where it is." The chaplain leaned in, keeping his voice low.

Left where it is? Did I hear him right? Everyone is too relaxed. Do more. Fix him now!

Frustrated and powerless, he struggled to trust all was being done to keep Harper alive. He did his best to keep up with the discussion going on between the hospital staff. Unless he was mistaken, they had determined the bullet would be removed and were preparing to move Harper to the OR. He caught glimpses of Harper as bodies shifted in front of him. His skin, what wasn't stained with blood, looked so pale and lifeless. The shirt he'd been wearing was gone, and the tie Ian had picked out the night before lay bunched up in the corner. Dark stains littered his navy suit pants. He felt the nausea returning but didn't have a second to think about it. Willie grabbed him by the arm and steered him further back into the room. Seconds later, they were moving Harper toward another set of double doors at the opposite end of the room. As if planned in advance, the process was stalled for a brief moment directly in front of them.

"Harper!" Ian cried out, while at the same time a strong hand landed on his shoulder, holding him back.

"ONCE Mr. Callahan is out of the OR, I'll be able to bring you to the recovery room. You can stay with him unless for some reason something unexpected occurs. Why don't you wait in here with your friend, and I'll stop back when he's been moved."

Ian exploded into the room and kicked a chair, sending it flying into the corner before realizing Spencer, Allison, and a stranger were all waiting with Andy. "They need to try harder."

"Ian." Allison jumped out of her chair. She took him in her arms and held him.

Ian couldn't hold back any longer. He began to cry in her arms. "They can't let him die."

"Ian, they're calm because they know what they're doing. They're very good at what they do here." Allison's words somehow managed to slice through his anger and provide comfort.

"He's alive," he managed to get out between sobs. "He's being operated on. I'm sorry I'm such a mess. Thanks for coming." Forcing himself to stop crying, he took his seat next to Andy, who wrapped his arm around him. "I saw him. I think he saw me." He fought to stay in control. "The chaplain told me, oh God, he told me it was going about as well as could be expected. He can't die."

Andy held him tight to his chest as he cried. He could hear Allison crying. Through tears he saw Spencer was holding her. The stranger was crying too. He didn't have anyone to hold him, he thought.

"Ian, this is Brent, Harper's assistant. He was with Harper at the courthouse," Andy explained after Ian had regained control.

Ian walked over to Brent, who stood and offered his hand. He ignored it and took Brent into his arms.

"Do you know what happened?" Ian asked, keeping his hand on Brent's shoulder as they sat.

"I saw Mrs. Flynn come up the steps. She's been at the firm several times in the last few weeks. I knew she was angry, but I never would have guessed.... I'm sorry." Brent shook his head from side to side. "I heard the shot, and at first,"—his eyes welled up as he continued—"at first I thought she had missed, but there was this splattering noise, and I looked down at the steps and my shoes, and they were sprayed with...." Brent leaned forward in his chair and fought to stay in control.

Ian took the young man's hand in his own. Something inside of him, as awful as it was to hear, wanted Brent to continue. He wanted, needed to know.

"Harper made this awful sound, and then he went down on his knees. I heard screaming, and people were running all around us. I dived behind Harper because I was scared...."

"It's okay." Ian patted him on the knee, struggling to keep the visual that was forming in his head from turning horrific. "All of us would have been terrified."

"Then I could see two men had the crazy woman restrained. About the same time, Harper fell backward, and I ended up with his head in my lap. He was moaning and swearing at Mrs. Flynn. I could tell he was in a lot of pain. I think he might have passed out, but I'm not sure because the paramedics got there. A man and woman. They asked me if I was all right, and I told them I was, and then they had me scoot out of the way. They asked Harper a few questions, but I couldn't hear what he said. They hooked him up to oxygen and some sort of IV. I just stayed there on my knees and watched them work."

Ian fought off images of Harper in pain, lying on the steps. It was more than he could deal with right now. He needed to get past this part of the story, so he asked, "Did you ride over here in the ambulance with Harper?"

"No. I wanted to, but they wouldn't let me. They asked me if I knew of any previous medical conditions when they were loading him from that board onto the stretcher, or whatever you call it. I didn't think he had any, I told them. Harper's never sick. Did you get to see him?"

"Yeah." He gave Brent's hand a squeeze. "At least for now, they have him stabilized. He was being wheeled into the operating room. I guess the bullet went through his arm and into his chest. They wanted to take it out. The chaplain said someone would be in to update us on his condition. How are you holding up?" Ian reached over and rubbed Brent's shoulder.

"I'm okay. It was so terrible. It all happened so quickly, there was nothing anyone could do to prevent it. Do you like the bracelet?" Brent pointed to Ian's wrist. "I helped pick it out."

"Yes, very much. I liked the toothbrush even better. Did Harper tell you what he did?"

Brent nodded and managed a small smile. "People don't know how thoughtful he can be until they get to know him. He's a great boss."

He could tell at a glance what Harper meant to this guy. "Harper has mentioned you several times. We haven't known each other for very long. You probably know that already."

"Harper talked about you in the car on the way over to the courthouse this afternoon. I could hear the happiness in his voice."

Brent's comment made him smile, but it quickly left his face when he realized the assistant's shirt was bloodstained, and so were his hands. Ian tried to talk, but he was incapable of forming words. He sat back in his chair and took in a few deep breaths. Everyone in the room traded silent looks. All they could do at that point was wait it out.

"Does anyone want anything?" Allison stood and walked to the door. "I'm going for a soda. Speak up. I have a half-million dollars' worth of loose change in my purse."

"Yeah, I'll take a soda," Andy said.

"Me too," Spencer and Ian both said at the same time.

"Brent?" Allison asked. "Can I bring you something?"

"Sure, I'd like a soda." Brent fished in his pockets, but Allison stopped him.

"I got it. No worries. Does everyone want diet something?"

Ian nodded along with everyone else. Allison stepped out of the room.

Lost in the moment, Ian glanced up at the clock. He was surprised to see it was past seven. He'd already been here for several hours. This whole thing was a nightmare. How many walls separated him from

Harper? Would Harper be paralyzed? Would he make it though surgery without any complications? His stomach cramped as he weathered the thought. Never before had he experienced such profound terror. And the strangest thing was, three weeks ago he hadn't even known who Harper Callahan was.

Allison returned with their sodas, and they waited another twenty minutes in silence before a noise outside the door of the waiting room caught their attention.

A tall, striking woman in scrubs with long red hair walked in. "I'm Dr. Elizabeth Monroe."

Her smile, Ian wondered. Was it a sign everything was going to be okay? Or was it a cover, a professional smile she used in times when news wasn't good? Strange thoughts raced through his mind as he watched the doctor organize her clipboard.

"Is Ian here?" she asked, surveying the group.

"Yes." Ian felt his lip begin to tremble. "I'm Ian Burke. These… they're my friends."

Dr. Monroe addressed the group. "I'd like a few minutes alone with Ian. I'll call you back here when we're finished." When the room had emptied, the doctor sat down next to him and placed her clipboard on an empty chair. "Let's talk about Harper first. If you have questions, I'll try and answer them for you."

He took a deep breath and forced himself to relax his hands.

"A single bullet entered and exited Mr. Callahan's left arm, and from there it continued on into the left side of his chest, midway between his waist and his shoulder. He was very lucky. Had the bullet entered lower, it would have most certainly taken a path through his spleen or, worse, his stomach. Any higher, and the bullet could have damaged a lung. When the bullet entered, it entered low, traveled several inches through his chest cavity, and shattered a rib. That's also where the bullet stopped its progression. Do you have any questions so far?"

Ian sat motionless. Images of Harper's naked, bloodstained torso flashed before him. He shook his head, too overwhelmed to think clearly.

"We were able to remove the bullet, and as of now, he is critical, but all vital signs are stable. As you can imagine, he experienced considerable blood loss. The next few hours will be decisive in determining his recovery. Honestly, I know you want me to tell you he's going to be okay, and Ian, I would like nothing more than to tell you that. However, there are certain complications involved with his wound that are challenging. The rib was nicked by the bullet, causing a portion of it to shatter into small, sharp pieces. We feel confident we were able to reduce the risk, but there still exists the possibility of his body being injured additionally by the movement of one of these rogue pieces of bone. If anything, find comfort in knowing we are keeping a very close eye on him and monitoring his vital signs continually. For the time being, he's my priority."

Ian had wanted to hear something encouraging. He clamped onto the hopeful portions of her comments and hung on for dear life. Every muscle, every nerve in his body had been poised for bad news. It was his nature to expect the worst. Another wave of emotion brought tears to his eyes. He needed to keep it together.

"We've moved him out of surgery and into a recovery room where we will be able to monitor for anything problematic." The doctor didn't acknowledge Ian's fragile state.

"Do you think I'll be able to see him tomorrow?" he found the courage and energy to ask, drying his eyes with his sleeve.

"Most likely you can see him tonight if you'd like. Your group is a little large to all visit at once, but you and another of your friends are welcome to sit with him. He's sleeping now. We administered anesthesia prior to operating. He'll come around sometime tonight, and it might be a very good thing for him to see your handsome face when he wakes."

He blushed. Her warm and caring remark caught him off guard.

"We're doing everything we can for him. He's in good hands. You'll have to trust that. Did the chaplain ask you if any family needed to be contacted? Because of the witnesses and the status of the case, Mr. Callahan's name has already been leaked by some of the news organizations. The front desk is getting calls regarding his status. If I can update our own staff on the family situation, it will make their jobs easier, and we won't run the risk of offending anyone while we protect the patient's right to privacy. In that regard, you'll have to determine for yourself what you want to share with your friends."

Ian nodded that he understood. "Is this the kind of thing that makes national news?"

"I would suspect so. Is there something we can do to help?"

He shook his head. "He's got a grandmother in Iowa. She'll worry if she doesn't hear from him. Maybe she's seen it on the news already. I'll need to get to her."

"If she's elderly, take my advice and tell her only good things. Tell her he's stabilized, the bullet has been removed, and he's resting comfortably. You might want to give her an exact time when you will get back to her with another update. We should know more in the morning, and certainly have a better idea of his progress by midday tomorrow."

"Thank you, that sounds good."

I wonder what happened to Harper's phone? I'll have to ask Brent.

Dr. Monroe stood and moved toward the door.

"Doctor, I can't thank you enough." Ian stood.

"How the rest of tonight goes will dictate my schedule. Here's a number where you can leave a message. I'll get back to you as quickly as I can."

He met her halfway and took the scrap of paper.

"They're usually good about tracking me down. I'll arrange for someone to give you an update if for some reason I'm not here. Hold a strong thought for your friend."

Finding a box of tissue on a corner table after the doctor left the room, he blew his nose and sat back down to collect his thoughts.

If anyone is listening, please don't take him.

He struggled to comprehend what had happened. Exhausted physically and emotionally, he'd almost forgotten he wasn't here alone. *Oh man, everyone's outside.* Ian went to the door and discovered his posse waiting in a small reception area a few feet down the hallway.

"We just have to wait. He's stable." He made it as far as Andy before collapsing into his arms. Allison and Spencer closed in around him.

"That's okay. If there's hope, that's all any of us need to know for now, buddy." Ian felt Spencer's hand rubbing his back. If there was ever a time in his life he needed his friends, it was right now. It took several minutes for him to work through this last wave of emotion.

"Where's Brent?" He looked around when he could finally step away and hold his own.

"I'm here." Brent scurried over to the group. "I was updating Harper's boss, Duncan Price. He wanted you to know that if there's anything he or the firm can do, we should let him know." Brent handed him the partner's card.

"The doctor said Harper's—" Ian took in a deep breath. "—stable. I like her. I think he's in good hands." He thought about what else he could say. There were a million bits and pieces vying for attention as he tried to make sense of it all. "Brent, I'm worried about Harper's grandmother. I don't have her number, but I know it's on his cell phone. Do you have any idea what happened to it?"

"It's here." Brent produced the phone from his pocket. "I took it from Harper's hand. I've talked to Grandma Callahan a bunch of times over the years. She's a sweet lady. I don't mind calling her."

As Brent stepped into the group, arms took hold of him. Ian shared the advice from Dr. Monroe regarding Grandma's update.

For the first time in his life, he thought as they swayed back and forth, he couldn't find a single thing funny about a group hug.

ALEX sipped his Dew and stared out the car window. The bonfire had grown over twice its original size since he'd left his friends and ducked back into Zits. The crowd around it had gotten larger too. Along with a handful of freaks plus a few stragglers from schools nearby, most of his class was present, getting wasted on keg beer. The party was strategically located in a remote tree farm outside the city limits. He dreaded these end of the year blowouts. Even this year, with his graduation a few weeks away, he wished he were anywhere but here.

Graduation—his life was about to change. He leaned his forehead against the window. He wasn't sure how or when the change would come, but he felt it looming in the air.

Big-time change.

He had never been a drinker. He saw enough of that at home to last a lifetime. And even if he were a drinker, tonight he felt like being alone. Alone with his thoughts. He was consumed by replaying what had happened that afternoon beneath the palisade. Back in his car at Norbert's, he'd felt ashamed for being so weak. He was starting to reevaluate those feelings.

I'm gay. It's because I live in this crappy small town I'm forced to sneak around, and that's what's making me feel shitty. Guys hold hands walking down the sidewalks in San Francisco. This town is fucked up, not me. If he could just hang on a little longer.

Audrey promised this summer he could start waiting tables during lunch if he agreed to keep his regular hours busing and doing the dishes during the dinner rush. The extra cash would help him with his grand exit. When the season wound down, he'd wave a big goodbye to the palisade and head west, maybe all the way to San Fran. He could live his life there any way he chose. For the first time all night, he felt the dark cloud of doom begin to lift.

Where did Colin and Sarah go?

It was after ten. Safe to go home. His dad would be passed out in front of the television. He scoured the crowd, looking for his best friend. *Dammit, Colin. I hate it when you ditch me like this.*

"Dude, what are you doing sitting in Zits?" Colin whipped open the car door and leaned in.

"You scared the crap out of me. Where've you been?" He watched Colin throw the remainder of a twelve-pack into the backseat.

"There's a party going on, if you haven't noticed. You okay?" Colin settled into his designated shotgun seat and slammed the door.

"Yeah, I'm fine. Not really into it, I guess. Where's Sarah?" Alex looked over to the fire to see if he could spot her.

"She's in the woods with Emily… crying." Colin sounded disgusted.

"Huh?" He needed some clarification on this one.

"I'm breaking up with her. Let's bounce! I'm not into this either."

"Whoa, when was this decided?" He was surprised. Captain of the wrestling team and the cute cheerleader; for some reason he'd just thought they'd marry and have a bunch of great-looking kids. *I didn't see that one coming.*

"Tonight. I just decided tonight. She was all in my face about going on a vacation this summer with her family, and I don't want to do it. Her dad's a dick. No way am I going to do that. There's other stuff too. Come on, let's go somewhere else."

Alex started up Zits and guided the car down the rutted road out of the tree farm and onto the highway.

"You hungry?" he asked when he could finally relax his grip on the wheel.

"Naw, I'm thirsty. Let's park somewhere so I can pound down a few of these brews before I go home and crash. Where should we go?"

"I know." Alex blushed, thinking he'd been too quick to solve the "where to" problem. "Let's see if the road leading down to the old palisade cabins is okay." *Returning to the scene of the crime?*

"That works, but try not to get Zits stuck. That would suck." Colin reached in the backseat and grabbed a beer.

Alex turned off the highway onto the road leading down to the lake. "Wow, it looks like somebody else has been down here recently." It felt strange to lie to his best friend. Strange and kind of empowering at the same time.

"Probably Sheriff Parker making sure no deadbeat out-of-work taconite dudes are living here. Oh man, I'm sorry!" Colin reached over and punched Alex on the shoulder.

"It's cool. He is a deadbeat… not a dad. You forgot to tack on asshole. I don't see anyone else around, do you?" He parked Zits in the same spot he'd been parked at with Mike.

"Nope! The coast is clear." Colin flashed him a thumbs-up. "I wonder if this beat-up old place will ever get reopened? Maybe it will get torn down and people will build those humongo homes here, like they did outside of Silver Bay where the Cozy Inn used to be."

Alex didn't have an opinion or an answer. They sat in silence for a few moments, staring out at the lake. He and Colin had hung around together for so long they could sit like this for hours without feeling the need to make conversation.

"Wanna get high?" Colin reached into his coat and pulled out a pipe and a ragged baggie.

"Yeah, sure." He enjoyed getting high if he was relaxed and felt comfortable. Colin always had weed.

"I can't wait to get out of this town," Colin said, passing the lit pipe.

Tell him. Tell him tonight.

He took a hit off the pipe and listened while Colin ran down his list of reasons for wanting to go away to school. For the most part, the list didn't change much. Occasionally there would be a new entry, like tonight.

"I feel like Sarah is strangling me." Colin took a huge hit off the pipe. "I like her fine,"—he attempted to talk while still holding in the hit—"but do I want to spend the rest of my life with her? This shit is really good." Colin emptied his lungs, filling the car with sweet smoke. "I don't think so. I'd end up in jail because I'd lose my temper and kill her dad." Colin took another hit. "Have you made any plans to boogie?"

Tell him. This is stupid. Tell him now.

Alex couldn't keep track of the times he'd come close to having this conversation with Colin. Today felt different. His experience down here with Mike had in some way validated once and for all what he had refused to admit. Whatever the hell the reason, tonight it felt right. He took over the pipe and cautiously inhaled. "Kind of. Colin, there's something I need to tell you."

"Are you finally going to find the balls to tell me you're gay? Sorry, I probably shouldn't have said balls." Colin glanced over with that droopy, goofy smile you had to love.

He was stunned. Blood rushed to his head. His vision blurred for several seconds and then cleared. When he'd had a moment to come to terms with Colin's frank deduction, he started to laugh. Colin exploded seconds later and then went into a coughing fit of epic proportions, causing Zits to rock from side to side.

"Oh man, I'm going to barf," Alex barely got out. Tears were rolling down his cheeks.

"Shut the hell up! Don't say another thing, I'm dyin'." Colin hugged his chest as he weathered another violent round of coughing. "You pole sucker," Colin taunted when he was finally able to breathe.

"How long have you known?" He couldn't imagine Colin had kept something like this quiet for long.

"Boundary waters." Colin looked over to Alex.

"Huh?" Alex didn't have a clue. "I'm not getting it. What does boundary waters mean?"

That was two years ago.

"My sleeping bag slipped off my pack into the lake when we were loading the canoe after that long portage. That night, remember we laid a tarp over my wet sleeping bag, using it as the bottom layer, and then shared your bag for a top cover. Do you remember that?"

Colin, you were sleeping. I remember, you were sleeping.

"Yeah, I remember. So?" His stomach tightened.

"You thought I was asleep. I wasn't. Dude, I felt your hand touch my ass… and stay there."

Alex looked away. He felt his face flush. Waves of shame swept over him. There wasn't a thing he could say. He remembered it in such detail it would frighten Colin if he only knew.

"I don't know what to say." He was humiliated and unable to look back over to his best friend.

"It's cool. You asked me how I knew so I told you. Honestly, I thought you were gay for a long time before, but that's the moment you confirmed it for me, dude. Hey, look, I don't care. If I did, you would have heard from me before now."

"You were snoring. I thought you were asleep."

"I'm great at fake snoring. I got good at it to keep my little sister from bugging me."

"I can't believe you let me get away with it." He finally found the courage to look over. He was rewarded with another droopy smile.

"I kind of liked it. But kind of didn't. I've had some time to think about this, and I think on some level, I understood what courage it took for you to make the move, and—" Colin punched him on the shoulder. "—I knew you needed to do it. Wanna beer now?"

"No, but I'll take another hit. Wow! This is amazing." He accepted the pipe, lit it, and took a nice, slow toke before passing it over.

"You need to get out of here. You need to go where you can be yourself, dude." Colin opened the window and emptied the pipe.

"Yeah, I know." *I need a plan. As soon as I have a plan, you'll be the first to know.*

"I'd invite you to come live with me in the Cities, but Eric and Ben will be there, and they're not going to let you be who you need to be. There's nothing for you here but trouble." Colin reached into the backseat and pulled out another beer.

"Thanks, Colin." He was overwhelmed by what had just transpired.

"Wanna touch my butt again? Just this once I'll drop 'em so you can get a nice squeeze."

"Fuck off!" he barely got out before they erupted into fits of laughter.

IAN sat next to the bed, and Andy sat in the corner of the small recovery room. Allison, Spencer, and Brent had gone home with the promise from Ian he would call if for some reason Harper's condition took a turn for the worse.

"Hey," Andy asked out of the blue, "how did you know it was that Flynn bitch who shot him?"

"You want to hear something really weird?" Ian looked over to Andy. "He's been having nightmares where he wakes up drenched. She's been in his nightmares. Chasing him. She's also called him at home, threatening him. The last time she called, he got mad at her and really let her have it. A few minutes later, the doorbell rang. I went downstairs to answer the door, and she was standing there. She'd obviously been in the neighborhood when she called. She's a freak. Never in a million years…."

"Wow! Yeah, who would ever think someone would get so mad they'd take a shot at another—"

Andy was interrupted by a nurse who came into the room. "Has he moved or opened his eyes?"

"No, not yet." Ian backed his chair away from the bed, studying the nurse for her reaction.

"Enough time has passed since surgery. He could continue to sleep once the anesthesia has worn off, or he might regain consciousness." The nurse made a quick tour of all of the monitors and devices hooked up to Harper. "If he does wake and you're still here, why don't you let one of us at the nurse's station know. We want to make sure he's resting comfortably and has everything he needs."

"Sure." His eyes met Andy's briefly before watching her leave.

"She didn't seem too upset or anything." He scooted his chair back up to the edge of the bed.

"Yeah, she seemed pretty calm. I would think there'd be a whole lot more going on if he was iffy. Well, you know what I meant," Andy whispered defensively after Ian had shot him the look.

"He doesn't look as pale as he did when I saw him in the trauma room before surgery. That was so scary. There was blood everywhere—"

"Ian!" Andy jumped up out of his chair. "He just moved his eyes."

"Wow!" Ian grabbed the metal rail of the bed and peered over for a closer look. *Oh please. Please let him wake up and be okay.* "Harper, it's me, Ian. Can you hear me?"

With Andy breathing down his neck, he began a scan of Harper in hopes of another sign that he was coming to. Minutes passed by, and Andy sat back in his chair. "Maybe it's just a reflex thing. I've heard of that happening before."

"I hope it wasn't just that." He petted Harper's hand gently. "Harper, we miss you. Everything is going to be fine. I love you." He looked over at Andy. "Are you hungry? I'm sure they have sandwiches in the vending area."

"His lips just moved." Andy jumped out of his chair again.

This time there was no mistake. Harper twisted his head slightly. His left arm rose for a moment and then went back down.

"Harper, it's Ian. Everything's going to be just fine. I'm here, I'm right here." He ran his finger through his boyfriend's hair.

Harper scrunched up his face and then relaxed it. "Ol kin," he mumbled after a few more seconds passed, in a small, weak voice Ian could barely hear. "Ol kin."

"I'm here, Harper. It's Ian. Andy's here too. What are you trying to tell us?" He waited for Harper to respond.

"Maybe he's talking in his sleep or something," Andy offered when Harper failed to respond to Ian's question.

"Harper, it's Ian. What are you saying?" He wasn't about to give up hope.

Seconds later, he was rewarded with more movement. First Harper's legs twitched under the sheet, and then his head moved from left to right. Then he said it again. "Ol kiiinnn."

"Andy, do you know what he's saying? I can't make it out." He was frustrated. "Should we go grab the nurse?"

"Ollll kiinnnn," Harper said louder and clearer.

"It sounds like he's saying oil can or something that sounds like it."

"Oil can?" Ian shook his head, exasperated.

"Yeah, like the Tin Man...." Andy stopped, slapping Ian on the shoulder. "I think your boyfriend is messing with us."

Ian looked back over to Harper in time to catch something so wonderful, so astonishing, tears welled up. Harper, with his beautiful, deep dark eyes twinkling like diamonds, flashed a devilish grin like no other. "Hey, guys."

CHAPTER

Six

IAN looked up from his magazine when an elderly man took the seat next to him.

"Excuse me, young feller, would you pass me the People?"

He looked over at the table and discovered the magazine the old guy was referring to was the one he was reading. *My magazine! You're too old to read this stuff. Here's National Audubon; run with your bad self.* The last thing he wanted to do was relinquish his rights to the hot photo spread on excommunicated Mormon studs and their smokin' fund-raising calendar to raise money in support of marriage equality. He'd never in a million years buy this to read at home. It was a special indulgence, something to pass the time away at doctor and dentist offices.

"Here ya go." He gave up, handing the magazine over.

"Oh, no, I can't take it from you if you're already reading it." The old man smiled thoughtfully.

"Nope, I'm done with it. It's all yours." He held the magazine out, and the man took it.

"When I was here on Thursday, I started reading an article on Mormons. They do a lot of charity work, is what it said. This year they're doing a calendar you can buy. The wife and I always get our calendar from our insurance guy, Roland Lesinski. Otherwise I might be persuaded to buy one. I don't know when I'll be back. Hopefully not anytime soon." He leaned over and whispered, "I've got a little skin cancer they're treatin'."

The small waiting area had become almost a second home. Ian had logged a lot of hours here over the last seven weeks, waiting while

Harper's progress was examined and his treatment adjusted. On a few visits, he'd brought his work along. Sketching garden layouts and making product lists. For reasons he couldn't explain, it was hard to concentrate here, and he found passing the time with a magazine his best bet. Whatever he could do to keep his mind occupied was of huge importance. On more than one occasion, the smell and the setting had joined forces to launch a series of painful memories. He fought valiantly to bury recollections of the shooting and those anxious days directly after. The day of discharge was one such memory he'd give anything to be rid of. After Harper had been wheeled out of the hospital, he had tried on his own to get up out of the chair, stumbling into Ian's arms, too weak to accomplish even this simple task on his own. A preview of the challenges they would face over the next days and weeks. It had been a long journey for them both.

Remarkable, when he thought about it, Harper's recovery. So far it had gone amazingly well. Initially, pain had been the main issue. How horrible to watch someone you loved so much suffer. Frequently he wished there was a way for him to absorb the pain, to relieve and give Harper a break. Medication and time had worked its magic, and soon the tide had turned. Awful days were replaced with not-so-good days. Not-so-good days eventually gave way to okay days. On almost a daily basis, Ian could see signs of improvement. Small gains in movement and flexibility. Harper struggled to perform tasks most everyone else took for granted. Dressing, eating, so many activities were either rendered impossible or very difficult by eliminating the use of his left arm.

Ian's recap was interrupted briefly when a young woman walked in. After checking in at the desk, she took the chair directly across the room from him. She looked familiar, but why? This would pester the hell out of him until he solved the mystery. *Damn! Who do you look like? It's right there. You look like.... Yes!* He had it. She looked like Maureen, the lead nurse on Harper's floor during his hospital stay.

Harper's arm had been repaired on the second day, after it was determined no vascular compromise or damage to his lungs had occurred. Maureen was always there, it seemed, and nothing got in her way when it came to making sure Harper was comfortable. Some of his finest Maureen memories were from late-night visits, when she'd pop her head in to check on Harper and say goodnight. Ian, despite Harper's protests, had opted to stay at his bedside, leaving only after he was certain his lover was sleeping soundly. Maureen, a little rough around the edges, had a way of telling it like it was that you couldn't argue with. "Honey, you'd better get that cute little butt of yours home so you can catch some rest. This man is going to be hungry for some lovin' when the time is right, and you'd better be ready to give it to him." It was part of her charm, her face expressive and warm. When it came to providing patient care, he couldn't imagine anyone doing a better job. Maureen collaborated with Dr. Monroe to go over the discharge process, making sure Harper understood all of the steps needed to ensure he was pointed toward the road to recovery.

He watched the woman page through her magazine. *What is she here for?* Her reading was interrupted when a nurse called her name. She was escorted through the door into the small individual offices, where Harper was now.

Knowing it would be at least another fifteen minutes before Dr. Monroe had finished her evaluation of Harper, he scrounged around the table for something else to read. The choices were limited to Field and Stream, AARP Magazine, National Audubon, and a real estate brochure for property on the North Shore of Lake Superior. *Oh, I love the North Shore.*

Paging through the publication, he was surprised by the number of homes for sale. Many of them were beautiful, with stunning views of the lake.

Maybe he and Harper would retire there one day. He leaned back in his chair, closing his eyes to nurture the happy visual he was creating.

They would open a bed-and-breakfast. Harper could handle the reservations and all of the financials; Ian could take care of the maintenance. But more up his alley would be the beautiful gardens he would create. He'd read somewhere that the moisture coming off the lake compensated for the short growing season, and plants did quite well. The landscaping would attract lodgers. It would be something unique for the area. They could serve up a simple but elegant breakfast each morning. Lemony light pancakes with powdered sugar and sausages made locally. *Sounds pretty whacked. Maybe in another life.*

This dream was a keeper, regardless of its practicality. He made a note to store it away for later. Maybe he would resurrect it on a cold winter night when he and Harper were snuggled together in front of the fire. It wasn't likely Harper would buy into running a B&B on the North Shore. *I wonder if Harper has any pie-in-the-sky dreams of his own?*

"Hey! You miss me, handsome?" Harper came around the corner with Dr. Monroe close behind.

"Hi, Ian, it's nice to see you. You've obviously been doing a tremendous job keeping your partner focused on his recovery. I'm impressed." Dr. Monroe looked radiant.

"Hi, Dr. Monroe. It's great to see you too. I'm a taskmaster, and he knows I mean business." He had no idea why, but the beautiful young doctor fascinated him.

"He's not lying. I haven't been able to slack off for a minute." Harper gave his shoulder a squeeze.

"Harper can fill you in on his progress. But really—and I know this involves you both—he's doing exactly what I had hoped. Keep up the good work. If you want, Harper, you could reduce the therapy down to three days a week. The muscle atrophy appears to be diminishing rapidly. Your overall strength in that arm will only increase with activity, so it's a tossup. Why don't I see you in two weeks?"

"Two weeks, sounds good." Harper walked over to the desk to schedule his return visit.

"Take care, you guys."

"Bye," they chimed in unison. Harper pocketed his appointment card, and the two of them left the waiting area.

"She's so cool. And that hair, man, you don't see hair like that often." He knew they'd already discussed this, but he couldn't stop himself.

"Maybe I should dye mine red. Do the carpet too." Harper reached over and gave his ear a tug.

"Ouch! Don't you dare. I'd never forgive you. I like the Goth thing you have going on."

Harper laughed, opening the door for him. "You very funny, meesta Ian!"

"I wonder if she's got a devastatingly handsome man in her life like I do. She could probably have just about anyone she wanted." He remembered the first time he'd seen her, how striking she was even in scrubs.

"She's got a devastatingly handsome woman in her life, if you need to know."

"Shut up, are you serious?" Ian was shocked. He'd never even entertained the idea.

"As a gunshot. She told me today her partner, Monica, is an OB/GYN in one of the 'burbs."

"A what?" He speculated this was a doctor of some type but wasn't sure.

"A doctor who specializes in delivering babies and treating girlie parts… I think."

"How convenient."

"Anyway, she and Monica are heading up to the North Shore tomorrow for a long weekend." Harper stopped at the curb to wait for a produce truck to lumber by.

The North Shore again. That's twice in one day.

"Have you ever been to the North Shore?" Ian thought most Minnesotans had been at one point or another. Growing up in Iowa, Harper might have missed out.

"Well, kinda sorta maybe. I stayed in Duluth one weekend for a bar association meeting. I loved it. These huge taconite freighters sailed in and out of the harbor. We should go there sometime."

"Yeah, once things have settled down, let's do that. I haven't been in years. It's beautiful." He locked arms with his man as they walked to the car.

HARPER pointed the remote at the television and surfed through his movie options. It was strange being at home during the day and not at the firm. A brief conversation a few days earlier with Duncan Price had reminded him he wasn't missing much. Just the sound of the partner's voice repulsed him. *How in the hell did I ever put up with those dickheads as long as I did?* Duncan had assured him he could take all the time he needed before returning, and he planned on doing just that and more. Although he hadn't voiced this to Ian or anyone else, his mind was made up. He wasn't going back. If there was a positive to pull out of the shooting, it was the strong desire for change that had emerged. It was more than changing firms. He somehow sensed that wouldn't be enough. No, he was talking big change here. But what that change would be, could be, eluded him. He needed to hash this one out a bit more before he went public.

And it wasn't just his job or career he was evaluating. *What have I done with my life so far?* To a certain extent, he reasoned, your life does pass before you when you come face to face with the prospect of dying. It's a sobering moment, and it forces you to evaluate. It forces you to do an honest appraisal of your existence to date, and in the process, you somehow become aware of ideas, concepts, things you'd never thought about. *I'm not sure, before all of this happened, I could even begin to understand or appreciate the value Ian's brought to my life.*

Settling on the epic *Cleopatra*, a movie he'd watched as a boy with his grandmother, he dropped the remote to his side and closed his eyes. His back ached despite the adjustable mattress. Everyone from his doctor to his physical therapist insisted rest was the key to a speedy recovery. Like an assignment in law school, he decided to strive for an A. It was working. The pain in his ribcage had subsided considerably, and he was gaining strength in his arm daily. *I can't wait for this nightmare to be behind me.*

Bored out of his mind, he preferred to actually sleep as opposed to rest, but today, like so many others before it, dozing off was a challenge. He had tried focusing on the image of his handsome boyfriend traipsing around somebody's yard in those hot shorts and boots. A counterproductive visual, he had determined, after spending the next thirty minutes trying to make his dick deflate.

How many millions did they spend on this film? Without looking at the television, he knew from memory that soon after the Overture was concluded, Cleopatra would make her entrance, rolled out of a rug at Julius Caesar's feet. If he fell asleep before that scene, he'd watch it later, with Ian. *Does he like movies like this? I should ask him.* He yawned, and his eyes watered. He wiped his face with his pillow. The volume was perfect, loud enough that he could plug in to the plot if he wanted yet low enough to ignore. The noise from a garbage truck in the alley battled Caesar and the gang before a single enemy threatened him on screen. Harper caught himself drifting off.

"THE dwarf lilacs look great. Is it a new distributor?" Ian revisited the design on his clipboard. He hadn't thought of it, but lilac might be the perfect solution for the Morrisons' driveway. Becca Morrison had requested a border shrub that would effectively create a barrier between the edge of her driveway and her next door neighbors', who she despised.

"Nope. I'm still getting them from Thompson's, the grower from Wadena I was complaining about last year. He's finally getting it—that I won't settle for his hand-me-down crap. I tell ya what, use them on your project and I'll knock off ten percent. I want to show him I can move his product if he provides me with plants I can sell." Andy pulled one of the shrubs out into the aisle for him to inspect closer. "Remember the pruning issue with these? They bloom on old wood so you have to be careful."

"Leave it to you to be an expert on 'old' wood," Ian quipped, stepping a few paces back to reduce any impulse Andy might have to belt him one.

"Why I oughtta…." Andy laughed. "So, you can take ten of these off my hands?"

"I've got the room to take fifteen. Deal?"

"Deal. I'll have Emmett pull them this afternoon. Is Harper coming to the game tonight?" They walked back to the office.

"Yep. He's been talking about it since the weekend. We sure had fun at Spencer and Allison's, by the way. Spencer grilled ribs. Man, he's got those nailed." His stomach rumbled at the memory.

"I was so pissed off I couldn't make it. Emmett and I were here until almost eleven Saturday night waiting for a semi full of annuals from that outfit in Iowa. By the time we helped unload it, it was midnight. I think the scumbag driver has a squeeze in every port, if you know what I mean. Anyway, I ended up taking Emmett out for pizza. I think all my efforts with the kid are finally paying off. Last week he kicked good-for-nothing Trevor to the curb and decided to try living on his own for the first time. I hate to go there, but man, it would be nice to have a mini-me by the name of Emmett around here I could trust. You know, so I could get away from the business now and then and not worry."

He heard something in Andy's voice just then that caused him to take notice. *Was he? Naw, it couldn't be.* This special interest his best friend was taking in the hired help, was there more to it?

"Well I've told you this a million times, but now with Harper in the picture, you still need to know I'll be here for you whenever I can."

"Thanks. What are you doing for the rest of the afternoon?"

"Well…." Sex hadn't occupied his thoughts to this degree even as a teenager.

"What's it like having Studly Do-Me-Right home at your beck and call?"

It was heaven. His man was on the mend, and life was good. "It's tough, but somebody's got to do it, and do it, and—"

"Okay, I asked for that. Go on with your nasty self, and I'll see you tonight. You're picking me up, right?"

"Yes, sir! Hey, do you know if Allison's coming?" Ian asked. "She's his new best friend."

"That's funny." Andy stopped and turned around. "She is coming. According to Spencer, the feeling is mutual. She likes Harper way better than she likes the rest of us. Later!"

LIGHTNING flashed far off in the distance. Steam rose from the warm cobblestones. A soft rain fell. Harper, a hood draped over his head, stepped tentatively out of the shadows and peered down the narrow alley and listened. The noise from a distant tavern spilled out into the street. Confident the coast was clear, he crossed to the other side and stopped inside a doorway. Around a corner he heard the drunken banter of men approaching. Hoping to escape notice, he backed into the corner of the jamb and lowered his body until his knees jutted out in front. He held his breath.

"I wonder if they've found him yet," a low voice asked only a few feet away.

"Trust me, we'd know if they had," another voice slurred close by.

Harper's heart pounded so hard he feared it would give him away. His strong legs ached at being forced into such a tight constraint. Worse, his nose began to itch, a telltale sign a sneeze was brewing. *Oh please, please keep moving.*

Inches from his hideaway, a powerful spray splashed against the brick, its pungent odor unmistakable. Moments later, a second spray took over as the first ebbed.

"If I get my hands on him," the slurred voice bragged with a noticeable tone of relief, "I'll castrate him and bleed him to death."

"That's too good for him," the low voice warned. "I'd cover him with honey, string him to a post in the field, and then let the ants and bees have their way. They'd drive him crazy before they ate him alive."

Harper pinched his nose, hoping to control the sneeze rising to the surface. His eyes watered as he trembled in the darkness. A few moments of sheer terror passed before the men crossed in front and continued down the alley, their sandals snapping against the wet pavers.

Harper removed his hand from his nose and eased himself back up. He peered out and watched the men increase their distance. When it felt safe to move on, he continued his zigzagging journey, crossing from doorway to doorway until he reached the top of the hill where the narrow alley forked. There were risks in either direction. Stepping back into the shadow, he contemplated his options. With apprehension, he chose a course to the left and what he hoped would be an opportunity to slip out of the city unnoticed. But first, he'd have to make it across the square undetected.

Approaching the large open area, he crouched behind a wooden cart and waited. It would be to his advantage to stay to the left as he worked his way along the wall of shops and residences. Light spilled out of a doorway midway between where he was now and where he wanted to end up, an added risk that could not be avoided. If he remembered correctly, the entrance belonged to a laundress. He would have to cross the pool of light. There wasn't another option—moving through the center of the square unnoticed would be next to impossible. Even with the hour being late, there would be merchants lingering about. If one of them recognized him, it would be all over. The reward for his capture was too enticing to ignore.

Filling his lungs to bolster confidence, he exhaled and dashed from the protection of the cart to the perimeter of the courtyard. Before he made another move, he stopped and listened. *Proceed with caution.* Tight to the wall, he crept stealthily along. A hissing cat darted out from behind a barrel, causing his heart to leap into his throat. He took refuge behind the barrel and waited for his breathing to calm.

Beads of sweat ran down his face as he resumed his journey. He approached the lit doorway. Close enough now to hear noises from within, he inched along the brick wall. The woman wasn't alone. He heard men's voices. They were arguing. Shadows in the light grew more frantic, and Harper flattened himself against the wall when the stooped figure of the laundress stepped out of the doorway, tossing a bucket of water into the street with the force of a woman much younger. As she turned to reenter the shop, Harper sneezed.

The woman stopped in her tracks. "Who is there?"

Harper froze.

"Brutus," the woman hollered.

Run or die!

Harper overcame his inability to move and dashed from the wall into the center of the plaza. Narrow walkways bisected the mass of makeshift shops and tents.

"Stop him!" a voice roared from behind.

"Kill him if you have to!" another shouted.

He overturned crates and carts in an attempt to slow his assailants but was forced to stop for a second to get his bearings. *Oh my God, which way? There's no exit on what side… Harper, what side? Try and remember; it's your life!* Catching sight of the enemy, a group of a half-dozen men, Harper collapsed a tent as he ran under it and prayed he was headed in the right direction. Rounding a pen of goats, he bolted past three men huddled over a small fire only to discover he'd chosen the wrong way. Like a caged animal, he searched in vain for an opening until a barrier of spears backed him into a corner.

"How long did you think you'd be able to hide from our queen?"

Harper's heart exploded inside his chest.

"Take him away. Take him to the queen."

His hands were bound behind his back with straps of thin leather. He was beaten by the shaft of a sword and forced out of the plaza toward the palace. Hauled up the steps of the great marble fortress, Harper was dragged through the halls and down a series of stairs lit by torches to the dungeon, where he was thrown to the floor. When he looked up, to his horror, he saw Ian, strung up from the rafter by his hands. His feet dangled off the ground, his body covered with lash marks.

"Noooooooooo! Iannnnnnnnnn! God… please… nooooooooooo!" A hard kick to the stomach silenced him. Before he knew what was happening, a foot plastered his face to the floor. Either his pulse or the sound of distant drums pounded inside his head.

"Well, what have we here?" Harper lay motionless, his vision limited to the surrounding sandals of his captors.

The sound of the drums increased. "I warned you. I warned you, and you chose not to listen." The voice, filled with anger, grew more forceful.

"Ian had nothing to do with this. He's innocent. Please stop hurting him." Harper began to weep. "Please stop…." The sound of a whip lashed through the air. Ian screamed out in pain.

"Did you not think I would have my revenge? How arrogant of you."

"Please don't hurt him anymore." Harper's vision blurred as he fought to stay conscious.

"Aren't you the valiant one, begging for your little boyfriend's life. You make me sick!"

That voice. That evil voice. It was so familiar. It wasn't the voice he had expected.

It's her!

Using every ounce of strength he could call upon, Harper pried himself up off the stone floor to confirm what he feared more than anything. Leering down at him from her gilded throne sat Queen Phyllis Flynn.

Harper bolted up out of the sheets onto his knees, his body drenched with sweat. Looking frantically around the room, his eyes settled for a second on the television. Cleopatra's barge, propelled by dozens of rowers, glided across the cobalt water. The buzz from a lawnmower in the neighborhood floated in through the partially open window. Collapsing onto his side, he moaned in agony. Hadn't he suffered enough? A gentle breeze fanned his steaming body, the terror his vivid nightmare had produced still a frightening reality.

Minutes passed. Anger replaced fear.

There is no way, no way in hell I'm going to allow Phyllis Flynn to have this kind of control over me.

Harper stomped down the worry that when his body was finally back to normal, he'd still suffer at the hands of this lunatic woman by way of these horrible nightmares. Something had to be done to stop this from becoming a bigger issue than it already was, but at this point, he didn't have a clue where to start.

"Harper?"

Ian's home. He can't see me like this. Harper climbed out of bed and rushed across the hallway into the bathroom. He splashed his face with water and rubbed it dry with a towel. "I'm up here," he hollered. Seconds later he heard the sound of footsteps on the stairs.

"Hey, sweetie."

Harper forced a smile for his handsome partner, placing the towel back onto the rack.

"Okay, what's going on? Harper? Talk to me. You just had a nightmare, didn't you?" Ian moved into the small room, pinning him between the sink and the door.

"No... I...." He stopped himself. *Why lie? Why lie to Ian?* "It was a really bad one."

"Phyllis again?" Ian reached for him.

"Yes." He melted into Ian's strong arms. "I can't go on like this."

"I know. We're going to get through this together. I want to be a part of the healing process. I want to help you, and you'll let me help, right?" Ian lifted his chin off his chest.

He was helpless to prevent the rogue tear that trickled down his cheek. He nodded, the sparkle in Ian's eye offering hope and comfort.

"Oh, honey, I'm always going to be here for you." Ian wiped the tear from Harper's cheek. "No matter what. I might not be able to predict these nightmares, and it might be some time before we can wipe them away altogether, but you can always, always count on me to be here for you. Like it or not, you're stuck with me."

"I like it… so much." He hugged Ian hard until his rib ached.

"Hmmm… now let's see if we can drive a stake through that nasty Mrs. Flynn's heart. I'm feeling more than a little inspired this afternoon." Ian led him by the hand back into the bedroom and up onto the bed.

Harper gasped when, unexpectedly, he found himself naked. Ian, smiling, triumphantly held the trophy boxers in his hand. "You're no match for me, Mr. Callahan, and the sooner you come to understand that, the easier this is going to be on us both."

He giggled, scooting over to his side of the bed. Ian tossed the boxers over his shoulder and began to strip, starting first with his T-shirt. Undoing his belt, he let his shorts fall to his ankles, followed with breakneck speed by his own bright red boxers. Using the headboard for balance, he stepped out of his clothes.

Harper clenched his pillow in anticipation. *Phyllis who?*

"I had an idea on the way over here." Ian opened the drawer of the bedside table and removed the familiar tube of gel. Kneeling on the bed, he leaned over and took Harper into his mouth.

"Oh God." Harper felt his cock turn to stone. "God, oh, that feels so good."

Ian slurped and sucked, nibbled and bit, until Harper begged him to slow his assault.

"I think it's time." Ian crawled onto the bed. Tossing a foot over his man, he straddled him. "For you to drive."

He watched Ian squeeze a dollop of gel into his palm. Bending down, Ian planted a kiss on his nose.

"Your body, it drives me wild. I'll never get enough of you. Not ever." Harper reached around to caress Ian's marvelous butt. "Oh God, your ass is heaven."

"I've been wanting this for a long time, Mr. Callahan." Leaning forward for another kiss, Ian prepared himself for his man. When he straightened back up, he used the remainder of the gel to coat Harper's stiff cock.

He looked on, mesmerized by the efficiency. Ian's own dick and balls rested patiently on his stomach. A slumbering giant, he thought.

"Wait, don't we need...?" Harper looked over to the bedside table.

"When you told me you were tested last week, and you were clean, I thought I'd better take care of that too. My test came back this week, and I passed with flying colors. We're both on the honor roll, babe." Ian locked eyes and began to ease himself down.

At first, Harper felt resistance, but after a moment, he entered Ian. "Oh wow." It felt so warm and tight, like velvet. "I had no idea this would feel so incredible. It's like we're one, you and I. By the way, you have the most amazing chest, did you know that?" Harper traced the dark circles outlining his lover's nipples.

"Of course I do, I hear it all the time." Ian winked, inching down further and further.

Ian's hard butt stopped its descent when it landed on his pelvis. During the journey, his hot lover never once lost the sparkle in his eye or his sexy smirk.

"How do you like your new home?" Ian kissed his lips.

"Snug as a bug in a rug comes to mind." He reached up and gave Ian's mop of hair a toss.

"Am I hurting you if I lean way back like this and then do this?" Ian began rocking his body from side to side and back and forth.

"Not at all. I... you feel great." *My dick feels like it's a foot long.*

"I love it both ways." Ian continued his gyrations. "We haven't had a chance to talk about that."

"I think I love it both ways too." He reached for his talkative partner's neck, bringing him down for another kiss. "Ian, you might not believe this...."

"First time batting?" Ian hoisted himself up and down.

"It's the first time I... yes, it's the first time." He looked away and instantly hated himself.

"Hmm...." Ian reached out for his hand, guiding it into place. "Make yourself useful. Why the hesitation?"

"Ian, I don't want to.... Okay." *Just tell him. He'll understand.* "I have tried this before, but it didn't go too well."

"Let me guess. Were there different parts involved?" Ian giggled.

"Yes, sir." He slid his hands under Ian's hot, tight butt, slowly lifting him up and then letting him fall back down. His apprehension over his performance dwindled by the second.

"I had the same experience. I lost interest. Does that ever put a damper on the party. So, you've never done this with another guy?" Ian reached for his hand and once again placed it on his cock. "Remember to multitask."

"Sorry." He petted and stroked Ian back to life. "Yes, but I'd had too many beers, and I wasn't inspired. Pretty much the same results."

"I love how you feel inside of me." Ian wiggled from side to side. "Ah, you like that? Here, what about this." Ian rocked back and forth in earnest. "Feels great, doesn't it?"

"Ian, I mean this in the best possible way. Shut the hell up."

"Huh?"

"This isn't a seminar. I'm getting the hang of it." Harper dug in his heels and bounced his gabby partner with so much force Ian caught air time.

"HELLO, Ms. Hardpecker. Fancy meeting you here." Harper stood to give his new best friend a hug.

"Hey, Harper! Sorry I'm late. I had a ton of things going today." Allison hugged him hard and then freaked. "Oh God, I'm so sorry, I forgot. Did I hurt you? What was I thinking?"

"Chillax. It hurt like hell, but I'm a man." He could hardly wait for the sassy reply he was sure to receive.

"Okay, I love role playing. So you're a man. Where are we? Are we here, at the game? Come on, give me just a little more to work with."

"Why do I even try?" He accepted a wine cooler. "I hate these, by the way, but I forgot to bring something else to drink, so thanks. I might want another one. I hope you come prepared."

"For me, preparing to cum is like packing for Europe. A lot of thought goes into it. I was thinking I hate these too." Allison sipped and savored like she was sampling an expensive wine. "We can blame my book club. Those broads suck these things down like they're sodie pop. I tell you what, next time you treat."

"Can we start over? I'm exhausted already." He laughed, understanding he'd met his match in Allison and then some. And he loved it.

"I'm kind of jazzed tonight, sorry. Spencer took me from behind in the kitchen while I was putting up soup. Makes me crazy when he does that."

"Woman, I'm serious, stop." He clutched his chest and roared. "Do you know no decency?"

"Gotta love this weather." Allison took another sip and winked.

The game was just getting started. It was a perfect night for baseball. These early mid-July evenings were his favorite part of summer. It stayed light forever, and the temperature was perfect. He and Allison sat in silence while they watched the Hornets take an early two-run lead.

"Those knuckleheads are starting to look pretty good," Allison observed while the Litigators came in from the field. Harper had heard about the Litigators, a team made up of attorneys, but this was the first time he had ever watched them play. Secretly he hoped the Hornets kicked their asses, and this had nothing to do with Ian.

"Spencer, Andy, Ian, these guys really love the game. It's so fun to watch, knowing how much they're into it." He felt blessed to call them all his friends.

"They really do. Spencer is so into it. He reads books about baseball in the winter. Being captain this season is something he's secretly wanted to do for a long time. Between you and I,"—Allison leaned in to rub shoulders—"this team will never have a leader as committed to the game as Spencer."

"Isn't it great to watch people enjoy something they're passionate about? You feel this vibe coming off them. It's humbling in a way." He thought back to his days in law school. There had been a time not too long ago when he'd had passion.

"Yeah, I pick up on that too. It's most of the reason I give Spencer such a long leash when it comes to this game."

"What's the rest of the reason?" He peered over at his new friend in hopes of catching a hint of where this was headed.

Doug Trebtoske pitched a lazy strike to make it a full count. His next pitch, a curveball, caught the hungry Litigator by surprise to retire the inning, bringing Harper and Allison to their feet.

"Spencer wants a wee little one. I'm not sure I do."

He weighed his response options. He felt honored Allison had trusted him with something so personal. He analyzed how he would respond and carefully chose the path of least resistance and then abandoned the strategy as being too careful. No doubt she had a need to discuss this with someone other than Spencer. Friends shared, and they relied on one another for support and advice. Allison was a friend. "That's a huge decision." *Oh come on, she deserves better than that.* "I'm not sure how I would deal with this if I was in your shoes." *That's better. At least it was honest.*

"Here's what I've been contemplating. I'm not going to close the door on this kid thing. I mean, it's a part of life, and we didn't marry with the agreement we'd never have kids. In that regard, it's not fair to Spencer to remove that option. But deep down, I'm not sure he's done a thorough job of evaluating what it is he likes about wanting kids of his own. Oh, here's another thing." Allison took an impressive swig of her cooler. "If we do end up going down that path, one wee little one isn't the route to go. We need at least two. A matching set. I'm not sure he realizes that."

Harper breathed easier. He had a tried and true response for her concern. "I don't know a whole lot about raising kids, but I'm not sure you're right about the two-is-better theory. I was raised an only child, and I don't think I suffered. My grandparents made sure I was around other kids my age. The other reason I don't think I suffered, they were really involved with me. School, homework, sports, they were there for everything. I almost think that's a more important consideration. Are you guys willing to devote the time?" *Whew!* It was his turn to take a swig.

"That's a good point. I haven't progressed that far in my thought process. But it makes sense."

The discussion stalled as they watched Snotty Scotty, at the top of the Hornets' batting lineup, hit a line drive along the inside of third base, successfully making it to first.

"That's the way to start the inning." Allison clapped and whistled.

Despite her grumblings, there was no doubt in Harper's mind she loved the game of baseball almost as much as her husband.

"Anyway, I was planning on proposing to Spencer he start volunteering his time at some type of organization that deals with kids."

"The Little League comes to mind. He'd be a great asset to them." He looked over for a reaction.

"Oh man, you and I do think a lot alike. Yes, exactly. I think it might help him sort out his priorities. Well, you know, help him to identify what it is about having children he's looking forward to. I feel like such a stick in the mud. Childbearing is on the top of the list for most women."

"I'm not so sure about that either." *This should be interesting. I bet she can't wait to hear a gay man's thoughts on women and pregnancy.* "I think many women go down that path because of the pressure from society. I say stick to your guns. Besides, if he likes taking you from"—Harper coughed to make sure his double entendre was fully understood—"behind, what're your worries?" Harper knew he'd scored a keeper with that last one.

"You're impossible, impossible in a really good way." She leaned over and pecked him on the cheek. "Wow, there's a 'from the behind' position for the ladies *and* one for the gentlemen. Well actually, there's *two* for the ladies and *one* for the gentlemen. We win!" Allison threw her head back and laughed.

Spencer cracked a ball down the center of the field, allowing him to make it to first and Snotty Scotty to advance to second.

He and Allison jumped up and down, screaming like children.

"So." When they had sat back down, he took charge of the moment. "I've got a little something I was hoping to test drive with you too." *Really? You're really going to unveil this one?*

"Are you talking a four-way? We'd probably try it once."

"Who's impossible? We wouldn't, so no worries. Nope, nothing like that. I've decided I'm not going back to McPherson, Price & Wabash. I'm not sure I'm going back to practicing law at all." *Wow! That felt really good to say.*

"Doesn't surprise me, Harper. I think being shot would tend to give someone a slightly different perspective on life."

The conversation was put on hold again. Ian was at bat. He and Allison watched with giddy delight. The pitcher for the Litigators, losing confidence, quickly got behind in the count. Ian connected with a pitch, sending the ball back into the left side of the stands, keeping him at bat.

"Come on, slugger," he hollered. "Oh man, I can't watch. I'll jinx it if I do."

"Come on, Ian," Allison cheered under her breath. "You can do it! You can do it!"

Harper bit his lip, knowing how much the game meant to Ian.

After surveying the bases for a potential steal, the pitcher wound up and delivered a fastball directly across center plate. Ian connected with it at exactly the right moment, launching it like a rocket out across center field for a home run.

"Holy shit! Did you see that?" Allison hopped on top of the bleacher, jumping up and down and cheering. The crowd, made up of mostly Hornets fans, went wild. He was beside himself with pride. Like lunatics, they cheered Ian around the bases. *What a little stud.* With a grin as wide as the Grand Canyon, Ian came lumbering into home to hugs and high fives from his fellow teammates.

Bursting with pride, Harper looked over to Allison. "Ian's playing the biggest role in my decision. Look, he's so comfortable with himself. He has his own business. Life seems so easy for him. He's made his own set of rules, and they seem like such a perfect fit." *Is that it? I hope that came out right.*

"Ian's changed in the last month, Harper. He never used to be this carefree. Oh, he's always been happy, but now, with you in his life, he's much more relaxed. You guys are good for each other. What do you think you'll do if you don't practice law? Any ideas?" Allison offered another wine cooler, which he accepted.

"I don't have a clue."

"Well, I have to be honest. Envisioning you planting shrubs in the hot summer heat is kind of a stretch. Not that you couldn't do it. Maybe I'm wrong on that one."

"No, that's Ian's thing. I have no talent for his line of work. Something will come along." *Oh, Allison, I don't have a stinkin' clue what I'm gonna do.*

CHAPTER
Seven

"CAN you hand me a cookie?" Ian pressed down on the pedal to pass the utility van bumbling along the freeway at half the speed limit. "Hey, a cookie please." He glanced over and confirmed what he had suspected. Harper, with his seat reclined, was sound asleep. *Never mind, sleepyhead.* With an arm functioning at less than one hundred percent and a rib that still ached, Harper had managed to wipe clean his grandmother's "repair list" during their brief weekend visit. But the effort had taken its toll, and Ian was happy to see him rest peacefully.

Reaching behind, he pawed the air until he made contact with a shopping bag on the backseat. Fumbling with it while still managing to keep his eye on the road, his flailing efforts were rewarded when he snagged the twist tie on a baggie he knew to contain incomparable, delectable treasures—Lollie Callahan's chocolate-chip-raspberry cookies—a work of culinary art bar none.

Lollie was no slouch in the kitchen. The weekend visit had been one continuous food fest. When they had arrived on Friday afternoon, she had just finished making her homemade egg noodles. They were draped over the dining room chairs to dry. She used them to make a marvelous chicken soup they ate for lunch on Saturday, using leftovers from the mouthwatering fried chicken she'd served the night before. Saturday night was pot roast, Harper's favorite childhood meal. It too was scrumptious. The beef was fork tender and the carrots and potatoes cooked to perfection. For Sunday's brunch, Lollie stepped it up a notch with baked eggs, an incredibly rich and tasty cheesy potato dish, slabs of thick-cut bacon, and for dessert, homemade coconut cream pie. The cookies were sent along to ward off hunger on the long drive home. *Where the heck did she think we were headed, Nova Scotia?*

He tried to compare Harper's upbringing to his own but found it almost impossible to come up with similarities. When it came to feeding her kids, Bernice Burke didn't stand a chance against the likes of Lollie Callahan. Bernice had worked steadily through his childhood and had had very little time to put a meal on the table. Having three children in the course of a five-year span didn't make it any easier. Casseroles, simple oven dinners, which more often than not used mushroom soup as the binding ingredient, were her best friend. It wasn't until he got to college that he realized what he'd been missing. *Really? There are spices other than salt and pepper?*

If possible, he thought as he changed over to the left lane to avoid whizzing past a stalled car on the shoulder, he was even more in love with Harper after witnessing the tender, devoted way in which he interacted with Lollie. The love the two shared for each other was obvious. He was her boy; there was no doubt about that. The fact he had made good, had become a lawyer, was something she was fiercely proud of, even if the profession had stolen him away from Iowa to the big city of Minneapolis.

Managing to undo the twist tie with one hand, he took a cookie out of the bag and tossed the tie into the backseat. Looking at his watch, he estimated they would be back to Harper's by six thirty. He'd have to spend an hour or so organizing his truck for the week ahead. He'd picked up two other jobs from the commercial. *Hands down, this is the best cookie I've ever had.* At Harper's insistence, he'd find the time to see about subletting his apartment until the lease was up in October. He had no argument there. Compared to Harper's house, his apartment was a rathole. Andy had mentioned Emmett might be interested in taking it off his hands. He'd check tomorrow to find out if Emmett wanted the place.

Finished gobbling down his cookie, he set the cruise control on the sedan they had rented for the trip and sat back. With a tiny Smart Car and a truck to choose from, it only made sense they rent a comfortable ride for the road trip to Iowa. A majority of the journey was spent on the interstate. Having cruise control was a real treat.

He was surprised at just how enjoyable the time had been, staying with Lollie Callahan. Although Harper had assured him she would be accepting of his new love, he was overwhelmed by her affection. In a quiet moment while Harper was upstairs showering, she had expressed her gratitude for being there when her boy needed him and for making him so happy. His health and happiness were her primary concern. As she waited by the window for them to arrive on Friday afternoon, you could see the worry rush out of her face when Harper got out of the car on his own and walked up to hug and hold her in his arms.

Before meeting her, he had speculated on why Harper didn't just move Lollie to the Cities where she could be closer to him. After spending time with her, he understood why this wouldn't work. Lollie was one busy lady with a network of close friends. They were her lifeblood now that her husband, Leonard, had passed.

"Where are we?" Rubbing his eyes, Harper stretched out his long torso as best he could in the confines of the car.

"We're in Minnesota. We just passed the border a few minutes ago. Did you have a nice snooze?" He reached over and ruffled his partner's hair.

"Yeah, but I had the weirdest dreams."

"Weird like scary weird, or just plain weird?" He looked into the rearview mirror to make sure the highway patrol car he'd just passed remained where it sat. He'd set the speed for a couple points past the limit, which should keep him from being singled out, but you never knew.

"Strange weird." Harper reached around to the backseat to retrieve his coat. "I'm cold all of a sudden."

Ian looked down at the controls and determined the settings were fine. He was chilled because he'd just woken up.

"Already into the cookies, I see." Harper reached over and patted Ian's stomach.

"I'd weigh three hundred pounds if I spent two weeks living with Lollie. Did she ever make anything you didn't like?"

"Hmmm, let me think. Yeah, she did. She occasionally made liver for Gramps. That stuff is just plain awful."

"Tell me about your dream." Ian relaxed into the seat.

"Well, you and I were in the woods... somewhere. It was warm. We were naked."

"I like where this is going."

"It might have been an ocean, or maybe a big lake, I can't remember. There were waves. Anyway, we were frolicking like kids on the beach. Throwing Frisbee, swimming, lying in the sun. Well, until…."

"Until what?" Ian looked over for an explanation.

"You got that look in your eyes."

"What look?" *I have a look?*

"The 'I want it really bad' look."

"My everyday look."

"Pretty much, yeah." Harper laughed. "So we ran into the woods."

"A beach and woods? Sounds awesome."

"It was beautiful. The sun sparkled through the trees, the birds were singing, the air was sweet, and we found this log." Harper scooted over in his seat.

"Log?"

"Yep. And without even the teensiest, weensiest protest, you bent over it."

"Me? Are you sure it was me?" *This is getting very interesting.*

"It wasn't me."

"That leaves me."

"I made passionate love to you." Harper's finger dragged across his chest.

"You did that, did you?" The story had Ian aroused. He had taken the lead early in their relationship, but he'd hoped Harper could be coaxed to drive more often. He'd proven himself quite skilled on several occasions in the leadership role.

"I did."

"Then what?"

"A rabid squirrel scurried up and bit one of your nuts."

"Whoa…." He exploded in laughter. Harper was already giggling so hard he was shaking.

When they'd stopped laughing, Harper leaned over, resting his head on Ian's shoulder. "I tried to scare him off, but I think he knew how tasty those meaty orbs were and wouldn't budge. That's when I woke up."

"I love your silliness, Mr. Callahan."

"I love your everything, Mr. Burke." Harper rested his hand on Ian's thigh, giving it a small squeeze. "Gram adored you, but you know that already, right?" Harper gave his leg another squeeze.

"Try that a little higher… please. I love Lollie. She's an amazing lady. I'd visit her anytime, say the word."

"Here?" Harper inched his hand up slightly.

"You're in the ballpark." He was surprised at how horny he was.

"Hmmm, how about here?" Harper walked his fingers up Ian's leg a few more inches.

"Close, but no cigar." He turned and caught a devilish grin. "I know *that* look."

"Cigar, a modest assessment if I ever heard one." Harper found what he had been searching for through Ian's jeans and tapped his finger on the tip.

"Bingo! Are you considering what I think you're considering?" It was Ian's turn to grin.

"Keep your eyes on the road, son. I'll handle the rest."

He relaxed back into the seat. Harper slowly brought down his zipper. With very little fuss, his cock sprang free of its plaid boxer restraint, and before it had much of a chance to take in the surrounding scenery, Harper leaned down and throated it to the root. *Woohoo!*

HARPER carefully tucked Ian back in.

"Oh man, you're good at that," Ian sighed.

"Wow, when did it cloud up?" Harper examined the sky, swiping his chin one last time to make sure he hadn't missed any of Ian's man goo.

Ian laughed. "About mid-blow."

He stared out the window, enjoying the scenery. How often had he made this trip alone, dreading the monotony? Too many times. What a difference it made having Ian along. And the best part, this was just the beginning. The beginning of what he hoped would be a lifetime of trips with impromptu blow jobs when the mood felt right.

Lately any thoughts of the future, with the exception of Ian, made him uneasy. He knew what he didn't want to do—go back to practicing law—but an alternative was nowhere in sight. The downside of having been so focused on his legal career was that it left him ill-equipped to do much else. It would take time, but he'd come up with something.

This would be a good time to let Ian know where you're at.

"Ian, I've been doing some thinking lately, some soul searching, and I've decided to step away from my legal career. I have savings, so financially it shouldn't impact us. But at this point, I don't know what I'm going to do."

"Really? I'm kind of surprised. Is it because of...."

"Sure. The shooting definitely plays a role in my decision. But honestly, I was headed for a change before that. I thought about switching firms, but something is telling me that won't be enough. The nightmares...." It was embarrassing to make those a consideration, but to ignore them would be a mistake. "I think I need some drastic type of change to refocus my attention. Something I can really sink my teeth into." He looked over to see if what he'd been saying was making any sense.

"You're welcome to give landscaping a try. I know there are aspects of running a business you'd be a big help with."

"Oh, I'll be happy to help you regardless of what I decide to do. I'd enjoy helping you, but landscaping isn't me. I need something that fits more into my whacked personality." *Like... like....*

"You mean like towel boy at the Y?"

He laughed at Ian's playful gibe. "So,"—he turned to face his partner—"Burke Landscaping, is that the dream? Is that where you want to end up?" He leaned back against the door, then bolted up to check to make sure it was locked, a fear dating back to childhood.

"It's funny. I would answer that with a yes and a no. The business is very new, so keep that in mind."

"Point noted." *Jeez, are you at the firm?*

"Before I had something of my own, it's all I thought about." Ian waited until he'd passed a semi to continue. "Now that Burke Landscaping has launched, I'm already thinking ahead to a time when I don't have to work in other people's yards. When I have someone on the payroll who can do the actual labor so I can concentrate on designing. I don't see that change coming anytime soon, though. Especially with your expensive tastes and us trying to survive now on one income."

"You don't really think that, do you? That now you're trapped in your landscaping job because of me?" *Crap, I'd never thought of that. Is he serious?*

"Well...." Ian burst out laughing. "You dolt, Harper. Damn, you can be serious sometimes. No, I don't think that. I'd have you out there selling Mary Kay before I suffered."

It was Harper's turn to laugh. Ian had played him beautifully. "Mary Kay, I never thought about that one."

The countryside had changed from flat fields of corn to rolling green hills. This was the best part of the year, he thought. Everything was so lush and beautiful.

"I'd love for you to have the time, the ability to concentrate on your landscaping design."

"Oh man. Well, that'll happen someday, I hope. Hey, I came across something last week that interested me. When you were being checked out by Dr. Monroe, I paged through a property brochure on the North Shore. This is really out there, but you asked."

"I don't care if it's out there. Hey, isn't it kind of strange that I came out and said that Dr. Monroe and her partner were going to the North Shore for a long weekend? Did you think that was weird I said that?" Now that Ian had brought up his interest in the North Shore, he thought the connection was kind of strange, strange timing.

"I just thought the brochure was Dr. Monroe's or something. I thought maybe they were looking at property around there."

"Oh, that works. Okay, so back to the North Shore. Whatcha got noodlin' around up there?"

"You and I running a B&B. I could be the groundskeeper, keep up with the repairs, and you could manage it all and deal with the lodgers. See, I told you it was out there."

Hoping to get a rise out of Ian, Harper crossed his arms and shook his head. "That's not out there, that's the stupidest frickin' thing I've ever heard." Was Ian gullible enough to think he was serious? He was all about the payback.

Turned out he wasn't. Before reducing their speed, Ian swerved the car over onto the shoulder and then applied the brakes.

"Ian, what the hell are you doing?" He gripped the door handle and braced himself.

"You wanna see stupid, I'll show you stupid." Ian activated the emergency flashers, turned the windshield wipers on high, and honked the horn as they came to an abrupt halt on the side of the freeway. "Take it back." Ian reached over to him and started bitch slapping him.

"I'm sorry. It's not stupid. Stop it, you maniac." He whacked back but was laughing so hard he snorted.

"Don't fuck with me, Mr. Callahan. When are you going to learn I am... the *master*!"

"Oh God," he squealed, "you are the master."

"I am the master." Ian proudly put the car back in gear, checked the mirror for oncoming traffic, and eased back onto the freeway.

A B&B on the North Shore, that's not that out there. It could have been worse.

He sat back in his seat and allowed a visual of what Ian had proposed to take shape. He pictured a beautifully restored old Victorian house with a large porch. Huge, glorious baskets of flowers hung from the beams. Rocking chairs and small seating areas were strategically placed for the lodgers. The view of the lake was exquisite. Yes, sir, Ian's pie-in-the-sky dream could have been a whole lot worse.

DRESSED in his finest suit, Harper walked through the doors of McPherson, Price & Wabash for the first time since being shot. "I know where I'm going." The receptionist was new; he didn't feel the need to introduce himself. *I can't wait to see the expressions on Duncan and Arthur. This is going to be great!*

"Brentster! Hey, buddy, how's it going?" Harper poked his head into his assistant's cubicle.

"Hey, Harper." Brent jumped out of his chair. "Wow, I had no idea you were coming in."

"You miss me, I can hear it in your voice." Harper chuckled.

"Are you back for good?" Brent stepped out from behind his desk.

"Are you in the middle of something?" Harper moved into the little space and slapped Brent playfully on the shoulder.

"Naw, just proofing a motion going out tomorrow. It can wait."

"Great, let's take a walk." Harper stepped out of the cube and waited for Brent to join him.

"How are you feeling? You look great!" Brent patted his boss on the back.

"I'm feeling pretty damn good. The arm is coming along, and the pain in my chest is almost gone. Hey, thanks again for the call right after Phyllis Flynn was sentenced. It looks like my impact statement did the trick. Hard to believe both she and Jasper are serving twenty-five-year sentences. His and hers." Harper laughed as he led Brent into a conference room and closed the door. "So what's been going on around here lately?" He sat and gestured for Brent to sit across from him. Before he paid a visit on the partners, he thought it best to get an update on the recent activity around the firm.

"Ronnie McPherson was involved in another car accident. He drove off the road and into a tree about a mile from home. Of course he was drunk." Brent did nothing to hide his dislike of the partner's spoiled son.

Harper wasn't the least bit surprised by the newest development in the Ronnie saga. A couple of years ago, he'd been snagged to represent Ronnie in court when he was charged with selling pot at a Guster concert. The kid was fined and ordered to put in a few hours of community service tidying up one of the local parks. It was a sweet deal that only money and legal influence could buy. To this day it remained a revolting memory. He hoped Ronnie was reaching the end of his legal nine lives. The kid would always be trouble as long as Daddy was there to bail him out.

"Old man McPherson assigned Brock Baumgartner, the new associate in med-mal, to represent him in court this week." Brent's disgust with the situation was palpable.

"You have no idea how glad I am not to have to go through the defending-Ronnie experience again. I guess it sucks to be Brock," he quipped. "Anything else going on? What kind of crap did they throw at you while I was out?" He hoped his assistant's survival skills would be enough to protect him from the onslaught of needy associates who would jump at the chance to have someone as competent as Brent at their beck and call.

"So far, I've been okay. I'm keeping myself busy preparing the McGuire file for closing. Which reminds me, with your blessing I want to gather up all of the client materials and send them back. They're in the way, and I can't think of a reason why we need to hold on to them any longer."

"Oh God, send them back. If I have to look at those stupid scrapbooks one more time, I'll vomit." Tammy McGuire was a cheerleader who had taken a prescription drug for birth control and, as a result, had died of a massive stroke. It was a tragic case. The family, in hopes of seeking legal and, much more important to them, it was soon discovered, a monetary reward, had stopped just short of supplying her baby shoes in hopes of bolstering their defense. During the trial the dad had become a monster to deal with, and even though the outcome had been highly favorable for his clients, the greed displayed by Tammy's family tainted any joy for him when it was all said and done.

"Thanks. I have everything packed and ready to send back." Brent giggled.

"No doubt." Harper laughed. *You're truly the only one I'm going to miss here.*

"Brent, I'm not coming back. I'm here to tell you first, and then the partners."

"Fuck!" Brent couldn't hide his disappointment.

"I wasn't happy here before. Well, you had to know I haven't really been happy here for a while. This seems like the perfect time for me to make a change." Harper felt a lump grow in his throat. He hadn't planned on this exchange with his assistant being as emotionally challenging as it was turning out.

"It makes sense. Fuck, I'm going to miss you here, Harper. You have to know that." Brent looked like he might break down.

"I've enjoyed working with you so much, Brent. You do an amazing job." *There must be more you can say, Harp.* "I'm sorry this is so abrupt. It's been something that has been on my mind for a very long time. I just wanted to make sure it was the right decision to make at the right time."

"Oh, I get it. I understand. I'm just...." Brent looked away.

"Hey, we'll stay in touch. You're a friend, Brent. Now that we don't have that strange working relationship thing between us, it's going to be even better." *Does he believe me?*

"Can I still be upset you're leaving?"

"As long as you don't cry, I'm fine. If you cry, then I'll cry."

"Can I whine?"

"Don't you always?" Harper hoped his humor would soften the blow.

"Fuck off!"

"There's the nasty Brent I knew you hid under all of that professionalism."

They shared a good laugh.

"Well, wish me luck. I'm off to tell the partners. Oh wait, I have a favor to ask you. If you don't have time to do this, no worries." He knew the answer but would never think to assume.

"What's up?" Brent sat back in his chair.

"I have a friend who's interested in purchasing property up along the north shore of Lake Superior. Would you search around and see if you can find a real estate agent who specializes in that area? I'm looking for someone really competent. My friend is interested in properties that have the potential to be turned into a B&B. If you can come up with a name or two by the end of the week, that would be great."

"Sounds like fun. Sure."

If Brent was pumped about a project, there would be no stopping him.

"Thanks. I appreciate it." Harper stood. "Come here, my friend. How about a hug?"

Brent got up, and Harper wrapped his arms around him.

"Let's talk soon, okay? I'd love to go out and grab a beer or two or three sometime soon." Harper broke the embrace.

"Back at you soon with a realtor. Oh, and Harper?"

"Yes, sir?"

"Make sure to say hi to Ian for me."

"Will do. Okay, here I go."

"Oh God...." Brent looked over his shoulder as he opened the conference room door.

"What is it?" Harper backed away from the opening.

"Here, I have to show you." Brent led him down the hallway toward the section of the firm that housed a majority of the partners. About midway down a bank of offices, he stopped.

"What?" Harper looked around for a clue to the mystery.

Brent pointed to the sign on the door. "Harper Callahan" was printed on the nameplate in gold lettering. Stepping into the office, he switched on the lights.

"Wow!" Harper was impressed. The office was furnished more like that of a senior partner than a first level.

"I got to help pick out the furnishings. How did I do?" Brent asked, unable to mask his pride.

"You did great, but you're a sly one, Brent. You were hoping this office would get me to change my mind, weren't you? I know how you think." Harper walked around, admiring the tastefully-appointed space.

"Harper?"

Harper looked to the door as Duncan Price waltzed in, smiling from ear to ear. "Welcome to your new office, counselor!"

Price extended his hand, which Harper shook.

"I'd better get back to work." Brent made a beeline for the door. "I'll talk to you soon, Harper."

"Well, what do you think?" Duncan gestured around the room. "Did we get it right?"

Why does everything I do have to always get so complicated?

"Duncan, close the door, please, and take a seat." Harper resisted the temptation to sit behind the large mahogany desk, instead opting for one of the guest chairs facing it.

Duncan sat his large butt down on the chair next to him and smiled. "Should we buzz Arthur to join us?"

"That won't be necessary." Harper crossed his legs and adjusted his tie.

"You look good, Harp. How are you feeling?" Duncan asked apprehensively, his smile fading.

"I feel great." Harper leaned over the arm of the chair. "Duncan, I don't want to waste your time or mine, so I'll get right to the point. I'm not coming back to the firm."

The partner was too seasoned to show much of a reaction. "Perhaps this decision hasn't been properly thought out."

Harper was surprised at how quickly this conversation had reached the fork in the road. He had two options: he could let loose years of frustration and anger at having to serve such an egotistical and pompous master, or he could hold it back and extricate himself from the situation without showing the slightest bit of apprehension or emotion. Just as quickly, he made his choice.

"I wish you and the firm the best of luck going forward." Harper stood and walked toward the door. "Whatever I need to sign to make this official, please have it sent to my home. I'll be prompt at returning it fully executed."

Wow! He laughed when he'd stepped out into the sunlight. *That felt even better than I'd expected. Harper Callahan, welcome to your new life!*

The trip back home felt surreal. So many things were bouncing off the walls of his mind. He had to check himself several times to make sure he was giving his driving the attention it deserved. As soon as he had a realtor they could work with, he'd plan a surprise visit to the North Shore. He and Ian could spend a couple of days away and, for fun, take a look at a few properties.

I wonder what Ian will think when he finds out I've picked up his idea and started to run with it.

"HONEY, Francine needs to head into Duluth for a dentist appointment. Do you feel comfortable being the only one on until Rosalie comes in this afternoon to prep for the dinner rush?"

Audrey was taking the long way around asking if Alex was comfortable being on his own so she could take off and have a break from the café before she returned to run the counter and the register until they took their last order at eight thirty. Like most mornings, she had arrived at six to begin baking the pies and muffins that had become a trademark at the Smacker.

"Oh sure." Waiting tables was a whole lot easier than he'd thought it would be. Alex was happy to have the opportunity to pull in some extra money, being the only one left on until the dinner shift hit.

"Thanks, darling. You're a true blessing." The owner of the Lip Smacker took off her apron and walked over to Francine to tell her she could leave whenever she needed to. Alex finished clearing table nine, the round seating six in the corner, and bused the bin of dishes back to Louie, an ex-Marine who manned the dishwasher until Alex took it over at five.

"Alex, my friend, how's it look out there? Is it slowing down?" For Louie, it wasn't about whether or not the sun rose or set, it was all about the volume of dishes dumped in his station. Louie's life was dictated by it either "picking up" or "slowing down." A picking-up report brought about a harmless rant of cussing. News that the dish flow would finally be slowing down produced happy whistling and smiles. Colin, an endless source of nicknames, christened the predictable dishwasher "Pavlov."

"It's all over for today, Paaa… Louie."

"Yes! Christ, I could hardly keep up for a while. Those fuckin' breakfast skillets are a bitch."

Leaving his tray of dishes on the brushed aluminum counter, Alex reached for one of the small round serving trays from the shelf and headed back out to the restaurant to start filling salt and pepper shakers, just one of the side tasks he was responsible for.

"Alex, are you sure you'll be okay?" Francine had a problem with both guilt and trust. Whenever she needed a favor, she felt guilty asking, and when you did your best to assure her it was no big deal, she never trusted you were being truthful with her. *How could you leave me here all by myself? You only think of yourself!* He made a note to self to have Colin reach into his bag of names for something fitting for Francine.

"I'm gonna be fine, Francine. You working tomorrow?"

"I open tomorrow, but if you want me to stay late for you, I can. All you have to do is ask." *Guilt.*

"Thanks, but I'll be good. See you tomorrow."

"Bye, Alex, if you're sure."

You witch! How could you do this to me?

"Bye, Francine." Unable to muster up another reassurance, he started down the row of tables, cleaning and filling the small silver-topped containers. The bell over the door rang when he had reached the far end of the dining area, signaling a new customer. Knowing the sign at the door instructed them to seat themselves now that Audrey had left, he kept on with his side work until the tables in the back had been refilled.

A single man had seated himself up toward the front of the restaurant. Alex filled a glass of ice water and headed over to greet his customer.

"Hey, how you doin'?" Placing the glass in front of the man, he backed up in his tracks after realizing who was seated at the table.

"Alex?"

"Hey…." *What are you doing here?*

"It's me, Mike. You remember me?"

"Yeah, sure. Sorry, I'm just surprised to see you."

His heart was racing. Mike had held a large portion of his thoughts captive since their first encounter. Secretly, he'd hoped they would cross paths again. Nothing had been planned. He'd been too freaked out by the entire experience to show any interest in hooking up again. Now he regretted how abruptly their time together had ended. Maybe there would be a next time after all. Was Mike interested?

"A good surprise, I hope?" Mike smiled, taking a sip of his water.

"Oh yeah, it's a good surprise. Are you heading home?" Where was home? He couldn't remember. *Somewhere north of Grand Marais, wasn't it?*

"Nope. I'm heading into Duluth tonight. Staying at the Best Western a few blocks off of Superior Street on second. Interested in hanging out together? I have to make some stops but should be checked in by four thirty."

Damn! There was no way he could get out of work tonight. It wasn't possible. "I can't hook up tonight. I'm working a double shift. It's usually after ten by the time I get outta here. I guess I could drive over to Duluth after I'm done."

"That's getting kind of late for me. I have to be back on the road early in the morning. Shoot. Got any other ideas?"

"Not at the moment. Do you want to see a menu?" There wasn't a chance he was going to let Mike leave without some plan to meet up. He needed time to think this one out.

"Yes, please. I'm really… hungry." Mike winked.

Alex grabbed a menu and placed it down in front of his handsome customer. "We have homemade turkey noodle soup today, and our sandwich special is meatloaf. Do you want something other than water to drink?"

"I'd love a diet cola. And to make it easy, I'll take a cup of the soup you mentioned and the meatloaf sandwich. Two of my favorites."

"They're both really good. I'll put in your order. Be right back."

Even if Pavlov would agree to work a double, which of course he never would, Audrey wouldn't approve of the switch. He was screwed.

Clipping his ticket to the order wheel, he filled a tall glass with diet soda and walked back to Mike's table.

"Here you go." With Audrey gone for a few hours and the rest of the diner empty, he sat down across from Mike. "I wish I could get off tonight, but it's just not possible."

"Oh, I understand. Don't worry about it. It would have been nice to spend some time alone together, but we'll figure something out soon. Would you like that?" Mike grinned, removing the paper from his straw.

"Yeah, I'd like that." His body was in total agreement. Like the time before when they'd been together, his jeans were beginning to feel tight in front.

"So," Mike picked up the conversation, "what kind of crazy schedule are you on here, anyway? Don't tell me you work double shifts every day."

"I work a lot. Right now I'm scheduled to work doubles Monday through Wednesday, I work late Friday and Saturday nights, and I have Thursdays and Sundays off, but I'll usually pick up a Sunday shift if someone else wants it off and I've got nothing going on."

Mike pulled his phone out of his pocket. While he was studying it, a bell rang in the kitchen, signaling Alex to pick up his order. "That's your food. I'll be right back."

Loading up the empty portion of the sandwich plate with chips and a pickle, he tossed a couple packets of crackers and a soup spoon onto the saucer with the cup of turkey noodle and carried it to Mike's table. Instead of sitting down after he delivered the food, he knelt on the seat across from Mike. He needed to make some headway on his side work, or Rosalie, the early waitress coming in for the evening shift, would chew his ass off. You didn't mess around with Rosalie if you knew what was good for you.

"Can I bring you anything else? I have a few things here I need to do before my shift is up."

"No, this looks great. I was looking at my calendar. I'm going to be headed back this way in two weeks. If I switch around my schedule a little, I could work it so I'm spending the night at the Best Western in

Duluth again. That would be two weeks from this Thursday, August 11. You're off, right? We could have dinner together and then…."

Alex didn't know if he could complete the sentence either, but he knew what Mike meant. There was no question he would be there. "That sounds like a plan. I'll stop back in a minute."

Darting around, he scrubbed and organized the beverage area. Pavlov was just finishing up the silverware so he could roll a couple dozen sets using the special order "Lip Smacker" napkins Audrey had ordered from that fancy paper company in Cloquet. While he waited, he stepped back into the diner to check up on his customer. Mike had finished his soup and still had half a sandwich to work through. He had gone over to the counter and grabbed sections of the newspaper left behind by previous diners.

"Everything okay?"

Mike looked up from his newspaper. "Oh yeah, the soup was amazing. Best I've ever had."

"Good to hear." *Why is he staring at me like that?*

"You're really handsome, Alex. I hope it doesn't embarrass you when I say that. But you really are. The fact you want to spend time with me is so fantastic. Any thoughts about how we can hook up on the eleventh?"

"Hang on, I'll be right back." He needed a moment to collect himself. Mike's comment embarrassed him. Hiding out in the kitchen, he remembered there was one piece of Audrey's banana cream pie left. He'd intended to chow on it himself but wanted to serve it to Mike on the house. Taking the tin out of the pie cooler, he topped it off with a small dollop of whipping cream. Grabbing a new fork—that was the fancy way to serve dessert—he placed it on the table. "This is on the house, by the way. It's my favorite."

"Your favorite pie is—" Mike took a closer look. "—banana cream? This is getting a little too weird, my friend. Our birthdays are a few days apart, and guess what? Banana cream is my favorite too."

He knew by the look on Mike's face that he was bullshitting him. "Do you know what time you'll be done on Thursday? I'll plan on driving into Duluth, and we can meet up at your motel or anywhere else you want. I know Duluth pretty well."

"Should be about the same deal. I'll be checked in about four thirty. I'm not sure what room I'll end up in, so why don't I keep an eye out for you. Say around five, does that work?" Mike placed his soup dish on top of his sandwich plate and moved his slice of pie into place. "I shouldn't be eating this, but what the hell. You've gotta enjoy life, right?"

Yes! You've got to enjoy life. I've got to enjoy life.

"You can plan on me being in the parking lot of the Best Western at five on the eleventh. Enjoy the pie. I'll be back in a minute." When he returned to the kitchen, Pav had finished the silverware. Alex carried the thick plastic container over to the waitress stand and tossed on a bundle of napkins. Filling a soda for himself, he brought the whole operation out into the dining room and placed it on the table across from Mike.

"This is the worst part of the job." He was bummed he had to waste his time with Mike doing this stupid side work.

"Trust me, I know. I waited tables to help pay for college. I did everything I could to avoid side work. This pie, it's a little bit of heaven. Does someone here make it?"

"Audrey, the owner. She makes all of our pies and muffins."

"That was sinful." Throwing his napkin down on his empty plate, Mike crawled out of the booth. "Well, I should get back on the road. I'm going to be counting the days until we can hook up. What do I owe you for this feast?"

"It's my treat." His heart raced. Snapshots of their time together in Mike's car flashed before his eyes. How good it had felt to be touched by this strong, masculine man. *I can't wait for you to touch me again.*

"Alex, you don't have to do that." Mike removed a wad of bills from his pocket.

"No, I want to."

"It was delicious." He extended his hand for a shake. "I'm so glad to have run into you."

Instead of shaking his hand, Mike held it. A wave of desire shot through Alex's body like nothing he'd ever felt before. Unable to hide his reaction, he broke contact and looked away.

"See you on the eleventh, then?"

"Yes." His throat was parched.

"Thanks again, handsome."

When Mike had pulled out of the parking lot, Alex went back to the table to clear it. A crisp twenty-dollar bill was hidden under the pie plate. His heart soared.

Maybe I've found my cowboy.

"YOU got to drive last time. Besides, this was my idea." Harper accelerated down the ramp, merging their rental car onto the freeway.

"Yeah, well it's *my* retirement dream." Ian swatted the dashboard.

"So? I stopped so you could get a bag of sliders, didn't I?"

"And admit it, you loved them, right?" Ian slid over and placed his head on Harper's shoulder.

They were good. Sinfully good, there was no doubt about it. The little square hamburgers covered with onion bits melted in your mouth. White Castle was another new experience Ian had introduced him to. How was it he had tolerated living under a rock for so long?

It was fun driving again. So far, his arm wasn't giving him any trouble. Ian had confessed in a weak moment how much he hated being a passenger. Playfully, he had badgered Harper to let him drive but had finally caved when he realized it wasn't going to happen. A wonderful sign that the carefulness of their new relationship was starting to fade away. They were starting to settle into each other.

The landscape was changing. Flat crop fields were being inundated by large, majestic pines. First just a few clusters planted here and there, most likely as a windbreak to protect the freeway from the fierce blowing snow that could make winter travel next to impossible. As they furthered their journey north, the wind blocks were replaced by an endless forest.

"It's starting to get really beautiful, isn't it?" The respect for the landscape was impossible to miss in Ian's voice.

"Yes. I can't believe how different it looks here, and we're only a few hours out of the city. Does it look like this where you grew up?" He had a million questions for Ian floating around in his head, and the answers couldn't come soon enough. He had been trained to replace unknowns with fact. The more he knew about Ian, the more comfortable and relaxed he would feel in their relationship.

"Yeah, in a way it does. What I miss most about home are the wooded hills and valleys and the beautiful clear lakes. You'll see. We'll plan a trip there sometime soon. If it works out, we'll try and make it back for the reunion. I haven't heard anything about it yet. Some years we just skip it. Not sure why. Our immediate family usually figures out a time in the summer to get together."

What was Ian's family like? He wanted very much to meet them. He longed to be included in their plans. To be a part of them. He'd heard bits and pieces here and there, but it wasn't enough. It was in his nature to speculate, to formulate an image, and based on what he'd learned from Ian, he pictured the Burke family as loving and caring. Simple, in a way meant to compliment. Ian had values, deep-rooted traits Harper recognized from his own upbringing. There were things in life that mattered and many more that didn't. He felt confident both he and Ian had been blessed with a knack for valuing what really counted. Maybe this shared knowledge would help them navigate through their years together with more joy than pain.

"Harper, what are we doing today?" Ian remained snuggled up close.

"I'm trying to sort that one out myself." He was thankful Ian had initiated the conversation. Where and how to fit it into the day had eluded him, but nevertheless, he knew it was an important talk they needed to have.

"Here's what I'm thinking." Ian moved himself over to his side of the seat. "I think there're some questions we need to ask each other, answer them as best we can, and go from there. The biggest one in my mind right now is, are we both willing to give up our lives in the city and relocate? I'll go first, if you don't mind."

"I don't mind. What've you been thinking?"

"We're relatively young. The way I look at this, it's nothing that has to last forever. To me, it's more of an adventure." Ian adjusted the air vent so it blew directly on him. "Where I run into a problem is when I think of this in permanent terms. I'm game for adventure, but I'm not necessarily seeking a permanent change. Some aspects of my life I could easily say goodbye to, others not so much. So if I approach this as temporary, it's easy for me to deal with now."

"Have you thought about this enough to elaborate?"

"Yeah, I think… so…." Ian sneezed. "Excuse me. I would miss having my friends close by. I really depend on them. Having you in my life will make being distanced from them easier, but it still would be tough. Does that make sense?"

Did it ever. Despite his attempts to not go there, it produced a pang of jealousy he was ashamed of. It brought to light the fact friends hadn't mattered much to him before meeting Ian. How could he have been so blind? "Ian, seeing you with your friends was a revelation to me. I hate to admit this, but on a very selfish level, it makes me kind of jealous. Well, jealous and sad. I should have paid more attention to nurturing friendships along the way."

"You don't need to go there, Harper. We're not identical twins, and I hope we never will be. We all have different needs. I can flip that around and admit jealousy in seeing how devoted and dedicated you've been to your career. I've never had that kind of focus." Ian reached over and squeezed his shoulder.

"Would not having your friends close by be a showstopper?" He braced himself for Ian's response.

"No. Part of me hates living in the city. I'm happy enough with all I have going on so I don't think about it that often. But I sure do miss what we're looking at now. I miss the north woods. It's a big part of who I am. Can you imagine growing up with all this beauty surrounding you? Some of the kids hated it. I didn't. You know, it's funny, I think that's why Andy and I became such good friends." Ian laughed. "You think we bopped each other in the woods and frolicked through the meadows naked. You were thinking that, weren't you?"

"It hadn't entered my mind until now. Did you fuck each other silly in the woods? That's kind of hot."

"Yeah, we tried everything. The woods were a great place to explore. Darn, now you ruined it."

"I did not ruin it. You did. You're kind of edgy and sensitive today, Ian Poo. What's up with that?"

His inquiry was met with silence. He had meant for his comment to be more of a tease, not an accusation. Now he wasn't sure how it had been received. Better to let this one flop around for a while before pursuing it.

"I'm thinking ahead." Ian shifted in his seat and continued to look out the passenger window. "In my mind, I already have us relocated to the North Shore. I can see us running our B&B as clearly as if we were actually doing it. I have a hard time separating fantasy from reality sometimes."

Owning and operating a B&B was an idea Harper was more than willing to pursue. Unlike Ian, he hadn't ventured much further than that. Ian had already projected himself there. *Maybe that's the way he processes change. Interesting.* "Ian, placing yourself in the scene isn't necessarily a bad thing." *I'll do the same thing, but it won't be until it's a done deal. Ian's test driving.* "In a way, you're already living the change. Contemplating and evaluating how this change will compare to what you have going on now. I think that's an amazing technique."

"Sometimes it can be a real pain in the ass. I get these preconceived notions of what something is going to be like, and when it's not what I've envisioned, well, I don't do so well." Ian chuckled, sounding relieved he'd gotten that off his chest.

"I look at today as a fact-finding mission. We have this idea that might work, might not. Let's see what… oh my God…."

"Oh God, what?" Ian swung his body around so he could see.

"Tiffany Marks. The billboard."

"Holy smokes, are those ever going to be lost on us." Ian looked over, awestruck.

"No kidding."

Tiffany Marks, the realtor Brent had hooked them up with, had clearly identified her marketing strengths—a pair of gargantuan breasts. Like marsupials nestled snug inside their mother's pouch, Tiffany's crowd pleasers stretched her fuzzy pink angora sweater to the limit.

"Wow!" He giggled. "I don't know what else to say. Does it have anything to do with storing energy to help get through the long winter?"

"Stop it, Harper." Ian laughed. "I can't go there or I'll never make it through our meeting. Besides, tits that big can be a disability."

"Oh, I know,"—he fought hard to control himself—"but something tells me she's coping just fine."

A small sign announced they were entering an accident reduction area.

"Don't say it." He and Ian weathered another round of uproarious snorts and silly laughter.

"Oh man, this is going to be tough," Ian admitted when he was finally able to talk again.

"How about you go in and I'll wait in the car."

"Not a chance," Ian protested. "We have to face our demons."

"Wow! I don't know, this could be bad."

"She's probably very sensitive to people's reactions to them," Ian cautioned.

"Shut up. You're not helping."

The tension in the car generated by Tiffany's big sisters was thick enough to slice with a knife. It got worse when Harper exited the freeway and turned onto the county road leading them to her office. He didn't dare chance a word for fear it would set off another round of debilitating hysterics. It was likely Ian had fallen silent for the same reason. One could only hope poor Tiffany had a good sense of humor. There was little doubt in his mind she was going to need it.

IAN braced himself. They had sat in the parking lot of Marks Realty for as long as they dared, until the fear of being noticed got the best of them.

"You ready?" Harper asked in a shaky voice a few feet from the entrance.

"I have a plan. If we go off in there, we'll make some dumb excuse a friend of ours called on the way up and told us something really funny."

Harper turned in his tracks and headed back to the car. "You call that a plan?"

"Come back here. This was your idea, not mine."

He waited for Harper to join him at the door. "Listen, we don't know this broad from Adam… Eve, I mean. If we blow this, we blow it. We'll just get up and leave. No skin off our butts, right?"

"Okay, I'm all over that. And we'll send flowers or something if it's real bad." Harper coughed and needlessly adjusted his T-shirt.

"Ready?" Ian stepped up to the door, rubbing his hands together.

"Ready." Harper stepped in front, opening the door, forcing Ian to enter first.

The little waiting area was tastefully decorated in a variety of beige tones. A large reception desk filled most of the room. A small seating area was arranged on the opposite side with a large potted plant separating the two spaces. There wasn't a soul in sight.

"Are you sure she knows we're coming?" He looked over to Harper for a confirmation.

"Brent set up the appointment last week. He's usually very efficient when it comes to this kind of thing. Let's sit down for a minute and see if anyone comes out." Harper sat in the seat nearest the window.

With an overabundance of caution, Ian took the seat furthest away from Harper. Several minutes passed before they heard the sound of a toilet flushing. No way was he going to chance a look in his companion's direction. Footsteps on the beige Berber signaled the arrival of someone. Once again, he braced himself.

Unless she'd undergone a radical makeover, the woman who entered the room could never have been confused with Tiffany. Gangly, she had absolutely no chest. Dark brown polyester slacks battled a turquoise and purple satin top. The lady's hair was stringy gray-blond, and if any makeup had been applied, it was impossible to detect. Thick round glasses completed the look.

"Hello, I hope you haven't been waiting long. Breakfast hasn't agreed with me, if you know what I mean."

Harper stood. "Hello, I'm—"

"Ian Burke." The woman cut him off. "Is that you, Ian?"

Harper looked over for an explanation.

"I'm Ian," he answered, unsure of what was happening.

"Ian Burke, well I can't believe it. You don't know who I am, do you?" The woman chuckled, stepping in front of the desk.

"I'm sorry, I don't. Do we know each other?" There wasn't a single thing about her familiar to him.

"Well, it's been a few years now, but we went to school together. I'm Eunice Larson. You haven't changed a bit."

Eunice Larson? Oh God, really? You're Eunice Larson?

"Of course, Eunice! Eunice Larson…. Harper, this is Eunice Larson." He hoped his face somehow communicated to Harper how unwelcome this unexpected reunion was. "She and I went to school together. Can you believe that?" *I can't.* "Eunice, this is my partner, Harper Callahan. Harper… this is… Eunice."

"It's a pleasure meeting you." Harper smiled, nodded, and sat back down, leaving Ian to deal with Eunice on his own.

I'll get you for this.

"Ian Burke, you look great. He probably knows this," Eunice purred. "I had quite the crush on this guy back then. He was such a stinker. Wouldn't have a thing to do with me."

"He's still a stinker," Harper piped back.

"Well, as you can see," Eunice warbled on, stepping around to the other side of the desk, "I wasn't about to confine myself to little old Buchannan. Not this girl. I need to be where the action is. Took some classes in real estate and never looked back."

"Well,"—Ian staggered over and sat in the seat next to Harper—"I'm glad things have worked out for you." There wasn't much he could say. Eunice had achieved her goal, and he was happy for her. She hadn't been given much to work with.

"Oh, Ms. Marks called a few minutes ago. She was tied up on a closing, but she's on her way back from Duluth. Shouldn't be more than a few minutes, I would think. Do either of you care for coffee? We have some diet soda in back too."

"I'm good. Harper?" He wasn't thirsty. He wasn't anything. He was numb.

"A diet soda, please."

"Be right back. Ian Burke, I can't believe it," she mumbled on her way out of the reception area.

"Wow. Small world, huh?" Harper jabbed him in the ribs.

"Too small." He slapped Harper's hand away. "Eunice Larson—"

"She's still sweet on you." Harper gave him another jab.

Before he had a chance to counter, the door to the office swung open and Tiffany Marks made her entrance.

"Gentleman, I'm so sorry for keeping you waiting. I'm Tiffany. And you are… let me guess, Harper?"

"Harper Callahan." Harper extended his hand.

"Nice to meet you. That makes you Ian, right?" Tiffany winked.

"Ian Burke, nice to meet you."

"Terrific. Has Eunice been out to greet you?"

"Boy, has she ever." Harper was on a roll.

"Good. Let's head back to my office, and we can discuss what you have in mind."

Ian shot Harper his best "you better behave yourself" look and followed Ms. Marks down the hall. Her boobs didn't seem quite as big in person. He made a note to ask Harper if he thought she'd had them digitally enhanced. He couldn't help but notice the restroom door was closed. *Poor Eunice.* Rounding the corner, Harper pinched his ass so hard he yelped.

"Everyone doing okay back there?" Tiffany asked over her shoulder.

"Just excited is all," Harper answered.

"Okay." Tiffany motioned them into her office. Another celebration of beige. "You guys take a seat, and let's get busy. What can I do for you?"

Ian shot Harper another look. He hoped, without any confusion, it would communicate to him he'd better start talking if he knew what was good for him.

"Ian and I—" Harper was interrupted by Eunice entering with his diet soda.

"Thank you, Eunice. Ian, are you sure you don't want anything?" Tiffany asked while Eunice hovered over him in neutral.

"I'm good. Thank you." Eunice grabbed her stomach and bolted out the door.

"Okay. Harper, you were saying?" Tiffany adjusted the legal pad she had in front of her.

"Ian and I have been entertaining the idea of relocating to the North Shore. One of the things we've discussed is purchasing either an existing B&B or a large enough residence that could be converted into one."

"Your assistant mentioned that. I have a few ideas. Any specifics? Do you guys have a wish list you're working off of?"

"Not sure we've gotten that far." Harper looked over and shrugged.

Ian had thought quite a bit about what he'd prefer. In his dream, he pictured fabulous landscaping with a view of the lake. A large Victorian structure with a huge porch. "We'd like the house to be on a good chunk of land. And if possible, either on the lake or with a view of the lake." It was his turn to look over to Harper, who nodded.

"Okay, well that helps. It limits the choices, but I still have some ideas."

Ian liked Tiffany. He liked her comfortable manner. She was warm, friendly, and at first glance seemed confident and competent. And the much feared boob issue was all but forgotten.

"Do you have an idea of what you'd like to spend?"

"We don't." Harper didn't wait for a signal to take the lead, which was fine. They hadn't discussed finances. "I'd like to shoot for the moon and then scale back if needed."

Where have I heard that before?

"Great. Why don't we do this. What are your weekends like in the next couple of weeks? I'd like to research what's available and have you come back this way for a few showings. Sound like a deal?"

"That works for me. Ian?" Harper looked over for his approval.

"Sounds great." He was pumped. Giddy. In the brief time they had spent with Tiffany, he'd realized for the first time that his dream to run a B&B could in all likelihood become a reality. How different life would be if Harper had been taken away from him. Ian promised himself to try and make every moment of their lives together count.

CHAPTER
Eight

"BOY, with all that work, I know you got money. Give me a twenty."

Only a few days before, Alex had handed over two hundred dollars to his dad so he could buy used tires. He wondered how much of his money had gone to the tires and how much had gone to cigarettes and whiskey. *You're not my father, you're a piece of shit. A living, breathing piece of walking shit.* He reached into his wallet and pulled out a twenty.

"Here. Any word on when they're going to bring you guys back?" He tossed the bill onto the table and stepped out of the room. The stench, sweat, and who knew what else made him gag.

"Oh, so you're the big man of the house now, is that it? Come here when I'm talkin' to you."

Alex made himself step back into the room. He couldn't remember the last time he'd spent time in here—sometime last year when the old man was still working.

"Big important man because you're workin' and I'm not. Don't test drive that uppity attitude of yours around here again if you know what's good for you. If I get out of this chair, you'll wish you'd never been born. You hear me, boy?"

The creature inhabiting the broken-down recliner looked nothing like the man that had married his mother. If he didn't get ahold of himself and lay off the booze, the chances of him getting on the payroll again were slim to nothing. Alex didn't care. He only had a few more months to go and he'd be long gone. If the drunken bum stopped breathing and sat rotting in that chair for a month, nobody would miss him. The lazy son of a bitch would be better off dead.

Now wasn't the time to get into it. He had places to go. "I was just asking, is all. I'm going to be late." Checking himself in the mirror, he was satisfied with the image looking back. The light blue shirt he'd picked up recently at Pamida looked good against his tanned skin. He hoped Mike would think so too.

Traffic was heavy coming from Duluth. Every other vehicle that passed was either an RV or pulling some kind of camper trailer. He was thankful to be headed in the opposite direction. Tourists could be pretty pokey, slowing down at each vista to gawk at the lake or, worse yet, jerking their car over to the side of the road and stopping to snap a picture.

Alex stepped on the gas, and old Zits rattled and shook as he sped toward his rendezvous at the motel. The last few days had been agonizing. He doubted there had ever been a time when he'd wanted or needed anything as much as this. In his mind, Mike was no longer a stranger. He'd replayed and expanded on their brief time together until he'd elevated them to relationship status and jerked himself raw in the process. Condoms tucked away in his wallet ensured he'd be ready for whatever the night had in store. He'd waited long enough. It was time. Time to embrace who he was and jump in with both feet.

Shortly before five, he pulled into the motel and parked Zits next to a white van. The plan was to hang out in the parking lot until Mike spotted him from his room. He refused to let his nerves get the best of him. This was easier said than done. The anticipation, the speculation, and the vivid memory of their previous encounter all seemed to gang up, choosing the moment he stepped out of the car into the parking lot to unleash their most enthusiastic attack on his confidence.

He hadn't expected the awkwardness that overwhelmed him as he waited. How many eyes were on him as he stood next to Zits, waiting? *Who gets out of their car and just stands here like an idiot?* On the verge of climbing back in, it occurred to him he hadn't spotted Mike's Range Rover. The motel parking lot was laid out like the letter L, wrapping itself around the building. Heading past the single row of parking spots nearest to the office, he turned the corner. There weren't as many cars parked this far back. It took only a moment for him to realize Mike's car wasn't here either. *Maybe he's running late? Maybe he has another car?*

Pangs of disappointment threatened to destroy his fantasy of what this night would be. On the drive over, he pictured Mike, eager, like he'd been before, peeking out of the window waiting for him. *Please show up, Mike. I need you.* Those eyes—he couldn't shake the feeling he was being watched and analyzed. Could someone peering out their window mistake his intentions? Are they watching their car, fearful he might be a thief? Unable to ward off the gnawing insecurity, he crawled back into Zits and waited.

It was five fifteen. *Why didn't I give him my cell phone number?* He'd picked up nothing about Mike to make him not want to trust the guy or think he might not be sincere. After all, he'd been the one that had initiated their first meeting and, at the restaurant, worked out a date and time for their next hookup. *Simmer down. Something came up. Traffic was heavy, and he'll be here soon.*

A man and a woman appeared out of nowhere in his rearview mirror. Each had an enormous ice cream cone. The man held the woman's cone while she fished their room key out from the pocket of her shorts and opened the door. He heard them laugh before they hustled inside, closing the door behind them. *Come on, Mike. Where are you?*

It was now 5:33. He remembered Mike telling him he would be at the motel sometime between four thirty and five. If that was the case, soon he would be a whole hour late. Something wasn't right. He'd gone back and written down the date and time they were to meet the minute Mike left the restaurant. There was no way he could have mixed it up. Frustrated and fighting off waves of disappointment, he decided to get out and walk around. If something unforeseen had detained Mike, he hoped it wouldn't screw up the entire night. He didn't care what time they…. As he stepped out of the car, a navy Range Rover whizzed past, turning the corner. *All right! He's here.*

No more waiting. Alex slammed the car door and walked across the parking lot. The butterflies were back. The big date was on. *Stay cool, Alex. Let Mike call the shots.*

Rounding the corner, he was stopped in his tracks when the door of the Rover opened and a middle-aged woman stepped out. *What the fuck?* He was stunned. How could this be? He watched her long enough to come to grips with the fact that she wasn't Mike before making a beeline back to his car.

It was now 5:54. *Please don't let this night go in the shitter. Please....* He felt like crying. He'd waited weeks for this. This was a special event. A milestone. An opportunity he'd fantasized about for as long as he could remember. And Mike, he liked Mike. He was handsome, and Alex felt safe with him. What about all of the different scenarios he'd envisioned them in—camping, traveling, having dinner together in nice restaurants. *Please, please don't stand me up. I'm a nice guy. I deserve this!*

He'd waited past six thirty before it dawned on him that the one thing he and Mike had in common was the Lip Smacker. Not having exchanged cell numbers, it was possible Mike had left a message for him there.

"Hi, Audrey. It's Alex."

"Alex, is everything okay?"

"I'm fine. Are you guys busy tonight?" Maybe if he chatted for a minute, she'd tell him someone had called so he didn't have to ask.

"We were swamped until about fifteen minutes ago. Everyone came at once. You know how that is. Just a second.... Thank you, please come again. Oh good. I'm glad you enjoyed it. Yes, I'll make sure she gets the change. Sorry about that, Alex."

"Audrey, did anyone call tonight for me?" She was busy. This was no time to chat.

"Not that I'm aware of. I've been by the phone for most of the night. Did you lose your cell phone, honey?"

"No, was just wondering, that's all. See you tomorrow."

"Okay, have a good night."

Miserable beyond words, he leaned his head against the window and watched a teenage girl plug money into the vending machine from his side mirror. When she'd retrieved her soda, she ran back up the stairs to her room on the second floor.

Unwilling to give up, he sat for another half an hour before he decided to try one last thing before throwing in the towel. Getting out of the car, he crossed the parking lot to the motel office. *What can I say?* He needed a reason for being there. He could say he was meeting someone about a job offer. *Yeah, that works.* He'd tell the person working in the office he was meeting someone here named Mike and then apologize for not knowing his last name. Hopefully the desk clerk would play along with him and look to see if any Mikes had reservations to stay that night.

A bell tinkled when he stepped through the door into the little office. The sound from a television drifted through the doorway. He walked over to a wire rack in the corner filled with sightseeing brochures.

"Hello, can I.... Alex?"

Startled to hear his name, Alex turned around to discover Peggy Munson, a girl he'd just graduated with.

"Peggy, oh hi." He felt like he'd been punched in the stomach.

"What are you doing here? Do you need a room?" Peggy laughed, knowing Alex lived only forty minutes away.

"No, I...." *What the hell am I going to say now?* "I was supposed to meet someone."

"A guest staying here? What's the name?" Peggy moved over to the computer at the end of the counter.

Devastated to the point of tears, he turned around and fled the office.

He heard Peggy calling his name as he fired up his car and tore out of the parking lot.

"I hate this motherfucking town! I hate my motherfucking life," he screamed at the top of his lungs. Several weeks of blissful anticipation made the disappointment of not having his evening with Mike unbearable. He choked back huge, angry sobs. A stream of steady tears clouded his vision as he fought to keep Zits on the road.

"IAN! Ian! Iaaaaan!" Harper led the cheering at the top of his lungs as Ian chugged his beer, slamming the empty mug down on the table.

The group of close friends gathered together at Merl's stomped and hollered their approval. After a tally of all the participating city teams, Ian had the best batting average in the league. A first for the Hornets.

"So, champ, how does it feel to be number one?" Andy blew beer suds in Ian's face.

"A lot better than it feels to be number forty-three." Spencer beaned Andy with a peanut.

"Hey, Harper,"—Ian gave him a playful shove while the gang recovered from their cheering session—"show these guys the picture of Tiffany's billboard. You guys,"—Ian poured a beer—"you have to check this out."

He complied, reaching into his pocket and pulling out his cell phone. "She's been blessed."

"Let me see." Allison snatched the phone out of his hand. "Holy shit!"

"Wow." Spencer wiggled his eyebrows after sneaking a glance. "Maybe we should look for some property up north, huh, babe?"

"You know, I'm not even sure you know what you're frickin' doin' with these babies," Allison slurred, thrusting out her chest and squishing her own boobs to make her point. "What the hell are you going to do with *those*?"

"Care for another shot, honey?" Spencer passed the phone to Andy.

"Sure, why the fuck not? What?" She punched Spencer in the arm and then cackled until a severe nasal snort silenced her.

Harper laughed. This was a side of Allison he hadn't seen before. Pocketing his phone, he poured himself a beer and signaled for the server to stop by.

"We'll have another pitcher. Allison, another butter shot?"

"What?" It was clear to the table Allison had met her match when paired up against the syrupy, butterscotch-flavored liqueur. "You guys suck. I mean… for real… you guys suck."

"That means yes," Spencer clarified. "So, are you officially ending the search for your north shore B&B?"

"It doesn't look good." Harper looked over to Ian for his response.

"I don't want you assholes to move. I'm dead serious." Allison banged the table with her fist, spilling at least two of their beers.

"Easy, hon." Spencer flicked his wife on the arm.

"Shut up, I don't. I can say it. I don't want you adorable assholes to move. There, I said it again!" Allison, changing up her pitch, accentuated her point by sticking her tongue out at her husband.

"We haven't been able find the right house on the right piece of property." Ian ignored Allison's drunken admission. "It's been one or the other. A great house with a shitty location, or a shitty house and a great location. But it was fun looking. And you guys,"—Ian filled his glass back up—"Tiffany was great to work with. She's really a cool lady. And now that she has a good idea of what we were looking for, she's agreed to stay in touch and call if something comes on the market we'd be interested in."

"And maybe we get lucky enough to have champ here on the team for another season." Andy raised his glass in a toast.

"Hey! Dude—"

The toast was interrupted when a man, obviously intoxicated, approached their table.

"Dude, I know you. You're the dude that was shot. You're the attorney dude who was shot. Guys, this is that dude I was tellin' you about." The drunk stumbled into Harper's chair as he waved for his friends to join him.

"Man, what's it like to get shot, huh?"

"I got this." Before anyone could respond, Andy was up and out of his chair. Grabbing the guy by the back of the neck, he forcefully escorted him toward the door. Spencer stood to make sure the guy's buddies didn't have any ideas about interfering.

"Honey, go make sure Andy is okay." Allison looked like she was going to cry. Spencer left the table but was back in a matter of seconds with Andy right behind him.

"Drunk dude sends his most sincere apologies," Andy reported as he and Spencer sat back down at the table.

"That's a first. And I hope a last. Thanks, guys." Harper felt embarrassed to have been the cause of the disruption sidetracking their celebration.

"Stupid dickhead!" Allison downed her shot. "Hey, let's go get a pizza."

"Hon, we still have a pitcher of beer." Spencer displayed his full glass.

"Okay… okay… you win. I never win." Allison slumped down in her chair.

Harper fished his phone out of his pocket when he felt it vibrate. "I wonder who this could be. Oh, speak of the devil, it's Tiffany. This is Harper," he answered, covering his ear. "Tiffany, can I call you right back? I can't hear you. Okay, I'll call you in a minute."

"What does she want?" Ian asked.

"I don't know. I couldn't hear her very well. I'm going to step outside for a minute and call her back."

"Drunk dude was staggering around in the parking lot when we left him. He shouldn't be a problem, but if he is, let us know and we'll take care of it." Andy looked over to Spencer, who gave him a thumbs-up. Allison had folded her bar napkin into a lopsided star.

Stepping outside, Harper couldn't help noticing how humid the night had gotten. *I bet we see a good thunderstorm tonight.* He punched the Callback button on his phone and waited for Tiffany to answer.

"Harper?"

"Hey, Tiffany. Sorry about that. We're having beers with some friends, and the bar is really noisy."

"I could tell. Wish I was there with you. I'm up to my elbows in paperwork. I don't want to keep you, but I'm calling because I think I may have stumbled upon a property you guys might be interested in. I know we decided to table the search for a while, but this, well, I think you should come and take a look."

Harper could hear the excitement in her voice. "Tell me more."

"Well…." Tiffany hesitated. "Here's the deal. I've been doing this long enough to know how a buyer's mind works. I'm going to ask that you trust me on this one. I don't want you guys to start dissecting and analyzing this until you've had a chance to see it first."

"Okay." Harper laughed. "That makes sense. Let me talk to Ian. I'm game, and I'm sure he is too. We'll need to take a look at our schedules." Harper looked over at the adjacent parking lot. He spotted his drunk friend leaning up against a pickup truck.

"Sounds good. I'm busy, but I'll rearrange my schedule. Call me tomorrow after you guys have had a chance to talk."

"Perfect. I'll call you tomorrow. Bye."

"Go back and party. Bye."

Harper glanced back to the lot. Drunk dude was nowhere in sight. *He's probably passed out under his truck.*

"What was that all about?" Ian asked when he'd sat back down.

"A casualty?" Harper pointed at Allison, who was leaning against Spencer's arm, fast asleep.

"She's gone to the land of ten thousand butter shots." Spencer smiled. "She'll rally if we get something to eat later."

"Tiffany has another property she wants us to look at." Harper slugged down half his beer.

"Really?" Ian belched loudly.

"Nice. Yeah, but she won't tell me anything about it. She asked that we trust her on this one."

"Can I go?" It appeared Tiffany had made quite an impression on Spencer.

"Back off, tiger," Ian cautioned. "When does she want us up there? I've got a busy week, but I can juggle a few things around."

"I'd like to juggle a few things around." Spencer wasn't giving up.

"Look at this piece of work." Andy cocked his head toward the team captain, "His wife's passed out, and Straight Cat's titty hunting."

"I'm curious is all."

"We'll talk when we get home." Harper downed the last of his beer. "I told her I'd call her back in the morning. I'm hungry."

"Whattaya say?" Andy looked around the table. "Should we grab a pizza at Luciano's?"

"Pizza!" Ian let rip another award-winning belch.

"Let's do it." Harper signaled for the tab. "My turn to treat."

"I'll pick up the pizza," Spencer countered. "Honey, we're leaving. We're going for pizza."

"Where are we?" Allison bobbed her head when Spencer gave her a shake. "I told her it wouldn't fucking fit. Oh...." Placing both hands on the table, she opened her eyes, surveyed the table, and vomited between her legs.

"TIFFANY, please, please tell me this place is located on top of that big rock. Ian, can you imagine the view from up there?" Harper opened his window, sticking his head out for a better look.

"Actually,"—Tiffany put on her blinker and slowed the car—"the property is located beneath the palisade."

"I've been to the top of the palisade." Ian squeezed his head between the two passengers in the front seat. "The view is amazing."

She turned off the freeway onto a dirt road. "Don't get all jiggy with me. The road's in rough shape, but that's fixable."

Did she say jiggy or jiggly? Harper made a note to run that one past Ian when they were alone.

"It's so pretty back in here. I love all the birch trees. Let's see, if I remember right, we go around this curve and... voila!" The realtor gunned the car, surging it up a small hill before stopping in front of a faded tangerine-and-white building. "Gentleman, I present to you the Palisade Beach Cabins."

Harper was speechless. *Is she kidding?*

"Follow me." Tiffany stepped out of the car and waited while he and Ian joined her. "This is the office. Down, closer toward the water, step over here, you can see better from here." He followed Ian over to the spot where she was pointing. "You can see the first couple of cabins. There are ten total stretching along the shore until the palisade begins. I know it's not what you originally had in mind, but as I got to talking with you, I thought maybe—well, I thought this had some potential if you were willing to expand your idea."

Ian looked at him and giggled.

What did that giggle mean?

"Let's walk down toward the water so you can get a better view. I have a key for the office. We'll check it out when we come back up." Tiffany, not waiting around to see if her plan was approved, pointed her guns toward the water and was off.

A busted-up concrete walk led down toward the cabins. Harper stopped in his tracks when the lake came fully into view. "Wow!"

"Wow!" Ian echoed. "Look, Harper, the units are right on the lake."

"That's, that's very cool." The view was stunning. The best they'd seen so far.

"Okay, as you can see, these cabins need some work. Well, a lot of work. But I think the cost to renovate would be comparable to the expense you would incur remodeling one of the older Victorians we've looked at. Maybe less, depending on how fancy you want to get."

"Any chance we can look inside one of these?" Harper's mind was racing a mile a minute.

"Yes, sir, but walk with me a little further before we go inside. I came down here yesterday. This is so cool."

Like a goose and her goslings, Tiffany led the way. The concrete walk stopped at the first unit. They walked on a combination of grass, weeds, and ferns. The cabins were spaced well apart. "I like how these things are spaced." His comment was met with silence. "Ian, what do you think about the spacing?"

"Yeah...."

Hmm, lost in our own little world, are we?

"If we walk down here toward the shore... this is it. Isn't it amazing?"

Ian gasped.

Standing in front of the last unit, the palisade towered majestically above them. Billowy white puffs of cloud floated overhead, contrasted by one of the bluest skies he'd ever seen. The slow-roaming clouds made it feel like they were moving. "This is one of the most beautiful places I've ever seen. I'm just amazed. Isn't this great, Ian?"

"Yeah...."

"I have a key for the first unit and the office," Tiffany announced. "Let's go have a look. In their heyday, each of these cabins would have had its own grill," she explained as they worked their way back.

Harper reached for Ian's hand, holding him back. "Tiffany, we'll meet you up ahead in a minute."

"Sounds good."

"So, how's this going over? I can see some possibilities. Where are you at?"

"I feel like crying." Ian looked away.

"Hon, what's wrong? Don't worry about me. If this isn't working, we'll just tell her. We don't have to stick—"

"It's working on every level for me. Harper, this place is magical." Ian turned and gestured back toward the palisade. "I'm.... I don't know what else to say. I see gardens. I see a walking path down by the water outlined with plants. Flower boxes on the cabins and pockets of formal gardens, each having its own theme."

"You don't see dead people, do you?" He couldn't resist the jest. Ian was so serious, so overwhelmed by the property. "Come on, sport. Let's rejoin the tour."

"Hey there." Tiffany was all smiles. "It's musty in here but not as bad as it was yesterday. I opened the windows while I toured the property." She held open the screen door as they entered the first cabin. "These aren't laid out that much differently than a standard motel room."

The inside was roomier than he'd expected. A small table with two chairs occupied the spot in front of the main window. Behind it was a frame for a double bed. Someone had made the wise decision to remove the mattresses when the place was closed down. The bright orange shag carpeting was garish and painful to look at.

"Behind the bed is the bathroom. Take a look. They're small. A stool, sink, and a shower unit. Nothing fancy. By the way, you like the carpet?" She made a sweeping gesture at the floor.

"I love the carpet. Not!" Harper rolled his eyes. "Who wants shag carpet in a cabin?"

"Tell anyone this and you die,"—Tiffany chuckled—"but I had the same crap in my bedroom when I was in high school. It matches the rust in the bathroom."

"Yeah, what's up with that?" The dark patches of stain disgusted him.

"It's the water. There's so much iron in it. It's a constant battle up here. You can control it if you use the right cleaning product. I have to be honest, I'm not really up on my stain control methods. But I'm sure there's a remedy. Anyway, the units are kind of cute, don't you think?"

"Yeah."

"Don't mind Ian. He's kind of… verklempt." Harper reached over and fluffed Ian's hair.

"I hope that's a positive." Tiffany held the door while they exited. "You haven't asked about the price yet."

"I'm too scared." He reached over for Ian's hand. "There's a lot of land here. I wonder what a developer could get if they cleared this place out and put up new homes. I'm sure the seller has thought that one through."

"Yes, they have. Sorry, no price details until we've finished the tour." The realtor locked the door, and together they walked back to the office.

She knows what we want to spend. Something's up here.

"I found out yesterday, talking to the guy who represents the seller, that there are two reasons this place closed. What might be the obvious reason, the one that first came to my mind, was the road construction that occurred a few years ago. When they put in the tunnels, the tourists avoided the area like the plague. Unfortunately, access to *this* place during that period was so difficult nobody wanted to bother with it. But that's not the biggest reason. During the same time, the owner lost his wife. With her gone, he just gave up."

"That's so sad." Ian shook his head.

"Okay, here we are. The office is in front, and surprise, there is a complete living quarters in back. Check it out." Once again Tiffany held the door while they entered.

The front of the building was exactly what he had expected. Like the cabins, there was a small seating area in front of the windows. Across from it was a wooden counter that stretched almost the width of the room—the front desk. At the far end was an opening to allow a person to move out from behind it. An archway behind the desk hinted there was more.

"It's your basic front office like you see in so many of the strip motels. Let's go behind the desk, and I'll show you the living quarters."

They followed Tiffany through the arched doorway.

"Okay, this is basically a small home. We're in the living room. The fireplace is a plus."

"I'd miss not having one." He hadn't thought about it, but not having a fireplace would really suck.

"It basically just keeps flowing back. The next room is the kitchen. I was surprised. It's been updated. At least in the last ten years. You wouldn't have to do anything with it unless it really bothered you the way it is."

"It bothers me, but only because I'm spoiled."

"There's no pasta faucet." Ian was coming around.

"That's strange, because I would have expected one," Tiffany joked. "And finally, the bathroom which has… ta-da! A built-in sauna."

"Wow, a sauna. Let's have a look." Harper opened the cedar door. "Wow! Ian, look! There are top and bottom benches." Raising his eyebrows, he flashed Ian what he knew to be his naughty smile.

"I'm not touching that one." Tiffany giggled. "Any questions, boys?"

"Now can we talk price?" Harper was starting to get excited. The last thing he wanted was for him and Ian to get all charged up and then have the whole thing quashed because of the price. The Palisade Beach Cabins could definitely work.

"Yes, we can. Here's the deal. Do you guys mind if we step back outside? The smell in here, it's not something I'm dealing well with." Tiffany must have expected the answer was yes, because before either of them could answer, she was on her way out.

"Thanks," she said when they had rejoined her. "I'm really sensitive to smells."

Not as sensitive as you are to naked jumping jacks, I bet. Harper giggled at the image he'd just created.

"There's a contingency to purchasing this place. For ten years after the purchase date, it *has* to remain rental cabins. The owner will not budge on this. He's hoping someone will step in and refurbish it to its original splendor, or better. He knows he could make a boatload of money if he allowed the land to be split up for homes, but he doesn't want that. He wants to do this in memory of his late wife. The asking price is $350,000, a little but not much over your budget."

IAN waved as Tiffany sped out of the parking lot of the little diner. She dropped them off so they could have some time to privately chat about the cabins.

"The Lip Smacker, that's a cute name, don't you think?" Harper followed Ian inside.

"This place is a lot like the restaurants we have where I grew up." He walked past the cashier's stand and into the dining room. "Is this okay?" He gestured to a booth along the window side.

"Sure. I didn't realize it, but I'm starving." Harper plopped down on the green leather upholstered booth. "How about you? Hungry?"

"Famished. Do you see a menu anywhere?"

"Hello." A woman greeted them from behind the cash register. "Your server will be right with you."

He looked around. There was only a handful of patrons. Checking his watch, he wasn't surprised. It was after one. The lunch rush for a weekday was over.

"Hi, I'm Alex." A young man approached carrying two waters and menus. "Welcome to the Lip Smacker."

"Hey, Alex. Any specials today?" He knew from back home the specials in these little dives were usually the route to go.

"Yes. Today we have a chicken potpie, and the soup is beef barley. Can I get you anything to drink?"

"A diet cola for me." Harper's nose was buried in the menu.

"The same for me."

"Got it. Be right back." Alex smiled and left the table.

"Anything look good?" Ian had already made up his mind to try the potpie and a cup of the soup.

"Lots of things look good. What are you having?" Harper looked up.

"Both specials."

"Hmm… okay. Me too. I can have a burger anywhere." Harper closed the menu and sat back. "Interesting morning, wasn't it?"

"Very." *Please, oh please, can we buy it?*

"I think there's potential there. But I have to be honest, part of the reason I think that is I know what your skills as a landscaper are capable of. There's little doubt in my mind you'd have that place looking like Covington Garden if you were cut loose."

Ian felt Harper's foot lift his pants leg.

"Quit." He sensed Harper was onto him. It took everything he had not to beg Harper for the cabins.

"Here's your sodas." Alex placed tall, thick plastic glasses and straws on the table. "Do you need more time with the menu?"

"I think we're both going to have your special, the potpie, and Harper? You want a bowl or a cup of soup?"

"Cup is fine."

"Make that two cups of soup."

"Great. The potpies take a few minutes. Do you want your soup out first?" Alex collected the menus from the table.

"Please, we're starving." Harper removed the paper from his straw and inserted it into his glass.

"Thanks." Alex dashed off.

"He's a cutie. Can't be much older than eighteen, you think?"

"That sounds about right." Ian surveyed the room, adding, "I hate saying this, but I just have to. I think he plays on our team."

"I got that sense too. Yeah, the whole gaydar thing, I don't like to go there. But sometimes, there's that little special, I don't know, something you connect with."

He felt Harper's foot lift his pants leg again. "I think it would be a special challenge to be gay up here, don't you?"

"He reminds me so much of myself." In hopes of finding a successful pestering maneuver of his own, Ian placed his foot up against Harper's crotch and then smiled.

"Why would you want to hurt Binky?" Harper looked down at his lap.

"I'm," he laughed, "I'm not going to hurt Binky. Binky is my friend. But if Binky doesn't keep his foot off my pants leg, he's going to get the squeeze."

"Huh?" Harper bent closer to his lap. "Binky says he loves you. Isn't that sweet?"

"Here you go."

Saved by food, he thought as Alex placed steaming cups of soup in front of them. "The potpies will be out in a minute. Do you need anything else right now?"

"I don't think so. Binky?" Ian chuckled.

"I'm good." Harper laughed.

"Great. Back in a minute."

"Maybe he has an Andy for a friend?" He blew on his soup spoon.

"Come again?" Harper ripped open a cracker packet and emptied it into his cup.

"Andy. If it hadn't been for Andy, I don't know how I'd have survived. Knowing we were *both* queer somehow gave us power. We felt more special than we did immoral. This soup is awesome."

"I wonder if he knows we are? Yum, this *is* good." Harper toasted with his spoon.

"I think there's a good chance he does, Bink!" They both laughed.

The beef barley soup kept them busy until Alex returned. "How's it taste?" From his tray, he hoisted two golden brown potpies onto the table.

"Very good. Thank you." Harper slurped another spoonful into his mouth.

"Careful, these are super hot. I'll stop back to see if you need anything else."

"Thanks." Ian rearranged the dishes in front of him. "I like this place." He felt like he was going to burst. *Say it! It's fine.* "Harper, I'm notorious for making decisions before thinking them through. You need to know that about me. But…." *Say it, you imbecile!*

"I think Brent will rent the house. I put out some feelers without letting him know what we were thinking about." Harper used his fork to tear the crust off his potpie. He mixed it in with the hot, creamy filling. "Ian, watching you this morning was amazing. Admit it, you were a goner the minute you stepped out of the car, right?" Harper blew on his fork. "Damn, he wasn't kidding. This is like molten lava. Be careful."

"Everywhere I looked I saw potential. I've seen dozens of these little cabin cluster outfits. They're all around up here. But I think we could bring something new to the table. I think we could make that piece of property… magical." Ian giggled, amazed at how passionate he sounded.

"I can't see what you can see. I sensed you envisioning it like you just described, but I can't see things like you do. I saw a geographically beautiful piece of property. That in itself set it apart." Harper savored his first bite now that it had cooled. "Oh man, this is tasty. I had an idea I could make it work just on that. Add to the mix your vision, and I don't know how we could go wrong. I really don't."

Ian sampled his own bite. The crust was light and rich with a buttery taste, the filling velvety smooth and savory. "What about the price? I feel bad I don't have more to contribute."

Harper, I'd throw every cent I had into this idea.

"I can deal with the price. That won't be a problem. Don't feel bad about your contribution. Look at it this way. I have the money up front, and you bring your wonderful landscaping skills, which I don't have. Trust me, hon, it's an equal trade-off."

"Okay." Ian saw the logic in Harper's reasoning, but it didn't matter. As hard as he tried, he couldn't escape the feeling of inadequacy. Even as a kid he had worked hard at establishing his own financial independence. The paper route, picking up the odd job here and there; if there was a penny to be made, he went after it. Faced with no other option, he was forced to trust Harper meant what he had just said. He'd compensate by working his ass off on the property.

"The other thing, I think I could get into the office bookkeeping angle of the business. The publicity. I think I'd enjoy that. And talk about placing the cart before the horse, but maybe we vacation somewhere during the long winter. Someplace warm. How's it sound so far?"

"How're the potpies? You guys doin' okay?" Alex, suddenly appearing at their table, seemed anxious for an opinion.

"I don't know how they could be any better. Delicious." Harper smiled.

"Compliment the chef for us. These could be addicting," Ian added.

"It's Audrey, the owner. I think she said hi when you walked in. She comes in early and makes them from scratch. She also makes all the pies and muffins."

He's proud. He's proud and not afraid to show it. "Tell me, have you worked here a long time, Alex?"

"This is my fourth season. Pretty much all through high school."

"Let me do the math." Harper wiped his chin with his napkin. "Did you graduate this year?"

"Yeah." Alex grinned. "I thought I'd never make it. Are you guys…."

"Together? On vacation?" They completed Alex's question in unison.

"We're thinking of maybe moving up here. At least for part of the year. Good idea? Bad idea?" Harper looked over and winked. "Give it to us straight, Alex."

Give it to us straight? Why the hell would he do that?

"If you haven't spent any time here before, I guess it's pretty cool."

"A waiter and a diplomat." Harper chuckled. "Very good."

"Well, I'll let you guys finish up. If you have room for dessert, Audrey makes a killer banana cream pie. Just let me know."

They both watched as Alex retreated into the kitchen.

"What a little sweetie. Hey, do you think he was fishing, you know, to find out about us?" Harper was serious.

"How many times do I have to tell you, Binky? He knows. He knows." They roared with laughter.

"Hey, Tiffany's back. She just pulled into the parking lot." He slammed a huge forkload of potpie into his mouth.

"Well, slugger, what do you think? Feel like owning some cabins?"

"Nothing's forever, right?" *Never in my wildest dreams would I have ever expected to be a resort owner. Andy is going to shit!*

"Right. So…." Harper held out.

"Will you be staying with us for one or two nights?" Ian bellowed for everyone to hear.

HARPER found it almost impossible to relax. There were too many ifs floating around, and they all hinged on whether or not their offer on the Palisade Beach Cabins was accepted. Almost every aspect of the after-dinner conversation was prefaced with some type of qualifier regarding it. An agonizing week had passed and still no word from Tiffany. Jazzed to make this happen, he and Ian had decided to offer the seller exactly what he was asking. He had spent the day after giving her the green light crafting a proposal, using many of Ian's preliminary landscaping ideas to communicate to the seller their intent to adhere to his wishes. Choosing his wording carefully, he hoped the document would demonstrate a respect for the property and its natural beauty, outline some of their ideas, and alleviate any fears the seller might have.

Despite a growing concern their offer might be rejected, they both had a good week. Ian continued his hitting streak, delivering a three-run homer in the ninth to give the Hornets a seven-five win over the Greasy Axles, a team made up of area car mechanics. If Ian was experiencing any remorse at the idea of relocating to the North Shore, he wasn't displaying any outward signs. If anything, he seemed to be growing more anxious and pumped every day.

The deep ache he'd experienced in his arm since the shooting had vanished this week. Wednesday morning he'd gotten out of bed anticipating the pain he'd come to expect while getting dressed, but to his surprise, it was no longer there. Throughout the day he had put the arm through various tests, and despite what he did, the pain refused to acknowledge itself. He couldn't tell if it was the excitement surrounding the cabins or another signal from his body, but his energy was back to normal too. The biggest achievement of the week—*Knock on wood!*—was that he hadn't experienced a single bad dream. *Bite me, Phyllis!*

"It's magical back here." Allison surveyed the yard in wonderment. "The lighting, I could sit here all night. The sound from the water is so soothing."

With everything going on, this was the first chance he and Ian had had to show off the new backyard. *Wow, does it ever feel good to have friends over to your own house.* With what little social life he'd had before Ian, it had never once occurred to him to host something on his own. Just didn't feel right, and of course, his yard used to really suck. *Thank you, Ian.*

"Hey, hon?" Spencer leaned over and pecked his wife on the arm. "When we get home, let's haul the futon out to the yard. Sleep under the stars, what do you think?"

"I love the romantic in you, sweetie. But somehow, it wouldn't be the same."

"You guys are welcome to stay here if you want. Harper, we've got an air mattress somewhere. Do you remember where we put it? I brought one over from the apartment. And we have sleeping bags." Ian was trying his hardest to feed into their dream.

"Seems to me it went into the basement. Seriously, you're more than welcome to it. Say the word." Harper, restless, stood up and stretched. Eager for a task that would take the cabins off his mind.

"Hon?" Spencer provided another "please" peck to her shoulder.

"Naw,"—Allison reached for her husband's hand—"every time I agree to something like this, I regret it. Besides, I've had a few mosquitoes bite me on the ankle. I bet they get worse as the night goes on. I don't do mosquitoes."

"Me either. I know size doesn't matter, but the dicks on those bugs are so damned small." Andy, who had been uncharacteristically quiet all night, suddenly came to life, cracking everyone up.

"If anyone would know, it'd be you," Spencer lobbed back, inciting more laughter.

Harper felt a pang of guilt. He hadn't given much thought to how their move might affect these guys. Realizing Andy had been so quiet all night, it occurred to Harper he would have the biggest adjustment to make. He'd be losing daily contact with his best friend. Did Ian worry about him? Had the two talked this out?

"Another round?" Ian stood, stretching his arms out to the world. "Allison, we've got butter shots."

"All right already with the butter shots. A girl messes up one time and she never lives it down." Allison had been raked over the coals for her butter shot binge at Merle's and had reached the saturation point.

"Okay, you're right. It's time to put that bad boy to bed." Ian collected some bottles from the table. "Wine cooler?"

"Oh, I don't think so." Allison looked over to Spencer. "If I do, I'll never get up. Spencer and I are finally going to tackle the garage tomorrow. There's been a rash of car break-ins in our neighborhood, and I need to get my car off the street."

"Sadly, it's the threat of our stuff getting screwed over that's motivating us. The thought of a clean, organized garage isn't enough." Spencer downed his beer.

"How about you, Andy? Up for another beer?" Harper strolled over and patted him on the shoulder.

"I'd love to, but I'd better get going. The garden center has been really busy lately."

"Okay, party poopers." He knew he'd be able to talk Ian into another glass of wine when everyone had left. "Don't leave before I run these bottles in and pee. Be right back."

The gang had moved toward the gate when Harper returned to the backyard. Ian was explaining some aspect of the water feature to Spencer. Allison and Andy were talking a few feet away.

"Thanks, you guys," Allison said after he crossed the yard. "Great food, great friends. Another perfect night." She made the rounds with hugs and kisses.

"It was our pleasure." Harper moved around and unlatched the gate leading out to the driveway.

"Andy, if you get in a bind tomorrow, give me a call." Ian followed the group out the gate, wrapping his arm around Harper's waist.

"Thanks, but unless someone calls in sick, I should be okay. It was a great night, you guys." Andy hugged them both.

"I don't want to go in yet, do you?" Harper asked once everyone had sped away into the night.

"No, these nights are priceless. I love it when the heat sticks around after the sun goes down. It's one of my favorite things about summer." Ian kissed his neck.

"Wine or beer?" he asked when they had returned to the patio.

"I better stick with beer. You running?" Ian pinched his butt.

"Ouch."

On his way back with cold beers, his phone went off. "I wonder who this could be?" Setting the bottles on the table, he fished it out from his pocket. "Harper Callahan."

"Hey, Harper, it's your night owl realtor, Tiffany. How's it going?"

He laughed. "We just said goodbye to friends."

"I guess that's what normal people do on a Friday night, have friends over. Me, on the other hand, I spend it chained to my desk because I was stupid enough to go after a real estate license. Boo hoo."

"Well, I bet you get plenty of Mondays off." Harper bit his tongue.

"Always looking on the bright side, you are." Tiffany chuckled. "I have news."

"Tiffany, I'm going to hand the phone over to Ian. Hang on."

"Harper, what are you doing?" Ian reluctantly accepted the phone. "Hey, Tiffany, how's it going?"

From the first words out of her mouth, Harper knew she'd received an answer from the seller. Unless he'd lost his knack at decoding subtext, he wanted Ian to hear what she had to say first.

"Harper, she heard from the seller." Ian began pacing around the table as he listened.

Old Tiffany was having some fun with this one. Ian had completed several tours before he put the phone to his chest and hollered out, "He accepted our offer!"

"That's wonderful!"

Ian continued his journey around the table until Harper intercepted, wrapping his arms around him from behind.

"Perfect. We'll discuss all of that and call you after the weekend. Thanks so much, Tiffany. We're thrilled. Bye!"

"Are we thrilled?" He nestled his nose into his handsome landscaper's neck. Several seconds passed, and Ian began to shake. "Ian?" He released his grip and turned Ian around in his arms. "Oh honey, you're cry-happy, aren't you?"

Ian nodded, melting into his arms.

"What else can we tackle in less than six months? Should we see if we can adopt a kid too?"

"God no." Ian giggled, wiping the tears from his face. "Man, we must be setting some kind of record here."

"You aren't kidding. I can see it now—boy meets boy, they fall in love. Talented garden boy turns untalented attorney boy's backyard into a paradise…." Harper paused to undo the button of Ian's shorts, letting them fall to his ankles.

"Garden boy has the pants charmed off of him by brilliant attorney boy," Ian picked up the thread where he'd left off, "but before brilliant attorney boy knows what he's gotten himself into…." Ian whipped off Harper's T-shirt with one hand and attacked his shorts with the other. "Garden boy has his way with him in the backyard because…."

"Because why?" Harper giggled.

"Because garden boy is the *master*!"

Harper made a run for it but stumbled out of his own shorts, crashing onto the grass with Ian on top of him.

"Stop!"

"Not on your life." Ian planted wet, sloppy kisses all over him.

"Ian, stop that! It tickles."

Ian had him pinned on the grass. "I love you so much, Harper."

"I can't imagine anymore what my life was like without you. You're the best thing that has ever happened to me, Ian."

Lying on the cool grass, they held on to each other, panting from their love wrestle, until Ian rolled over on his knees and tugged Harper's boxers down to his ankles.

"Hey!"

"I hope," Ian said with a mischievous grin, "you still think that in the morning when I scrub the grass stains off of your ass."

THE drab conference room provided a stark contrast to Ian's festive mood. Everything—the cheap blinds, the plastic chairs and table, the dull white walls and tan linoleum—reminded him of one of those scuzzy computer learning centers in a suburban strip mall.

"We'll wait a few more minutes, and then I'll start calling around. Did you guys have a nice weekend?" Tiffany, anxious to get the signing process underway, reorganized her paperwork.

Ian was anxious too. He and Harper had gotten up early so they could have breakfast on the way up. They chose a truck stop outside of Pine City and were not disappointed. With a hearty breakfast under their belts and all of the "do you think this is the right thing to do" discussions argued and analyzed, neither was experiencing any apprehension with their decision. Like their blossoming relationship, everything about buying the Palisade Beach Cabins felt right. This had the potential to be one of the biggest days of their lives together. Provided the seller showed up.

"Who suggested the meeting time?" Harper checked his watch, leaning back in his plastic bucket chair.

"The seller." Tiffany reached for her phone.

In the process of dialing, she stopped when a middle-aged man wearing a checkered sport coat and white slacks entered the room followed by a woman with an armful of documents. "Sorry we're late. I'm Forest. Forest Criberts, representing the seller. He's in the bathroom."

"Hello, I'm Missy Talbert from Tundra Title. It's my fault we're running late. I had some last minute glitches with the paperwork."

"Let's wait until the seller joins us to finish introductions."

The slight tone of annoyance in Tiffany's response was meant to admonish the other parties for making her party wait. Ian couldn't help but notice the difference in energy levels between the two groups. Forest could easily have just crawled out of bed. Missy, well, he wasn't sure, but she wasn't exactly a bundle of energy either. Tiffany, a veritable Formula One, sat patiently at the starting line, revving her engine. Ian chuckled—an image of Forest attached to jumper cables popped up out of the blue.

"What's so funny?" Harper reached over and flicked Ian's shoulder.

"Ah, nothin'." He was used to not being able to share his images with the world. Not only were they hard to explain, but for some unexplainable reason, the translation almost always seemed to get lost.

"Come on." Harper flicked him again.

He chuckled. *Just let it go, Harper.*

"Someone's excited, I think." Tiffany shared a wink with Harper.

"Sorry, folks. I hope I haven't kept you all waiting too long."

Ian was thankful to have the focus shifted away from his meaningless visual to the seller, who appeared in the doorway looking like.... *It's Santa Claus wearing rainbow suspenders. My word.*

"There he is." Forest rose out of his chair. "This is Floyd Hutchins, the seller."

"Nice to meet you, Floyd. I'm Tiffany Marks." Tiffany stood and shook his hand. "I represent the buyers, Harper Callahan..."

"Pleased to meet you." Harper stood and initiated a handshake.

"... and Ian Burke."

Ian bypassed any verbal exchange, choosing instead a hearty nod to accompany his shake.

"Okay." Not unexpectedly, Tiffany took the lead. "There's a lot of signing to do, so let's get going."

"You boys have your work cut out for you." The seller took a chair directly across the table from Harper.

Floyd obviously needed to connect. As big a day as it is for us, Ian thought, it's probably an even bigger day for him. The end of an era.

"Miss, I'm sorry, but I've forgotten your name."

It took a few seconds for Tiffany to disengage and look up from the mounds of paperwork before her. "Tiffany," she answered dryly.

"Tiffany, if you would be so kind, let me have a minute to say a few things before we whiz bang through all of the official business."

"Ah... sure."

Ian detected a hint of impatience. She folded her hands on top of her papers and sat back. You could almost hear her engines idling.

"Rosie and I weren't much older than you boys when we bought the property the cabins sit on."

It was clear, looking over at Floyd's realtor and Missy from the title company, that his story had already made the rounds. Perhaps as recently as the ride over in the car. Add to it, Ian thought, he wasn't the easiest guy in the world to look at. Like a poorly kept yard, there were weeds popping up and out of cracks all over Floyd. And those rainbow suspenders. *I wonder what old Floyd would think if he found out he was sportin' the universal brand for all things gay.* Ian covered his mouth with his hand, fearing the potential to appear disrespectful was too great.

"We never went into it with cabins in mind. Nope." Floyd laughed. "After owning the land for a few years, we saved up enough to start to develop it. And you know what we did?"

Before Ian had even registered the fact he'd been asked a question, Tiffany zinged out, "Not a clue."

"Me and the wife, we opened up a trailer park."

"Isn't that something?" Harper, who must have felt he was running the risk of being impolite by not engaging, laughed and banged his fist on the table.

"It's always nice to have a little background on the property—"

"We worked like dogs those first couple of years. Dogs!"

Tiffany's attempt to wrap up Floyd's history lesson was completely ignored. He'd asked permission to say a few words, and it was clear he wasn't giving up the floor until he'd said his piece. "The office, well, it was in the same spot the office is now, but attached to it we had showers and, on the other side, a small store Rosie kept stocked with the essentials. We tried to think about what people would need once they settled down for a stay with us so they wouldn't be forced to head into town. It was harder for folks to run an errand back in those days because not only did they usually have to undo the rig they were haulin', but there wasn't much between the palisade and Duluth."

"How long did you keep the property a trailer park?" Harper asked.

It was no surprise to Ian that Harper would be eating this up. He just knew this to be right up his partner's alley. If he shifted his focus away from looking at Floyd, he had to admit he found what he was hearing interesting too.

"I'd have to look back at the bookkeeping, but I would suspect it was close to ten years. Rosie had been itchin' to change the land over to cabins, but she wanted to do it right. When we were able to figure out a way to get running water piped in, both hot and cold, we made our move. We were the first ones up in these parts to have modernized cabins. Rosie was damn proud of that, she was."

"She sounds like a wonderful person." Harper smiled, looking around at the others.

Harper was moved. Ian could hear it in his voice. Mister wheelin' and dealin' attorney was a big ol' softy deep down. This made him smile.

"When she passed...." Floyd paused. The thought of his beloved wife gone from his life still choked him up. "The fun went with her. She was the planner, you know. She had this dream, and I helped her to get there. If she was around... well, she'd never admit this to your face, but she was the mover and shaker. I'm sorry, I miss her like she left me yesterday."

The room went silent. Love: it was an amazing emotion. Ian choked back the lump in his throat. It wasn't the same, but nearly losing Harper was one hell of a primer.

"Oh, well I didn't mean to get all mushy on ya. Sometimes I can talk about this stuff and sometimes I can't. I wish you boys luck. I truly do. And remember, you're apt to have Rosie lookin' out for you too. So if the doorknobs start to move or blinds snap up unexpectedly, it's probably Rosie letting you know how she feels about something. Make her proud, boys. That's all I ask."

CHAPTER
Nine

IAN sat on the chair and stared into the fire. *I'm exhausted.* It was the first time all day he'd been off his feet for more than a few minutes. *A perfect time for reflection.* He smiled, unable to remember the last time he'd thought about Pastor Erickson and the church he'd attended periodically as a kid growing up. If the Burkes missed church, it was no big deal. They made it a point to show their faces on the big ticket religious holidays.

It was fun being back home. Clearing his schedule so he and Harper could spend the week up north, their first stop had been to see his parents in Buchannan. This being a non-family-reunion year, the immediate family, including his sister, her family, and his brother, had gathered at Dickenson Park on Lake Walburn for a picnic. Harper charmed the socks off of everyone. It was a blast watching his new beau work the crowd. Confident, charming, his special brand of silly fit right in. Ian was most amazed at how his father had warmed up so quickly to Harper. Bernard Burke, the typically reserved head of the family, had been animated and welcoming in a way Ian didn't recognize.

From Buchannan, they drove to Duluth. He was surprised to see so many patches of spectacular fall color this early. Radiant reds and brilliant yellows contrasted starkly with dark evergreens made the trip breathtaking.

After checking in to their motel on the bluff overlooking the harbor, they headed over to The Main Club. The popular watering hole across the bay from Duluth in Superior, Wisconsin, was a huge hit. He'd heard about it from friends, but this was his first visit. They'd stopped in for a beer and ended up closing the place down. Darts, pool, and some of the friendliest locals you could ever run into made the night memorable. The next morning, Harper was filled with promotional ideas linking their new investment and the venerable Twin Ports gay bar.

They had agreed to meet Andy, Spencer, and Allison at the Lip Smacker bright and early Saturday morning. After breakfast they headed over to the cabins and got busy tackling a list of chores. The goal was to make the office apartment livable, as well as cleaning and setting up a few cabins so the gang all had a comfortable place to crash. It had been a busy day. Spencer and Andy helped Ian tackle the larger apartment where he and Harper would be spending the winter, while Harper and Allison cleaned the cabins. Spencer grilled burgers for dinner, and once the sun had set, the group found themselves congregated around the fireplace in the tiny living room of the apartment.

"The entire winter, you guys are going to live in this? For the entire winter?"

"That's the plan." Ian wished he'd hesitated before answering Allison's question to see how Harper would have responded. Allison couldn't seem to wrap her head around the fact they were entertaining the idea of spending a long, cold winter in the little back-office apartment.

"I mean, what if it snows so much you can't get out? What if you lose your power?"

She had valid points. Perhaps in their enthusiasm to jump into this project hook, line, and sinker, they'd gone too far. Nobody said they had to tough it out here over the winter. It had seemed like part of the adventure. Now he wasn't so sure it was the best idea. Snuggling up to Harper for five months didn't sound particularly grueling, but anything could get old after a while. He wondered how the previous owners, Rosie and Floyd, had passed the winter months. Something told him the cribbage board saw more action than their mattress. It was just a guess.

They would have to winterize before the bitter cold set in. The windows would need to be covered over with clear plastic film, particularly those in the bedroom and the bathroom. Andy inspected the tiny furnace and thought it would be fine.

Ian glanced around the room and sipped his pinot noir. Spencer seemed lost in thought, parked down on the floor between Allison's legs, staring into the fire. He and Andy had spent all day going through the apartment, pulling out all of the appliances and giving them a test to make sure everything was still working. Ian and Harper and Allison had finished sprucing up a few of the cabins. By afternoon they had moved over to the office apartment, emptying boxes and organizing as much as they could.

"My frickin' back aches." Andy launched into a series of stretches.

"My everything aches." Allison slumped in her chair.

"Please don't say that. Please don't shut the door on Mr. Wally's Fun World," Spencer pleaded.

"Easy, tiger. Who said anything about shutting down Wally's? What the hell did you just say?" Allison and everyone else in the room roared. "That's the most pathetic, desperate thing I've ever heard."

"For you, maybe," Spencer whined.

"A back—forget that, a *body* rub will gain you unlimited access to Wally's... whatever." Allison reached over and ruffled her husband's hair.

"Yes!" Spencer launched into a sit-down version of his happy dance.

Everyone was comfortably exhausted and tipsy off red wine. The temporary silence was broken by Andy's cell.

"God, I hate these things sometimes." He stood and fished the phone out of his pocket. "This is Andy. Hi there!"

Andy sauntered off to the kitchen to take his call.

"Who's that?" Spencer yawned, reaching for the half-empty bottle of wine on the table, filling his glass, and then passing it over to Harper. Harper sat on a folding chair in the corner with a sloppy grin on his face. The day's activities appeared to have finally caught up to him.

God, I love you. If spending the winter here is what you want, my handsome man, I'm there.

Little snippets of Andy's conversation floated into the room, but not enough to determine who was on the other line.

Ian got up and walked over to Harper, planting a kiss on the top of his head. "You doin' okay?"

"I'm perfect. You?" Harper reached up and stroked his cheek.

"Yep. I love you."

"I know you do." Harper smiled, tugging him down for another kiss. "And I love you."

"Another bottle?" Ian plucked the empty from Harper and looked around the room for a consensus.

"Why not?" Spencer sat up and kissed his wife's knee.

"I think we can manage the walk over to cabin five without too much trouble." Allison leaned down and planted a smooch on Spencer's forehead.

Ian strolled into the kitchen, expecting to find Andy on his phone, but his friend had ventured deeper into the apartment.

"Right. Just leave what you'll need to open with tomorrow morning in the till, and put the rest of the cash in that box in my office."

Ah, he's talking to Emmett.

The summer had been a productive one for Emmett. He'd blossomed into a reliable, trusted right-hand man. Andy had worked a miracle.

"Oh God, really? I should have warned you about her. She can be really picky. Sounds like you handled her just right."

Ian smiled. He didn't mean to eavesdrop on his friend's conversation, but he was fascinated by the turnaround. How did Andy know Emmett was worth the effort? How did he find the patience?

"I'm so proud of you, Em. Thank you. I miss you too. What? Okay, look in the sky, and I'm the brightest star. I'm always watching over you. I love you too. See you tomorrow afternoon. Oh, and Em, call me if you run into anything you're uncomfortable with."

Ian was stunned. There had been little hints here and there, but he'd always dismissed them. There was nothing substantial enough for him to suspect Andy and Emmett were lovers.

"How long have you been standing here?" Wearing a sheepish grin, Andy walked over and wrapped his arms around Ian.

Ian eased the cork out of the bottle. "Long enough."

"I was going to tell you."

"Just not tonight, right?" Ian turned in his friend's arms and smiled. "You're such a dick sometimes."

"I thought you'd never let me live it down."

"Oh, that's a given. I mean, whose boyfriend gets let off the school bus on the corner each day? It's like you're dating Beaver."

"I hate you." Andy chuckled, resting his head on Ian's shoulder.

"So, is this just between you and me?" There would be plenty of opportunity down the road for him and Spencer to tease. Andy's happiness was much more important.

"Naw, let's do it." Andy stood up and reached for the new bottle, guzzling a healthy portion of it before setting it back down.

"You want me to do the honors?" Ian picked up the bottle.

"In the worst way. God help me."

Ian linked his arm with Andy's and walked him back into the living room.

"Everyone, listen up. After Andy picks Emmett up from Cub Scout camp, he takes him home and fucks his brains out. They're registered at Target, Homo Depot, and Sly's Fantasy Leather Hut. Please join me in wishing them the very best."

LEANING over the edge, Alex released his grip on his soda can. From his perch on top of the palisade, he watched its long, silent journey to the rocks below. The sun was beginning to set. The breeze coming off the lake chilled him. In the last hour, the waves had built to twice their size and were now crashing steadily against the jagged rock. The view from high above was mesmerizing. He hugged himself to stay warm.

Occasionally laughter drifted up from down below. Earlier he'd walked over to the right side of the lookout and spotted several lights shining from the old cabins below. Two guys from the Cities who had been in the café recently had bought the property. Rumor had it they were going to restore and reopen the cabins next spring. He'd waited on the handsome dudes several times now. They were big tippers. And they were funny. Especially the guy with the short black hair. He was always up to no good. Harper, that was his name. The other guy was quieter but nice too. Ian, was that it? Harper and Ian. He'd caught them holding hands one night. Neither of them seemed fazed in the least. About time the area got a look at some gay guys. Just what we need around here. It could be tough for them, but if anyone could make it work, they could. Too bad he wouldn't be around to get to know them better.

His thoughts drifted to Mike. For days after their planned meeting in Duluth, Alex had expected to see Mike at the restaurant. Or at least some kind of a message left there for him. He'd heard nothing. What could have happened? Maybe something bad. An accident? Was he sick? So strange of him not to show. He was the one who had initiated the whole thing. Nothing Alex could do about it. It hurt. Stung bad. He couldn't remember ever feeling this shitty over something. *That's not true, Alex.*

When Mom died. That was really bad. He'd just turned twelve. The cancer got her quick. Quicker than anyone had been prepared for. There was nothing he could have done about that either. For the first year or so, his dad stepped up to the plate. But the drinking increased at a pretty good clip soon after, and his parenting went from just adequate to fucking awful. It was downhill from there. But as miserable as life was around here, Alex had managed to navigate the bumps pretty well. Colin had been gone almost a month already. *Damn, I miss you, bud.* Maybe he'd spend a night or two in the Cities before he journeyed west.

Climbing back into Zits, he drove the short distance home.

At least something is going my way tonight.

The old man's car was nowhere in sight. Maybe he'd gone up to Grand Marais to fuck that skanky redhead he'd had over several weeks ago. *What a trash bucket. Exactly what you deserve, you drunk.*

The house stank. It had gotten really bad lately. He'd given up on trying to keep the place clean. His bedroom and the bathroom were the only spots in the house he bothered with anymore. Lately he'd been taking his laundry to work. Audrey wouldn't mind. Hell, if he brought it up, she'd probably offer to do it for him. He didn't want that. She did enough for him. Last week there had been an envelope on his time card, and inside, a crisp one-hundred-dollar bill. The card read "Thanks for working so many shifts for me. You're one in a million, Alex." If business didn't slack off too much in the next few weeks, he'd have what he needed to escape the palisade. The increase in business because of the fall colors on the shore was worth waiting around for. The leaves were awesome this year.

He thought about catching some television, but the thought of sitting in that pigpen living room disgusted him. Opening the refrigerator, he pulled out a can of Dew. His dad hated the stuff and left it alone. Switching the light on in his room, he closed the door and locked it. It was the only way he could relax. He fired up his laptop. It used to be Colin's. His parents had gotten him a new one for Christmas. Colin had helped him run a phone line into his bedroom without his old man knowing it. It was slow going accessing the Internet this way, but it was better than nothing. It was a miracle the old man's phone hadn't been cut off by now. He knew he was running on borrowed time. *I've got to research my escape.* The last couple of nights he'd been looking at motel rates in San Francisco. *Fuck! Are you kidding me?* I've got to find a place to share with someone. It's the only way I can make it work.

Reaching into his pocket, he hauled out his tips from today's lunch. Altogether, he had thirty-one dollars and change. Not the best, not the worst. Jotting down the amount on a piece of paper, he scooped the money up in his hand and walked over to the old dresser in the corner by his bed. Tucked in back of it was a slender gift box he had rigged to slide in and out of a cardboard sleeve. It was the Bank of Alex. Unless he was mistaken, today's deposit brought him within a few dollars short of four thousand. *Not bad.* It was enough to keep him going for a month or two once he left. More if he picked a place cheaper than San Francisco. If he had any luck at all, he'd add another thousand to it before he blew town.

Jimmying the dresser away from the wall, he reached back for the box. His hand slid right into the cardboard sleeve where the box should have been.

What the fuck?

Pulling the dresser out further, he wedged his head between it and the wall and confirmed his worst fear—the box was gone. *The fucking box, my money, it's gone. He's fucking taken it!*

Stumbling backward until the edge of his bed forced him to sit, he clutched his stomach and began to rock back and forth. He struggled to breathe. His eyes welled up with tears. *Where did the drunk fucker go? It was him, it had to be him. He must have....* Alex stood and looked around the room. He hadn't noticed it before, but it had been given the once-over. The mattress was slightly off its frame. The two lower drawers of the dresser hadn't been shut. His desk.... *How could I have missed it?* The stacks of magazines and check stubs were all mixed up. *Christ, the fucker hadn't even tried to cover his tracks.*

The money had been there last night. If he caught up to his dad soon, chances are he'd still be able to retrieve most of it. And he would. He'd kill the fucker if that was what it took. Racing out of the room, he jumped into Zits and screamed down the dirt road to the highway.

SITTING at the vintage Formica table in the tiny kitchen, Ian compared his sketch to the photograph he'd placed beside it. There was so much potential here it was maddening. After talking to Andy, he'd decided the best approach would be to identify areas throughout the property where the look of established growth was needed—clusters of shrubs, trees, and various vines. It would be important to get those planted as soon as possible so it wouldn't take so long to realize their benefits. Maybe just a season or two in some cases. Except for adding ornamental trees here and there, the property already had an ample amount of large shade trees. Almost too much, but that was a problem he'd happily work around. It was all about the North Shore experience, and the wooded setting played nicely into that. The guests would also benefit from the shade on those rare days when the thermometer climbed up into the nineties. It didn't make sense to air-condition the units because, for the most part, it wasn't needed.

"There's something about this deal we need to talk about." Harper walked out of the bedroom, drying his hair with his bath towel.

"Shoot." Ian knew by the look and the hesitation in his voice, Harper had something serious on his mind. He had noticed in the short time they'd been a couple that Harper's words were chosen for accuracy and precision. Once the idea had been baked to Harper's liking, was there room for negotiation? *I guess I'll find out.*

"I know this is all very new to us, but I have to be honest and tell you I can't live here… in this. I just can't do it. I won't be happy no matter how much we fix it up."

"Okay." Ian pushed his chair back from the table. *I called the serious part right. Wow!* "I don't know what to say. I mean, I guess I just assumed we'd give it a shot. I can't see us running this operation from Minneapolis. Can you?"

"No. Sorry, I started this out poorly. Let me start over." Harper took the seat across from him.

Please don't tell me you can't make the whole idea work. "Talk to me, hon."

"Well, I have to be honest. From the minute we looked at this place and toured the living quarters, I knew it would be impossible for me to be happy here. I didn't want to say anything at the time because everything else about this place seemed so right, and, well, I didn't have a solution to my problem. I wanted to spend a few nights here just to make sure, and I'm sure. This isn't going to work."

"I guess I'm confused. You mean the whole cabin rental idea isn't going to work, or just the living situation? It's a little late in the game to question the whole idea of running the cabins, isn't it?"

"It's a wonder I ever set foot in a courtroom. Not sure what's happened to my presentation skills, but I'm failing this one miserably. Okay, let me try this again. I think we should build ourselves a home here that is comfortable, modern, and a welcome retreat from a day of pleasing our guests."

"Well, I wish rainwater was beer, but what the hell? Harper, how do we make something like that happen? I'm sorry, I don't mean to be snotty here, but I don't see how we could make something like that happen. We haven't even figured out the total cost of bringing the cabins back to where they need to be. Or the cost of landscaping and, well, with all we need to do here, where's the money going to come from to build ourselves a home?" As much as he understood where his partner was coming from, the alternative, what was being proposed, was impossible. Unrealistic.

"Me."

"Huh?"

"I have money. Plenty, actually."

A wily smile blossomed over Harper's face. Ian had seen this smile a few times before, but up until now, it had never been produced with such a definitive sparkle. He laughed nervously. "What are you trying to tell me?"

"The plane crash that killed my parents, there was a settlement. My grandfather invested it. Turns out he had a knack for making good decisions. I'm worth, well, I feel kind of creepy for not telling you this before. The last time I checked, I was worth over several million."

"Hang on, I might have just pooped my pants." *Didn't see that one coming.* This unexpected development was more than Ian could process sitting down. Getting up, he began walking a tiny circle in the kitchen.

It was Harper's turn to laugh. "My grandparents kept it a secret from me for the longest time. When Gramps first got sick, he sat me down and went through all of it. Of course I'd already worked my ass off in law school, bartending and everything else it took, but I guess that was the plan. I'm a hard worker, but I have a small fortune in the bank if I need it. I'm tellin' ya, Ian, we need some of it now. Are you mad at me?"

"I'm not sure yet." *Why am I just hearing this now?*

"Are you okay?" Harper laughed.

"I guess I'm not okay. I'm trying to think of reasons you might have had for not sharing this little piece of information with me. Was it by any chance because you didn't trust me?"

"Ian, no. God no. I'm kind of freaked out by the money." Harper made a move toward him.

"Not as freaked out as I am. I mean, come on, this is pretty big news, Harper." Ian moved further away.

"I don't know what else to say. I guess I never thought it would be a big deal." Harper leaned up against the counter.

"Do you have any idea how crappy I've felt for not having the money to match your investment? I've spent nights laying awake trying to think of ways to cut costs so you won't be pinched so hard."

When Harper failed to respond, Ian continued, "Do you think I was looking forward to living in this piss hole all winter long? I was fired up to do it because I didn't think we had a choice. God, I feel like a fucking idiot right now."

It was Harper's turn to walk in circles. "Okay, I made a terrible mistake in not telling you. I had no idea this money thing.... I had no idea how sensitive you are about it."

That was the wrong thing to say. The wrong thing. "I'm not that sensitive. You didn't level with me. I'm more sensitive about that. I'm really pissed off." Before he could check himself, he turned his back to his partner and slammed his fist down on the counter.

Minutes passed. Neither of them moved or said a word.

"I don't blame you for being angry."

I know you didn't mean it. I can't explain to you why I feel this way.

"I know you didn't mean to offend me." Ian turned around and backed into the counter. He found it impossible to make eye contact. "I can't explain why this makes me feel so crazy."

"You have a huge sense of pride, Ian. It's one of the things I love so much about you. I offended your pride, and I'm deeply sorry. I don't know what else to say. I love you so much, I'd never intentionally hurt you. Do you believe that?"

Ian looked up from the floor. He hated the distressed look on Harper's face. "Yes, I know that."

"I don't want you to walk away from here without getting it all out. Is there more fueling this? I'm not patronizing you. I want you to let me have it. I deserve it."

"No,"—Ian couldn't help but chuckle—"that's pretty much it." It felt good, for some reason, to have these feelings surface.

"Will you let me hold you?" Harper took a step forward.

Ian chuckled again. "Yes, you can hold me." *I feel like I'm twelve.*

Harper took him into his arms. "I hate seeing you upset. I promise to do whatever I can to not let this happen again. Well, at least until the end of the week."

"Does this mean I get a raise in my allowance?" Ian broke the embrace and traced his finger innocently up and down his partner's chest.

"You're going to get a raise out of me, but it won't be your allowance."

Ian laughed. "That works."

Harper went for a beer. "Want one?"

"Like you'll never know." Accepting the cold beer, Ian sat back down.

"What's changed is that we have some money up front to invest in our dream. We still have to recoup our investment. I want this place to make us money. And you know what? I think once you get it looking like it already does in your mind, we'll be well on our way to making that a reality. I believe in you."

"Man, Harper. I'm still digesting the fact you're a millionaire."

"I know. I pooped myself too when I found out. You know what's funny, well, funny in a weird way?"

"Huh?"

"Had I not survived the gunshot, a small library in central Iowa would have been the happy recipient of one big-ass testamentary gift. That's the Lollie way." Harper raised his bottle in a toast.

"I love Lollie, but I'm so much happier things turned out differently." Ian returned the toast. "Testamentary gift?"

"Yeah. I only know that because of a case we had a few years ago when the surviving members of a family contested their mother's will."

"Gotcha. So, what's plan B? Were you thinking we'd tear this little apartment down and rebuild it?" This should be interesting. No doubt, Harper had a plan.

"No. I think we leave it for a while until we figure out what to do with the space. I don't think we should alter the place much. With the exception of the money we spend on landscaping the property, I don't want people to think there is big money behind this enterprise. But that doesn't mean we have to live like slum dogs either."

"That's a good point about the money thing. Besides, this place has its own charm. I think we can build on that and make it better without having to change it much." He looked at his sketches.

"Let's take a walk." Harper got up and gestured for him to follow. "Okay," he said when they'd both stepped outside. "The left side of the property is all about the guest cabins. But the right side, the piece we were thinking of using for trails? Follow me." Harper grabbed him by the hand and marched over to the edge of the woods. "Let's build something nice in here. Let's build a home we'll be comfortable in year round. Not ostentatious, but comfortable. If we locate it back here somewhere, we'll have privacy from our guests. We don't know it now, but trust me, by the end of the day I'll bet we'll have had our fill of them. It's hard to imagine, but all it takes is a few difficult guests to suck the fun out of life. Consider this our sanctuary. Off limits to everyone but us."

"Wow!" Ian giggled. "I like it." He peered up to the top of the huge trees. "It's already fall. Is this something you think we should start next spring? We need time to plan, right?"

"Let's go back inside." Harper took the lead back to the apartment. Ian sat at the table.

"Don't get mad." Harper moved to the end of the room. "This isn't another secret I've been harboring. It's something I just stumbled on when I was trying to come up with an alternative to living here. Wait, I'll be right back." Harper went to the bedroom and came back with a folder. He took his chair and moved it over to Ian's side of the table. "There's this place up here that manufactures prefab homes. The homes are built at the plant and then moved onto the site. They come in all shapes and sizes. You can customize the interiors to however you like. Here's one I've been looking at."

Moving his designs, Ian made room for Harper to lay out his materials.

"Here, what do you think of this one? Isn't it cool?" Harper presented two color photos: the outside of a large two-story, log cabin-style home and an interior shot showing an awesome kitchen connected to a spacious great room.

"This is a prefab house?"

"Yes, isn't it amazing?"

Together they hunkered over the photos. He couldn't believe it. The home was beautiful.

"I love you, Harper Callahan. You're rich, clever, and when I get those clothes off you like I'm about to do in a second, you're all mine. And you know why that is?"

"I'm all ears." Harper giggled.

"Because"—Ian stood and hovered over his man—"I'm the *master*!"

"Oh God…."

Ian picked him up from the chair and carried him by the waist into the bedroom.

"No. Nooooo!" Harper hollered. "You're a… scrappy little thing… you know that?" He was laughing so hard he could barely talk.

"Little? Hmmm, we'll see about that." Crashing them both onto the bed, Ian smothered him with kisses.

"Ian." When they had settled down, Harper rested a finger on his lips to halt the kisses. "Make love to me."

"I'd planned on it. I want you so badly, my boxers are coated with happy gel." He'd been leaking since they'd hit the bed.

"Let me see." Harper thrust his hand down the front of his pants. "My word."

"Told ya." Ian reclined.

"We've got to do something about that." Harper kneaded his balls.

"We?"

"Sorry, I forgot you're the *master*. Here, let me service you properly, Master Ian."

Ian watched Harper undress him, beginning with his shoes and socks. Crawling back onto the bed, Harper cupped his hand behind Ian's neck, raising him gently until their lips met for a passionate kiss.

Ian felt himself harden in anticipation. His shirt came off next. Harper tossed it over his shoulder. Naked from the waist up, he was gently pushed back onto the pillow. To his delight, a tongue traced around and over his nipples.

"Oh God, yes, bite 'em, hon. Bite my nips." Ian arched his chest. Harper responded as requested, nibbling on each nip until he purred with pleasure.

"That's what I'm talkin' about. Oh yeah, harder, harder!"

Harper bit down, holding each tender nipple between his teeth until Ian begged for release, pounding the bed with his fists. Harper finally relented, gliding his tongue down Ian's stomach, making lazy circles around his navel.

"You're driving me crazy. I'm going to fuck you like you've *never* been fucked before, Mr. Callahan."

Unbuttoning his jeans, his handsome partner knelt on the edge of the bed and pulled them off in one fluid move, exposing his wet, stained boxers.

Making a move for his own crotch, his hand was slapped away and replaced by Harper's mouth. "That wasn't niceeee… oh yeah… oh yeah… that's it." His trapped cock was being sucked through the thin cotton fabric. He throbbed where teeth held him captive. "I'm so…." Before he could finish his sentence, his boxers were whisked off and his cock shoved deep down his lover's warm throat.

"Fuckin' yes! Yes! Yes!"

He could hear himself pant. He could feel his prick pulsate, begging for attention. Seconds later, Harper backed him out of his throat until the head of his dick was squeezed tight by lip-covered teeth. Lifting himself off the pillow, his eyes locked with his devilish sex slave. "Please don't bite it off."

Harper's tongue circled his cockhead. Turning dry, the tongue scraped over and over his scar. He squirmed, attempting to manage the powerful sensations rocketing through his body. "Please take me deep. Take me deep, I can't stand it any longer. You're driving me crazy."

He gasped when he was suddenly throated to the root. Placing a warm palm on his hard stomach, Harper bobbed up and down on his rock-hard shaft until it was sloppy wet.

"Babe, I'm so hot for you." Knowing he wouldn't last much longer, he reached for his lover and gently pulled him off. "You're amazing."

"I love pleasuring you." Harper crawled on top of him for a kiss.

"It's my turn." Ian scooted up from under and stood by the edge of the bed. "You want my Tina Turner?"

"Not sure, but probably." Harper's laugh was spiced with innocence.

"The Tina Turner starts out nice and easy, and then we finish it rough."

"Oh, Daddy, bring it on."

Ian wasted no time removing Harper's clothes. He was dripping with anticipation, and despite the wonderful foreplay he'd just been treated to, servicing his partner in the same loving, leisurely way just wasn't going to happen. *I need to fuck you and I need to fuck you now!*

"Ian, I can't wait any longer. Fuck me."

Thank you, penis god!

"I can't wait to feel you deep inside."

Ian grabbed Harper by the feet and dragged him down until his ass was on the edge of the bed. Placing his feet up on his shoulders, Ian took Harper's dick in his hand while painting his partner's tender ring in preparation for *the biggest fucking hard-on I've sported in my entire fucking life!*

Unable to hold back another second, Ian leaned forward and planted his dripping cock at the center of the target. "Don't worry. I'm still in gentle Tina mode." Leaning into his handsome partner, he broke the seal, stopping after the engorged head of his dick had disappeared. "How're you doin'?" He looked down and smiled.

Harper gripped Ian's powerful arms until his body relaxed. After a few steady breaths, he smiled back. "I'm ready for more."

Locking eyes, Ian pushed again, sliding deeper until he could go no further. "I'm going to make this one memorable." He leaned forward until their lips met. His cock throbbed, nagging him to pick up the pace.

"You're the greatest thing that will ever happen to me." Harper stroked his chest.

Their tongues melded and twisted until passion won over and the kiss intensified. Ian pumped with deliberate thrusts, almost completely removing his dick and then shoving it all the way back in. The expression on Harper's face told him everything he needed to know. He could tell when his plump head with its flared scar scraped across his sensitive gland, sending waves of ecstasy raging through his lover. He rocked his body from side to side, continuing to monitor its effect.

He pumped harder, faster. Harper pounded and slapped his arms in response. "I'm so hot for you, baby." Ian threw back his head, savoring the sensations from the friction on his swollen cockhead as it moved up and down Harper's warm, tight chute. As the pace increased, juices flowed freely, and he began to glide effortlessly in and out.

"Harder, Ian. I'm ready for rough Tina."

"Wrap your legs around my waist, babe." Without completely pulling out, Ian waited until Harper had them linked snugly. Placing his hands under his partner's back, he lifted him off the bed.

Laughing madly, Ian spun him around the room. When he'd made a complete circle, he marched them into the kitchen and deposited his man on the kitchen table.

"It's cold." Harper winced.

"It won't be for long." Unwrapping Harper's legs, Ian pushed them back as far as they could go. "Ladies and gentlemen, I'd like to introduce to you Rough Tina!" He slammed his dick in hard.

Harper gasped, shaking his head back and forth.

Ian pulled out and slammed back in again and again. He increased his effort until his balls slapped the round, pert ass he penetrated. Holding nothing back, he increased his assault, causing Harper to moan and whimper. The table jumped across the floor until it crashed against the refrigerator.

Pausing long enough to coat his hand with Harper's precum, he took his mate's cock in one hand, pushed his leg back with the other, and banged with newfound enthusiasm.

Harper thrashed and pounded the table with his fists, his head scrunched against the door of the fridge. Ian pummeled his ass relentlessly. Their naked bodies glistened with sweat from head to toe.

"Oh God, I'm getting close," Ian hollered, jacking Harper's rock-hard shaft furiously.

"Ian... Ian... oh fuck...." Harper gripped the table on both sides.

"Oh, baby, I'm going to fill you up. I'm...." Ian steadied his stance; he was there. "Oh fuck, I'm cumming," he roared, squirting his load deep.

"Holy shit!" Harper's cock exploded, sending jets of thick white cum high into the air.

Ian slowed his thrusts, his body rocked to its core as he milked himself dry.

Harper ripped Ian's hand off his cock. "I can't take it anymore."

Still buried deep, Ian collapsed on top of his lover, spent and panting. "How'd that work out for you?" he asked between breaths.

"Your... Tina.... It was spot on."

"COME along, sissy pants." Ian had reached the clearing and stood with his arms folded, waiting for Harper to catch up.

"I'll give you sissy pants." Harper swatted away a bank of spider webbing he had managed to walk through. "Oh, not sure you noticed, but there were a whole bunch of snakes back there."

"No there wasn't. You're just trying to scare me."

"I thought you were the *master*." Harper laughed when he'd reached the clearing.

"I am the *master*. Don't you forget it. How much further do you want to walk?"

Harper glanced around to get his bearings. "I think this could work, right here. What do you think?"

"You're thinking the house sits right about here?" Ian turned in a three sixty.

"Yeah. What is this, southeast we're facing? We'd have the morning sunrise, and the hot afternoon sun would be on the back of the house where we position the driveway and garage. How does that sound?" Harper took delight in watching Ian scope out the property. A mere twenty-four hours earlier, he'd been charged to live in the tiny little apartment. *What a trouper.* Now the floodgates had been opened. The sky was the limit. It was important he let Ian make the decision here. There'd already been a few signs of insecurity regarding Harper's substantial wealth. This had to be a collaborative effort. He didn't want to come off as being the one who had the final say in how things should go because he was the one footing the bill.

"Harp, that's what I think too. We don't want any of this great view compromised by a car or a garage. Hey, what do you think about a large screened-in porch? Wouldn't it be nice to sit out here in the middle of the woods at night with nature all around us and not get eaten alive?"

"Oh, I really love that idea. Ian, not that I want to start downing trees left and right, but the view to the lake, I'm kind of thinking I'd like it to be more open."

"I'm with you on that one too."

Harper wasn't sure how sensitive his partner would be when it came to saying goodbye to majestic pines and birch to make way for a house. The property was too wooded. They would have to clear a spot but, if they planned it right, only give up what they had to. "Let's go into town and have some breakfast. We can pick up some supplies at Pamida and come back here and mark off where we want the house to sit before we head back home."

"How in the hell can they get an entire home back in here?" Ian asked, doubtful.

"I did some research on the web. They require about thirty-five feet on one side of the foundation for the crane to lift the sections of house into place. It sucks to lose more trees, but it's the only way this will work."

"I hate to see them go, but hon, we've got plenty of trees around here. I don't think we'll miss a few more. What do we do, call them up and order a house?" Ian laughed. "This is crazy, Harp. Fun crazy."

"We have to draw up a rough floor plan. When we have that, then we make an appointment and go in and try to fit our plan into theirs. From there, it's kind of like planning to have any house built. You pick out fixtures, appliances, everything. The only difference is it's built indoors and then moved in chunks to here. I figure while you're working on your garden plans this winter, I can work on the house. We can share our ideas as we go."

"This has to cost a fortune. I know what you're going to say, but still."

"Ian, I'm told it will cost less per square foot than a home built on site. I promise you, that's what I've read on the Internet. What do you think? Should we start working on a floor plan?"

"Yeah, okay." Ian laughed. "It probably wouldn't have been the best, but I'd have survived a winter in the apartment with you."

"I know that. I need food."

Ian started back toward the cabins. "You were kidding about the snakes, right?"

THE Lip Smacker did a respectable breakfast business. Most of the tables were full, and the ones that weren't hadn't been cleaned off yet. They waited by the sign instructing a hostess would seat them.

"Eggs Benedict. That's what I'm thinking." Harper looked over to Ian for a comment.

"That could work. The meat skillet thing is good too. With maybe a pancake. Hey, is that Alex back there sitting in the booth with those cops?" Ian stepped over to get a better look.

"What? Where?" He looked over Ian's shoulder. It was. Alex looked like shit. "Oh God, I hope the kid didn't get himself into trouble."

"Good morning, boys. Give me just a minute and I'll have a table cleared for you." Audrey looked like shit too.

"Oh, we're in no hurry, Audrey." He came close to asking if everything was all right but held back.

He and Ian moved over to the door while a couple paid their tab. When they turned to leave, Ian's curiosity got the best of him and he made his move. "Audrey, everything okay with Alex?"

"Honestly, no, it's not. He's had a terrible thing happen. Let me get your table ready."

Ian looked over and frowned. "Doesn't sound good."

Harper was curious to find out what was going down. If Alex was in some kind of trouble and needed legal assistance, Harper would be more than happy to help the kid if he could.

"Okay, follow me." Audrey led them over to a table in the middle of the dining room.

"Audrey, I don't mean to be nosey, but if Alex is in some kind of trouble with the law, I'm an attorney, and maybe I can help him out."

"Well, I just lost a bet." Audrey placed the menus down in front of them. "I had you pegged for a teacher. You just kind of looked like one. Silly me, I don't know why I think the things I do."

"I'm not smart enough to be a teacher. Anyway, I'd like to help if he's in some kind of trouble. He seems like a good kid." Maybe it was because they suspected Alex was one of their own that he felt a pang of responsibility. It surprised him.

"Alex is a blue ribbon kid, no question about that. He's been working his tail off all summer long, saving for something big. Not sure what, he's a touch on the quiet side. Anyway, I guess his father made off with all his savings. He's been driving around the last two days with no sleep trying to find him. When he came in to work this morning, I took one look and made him come clean. I called the police."

"You've got to be kidding me." Ian was practically out of his chair.

"Hard to believe, isn't it? Who does that to their own kid? Dad's a piece of work, let me tell you. If only his mother was still around. She'd'a never let a thing like this happen, that's for sure. Coffee for you both?"

"Yes, please," they answered in unison.

"Can you believe that shit? God, I feel terrible for the kid." Ian looked over, incredulous.

"It's a cruel world out there." Harper knew as much from spending so much time in the legal profession. Just when you thought you'd seen it all, a new twist on ugly reared its head.

Audrey returned with their coffee. "I've got to find him a place to live. I'm afraid if his old man comes back with empty pockets, the kid is going to kill him. Knowing his dad like I do, I have a feeling we won't see him around here until the money is all gone. That son of a bitch. Excuse my French. Do you know what you'd like?"

"Eggs Benedict for me. Ian?"

"Is it too early to get a cheeseburger?" Ian displayed a special look when he knew he was being troublesome. He wore almost the identical look when he was sitting on the toilet.

"Not at all, honey. You're like me. I have to be in a special mood for eggs. A cheeseburger it is. You want bacon on that?"

"Great!" Ian's face lit up. "Yes, please."

"No fries this early. Are hashbrowns okay?"

"Please." Ian waited for Audrey to walk away. "Harper, are you thinking what I'm thinking?"

"You mean am I as happy as you are you have a cheeseburger coming? Oh, I guess so. Hadn't really thought about it that much. Why?"

"Ah, come on, you goofball. I'm talking about Alex."

They were on the same wavelength, there was no doubt about it. "Wait. I think something is beginning to surface…." A lot was beginning to surface. And at breakneck speed. "We hire Alex to caretake the cabins over the winter. As part of his salary, we let him stay in the office apartment. In the spring, or when we get the cabins up and running, he can decide if he wants to continue to work for us, or work here, or a combination of both, or something completely different. Is that what you were thinking?" Harper laughed, knowing he'd blasted the socks off Ian with his reply.

"I love you, but I also want to slap you. I want to slap you really hard." Ian couldn't help laughing.

"Why? It all came together for me in one complete burst. Sorry for living."

"The Snyders aren't expecting me at any particular time tomorrow. I told them I would call in the morning to set up a time for a walkthrough. Depending on what Alex has going on today, maybe we can make some of this happen before we leave."

"I'm game. Let's run it past Audrey when she comes back." This wasn't something he necessarily felt they needed, Audrey's approval, but it couldn't hurt.

"Top off your coffees?" Audrey stopped by with a steaming pot.

"We've got an idea we want to run past you."

Ian did a solid job of explaining their need to have someone around the cabins this winter, and thought perhaps it might be the solution for finding a place for Alex to hang his hat. At least until he figured out something else.

"I don't know where he's going to come up with a better offer. I'll stop by their booth and tell him you guys want to talk when he's through giving the police the details."

"Great. Audrey, is he supposed to be working right now? We thought if he was free, we could help him get situated before we head back to the Cities." He hoped if Alex was on the schedule, Audrey would figure out a way to do without him.

"I got the bases covered. You guys are saints, I hope you know that. Be right back with your food."

They'd almost finished eating when the two officers that were talking with Alex walked by. A few minutes later, Alex approached their table. "Audrey said you wanted to see me."

"Have a seat." Ian pulled out a chair.

Harper winked at Ian and took the lead. "Alex, I'm an attorney. When we came in this morning and saw you talking to the police, well, I thought if you were in any kind of trouble, maybe I could help you out. We asked Audrey if everything was okay. She kind of let us in on what happened between you and your father." *I wonder if the kid resents what I'm saying.*

Alex nodded.

"Ian and I had planned to spend the winter living in the apartment behind the office but, after thinking our plan through, decided it would probably be best for us to remain in the Cities. Anyway, because we're not going to be around, we're looking to hire a caretaker over the winter. We'd feel even better if the person we hired actually lived in the apartment. You know, to keep a better eye on the place. Would you be interested?"

Alex looked exhausted. He nodded several more times to show them he understood but was having a hard time looking them in the face. A few moments passed before he lifted his head, looked them both in the eye, and said, "Yes."

"Really? That's fantastic." Ian sat up in his chair. "If you're up to it, do you want to follow us back to the apartment? We can show you around. It's yours starting today if you want."

Harper reached over and squeezed the boy's arm when his lower lip had began to tremble. "You're doing *us* a huge favor."

Alex wiped his face with his sleeve. "I'd like to stop at my house to pick up a few things."

"Works for us." It suddenly occurred to him that the kid might be walking into a dangerous situation. "We have to stop at Pamida. Would you like us to come with you? To help?"

"No, that's okay." Alex sat back in his chair. "He's not going to be there."

"Okay." Ian removed the napkin from his lap and tossed it on his plate. "Take all the time you need. It'll give us a chance to write down some instructions for you." It was Ian's turn to give the boy a pat. "Harp, you ready?"

"See you later, Alex." The three of them stood and walked out of the café together.

"What do you think we should pay him?" Harper asked when they'd gotten into their car.

"Let's ask Alex."

"That's a great idea."

BACK at the apartment, Ian hustled around gathering up their clothes and a few other personal items and began loading up the car. Harper, once he'd marked off the lot for the new house, looked through a stack of appliance manuals and reorganized them for Alex in case he ran into any trouble. He also included both his and Ian's cell phone numbers. About an hour later, Alex drove up and parked.

"Alex is here," Ian shouted from where he was loading the car.

Harper chuckled. The kid must have moved with lightning speed because his car was jam-packed. "Hey, let us give you a hand with this stuff."

Together the three of them unloaded the car. After they'd finished, Ian suggested they sit around the table and talk.

"Alex, we have no idea what to pay you for caretaking the grounds this winter. Any ideas?" Ian looked over to Harper before adding, "Do you have an amount in mind?"

"I… I don't. I was thinking I'd maybe have to pay you guys rent or something to live here."

"Are you planning on working at the Lip Smacker through the winter months?" Harper was curious if Alex had had any kind of plans made before the shit hit the fan with his dad.

"If Audrey does the same thing this year, she'll only open for breakfast and lunch. I'm sure she'll have shifts for me. Yeah, I'll work there, I think."

"How about a thousand bucks." Harper thought it sounded fair.

"For the whole winter?" Ian appeared shocked.

"Sorry, no. A thousand bucks per month, and we won't need anything for rent. It's comforting to know you're here looking after everything." Harper could tell by the expression on Alex's face he'd happened upon an acceptable wage.

"Wow! Sure! I mean, are you sure?"

"We're sure." Ian chuckled. "Harper, you know what we forgot about?"

"What's that?"

"We have that satellite dish scheduled to be installed."

"We do? Oh yeah, that. Alex, are you okay with satellite television? That's what we had planned on putting in if we were going to stay the winter."

"Oh heck yeah, that sounds great!" Alex launched his first big smile of the morning. "You guys tell me where you want it installed and I'll make sure it happens."

"Great. We left a flatscreen television in the bedroom. Move it wherever you want. Ian, did you decide where you wanted the satellite placed?"

"Place it in the spot that provides the best reception. If it doesn't matter, tuck it in back somewhere so it's out of our guests' view."

"Sure. I'll try to have it installed somewhere out of sight." Alex began tapping his finger on the table.

"Let's see, I'm trying to think if there's anything else we should cover." Ian looked over to Harper.

Something was up with Alex. He'd begun to fidget in his chair. "Alex, is there anything you want us to go over before we leave?" Harper asked.

"You guys"—Alex looked across the table—"I'm gay too."

"Go on!" Ian did a really shitty job of feigning surprise. Shocked and amused in equal amounts, Harper burst into laughter.

"Ian! Behave yourself. Don't mind him, Alex. He's impossible."

"At first"—Alex giggled—"I thought you guys were straight."

"Go on!" Ian went for round two. "What changed your mind?"

"You called Harper Binky or some shit like that. And your bracelet." Alex pointed to Ian's bracelet.

"It takes a real man to wear a bracelet." Ian smiled and scooted back over to his own spot at the table.

Excusing himself, Harper went into the bathroom. Opening his wallet, he counted out a hundred dollars. *The kid's going to need grocery money.* Flushing the toilet, he walked back out and placed the money down in front of Alex. "Here's an advance on your first month. I'll mail you a check when we get home tonight. You should have it in the next day or so. You'll need some grocery money, right?"

"This morning I wanted to kill myself. Things are looking up." Alex was showing signs he might just make it through this horrible incident without it causing any more damage to his self-esteem than it already had.

"Hey, Alex, I was joking with you before." Ian moved his chair back to its original spot. "Can I ask you something personal?"

The young man didn't hesitate. "Sure."

"Are you out? Do others know you're gay?"

"Just my best friend, Colin. He's the only one I've told so far."

"Well, take it nice and slow. Next spring we'll be around to offer our support. Hey, what's your last name? I'll need it when I write the check." *Paulson, Emerson, Henderson, something with a son on the end.*

"Stevens."

"Stevens, got it. I'll send the check to the Lip Smacker until we figure out the mail thing here. Hey, would you mind checking into that for us?" Harper stood up and stretched.

"You drivin', Binky, or am I?" Ian winked at Alex.

"Stop with the Binky already. I'll drive. I don't have to work tomorrow, and you do. Call us if you need anything. There's an extra set of keys on the dresser in the bedroom for the office, and in the top right-hand drawer of the counter out front, you'll find keys to all of the cabins. We'll be back in probably a week or so to check in. Not sure how it's all going to work out yet, but I think we're going to be putting up some kind of house back in the woods. Any questions?" Harper shared a glance with Ian to make sure he hadn't forgotten anything.

"I really appreciate this. You guys can count on me." Alex stood and offered his hand.

"I know we can." Harper and Ian both shook it enthusiastically. "Remember," Ian said as they walked to the door, "call us anytime."

CHAPTER

Ten

"IT SMELLS so... *new.*"

"Excuse me?" Harper reached down and pulled Ian's head up from under the covers where he'd been teasing and coaxing, licking and sucking him into another spirited round of butt bumping.

Ian laughed. "I thought about this when we went to bed last night, but I forgot to mention it before I fell asleep. The house, it smells so new. Like a car. It's really beautiful, isn't it?"

"It's exactly what I'd hoped for. And having you here, next to me in bed, complimenting me on how fresh and new my dick smells, is one added plus I could have never imagined." He leaned over and kissed his partner's forehead.

"Actually"—Ian propped himself onto his elbow—"what I smell is bacon."

"Yeah, so do I, come to think of it."

"It's Allison. Either Allison or Spencer or both. They're in charge of breakfast this morning, remember?" Ian hopped out of bed and into his boxers. "Come on, sleepy head, we have a full crew we're supposed to be leading today."

Harper sat on the edge of the bed and yawned. "That's right. Okay." He pulled on his own boxers. "I'm fired up. Yes I am. I'm fired up to... what am I supposed to be doing today?"

"You and Allison are painting cabins." Ian tugged his signature hooded sweatshirt over his head.

"Ah yes, painting with Allison. How could I forget?"

"Yep, and if I hear you guys screwing off there's going to be trouble. We have a shitload to get done today." Ian held the bedroom door open. "Let's move it, Bink. You can shower after breakfast. I'm going to be playing around in the dirt so it doesn't matter."

"I'm coming." Harper yanked his jeans up and grabbed a sweatshirt.

When they walked into the kitchen, Allison was picking out strips of bacon from a frying pan and putting them onto a plate lined with paper towels. Spencer was ladling pancake mix into a skillet. They both were sporting paper hats commonly worn by short order cooks.

"I bet the aroma of bacon woke you up, didn't it?" Allison hooked the remaining pieces of bacon and topped off her platter.

"There were a few smells this morning that got us rolling." Harper smacked Ian on the back of the head.

"Ouchy, stop. Good morning, guys. I love the hats." Ian plucked off a piece of bacon as Allison carried it over to the large table in the great room.

"We love this kitchen, by the way. The pasta faucet is a nice touch. Do you know if Andy and Emmett are up yet? Someone should tell them breakfast is almost ready." Spencer expertly flipped his skillet, sending a pancake somersaulting into the air and miraculously back into the pan.

"You'll have to teach me that trick someday, Straight Cat." Harper stood behind him and watched with awe.

"It's in the wrist action." Spencer flashed an evil grin.

"Not going there. I want to, but I'm not going there. I'll run up and check on Andy and Emmett."

Harper raced up the stairs. They had given Spencer and Allison the room on the main floor. Further down the hall on the second floor past the master bedroom was a second guest room. It became apparent as he approached the door that Andy and Emmett were awake. The distinct sound of flesh being slapped was unmistakable. *What the hell?*

"Has Daddy's little boy been naughty?" a voice, Andy's, asked prior to a set of rapid slaps.

"I'm sorry, Daddy. I'll be good, I promise," a smaller voice answered.

"You bet you'll be good," Andy stated with authority. "You'll be a good boy once Daddy has spanked your bare butt good and hard."

So that's how they roll. Wow!

Covering his mouth, he giggled all the way down the hall.

"Are they up?" Ian asked when he'd returned to the kitchen.

"Oh yeah, they're up. Should be down...." Unable to hold it in, he burst into laughter. "Sorry." *Oh my God, I'm dying here.* "I... I was just thinking of something funny."

"I never thought of it before, but it might be fun to have intercoms between the rooms. That way we wouldn't have to run up and down the stairs all the time." Ian looked around for a response.

"Oh, that *would* be fun." The image of everyone seated around the table eating breakfast listening to Andy spank Emmett was more than he could take. He lost it again, bursting into hysterics.

"Okay, what's so funny?" Allison insisted on being let in on the joke.

"Oh man, I can't explain it, I just can't." *Time to change the subject.* "Hey, has anyone seen or spoken to Alex this morning? I invited him to breakfast."

"He strolled by earlier carrying a flat of plants." Spencer proudly walked his platter of cakes over to the table. Allison followed with a bowl of cut-up fruit in one hand and a pot of coffee in the other.

"Alex," Harper hollered, walking out onto the screened porch, "if you can hear me, breakfast is on the table. Come and get it."

"Be right there," a voice hollered back from a distance.

Returning to the table, he plopped down next to Ian and poured a glass of orange juice. "Thanks, you guys, for making breakfast. This looks great. Should we wait for the other two?"

"No need. Here come the lazy sots now," Ian chimed.

Andy came bolting down the stairs two at a time with Emmett right on his heels. They bounced into the room like Keystone Cops.

"Good morning, everyone," Andy hailed. Emmett, wearing a mile-wide smile, peered around Andy and waved.

"Morning, guys. Grab a seat and help yourself." Allison poured from the steaming pot. "Let me know what you think of the coffee. It's a special blend a friend of mine suggested. Sure smells good."

"How did everyone sleep?" Ian took three pancakes off the platter and passed it to Emmett.

"Great." Andy stacked cakes on his plate after Emmett. "Our bed was really comfortable. Didn't you think so, Em?"

"Yeah." Emmett was a man of few words. Ian had mentioned he was shy. Shy, and apparently very, very naughty.

"Hey, everyone!" Alex came strolling in from the porch. "Ian, I moved the plants you picked out last night over to the garden by cabin one. What do you call the little flower plants?"

"Annuals? You're talking about the packs of four plants in the plastic flats, right?"

"Annuals…. Anyway, all of those have been moved up to the house."

"Awesome! Sit down and have breakfast." Ian moved his chair over and pointed to the empty seat next to him.

"I just got off the phone with Colin. He'll be over in a few minutes to help. He's out to breakfast with his folks."

"Thanks so much, Alex, for drumming up some more help. We can sure use it." Harper poured a cup of coffee.

"Colin wants to meet you guys. I've told him so much about you."

"And he *still* wants to come over? Wow, he's one brave lad." Harper winked.

"You think you're safe planting annuals now?" Allison reached for the coffee. "Load up your plate, Alex." She passed the bacon across the table. "Do you drink coffee?"

"I'll stick to juice, thanks."

"No, it's too early to plant them. Now that they're off the truck and near the house, we can either bring them in or cover them, depending on how low the temperature gets. Something tells me we're in for some pretty hard frosts yet."

"The lake could temper that a bit." Spencer reached for a second helping of bacon. "Where'd you get this bacon, honey? It's the bomb."

"Everett's. I think so too."

"Hey, Alex," Spencer asked between bites, "what were all those people fishing for? We saw a ton of cars along the side of the road when we drove up. Salmon?"

"Smelt." Alex downed his glass of juice.

"Smelt?" Spencer looked around the table. "Anyone heard of smelt before?"

"They're small fish. People catch them by the bucketloads. They dip them in egg and roll them in some kind of batter and fry 'em up with the skin, heads, everything still on."

"Yummy! Not!" Allison wore a look of disgust.

"If you know how to cook smelt right," Alex said, unfazed by Allison's harsh reaction, "they're great. You'll see, bars in the area have smelt fries. It's kind of a specialty around here. Check it out." Alex appeared proud of the fact he could speak so extensively on something nobody else knew about. "I heard someone up at Norbert's mention they were running this weekend."

When they'd finished breakfast, Ian led the group in a short meeting where they outlined their hopes, wishes, and dreams for the day. Emmett, Ian, Alex, and Colin would be working up the gardens and planting. Harper and Allison were on painting detail. Andy and Spencer were in charge of building the small brick fireplace grill units Ian had designed for each cabin. This was the best idea yet. Besides grilling, their guests could pull up their chairs and enjoy a campfire. Clumps of shrubs would offer each cabin more privacy than they'd had in the past. The guests could roast marshmallows and warm themselves during the early spring and fall months. Harper and Ian hadn't decided on what their seasonal schedule would be. At some point they'd planned on closing the cabins during the coldest portion of the winter. No doubt they'd need a break, and the two had planned to travel and energize themselves for the next season.

"I can't believe these actually had orange shag carpeting." Allison dipped her roller into the pan and began covering the surface of the small wall with the soft lemon-colored paint Harper and Ian had picked out at the hardware store in Silver Bay.

The cabins, with all of the shade from the surrounding trees, had seemed too dark. The lighter color on the wall would help. That and the sand-colored industrial carpeting they'd chosen. Over the winter, Alex had yanked out the orange shag from all of the cabins. Once the interiors were painted, a professional carpet outfit out of Duluth would sweep in and lay it all in a day or two.

"When do I get to use a roller?" Not having much experience with painting of any kind, Harper agreed Allison could be team leader.

"Maybe never if you don't get crackin' on that trim. Let's pick up the pace, counselor."

"You know it's funny, I hardly think about the firm or the work anymore. I think I was so disgusted for so long, it's somehow evaporated from my mind."

"You haven't talked much about it, but did the firm try to change your mind and get you to come back?" Allison handed over the roller. "Here. I think I can do the trim faster."

They exchanged spots in the room. "They didn't get the chance. I met with Duncan Price, and he pissed me off almost instantly, so I got up and walked out. That was it. Anyway, it's so funny to hear you call me that because my past life, even though it's been such a short time, seems like a million miles away right now."

"I swear to God you and Ian could go into the book of world records for how fast you've moved from point A to here, to now." Allison ripped off a strand of blue masking tape and tossed it into the garbage bag in the center of the room.

"It seems more right than it does fast, if that makes any sense. This roller really works." He'd only been at it for a few minutes and already he'd completed an entire wall. "Come to think of it, the only thing faster than Ian and me is this roller. Wow!"

"Well, for what it's worth, Harper, the consensus is you are fast *and* right for each other. If *that* makes any sense. I don't think what happened with you guys is very common, but why fight it because people can't wrap their minds around it. Honestly, I met Spencer out one night with some friends at a little bar off campus. I knew. I knew at that moment I wanted to spend the rest of my life with him. Of course, we had to conform to the norm, not sure why, but we did. We went through the entire dating ritual to satisfy our friends and family. You guys just skipped that part. And…."

"And?" He poured more paint from the can into the tray.

"And we feel blessed to have gotten to know you. Had you guys stuck around in Minneapolis, Spencer had planned to campaign hard to get you onto the Hornets. He didn't give a shit how good you played. He just wanted you around."

"Seriously? Wow, thanks for sharing that. But there's no way in hell I'd ever give up our bleacher time together. It's sooooo annoying."

"YOU guys are doing a good job. If you have any extra hostas left over, bring them back to the truck. It's kind of our regrouping station." Ian surveyed the progress. Alex and his friend Colin were planting like gangbusters. It had been a good idea to give them both the "don't be too careful" speech. Hostas were basically indestructible. He frequently sawed through large clumps to create new smaller plants. They recovered quickly and barely skipped a beat. Emmett was up at the highway planting a mixed bed of perennials and low shrubs in the spot where the new sign would go.

"Colin, Harper and I sure appreciate you coming by to help."

"Oh, no problem. I came up from school to spend the weekend with my parents. Basically all we do is hang out and eat."

"You're at the University of Minnesota, right?"

"Yep. I live in Dinkytown with some guys I went to school with up here."

"Cool. Do you actually get any studying done?" Ian laughed, imagining party central.

"We don't do too bad. You'd be surprised. I've got my sights on premed, so I can't really be a fuck-up. I'd sure like to."

"Wow, very cool."

The sound of a car caught Ian's attention. He watched a jeep turn the corner, drive up the small hill, and park in front of the office. "I wonder who that is? Alex, any idea who this might be?"

Alex got up from kneeling on the ground and looked over to the office. "Not a clue. Want me to go over and check it out?"

"I tell you what, let's all take a break. I need to portion out some ferns for our next bed." Because the office was also Alex's home, they followed him up to the car. "Hello, can I help you?"

A dude wearing dress pants and a crisp white shirt was standing near the office door. A woman, still seated in the passenger seat, waved and smiled.

"You're Ian Burke, right?" The man walked over to meet them.

"That would be me. And you are…?"

"I'm Steve Gilmore. This is my wife. Honey, come on out for a minute." The guy gestured for the woman to get out of the car. "This is my wife, Debbie," he said when the door had opened. "She's expecting, but it will be good for her to move around some."

Ian and the guys watched with amazement as the small, pale-faced woman swung her legs around the seat and, after a wobbly second or two, took a step forward. "I'm Debbie."

Good lord! She's expecting what? Three watermelons?

"I'm Ian. Pleased to meet you." He gestured behind him. "This is Alex and Colin. Sorry, we're kind of busy today getting everything planted. What can we do for you?"

"Well," Steve said, clapping his hands together, "I was hoping I could convince you to play ball on our team. I'm the team manager. We're the Taconknights out of Duluth. We play in a league that includes some of the surrounding cities. Any interest?"

"Wow! Can I ask how you found me? We've only been up here for a few weeks now." *This is wild.*

"The wife's brother lives in the Cities not too far from where you guys play. I've watched several of your games. Damn, you can hit. Anyway, I got a call from some guy named Spencer a few weeks ago who told me where you were and to give you a shout if we were recruiting new players this season. Debbie and I were looking for a drive today after church, so we thought, hell, let's just bop over and talk to you in person."

Spencer.... Ian shook his head. "I'd be lying if I said I wasn't interested. I just can't commit right now. As you can see, we've got one heck of a project on our hands. When do you need to know?"

"Look, Ian, I'll be honest with you." Steve took a step forward. "The Taconknights aren't the Hornets. We play hard, practice hard, but we're not in the same league. Honestly, if you showed up midseason, it'd still be a boost. Listen, I know you're busy. Give it some thought, and if you're interested, here's my card."

Ian waited while pregnant Debbie fished a card out of her purse.

Steve extended his hand for a shake. "Good luck with the cabins. Sure is pretty down here."

Debbie smiled while her husband opened the door for her and helped her swing her legs inside. "Could happen any day," Steve joked as he got in from the other side.

Any second is more like it. Whew!

"I'll see you guys in a minute." Ian strolled down to the last cabin, Cabin 10, where Spencer and Andy were putting the finishing touches on their first firepit of the day. "Looks good, you guys."

"Thanks." Spencer wiped his brow. "I'm sure as hell glad it's not too hot out. It's been a long winter. Fuck, am I out of shape."

"We should be able to crank a few more out today. It took us a while to organize." Andy plopped down on the grass and sipped his soda.

"Say, Spencer."

"Say, Ian."

"Say, Spencer and Ian," Andy piped in, followed by a belch.

"I just had a visitor up near the office I think you might know a little something about."

Spencer looked over to Andy, and they both came back with blank looks on their faces.

"Testing the sports agent waters, are you?" The two bozos in front of him couldn't have looked more guilty.

"It was Andy's idea." Spencer threw his firepit-building partner under the bus.

"You dick, it wasn't my idea. Spanky, it was our idea. We just couldn't see that talent of yours wasted." Andy stood up.

"Besides, we didn't do it just for you. We have ulterior motives." Spencer crossed his arms proudly.

"We do. We have ulterior motives." Andy mirrored his friend's stance.

"We thought if for some reason, and trust me we really don't think this, but if for some reason this cabin shit doesn't work out for you guys and you come back to the Cities, we want you to be in shape." Spencer looked over to Andy, who nodded back.

"You guys don't want this to work out, do you?" If they'd each worn the face of guilt before, it had nothing on what Ian saw now. "I have a feeling you're both secretly hoping we lose our asses on this venture and come back home with our tails between our legs."

"Okay, enough of this shit. It's about time we had this one out." Spencer threw his can into the pit. "Ian, I love you more than you'll know. And not in a way you'll understand because it's a love you do with your clothes still on. I'm jealous you get to have this adventure. I'm sad you won't be on the team next year. I knew I was in trouble when I realized I was jealous of you meeting Harper. I know it's wrong. I know it. I just can't help it. Andy, care to add anything?"

"I loved him once without clothes on. It wasn't all that great. With clothes on is the way to go."

The three of them lasted slightly longer than a split second before they roared with laughter.

"Look," Ian began, even though he was still laughing so hard tears were rolling down his cheeks, "you have no idea how much I'm going to miss you guys. Yes, I love Harper. We have an adventure here, you're right. But you guys make me tick in a way he can't. We have history. Come here, you crazy lunatics!" Ian opened his arms.

"We'll try harder to want this to work for you, promise." Andy reached over and pinched Ian's butt.

"Nice." Ian shook his head. "You tools, you're always thinkin', you two. Anyway, it was pretty damned nice of you to line me up with some ball, no matter what your motive was. I appreciate it."

"So, you going to play up here?" Spencer raised an eyebrow.

"I'm going to talk to Harper and see what he thinks. This place could get crazy, and I don't want to leave him high and dry with all this to deal with."

"He knows. He said you could." Spencer flashed a sheepish smile.

"You guys are like frickin' four-year-olds. I *want* to play, and probably *will* play. I just want to talk it out with him before I commit."

"I LIKE those guys. You'd never in a million years know they're fags—I mean gays." Colin sipped his beer.

"Yeah, they're really great. They couldn't have come around at a better time." Alex downed half of his Dew.

"Ian, he's cool, man. When he was telling us how to do stuff, it wasn't like he was bossing or anything. Just matter-of-fact. He must know a lot about plants and shit. And what's the other dude's name, Harper? He's hysterical. So they're kind of like married, right?" Colin sat down at the table near the window.

"They're partners."

"What about Fred and Barney?"

"Fred and Barney?"

"Yeah." Colin laughed. "You know, Fred and Barney, the Flintstones?"

"Oh." Alex laughed. "That's a good one. Fred is Andy. He owns a garden center down in the Cities, and Barney is his partner, Emmett. I've met Andy before, but this is the first time he's brought Emmett."

"Okay, and Dick and Jane?"

Colin was on a roll. It was so much fun having him around. Alex missed him like crazy. When Colin had mentioned he'd be up this weekend from school, Alex had been bummed, knowing he'd be too busy to hook up. It had been Colin who'd volunteered to come over and help so they could spend time together. *Will we be friends for life?*

"That would be Spencer and Allison. They're really good friends. Everyone, they're all really good friends. It's cool."

"What about leaving the palisade? Do you still want to head west?"

"I don't know." He felt comfortable discussing almost anything with Colin. Always had. But they didn't have the same friendship they'd had a year ago, that was for sure. It had changed. Alex detected a distance. For the first time since they'd been friends, he didn't know everything about Colin. They'd gotten together several times over the past year, but it had always been so rushed. Or there were a ton of people around. Colin remained popular here even though he'd been away for almost a year. "I've got the money now. It's ridiculous what these guys pay me to sit here. I've agreed to help them open this place up and work through the summer. I want to do that. They're cool to be around. They make me feel good."

"You guys don't sleep together and shit, do you?"

"Colin, so help me, if you don't stop it I'm going to kick the crap out of you. These guys are awesome."

"I know, I'm just jerkin' your gherkin. Hey, can I ask you something?" Colin leaned across the table.

"Sure." Alex looked out the window. Ian walked by on his way to the truck and waved.

"You're not going to like it."

He knew where this was headed. Colin needed to know. It was the way he was. "You want to know if I've talked to my old man."

"That'd be it. My dad asked me about him this morning. I guess he saw him at Norbert's a few months back and he looked pretty rough."

"The answer is no. If I see him, I'll hurt him."

"Dude, don't you need to resolve this? It's not good to let shit like this just hang." Colin sat back in his chair, frustrated. "He's your dad. I know he's an asshole, but he's your dad."

Ian tapped on their window as he passed by with a flat of ferns.

"I'll go over there with you if you want. I'm serious." His friend stood and downed the last of his beer. "We'll just stand there and you can scream and holler at him and tell him what a prick he is and then we can leave. You can leave forever."

"Thanks, but I want him out of my life *now*. I'm working really hard to move on, with a bunch of stuff." Alex finished his soda and walked out, holding the screen door for his friend.

"MORNING, Audrey." Ian waltzed into the Smacker with Harper close behind.

"My two favorite fellas. I wondered if I'd see you this week. Are those cabins open yet? When they are, I'm going to rent one for two weeks and never even set foot in this damned parking lot. Even if the place burns down. And this is just the start of the season. How am I ever gonna get through it?"

"Just say the word. We'll give you the good neighbor rate. Hell, it'll be so cheap you might want to stay a month." Harper loved how they were starting to have relationships with the locals. Audrey and the Lip Smacker were their ground zero.

"Seriously, boys, how's it going?"

"We're several weeks out, but things are moving right along. We had a whole crew up here from the Cities this weekend helping out. Surprisingly, we actually managed to get a few things done." Ian heard his stomach growl. "I'm starving."

"Looks like your booth is open." Audrey handed them menus, even though by now they weren't needed. "Head on over, and I'll have Francine bring you coffees."

Breakfast appeared and disappeared in record time. When their plates had been cleared and their coffee mugs refilled, Harper slid the legal pad he seemed to carry everywhere these days into place. "So, where are we?"

"I've been thinking more about the opening." Ian brought his leg up onto the booth to make himself comfortable. "The grounds, at least the first round of landscaping, should all be planted by next weekend.

Andy's coming up alone with another truckload of product Thursday. Depending on what they have delivered at Jungle Gems this week, he'll decide if he can stay a day or two and plant with me. Anyway, I think our guests will appreciate how things look after this next weekend. So we can scratch that off the list."

"I think it looks amazing already. I'm so glad we took all those before and after pictures. It'll be fun to look back on this little adventure and admire all of our...." He couldn't get another word out. If he tried, he'd make an ass out of himself. Scrunching his face up in a ball, he weathered the unexpected wave of emotion.

"Harp, what is it? You okay?" Ian looked around as if something in the restaurant may have upset him.

Harper shook his head. Taking a few sips of water, he felt tears well up in his eyes.

"Harper, what's going on? Is it something in here?"

"I'm sorry,"—he wiped his eyes with a fresh napkin—"I don't know where that just came from." Several seconds passed before he felt it safe to continue. "Ian...." *Okay, this is just fucking nuts!* "I'm so in love with you. Really." He laughed at how absurd he must be presenting. "When you were talking a minute ago, I had this overwhelming feeling of joy. I'm so completely in love with you it makes me cry. It's so powerful, I don't know what to do with it yet."

Ian laughed and reached for his hand, giving it a squeeze. "You *are* worse than I am. I didn't think that was possible. I have moments like this too. Maybe it's all starting to catch up to us in some way. Damn, think of the speed we've been traveling at."

"It's probably a lot of that. It's also this whole cabin thing. I know we're just getting started with it, but it's already been so rewarding to me. And I guess here's where I get all crazy." *Get a fucking grip, Harp! Honestly!* "It's so intoxicating, is that the right word? It's so potent going through this with you. I've always been on my own. Everything I've ever done has been solo. I had no idea...."

"I feel the same way. Wanna cry for a few minutes and then we'll get back to the list?"

"I hate you."

"Do not. You just said you loved me." Ian gave his hand another squeeze.

"Okay, I'm over it." Harper laughed, wiping his eyes again. "Wow, I don't think I've ever had anything like that happen before."

"It's because I'm so special. Happens to people around me all the time." Ian looked away as if bored.

Before Harper had a chance to respond, three guys sat down at the table directly across from their booth.

"Okay," Ian forged on, "let's talk about the cabins. We're halfway done painting. Do you want to keep going this week? You can have Alex as a painting partner. I'll concentrate on the grills when I'm not planting. Wait, let's do this. I have a better idea."

Out of the corner of his eye, Harper caught something at the next table that put him on high alert. He hoped it wasn't what he thought it was. "What's your idea?"

"The soft opening we talked about. Let's make sure we have two or three units completely finished and the rest almost done before we try and snag our first customers. We can test drive a few guests for a week or two until we feel we're ready to open the place up completely."

Ian seemed apprehensive at the thought of having to handle a full house this early in the game. He needed a little push. "Okay." Harper thought for a second. "But I think there's merit to jumping in with both feet too. But the units definitely have to be finished before we do that." Another thought popped into his head, but he put it on hold when the table of guys burst into laughter. This time there was no mistaking it. The not-so-subtle looks in their direction were bordering on harassment. Pissed off at the fact these dimwits were taking a shot at destroying this wonderful morning, he looked over and asked, "Is there a problem?" There was no mistaking what he'd seen before. The burly dude sitting between the other two was putting on a show. The exaggerated limping of his wrist was meant to be only one thing. The dude was making fun of them because he'd probably heard from someone they were gay.

"You're the girls...." The table burst into a round of snickers. Only the fat pig in the center was able to make eye contact with him. "I mean, you guys are the ones who are opening the old beach cabins, right?"

Harper was ready for this one. He'd rehearsed an encounter like this before in his mind. He had endless avenues to go down. "You just called me a girl. Are you an idiot? You kind of look like an idiot. They all look like idiots, don't they?"

"Harper, let's just go." It was obvious Ian wasn't geared up for a confrontation.

"I'm not going anywhere. Sorry," he whispered, "I'm not backing away from this one. This is our home now. If they sense fear, we're goners. I'll explain that to you later."

"You uppity rich fairies think you can just move in wherever you want." The fat pig seated in the center glared across the table.

"Uppity rich fairies?" Feeling the need to display a sense of calm despite the fact that every nerve ending in his body was making itself noticed, he sipped his water. Ian, refusing to look over at the table, slowly shook his head. *I know, this is one of those times where you're fucked if you do and fucked if you don't. I choose to be fucked if I do.*

"What exactly is a fairy?" It was a fair question. Looking over to the table of Neanderthals, he smiled. *Come on, boys, collectively you should be able to come up with a clever answer.*

The ringleader was robbed of an opportunity to respond when, like magic, Audrey appeared at their table. "Luke, Earl, Adam, how's the breakfast this morning? We do a good job for you?" It wasn't lost on him that Audrey had strategically placed her hand on the center pig's shoulder, who he guessed to be Earl.

"Real good, Audrey." All it took were those few words out of Earl's mouth for him to see what a pansy-ass suck-up this guy really was. Like being caught red-handed by the teacher, Earl did his best, which wasn't a half-bad effort, to cover up for the shit storm he'd entered into. *Story of your life, huh, Earl? Too stupid to ever catch on? That's it, isn't it. You're an eating, shitting machine that will never contribute an ounce of value on this earth. You're pathetic.*

"Well," Audrey continued in an even voice, "if you ever want to eat breakfast, lunch, or dinner in the Smacker again, you're going to apologize to these wonderful gentlemen for your rudeness. You got about one second to make up your mind which it's going to be. Apologize or pay your bill and leave here for good. Your business won't be welcome anymore."

Harper fought to keep his inner smile from surfacing. Audrey, what a peach. Damn, the woman had balls.

"I'm sorry," the younger of the three said, to Earl's left.

"Not good enough. You look over to these fine gentlemen and give them a proper apology."

"I'm sorry." This time the dude looked up for a brief moment before staring down at his coffee cup.

"That's barely acceptable, but I'll take it for now. Adam, you want to give it a try?"

The guy on Earl's right nervously rubbed his mouth and nose before looking over. "I'm sorry."

"That's better." Audrey moved from behind Earl over to the side of the table. "Now, Earl, I believe it's your turn."

Earl, his face beet red, looked as if he was going to explode. He was fucked and he knew it.

"I'm... sorry."

Audrey walked over to their booth and snatched up the ticket Francine had left earlier by Ian's coffee cup. "This one's on me. No reason you have to put up with that kind of crap in my restaurant. It won't happen again. If for some reason it does, and I don't know about it, I'm going to trust that you let me know. You guys are the best thing to happen to this community in a long time. Even if some of us are too stupid to realize that." Audrey looked over her shoulder to make sure her point had landed on her intended targets.

"It was one big misunderstanding, Audrey." Harper crawled out of the booth and stood. "Guys, I'm sorry we got off to such a bad start this morning. I hope there's no hard feelings. Earl, is it?" The burly dude nodded at him apprehensively. It was clear he didn't have a clue he was being manipulated. *Ah yes, the Callahan touch.* "May I see that piece of paper by your elbow?" Earl fidgeted in his seat. "Yep, I'm talking about your bill. Can I see it?"

Seconds passed before Earl's mind caught up. When it did, he picked up the bill and surrendered it.

"We're up to our elbows in alligators trying to get these cabins open. It's taken a big chunk out of our savings, but you know what?"

Nobody seemed to have an answer for him. Harper chuckled to himself. Hands down, the face wearing the most lost look was Ian's. *Keep going, you're nailing this one.* "Audrey, let me see the bill you just picked up off our table, please." Audrey handed it over. "Thank you." *Okay, seal the deal. Bring it home.* "Guys, despite the fact we are up to our necks in bills right now, breakfast is on Ian and me. Audrey, we very much appreciate you offering to pick up our tab this morning, but we're all here to make a buck. Enjoy the rest of your day, guys. I look forward to meeting you again. By the way, I'm Harper. Harper Callahan. And this is my partner, Ian. Ian Burke." Part of sealing the deal was walking around the table and shaking the hand of each one of these douchebags. *The Callahan personal touch. Addicting.*

"Come on, Ian. We've got a hell of a lot of work to do today. Audrey, let's you and I settle up at the cash register."

"Well, that was pretty amazing." Ian hadn't said a word until they were just about to the car.

"What's even more amazing"—he stopped to make his point—"is the restraint you showed back there. I'm very impressed. In the back of my mind I was waiting for the detonation to go off."

"I guess I was just surprised by the whole thing. Shocked." Ian shook his head in disgust.

"I was shocked too. The Smacker feels like home."

"When I finally recovered and felt the anger beginning to surface, Audrey appeared."

"Here's the deal. I give what I did back there a better than fifty-fifty chance of working. Hopefully, we just smoothed over some of their rough edges. Now, they could be even stupider than they look, which, frankly, is really hard to imagine, but if they are, then they'll still want us out of their playground. Let's hope for the best."

CHAPTER

Eleven

HARPER crawled out from under the office desk where he'd been connecting cables to the new POS system. "There! Try it now."

Alex powered up the server. The screen blinked a few times before the system began to load. "Looks like that did it. Are you sure you want me to go through the training on this?"

"Positive." He knew he didn't want to give up time hanging on the phone while a sales representative located in God-knew-where walked him through Reservations 101. "You're going to be the point man at the desk most of the time. I want you to be the expert. Get to know the folks we bought this system from, and then you can train me, and probably Ian, as a backup on it in a language he and I can understand. Neither of us is terribly technical." *Like I'll ever find the patience to plow through that owner's manual. Yikes!*

"That's cool. I get into this stuff." Alex fearlessly paged through the manual.

"Oh, I almost forgot." Harper picked up his trusty legal pad and browsed through the notes he and Ian had made at breakfast. "There's a photographer coming by sometime this afternoon to take photos for marketing. Ian's all over that, so if he's not around or out working the gardens, call him on his cell. The guy charges by the hour so we don't want to keep him waiting around."

"Got it. I plan on being here all day."

"We need to talk about your schedule too. Have you finalized your hours at the Smacker?" He and Ian wanted Alex to be involved in the business as much as possible. Knowing that waiting tables at the Smacker had been a reliable source of income for him in the past, for at least this season, they'd work around whatever schedule he came up with.

"I was hoping to work just here, if you thought there would be enough for me to do. Ian mentioned he'd have his hands full gardening and could use help keeping the grounds up. The Smacker's great, but I'm ready for a change."

"That's exactly what we hoped. Let me talk to Ian, and we'll work on putting together a salary package that includes health insurance. Which brings up something else I want to talk to you about. Any chance you have an extra Dew in there? Let's sit down for minute."

Alex had spoken on several occasions about heading west. There hadn't been much talk of it after his dad had made off with his money. He and Ian thought the timing might be right to see if they could get a more solid commitment out of him. If he was amicable to their little industry, they'd make it worth his while.

"Oh yeah, sure. Be right back."

Harper sat down at the small table across from the front desk. *We need some art in here. That's it! Maybe we can feature local artists and have a revolving gallery. We could sell their work.*

"There you go." Alex popped the top on a soda and handed it over.

"Thanks. I don't drink soda that often, but I like the caffeine rush I get from this stuff. Makes the hair on the back of my neck stand on end." Harper took a long pull from the frosty can.

"I went to the dentist this winter. I have to find something else to drink. This stuff is lethal. He told me I'd wake up one morning and my teeth would be on my pillow." Alex laughed.

"Are you serious? He actually said that to you?" *Wow, he's using the scare tactic big-time.* "So, Alex...."

"Yeah, what's up?" Alex had relaxed considerably around both him and Ian. At first, the young man had seemed on pins and needles when they were together. It was nice to see him act naturally.

"Let's talk future. Any idea what your plans are going forward? You mentioned you'd at one time thought about heading west. You still noodling that one?"

"Naw, not really."

Harper was surprised to see his comfortableness fade a few notches. Alex fidgeted and broke eye contact.

"Look, we love having you around. You're a great guy, and we need a right-hand man around here who gets what we're trying to accomplish. Unless you can tell me otherwise, we think we've found him." *Come on, Alex, what's on your mind?*

"I like being here, being around you guys. It's just that...."

"I'm not going to judge you. I'm an attorney at heart, so you might hear an unsolicited opinion or two, but like Ian's learning to do, just ignore it."

"Harper, can I ask you something?" Alex resumed eye contact. A good sign.

"Sure."

"How did you and Ian meet?"

"I hired him to landscape my backyard."

"Huh?" Alex laughed, not understanding.

"I saw this landscaping commercial late one night, and this stud was in it who turned out to be Ian. I called the next day and he came over to discuss my yard. We've pretty much been a team ever since." This didn't appear to be the answer Alex had hoped for. "Hey, wait a second. Are you seeing someone? I've noticed Zits has been gone several nights lately."

"I wish." Alex was back to staring at his soda can.

"You on a bowling team or something?" He was happy to see a smile back on the young face. "If you're seeking out 'finding the right man' advice, I'm sorry, but I'm the last person you should be talking to. I wasn't even trying to meet someone when Ian walked into my life. It just happened."

His last comment wiped away the smile. Hopefully not for good. *What is going on with this kid?* Confident there wouldn't be any more clues forthcoming, he forged on. "Look, you're a handsome, charming dude. I can't imagine there aren't guys your age just waiting in line to date you. Are there places you can go to meet other gay dudes?"

He'd never thought about it. It could be a whole different ballgame meeting guys up here. He couldn't be sure about this, but there probably weren't the opportunities for Alex that guys his age had back in the Cities.

"I've been hanging out at Norbert's more."

"Yeah, so? I don't get it." *Norbert's, what the hell did that have to do with meeting guys?* It was a tacky convenience store.

"I've met a few guys there."

"You meet guys at Norbert's? How does that work?"

"There's a magazine rack in the back of the store. Every now and then someone will stand next to me. I just stand there for a few minutes pretending I'm reading. Then I put the magazine back and walk out. If they're interested, they follow me and we hook up." Released from his apparent burden, Alex once again looked up. "We get in the car and—"

"*You do what?*"

The look of horror displayed on the young man's face at Harper's reaction was, in all likelihood, a mirror image of what Harper's own face displayed. "Alex, I'm sorry, but do you mean to tell me you get into a stranger's car and you go somewhere and diddle each other?"

"Sometimes they get in my car, but not very often."

"I think this is the first time I've ever had my parent gene kick in. Wow! Sorry." It was his turn to look away. The idea of Alex getting into a stranger's car, the risk involved, was more than he could process at the moment. "I'm not judging you. You're likely doing what you have to do, or need to do. I'm just more than a little freaked at the reality of it all."

"It sucks."

He didn't need to know any more details. Sipping his soda, he stared out the window. Ian had positioned a rock garden just a few feet away from the office entrance. Although the plants were small, many of them were blooming. It was soothing. His heart ached for Alex. Here was an amazing young man who hadn't been given a single break his entire life, as far as he could tell, who was still out there smiling, working, keeping himself up. The alternative—Donnie McPherson came to mind. The spoiled snot son of the senior partner who had been handed everything in life didn't have a speck of the drive and character the young dude seated across from him had. *What a shame. What can I do? Can Ian and I do anything?*

A redheaded woodpecker landed on a stately pine about ten feet from where he was sitting. It immediately started pecking away. "Hey, look at that. Can you believe how red the head is on that bird?"

Alex leaned over the small table to get a look. "Wow, they're so cool. We have the large ones up here too. I think they're called pileated woodpeckers or something like that. They're huge. Somebody, it might have been a teacher at school, told us they're endangered or close to being endangered. I'd give money to save them."

They sat for a few moments in silence. The woodpecker circled the trunk of the tree and then, after looking around, flew off. *Hell, I'd give some money to help Woody out too. I'd give some money to help you out.*

That's it! "Alex, I feel the old Callahan genius kicking in. And when that happens, look out, dude! I'm unstoppable."

"Okay." Alex laughed nervously.

"You're looking for a safe, respectable way to meet guys up here your own age, right?"

"Yep."

"The first thing we need to do is check around the area to see what, if any, organizations exist for men only. I have no idea, but your problem is universal, and I can't help but hope others before you may have made an effort to lessen the burden on other young dudes coming up the ranks. So, first, we check out the area for healthy, safe groups you can latch onto for socializing. Curious, have you ever looked into what is already out there for gay men?"

"Not really. I know the bars sometimes have underage nights, but I usually find out too late. And before I wasn't sure who I wanted to know I was gay. I don't give a shit about that anymore."

"The other thing I'm thinking about...." Harper had to figure out a way to introduce his idea without giving away the fact that he had substantial wealth and, for tax reasons, a motivation to find a charitable organization he felt good about being the benefactor of. *This is the perfect fit.* "If the Palisade Beach Cabins are a success, and the community turns out to be supportive, accepting, Ian and I would like to give back to it in some way. We've talked about a couple of ideas. Ian's gardening skills and knowledge are substantial. Maybe create, fund, and manage a public space that everyone around here can enjoy. That's Ian's thing."

"We used to have something like that next to the gas station in town, where the vacant video store is now."

"Nice." *Nothing's as soothing and enjoyable to look at as an abandoned video store.* "My thing, something that would interest me, would be to help out the gay community in some way."

For the next hour, and another round of Dew, he and Alex took his sliver of an idea and built on it. The area would benefit from a men's center. Perhaps starting with gay men, but most certainly adding gay teens. A safe place to meet others. It would be a place where there would be gay-orientated events. Maybe dances. He'd heard about a similar men's center in the Cities. Ian had told him about it. They sponsored all sorts of activities. Biking and hiking groups, a variety of events where men could enjoy the company of one another and meet others. Forge friendships, and from there, relationships. Or, like he and Ian, go right into the relationship thing and bypass the friendship phase.

"Wanna do this with me? Is this something you could see yourself being interested in?"

He hoped Alex would respond positively. If he didn't, Harper would understand. He had learned a long time ago that his ideas, his views, weren't always shared by those around him. Sometimes his physical attractiveness had worked against him when it came to garnering support. For the wrong reasons, people agreed to things only because they were swept up by his looks and apparent charm. The concept didn't have a home in their hearts like it did in his. Whether they knew it or not, their motives were insincere. By nature, he wanted to give his ego a good thrashing for thinking his very being had this kind of influence on people. But it was true. He'd watched it happen many times. *And it's not my fault, dammit!*

"I would kill to have something, a place to meet guys like that here. Very cool. It's a great idea, Harper."

Yes! Baby steps. That's the way to go.

"In all likelihood, Ian's going to be gone a few nights a week during the summer playing baseball. Let's team up on our idea and take a night during the week to work on this. See what we can come up with." He was charged. Just like Ian, who could visualize so clearly the landscaping when they first toured the cabins, he could envision bits and pieces of his men's center.

"Sounds great. Sure, I'll do that." Alex appeared to be pumped for a minute, but like before, the joy suddenly vanished from his face. Harper had lost his young friend to some dreadful thought.

"Dude, you're looking at your soda can again. What are you thinking about? Talk to me. I'm prone to hollering, but I don't bite. Promise."

"I was thinking about Norbert's. I'm...."

"Hang on. It's me that has a problem with you luring innocent men into your web of passion. Wow, did I just say that?" Harper giggled.

"That's some shit." Alex laughed along with him.

"Do what you have to do. Be safe. Use your head. I mean the one on your shoulders, and hopefully, you'll have an option or two to replace cruising the magazine rack at Norbert's soon. Maybe there's something already around here we don't know about. We've got our work cut out for us, my friend. Now, go learn how to use that reservation system so when our first guest checks in, we can look like we know what we're doing. I have to head into Duluth to pick up some bathroom fixtures we ordered for the cabins."

"I'll get cracking on this software. Hey, Harper?"

"Yes, sir?"

"Thanks. I really appreciate all you're doing for me."

"It's our pleasure. Alex, Ian and I really enjoy having you around. Besides, haven't you figured it out yet? You're a better investment than the cabins. We think you're going places. And I'm not talking about out west, either. Later, dude!"

"DID you git 'er done?" Ian looked up from the computer screen. His "checking a guest in and out" lesson was just concluding. Alex had the patience of Job.

"Yep, Mater. We are... *open!*" Harper flopped the plastic tarp they'd had covering the new sign onto the desk and went along the room accepting high fives. "I can't believe it. And you guys, the grounds look great. Walking back from the highway, it's like you're strolling into the land of Oz or something. You'd never guess this place would look as cool as it does. I like that surprise element. Hey, let's celebrate. Alex, do you have plans tonight?"

"Of course not." Alex flipped a page in the manual he'd had his head buried in.

"This kid has been hanging around us too long, Ian. He's starting to sound like we do."

"Like you. He sounds like you. I'm always bright and cheerful." Ian patted Alex on the shoulder.

"Remember that one, Alex. We can use it as ammunition down the road. Anyway, I was thinking we should go into Duluth for dinner. Find the biggest and best steak in town. Whattaya say, fellas?"

This is going to be good. It hasn't sunk in yet. Walking over to the tarp on the counter, Ian picked it up and handed it to his partner. "Here."

"Huh." As expected, Harper appeared clueless.

"Put 'er back on, Mater."

Alex, hovering over the computer, chuckled. He got it.

"Oh." Deflated, Harper sat down in the chair with the tarp on his lap. "We're open, I get it."

"Yep. Life's going to be a little different from here on out." Ian moved from behind the desk and took Harper by the hand. "Come here, Binky. We love you." Wrapping his arms around Harper, he held him in a tight embrace. "You should have seen the look on your face. It was priceless."

"Binky wants steak, a big, juicy steak with mushrooms," Harper sniveled on his shoulder. "And a baked potato. And wine, Binky wants wine."

"But Binky is an innkeeper, or cabinkeeper, now. And he's subject to a whole new set of rules. There, there, we'll get through this together." Ian gave Harper's ear a gentle tug.

Another round of laughter exploded from Alex.

"Someone's laughing at poor Binky," Harper sniveled even louder.

"That's because Binky is a moron and very forgetful."

"A moron? Did you just call me a moron?" Harper stepped back, appalled.

"I did. But in a loving, tender kind of way, Binky."

"Well, okay then, I guess."

Ian and Alex watched as Harper carefully folded the tarp up for storage. "We're open now. The Palisade Cabins are open. But hey, I have an idea."

"Did you hear that, Alex? Bink has an idea. Let's hear it, Bink. What's your idea?"

"Takeout! Ta-da! How about Alex and I make a run into town for steak takeout?"

"Steak takeout? You mean like in a bucket or something?" Ian laughed. "With a couple sides of coleslaw?"

"No, silly. Like I call the.... Alex, what's that supper clubby kind of place on our side of Duluth?"

"Pickwick?"

"That's it! I'll call Pickwick and have them package it all together for us. I'll order the 'we just opened our resort cabins meal' for three. Big steaks, baked potatoes, salads...."

"That sounds awesome." Alex was pumped.

"Works for me. I'll hold down the fort." Ian slapped Binky's butt, sending him on his way.

"Oh, that reminds me...." Harper stopped midsentence.

"Slapping your butt reminds you of something? This should be good." Ian chuckled, looking over to Alex.

"I thought it reminded me of something, but Binky *is* a moron. So never mind."

"Okay." *What the heck was that one all about?* "Well, I'm going to run up to the house for a minute. Call me when you guys decide to leave, and I'll come back down."

Tonight needed to be special. Ian decided they should dine at the table. He carefully went about setting it, chuckling when he remembered the erotic penis napkin fold Andy had taught him one night when they were three sheets to the wind. *Perfect!* He'd just finished putting the water glasses on the table when Harper called to tell him they were headed into Duluth.

"Okay, hon. Drive safely. I'll head down to the office in a minute." *Wineglasses. Alex can pour his Dew into a wineglass if he wants.* Ian surveyed the table. The penis napkins were definitely the perfect touch. He giggled.

As he walked back to the office, the surrounding beauty stopped him in his tracks. *This is paradise.* Leaves were beginning to explode everywhere he looked. And the smell of spring: intoxicating. The shadows were long, signaling the end of the afternoon. *What a gorgeous day.* To pass the time, he reviewed the software lesson he'd just gone through with Alex. A thought occurred to him. How many hours would he have logged in this office when it was all said and done? Would it be hundreds? Thousands? The cabins, the grounds, already seemed like home to him. He couldn't wait for the first time they were up and running to capacity. The bustling activity. The aroma wafting through the air from all the different kinds of dinner being cooked on the grills he'd designed. The sound of happy, maybe even tipsy voices as they enjoyed their time away from home in the garden paradise he'd created. *Life is good.*

He'd just completed a trial run of the "check-in" program when he heard the sound of a car pulling up outside. *That was fast. Wow!* Car doors opened and slammed shut. The sound of a child's voice confirmed for him it wasn't Harper and Alex. Seconds later a little girl, maybe six or seven, appeared outside the screen door. "Hellooo," she said.

"Well, hi there. What's your name?"

"Tiffany." She smiled and rubbed her nose against the screen.

"Tiffany? Wanna hear something funny? I know another Tiffany, but she's bigger." *Much bigger.* He chuckled. "Do you want to come in?"

"I can't. Not until my daddy and mommy come."

Adorable. A moment later Daddy appeared. "It's okay," he instructed her, "you can go in."

The little girl and her father entered the office. A split second later, Mommy joined them.

"Welcome to the Palisade Beach Cabins. I'm Ian. Can I help you?" *Wow, was that ever strange to say.*

"We were just driving by"—Dad moved to the side to allow Mom to join him—"and saw your sign. You're open, right?"

"We opened today. Your timing is perfect."

"You have a beautiful place here. Just beautiful." Mom was impressed. Sweet!

"What are your rates?" Dad didn't appear to take into consideration how taken Mom was with the property. He was all business.

"Here, why don't you take a look at this." Ian reached under the counter and pulled out one of the newly laminated price sheets Harper and Alex had created. "This should tell you everything you need to know."

He was thankful for the pricing cheat sheets. Although they'd discussed the rates back and forth, honestly, he couldn't recall what they had decided.

"This works." Dad nodded his approval, handing the sheet over to Mom. "Preseason rates apply?"

"Ah, sure." *Ian, stop sounding so tentative. Check the damn sheet yourself if you don't know.*

"We drove up from Iowa this morning. Thought we'd just wing it." Mom giggled at how adventurous she thought they were being.

"Really? That's a long drive. My partner is from Iowa."

"What do you think?" Mom smiled her answer back to Dad. "Can we look around a minute?" Dad guided Mom toward the door.

"Sure. I tell you what, talk it over and I'll pop out in a minute with a key to one of our cabins. Maybe that will help you decide." Ah yes, he was hitting his stride.

After a few minutes, he grabbed the key to Cabin 10, their finest, the one closest to the palisade, and headed out the door. The family had strolled down to Cabin 1 and were inspecting the firepit. "What do you think so far?"

"This works." Dad's vocabulary left something to be desired. *He's kind of cute, though.*

"Great! I grabbed the key to Cabin 10. It's the one closest to the Palisade. Follow me." Ian led the family down the woodchip path. *Tiffany.* He and Harper would have a good laugh over that one.

"Who does your gardening?" Mom asked when they'd reached the cabin.

"I do most of it. I've got some help."

"I wish I could get my garden at home to look like these."

"Here we are." Ian held open the door. Even though they'd left the windows open for a few days, a hint of fresh paint lingered in the air. He followed the family in. "The cabins are basically set up like your standard motel room." Ian recalled Tiffany's selling points when she'd shown the cabins to them the first time. "The bathrooms have been upgraded this year. You have satellite television. We also include complimentary charcoal for the firepits, and,"—Ian focused the last part of his pitch on little Tiffany—"we have little S'more kits as a thank-you for staying with us. Each room has a list of amenities and cleaning services we provide. The office is staffed twenty-four seven. I'll wait outside."

This was fun. What were the odds that after only having the sign uncovered for an hour or so, they'd snagged their first customer? Or at least it looked like they did.

"Any chance you have a cot or a small bed for the girl here?" Dad had one final hurdle for Ian to hop over before he'd commit.

"We do. I have a few cots and extra bedding up at the office. We'll be happy to set it up for you and make the bed while you enjoy the grounds."

"We'll take it." Dad was sold. Mom was all smiles, and Tiffany—where was Tiffany?

"Did we lose Tiffany?" Ian asked as they waited outside the cabin.

"She had to tinkle," Mom informed him.

"Oh, I understand. So, Cabin 10 for one night, is it?"

"Three nights." Dad confirmed this by a brief smile directed at Mom.

"Great," Ian said when Tiffany had joined them outside. "I'll need a major credit card, and we're in business. We'll charge you with one night now, and the remainder will be charged to your card when you check out."

Ian was processing the card when Harper and Alex pulled up. "There you go. Follow the road behind the office, and it will take you down to Cabin 6. I'm afraid you'll have to walk the rest of the way to Cabin 10. Will you need help?"

"We'll be fine." Dad took his receipt and led the family to their car. Seconds later, Alex and Harper came bounding in the door.

"Don't tell me...." The prospect of having their first guests this early in the game was clearly something Harper hadn't counted on.

"I know, I can't believe it. And guess what? It's not just one night. They're staying for three." Ian could hardly believe it himself. He'd had visions of weeks passing by without any bites. "Alex, can you run one of the cots and bedding down to Cabin 10 for little Tiffany? And ask if you can make up the bed for them. We're all about service here."

"Tiffany, are you kidding?" Harper chuckled. "Please don't tell me she's...."

"Nope. She's too young to be sportin' floaters. Oh, and don't forget to bring them a S'more kit. They perked right up when I mentioned it."

"I'll run the food up to the house. Alex, meet us there when you get the.... Do our guests have a name?" Harper looked in the direction of Cabin 10.

"The Bergstroms, from Ames, Iowa," Ian announced proudly.

"Ames, Iowa? Way to go, Iowa!" The significance of their first guests being Iowans delighted Harper.

Alone in the office, Ian placed a card on the desk informing anyone who happened by to call his cell and someone would be right down. When he got up to the house, Harper was well on his way to having dinner organized.

"The table looks great, hon. I'm lovin' the provocative napkin design. Let's hope young Alex doesn't mess himself. Do you want wine or beer?" Harper had already poured himself a glass of wine.

"I'll take wine too. Wow, those steaks look wonderful. What a great idea." Ian surveyed the extravagant takeout Harper was plating.

A few minutes later, Alex showed up at the door with a couple of Dews in his hand.

"How're the Bergstroms?" Ian asked, pouring his wine.

"The Bergstroms are well. He's kind of grumpy, but the mom and the little girl are very nice. They're off for a walk. I showed them how to light the grill and made up the cot."

"Perfect, Alex. Tonight's a special occasion, what with our opening up the joint and having our first guests. Would you like a glass of wine?" Ian held up the bottle for Alex to inspect.

"Naw, I'm good. But thanks. Wow, dinner looks incredible. Can't wait."

"We don't need to wait. Let's chow while the food is still hot. Alex, there's sour cream and butter for your baked potato on the table. Here's your porterhouse. Wait, this isn't a porterhouse, it's half a cow." Harper handed over a plate with a piece of meat on it the size of Texas. "And for you, Ian, the petite filet and cottage cheese with a peach half." Harper slid a plate in his direction with the largest filet on it he'd ever seen.

"Holy shit! This looks awesome." Ian carried the plate and his wine to the table.

"Here's to the first day of business, and hopefully not the last," Harper toasted.

They managed to empty a bottle of wine during dinner. Alex decisively proved his eyes were not bigger than his stomach, being the first of the three to reach the clean plate club.

"Wow, that's seriously impressive." Ian picked up Alex's empty plate on the way into the kitchen for another bottle of wine. "We're going to have to warn guests with small animals to make sure they're kept inside with this guy around. They could end up being a little midnight snack."

"I couldn't stop." Alex chuckled. "That was the best steak I've ever had. Thanks, guys."

"Thank you. It's great having you on board. We really appreciate your effort and hard work to help make our dream come true." Harper pushed his chair back, tossing his mangled dick napkin onto his plate.

"Me too. I'm done." Ian coaxed, nurtured, and released a monstrous belch, declaring a total contentment even he found impressive.

"You and I are going to have ourselves a little talk about your table behavior." Harper tried valiantly to keep a straight face but lost the battle. "It's disgusting."

"Sorry, hon. Sorry, Alex, if I offended you in any...." *Belch!* "Dang, sorry again." Belching was a habit, and he'd need a more convincing argument against it before he'd consider doing away with it. And it felt good.

"What should we do now? Wanna play a game or something?" Harper looked across the table to see if there was any interest.

"Would you guys mind if I excused myself?" Alex began busing their table.

"You don't have to do that. Just leave it and relax," Ian protested.

"You guys relax. I'm going to go back home and hang out at the office. I think someone should be there in case our guests need anything."

"Okay, but we'll take turns evenings like we discussed." Ian felt a pang of guilt for giving up so easily, but he was looking forward to some cuddle time with his partner.

"Sounds good. Thanks again for the awesome meal. Have a good night, you guys."

"Night, Alex. I'll have my cell by me if you need to get ahold of us for any reason." Harper stood and gathered up the napkins when Alex was gone.

"You have that look, Ian."

Ian knew he had that look. He'd lusted after Harper all day, and now, with nothing else left in his way, it was time to act on his relentless desire. "How about we grab our wine and start out on the screened porch. Once the sun sets, we can move upstairs and, let's see, what are you in the mood for tonight? Should I introduce you to my Harry Belafonte? It has aspects of my Tina but with a Caribbean flair. And there's a calypso finale that will shiver your timbers. Trust me, you'll like it."

"You know me, I'm willing to try anything once." Harper grabbed the bottle and his glass and led the way. "Hey, you know what I'd really like to do?"

"What's that?" Ian was right behind him, watching his hot butt shift from side to side. *Daddy needs him a piece of that tonight.*

"Can I talk you into a slow dance out here?" Harper stopped in the middle of the big open porch.

"Hmm, with or without clothes on?"

"I have a feeling I'm in for one hell of a night." Harper grabbed him and pulled him in for a kiss. "All good things come to those who wait."

"Oh do they, now." He reached down between Harper's legs, confirming what he already knew. "Sure. I'd love that. You want me to put on some music, or do you have something in mind?" Ian placed his wineglass on the bar.

"I've got it covered. Be right back."

A few minutes later, Sinatra oozed out of the speakers. Ian could feel himself begin to leak. Sex with Harper hadn't lost an ounce of its passion or satisfaction. It kept getting better and better as time went on. He loved how willing his partner was to try new things. How Harper, like him, tended to approach making love with an element of athleticism. They could bounce a bed around a room with the best of them.

"There, how's that? You like?" Harper waltzed back in and retrieved his glass and sipped.

"Would you allow me the pleasure of this dance?" Ian did his best to bow with grace.

"I would be delighted to accept, Lord Hardenlong. Come here, you goof." Harper took him by the hand and led him into the middle of the room.

Our first slow dance.

It felt awkward in the beginning, but relinquishing his need to lead, Ian relaxed into his handsome man's arms, resting his head on Harper's chest as he was gently waltzed around the room. "Oh yeah, you definitely know what you're doing," he purred when Harper reached around and cupped his butt in both hands.

"There'll be more dance lessons, if you'd like." Their lips met; their bodies swayed back and forth.

"Harp, do you think we're luckier than most?"

"What do you mean?" Harper squeezed his cheeks, drawing him up tighter to his body.

"I mean, well, I can't imagine being happier."

"Ian, my love for you, it's so intense. I think about you constantly." Harper eased Ian's head off his chest and lifted Ian's face up to meet his own.

"Is it possible to cum just dancing like this?" He probed Harper's lips with his tongue until they parted, allowing him to push deeper.

Harper paused, allowing the kiss to intensify. When they finally released, his eyes were moist. "It's possible, when your dancing partner is a hot little number like you." Harper guided him back into the dance.

"Our first day in business. Pretty cool, huh?" Ian savored the sensation of Harper caressing his butt, dancing him around to the rich, masculine sounds of Ol' Blue Eyes.

"I think this is going to be a wild ride, Harp." Ian snuggled his head on his partner's chest but wasn't allowed to keep it there. Harper reached down, guiding him by the chin until their lips met again.

"Can I drive tonight?" Ian had plans.

"Of course, just don't speed." Harper gave his butt a hefty squeeze.

"I won't. Promise."

Ian was surprised when Harper suddenly broke their embrace. "We have an audience."

He looked over to see the little girl, her face covered in S'more, staring at them from the pathway.

"Just a guess, but could this be Tiffany Two?"

"Bingo." He walked over to the screen and asked, "Tiffany, do your parents know you're here?"

Tiffany turned in her tracks and sped off toward the cabins.

"Do you think I should follow her back?" Harper walked over to the screen to see if he could spot her on the trail.

"Naw, it's still light out." He grabbed his partner's hand, pulling him back into the center of the porch, and whispered, "Hell, maybe Mom and Dad were hiding in the next bush."

"She's probably a lot like I was when I was her age." Harper laughed. "A little on the independent side. Had my rump whacked a few times for it too."

"Speaking of…." Ian took Harper's hands and guided them back to his own rump.

"ALEX, what's wrong? It's so early." Harper sat up as he listened to Alex whisper into the phone.

"The Bergstroms. They're checking out. He wants his cabin fee for last night refunded. One of you guys better get down here quick."

"I'll be right there." Jumping out of bed, he slid into his shorts and T-shirt. "Ian, we have trouble."

"Huh?" Ian rolled over, rubbing his eyes.

"Something's wrong. The Bergstroms, they're checking out and they want a refund."

"What?" Ian bolted up. "Hang on, I'll go with."

Harper waited for Ian to dress. Together they ran down to the office. Rounding the corner, they could see the mother and Tiffany walk out of the office and head down toward the lake.

"Mr. Bergstrom, what seems to be the problem? I thought you were staying with us for three nights," Ian panted, entering the office and scurrying behind the counter to join Alex.

"Just clear the charges for last night from my card and there won't be any problem."

"Why, I don't understand? Was there something wrong with your cabin?" Ian glanced at Alex, who looked as if he was going to cry.

"Look, I don't want to get into it with you people. I just want my money back. You're running some kind of.... I don't know what the hell is going on here, but I'm not going to subject my family to it. Not on your life. So run a refund and we'll be on our way."

Harper's mind raced. Given the little he had to work with, it finally dawned on him what might be going on here. "Does this have anything to do with the visit your daughter paid us last night?" He could tell by the way Bergstrom puffed up his chest that he'd hit on it. Tiffany, his daughter, had probably run home and reported, in detail, who knew what? How long had she been watching their slow dance?

"Look, whatever you perverts do behind closed doors is out of my control. But out in the open, where a seven-year-old girl can see, it's sick. Now the wife and I have to go home and try to somehow get her to forget what she saw. It's filthy and disgusting. You should be ashamed of yourselves."

Ian's jaw was halfway to the floor. "You have got to be kidding me. You're the one who's sick. And you think we're going to give you your money back because you're a bigot? Not on your life!"

"What did you call me, you faggot?" Bergstrom made a move for Ian over the counter.

Harper knew what he had to do. "Alex, run his card and credit him for last night's lodging."

"Not on your life, Alex. This piece of swamp scum isn't getting a nickel of it back." Ian stepped up to the counter, ready for whatever this guy had in mind.

"Ian, please leave. Now!" Harper understood the effect what he'd just said would have on Ian. It would be far less damaging than a physical altercation, or worse, a lawsuit.

"Harper, what the fuck? Grow a few, will ya?" Ian wasn't backing down.

"Ian, I'm going to ask you one more time. Please leave. I'm the office manager. I'll deal with this. We can talk later!" *Please leave, Ian.*

"Fine! Throw your fucking money out the window. I don't care." Ian stomped toward the door, his face flushed with anger. Turning to face Bergstrom, he hissed, "You're goddamn lucky I didn't hop over that counter and beat the shit out of you, you ignorant pig." Banging his fist against the wall, Ian exploded out of the office.

"George, is everything all right?"

Mrs. Bergstrom, with Tiffany at her side, peered into the office through the screen.

"Everything's fine, honey. I'll be out in a minute." Bergstrom waved them away from the door.

"Alex, how are you coming with his refund?" Harper walked behind the desk to observe the process.

"Just waiting for it to finalize. Another minute or so." Seconds seemed like minutes as they waited for the machine to print out a receipt.

"Mr. Bergstrom,"—Harper walked back out into the office—"I know you're upset. On some level, I guess I can understand it. But I have to ask you, what exactly was it your daughter spotted Ian and I doing?"

Bergstrom shifted his stance and stared at the floor.

"The reason I'm asking is that for the life of me, I can't remember Ian or myself doing anything inappropriate, and trust me, I'm well aware of the items you most likely have on your list."

"You were kissing. You were dancing… and groping each other."

"Your daughter knows about groping? Amazing."

"Just give me the goddamn receipt." Noticeably uncomfortable, Bergstrom slapped his hand down on the counter.

"How's the refund coming, Alex?"

"Sorry, the computer is really slow this morning. Shouldn't be much longer."

"The world's a pretty diverse place." Harper leaned back on the counter. "You can run from us today, but if you don't at least make the effort to hit some middle ground, and by that I mean at least accept the fact there are good, upstanding gay people everywhere that deserve your respect, you're going to spend a huge portion of your life miserable and, in the process, make the rest of your family unhappy. I feel sorry for you, Bergstrom. Even more so for your daughter. It's going to be tough for her when she gets out from under your wing."

"Hi, Daddy!"

"Tiffany, go back and join your mother." Bergstrom made a move for the door.

"Here you are, Mr. Bergstrom. The bottom copy shows the refund." Alex slid the receipt and a pen across the counter. "All we need is your signature."

"Daddy, can we walk down to the lake?" Harper waved and smiled. Tiffany giggled and waved back.

"Tiffany, I told you to stay by me. Shame on you." Mom grabbed her by the hand, and she was gone from the screen door.

"I'm sorry you had to cut your stay with us short. Have a safe trip to wherever you're headed." Harper smiled, gesturing to the door.

Bergstrom slid the receipt into his pocket and walked out without saying a word.

"You okay?" Harper walked behind the desk and rubbed Alex's shoulder.

"Yeah. Wow, what a dick."

"I'd be lying if I told you this isn't ever going to happen again. But I'm pretty sure it's not going to happen very often. There's only so much scum on this earth, know what I'm talking about?" Harper chuckled, relieved to hear the Bergstroms' car pull away. "Hey, can you take on another small project for me?"

"Yeah, sure."

"Call the sign company we used in Duluth and have them make something permanent for the path leading up to our house. It should say… it should say 'Private Residence. No Beach Cabin Guests beyond this point. Thank you!'"

"Sure, I'll call them this morning."

"Thanks."

"Ian, is he going to be all right?" Alex looked worried. "He would have kicked that guy's ass, no doubt."

"I'm not sure. This is our first disagreement. Whoa, that date, is that really today's date?" They both looked over to the Rolodex calendar on the far side of the counter.

"Yeah, I changed it first thing this morning." Alex adjusted it to where he thought it should be facing.

"Well, it's either a good sign or a bad one. Today's our anniversary. I'd better head out and try to patch things up with my partner. If you hear lots of slapping and me crying, I'm getting my payback. Not to worry. See you later. If Ian comes around, let him know I'm looking for him, okay?"

"Will do."

He'd try back at the house first. Harper started up the path. *You embarrassed him. You trumped him. Ian's reaction was an honest one. Maybe he was right. Maybe I do have to grow a couple. Damn, why the hell did something like this have to happen?*

"Ian, are you in here?" He waited for a response, although he wasn't really expecting to get one. As Harper searched through the empty house, his heart sank. *Where did he go?* Both cars were still here at least.

"Ian!" he hollered toward the lake. "I'm sorry. Binky is sorry." Nothing. He'd try the road leading up to the highway. *God, he didn't ambush the Bergstroms on their way out, did he?* It was a good twenty-minute hike from the lake up to the turnoff. When the sound of cars passing by told him he was nearing the busy highway, he quickened his pace. Maybe Ian was headed down the side of the road to the palisade overlook. If he hustled, he'd be able to see him up in the distance. There wasn't that much time separating them. Reaching the highway, he was disappointed to find the shoulder empty on both sides.

"Wait!" *The snowmobile path. I bet he's walking it, trying to decide on the best way to thoroughly ream me out.*

About two hundred feet from the highway back down their road, he and Ian had discovered a snowmobile trail. They'd walked it one morning. It was a beautiful, rugged trail that eventually led them down to the edge of the palisade. Very near to where Cabin 10 sat. Taking a deep breath, he entered the trail, soon discovering that if he didn't walk very fast, he'd risk being eaten alive by mosquitoes. *Bastards!* The recent rains had left the trail much soggier than when they'd first explored it. His shoes and socks were soaked. "Ian, are you back here?" *Of course he's not back here. He's not as stupid as you are.*

It was too late to turn back; he'd come too far. He tried running, but the muddy trail soon put a stop to that when he slipped and fell. His ass was now covered with slimy forest yuck. *Great! I deserve this.* Careful not to fall again, he kept the pace as brisk as he could without losing control, slapping away the ferocious little devils whenever he felt a bite.

Forced to wade through a small stream, the result of all the rain coming down from the hills to the lake, he was relieved to finally hear waves. He was close. Up one more gentle incline and around a gully of ferns, he finally reached his first patch of loose rock, the beginning of the palisade.

Hunched over, he fought to catch his breath. The mosquitoes were relentless, following him out into the open. Walking down to the lake, the wind eventually eliminated most of the tiny beasts. Stepping out of his shoes and peeling off his wet socks, he splashed the chilly water onto his skin, temporary relief from all the bites he had sustained. Still no Ian.

With his shoes in one hand and his soggy socks in the other, he walked past Cabin 10. Peering through the screen, he spotted the cabin key on the table. Careful not to track anything onto the carpet, he walked in and grabbed it and, in the process, discovered a piece of paper wedged between the chair and wall beneath the window. He was surprised to find a crayon drawing of two men dancing. Tiffany had captured the moment beautifully in that honest, innocent way only a child was capable of. He smiled, folded it carefully, and stuck it in his pocket. He toured the rest of the cabin to see if any further evidence of the Bergstroms' stay had been left behind. Not finding anything, he closed the door. Alex would be down later to service the cabin. When he reached the motel office, a large truck was parked in the little adjacent lot. He heard Ian's voice and then his unmistakable laugh. *Huh?*

Peering into the office, he discovered an even bigger surprise. Big Earl. The homophobic lug from the Lip Smacker the other morning stood at the counter flanked by two women, one somewhere in the vicinity of Earl's age and one much further on in years.

"Harper, there you are." Ian was all smiles. "Remember Earl?"

"I sure do. How could I forget Earl?" Dropping his shoes and socks on the grass, he opened the screen and stepped barefoot into the office.

"This is Earl's wife, Penny, and his mother… I'm sorry, what was your name again?" Ian leaned forward across the counter.

If you say Tiffany, I'm going to shit my pants.

"I'm Dorothy. Dorothy Snughauser from up near International Falls."

"Well, I'm pleased to meet you all." Harper stood off to the side so as to stay out of everyone's way.

"Earl has some construction going on over at his place, and he thought it might be better if Dorothy spent her nights here with us. Isn't that great?"

"You guys have the nicest place now until you get to Duluth." Compared to the last time he'd had an exchange with Earl, the big guy sounded almost happy.

"Well, thanks for thinking of us, Earl." He hated to admit it, but Earl's arrival couldn't have come at a better time. His "win them over with kindness" campaign had taken quite a beating this morning. "Alex, make sure to give Earl our friendly neighbor rate."

"Will do."

Remembering his wet, muddy ass, Harper backed up toward the screen door. "Don't worry, Earl, we'll take very good care of her for you. Dorothy, you make sure to let us know if you need anything. It's a pleasure having you here as our guest. Ian, I'll be back at the house."

Trying not to look too awkward, Harper backed out the door, picked up his shoes, and headed down the trail toward home.

"Harper, wait up." Ian came out of the office. "Wow, your butt's all muddy. What happened?"

He stopped for Ian to catch up. "I'm sorry for trumping you back there, but you were headed down the wrong path."

"This isn't somebody else's restaurant. This is our investment. Notice how I used the word 'our'? Why should I let some asshole short us what he owes because he's got some morally fucked idea we're filth? He needed his ass kicked good and hard." Ian crossed his arms, jutting his head out to make his point.

"Oh, I agree with you, he's scum." Harper looked down the path, taking a minute to collect his thoughts. "Ian, you have every right to disagree with me. We feel differently about this, and that's fine. Besides thinking ahead to a potential lawsuit if you decked him, I was thinking about our time. If it costs me a few bucks to get that asshole out of our faces, I'm all for it. It's money well spent."

"Dammit." Ian stomped off toward the house.

"Ian, don't walk away. Let's try and get past this. I was trying to avoid a physical confrontation. I was taught to avoid those at all costs."

Ian turned, pointing his finger. "Now I'm mad because you're right. Fuck, you have no idea how much that pisses me off."

Harper laughed. "I didn't mean to embarrass you this morning."

"Nope, now that I've thought about it, I'm glad you did what you did. I'm not used to having my safe, friend-insulated world threatened. Living in the city, I'd forgotten what kind of ugly is still out there. Your way was the right way. Why are you still standing there?" Ian stuck his hands deep into his pockets.

"Hell, I don't know." Harper chuckled and caught up. "Let's stomp this one into the ground and never look back. Hey, pretty cool, huh? Earl coming around?"

"You could have knocked me over with a feather when he drove up. At first I thought, oh man, he's here to get even. But then I saw who he brought along for backup, and I thought…." Ian was laughing his head off. "I thought… goddamn, Earl, you're stupid, but you're not *that* stupid, are you?"

Harper threw his head back and roared, "You never know, do you? Come on, hon. I don't know about you, but I sure could use a warm shower. Oh, I almost forgot." Reaching into his pocket, he pulled out Tiffany's drawing. "Maybe there is hope for her after all?"

"Oh my God, that's amazing. Where did you find it?" Ian took the drawing from him.

"It was on the floor, between a chair and the wall. Mom and Dad must have missed it. Hell, this could have been the cause of it all, come to think of it."

"I'm thinking we frame this. Sound good?" Ian held it out in his arms once more so they both could get a better look.

"Perfect. It's priceless."

Ian linked arms as they walked to the house. "Hey," Ian asked as he followed him up the steps, "seriously, how'd your ass get all muddy?"

"I thought you might be on that old snowmobile path, so I hiked it back from the highway. Had a little sliperoo on the way."

This cracked Ian up. "I'm sorry, but wow, the image of you alone walking on that path is very funny."

"Is it? I was bitten by a million mosquitoes, and I could have malaria for all I know."

"It's not funny, I'm sorry." Ian pushed him through the door.

"Okay, maybe it's a little funny."

When they were naked and standing together in the shower, Ian lathered up his man from head to toe. "God, I never get tired of seeing your black hair wet and matted. It's got to be the sexiest thing in the world."

"Glad I'm at least good for something. I'm kind of thinking it might be fun to crawl back into bed for a few hours." Turning so Ian could see the effect Harper's scrubbing was having on him, he banged his rock-hard cock against his partner's leg. "Binky wants to play hide and seek."

"I think we should do whatever Binky wants." Ian shut off the water and stepped out of the shower. "Come here, my handsome prince. Let's get you dried off."

He stepped out of the shower into a warm towel. After they'd dried each other, they moved into the bedroom. Harper guided Ian onto his stomach and crawled on top of him. "Do you want to try my…." He started to giggle. "I can't think of anyone right now."

"I want my usual, the Harper Callahan with extra sauce."

"You got it. Hey, I almost forgot."

"Forgot what?" Ian looked back.

Harper rolled over onto his side and took Ian into his arms. "Happy Anniversary! It's been one year since a very handsome man dressed in a Hornets baseball uniform stopped by to give me a quote on my backyard and walked away with my heart."

CHAPTER
Twelve

"You want two cabins next to each other?" Alex used the keyboard to toggle to another view on the reservation system. "The earliest opening we have is the last weekend in July. Wait, I have a few nights at the end of this month, but it's the middle of the week. A Wednesday and Thursday, June 23 & 24. Right. For the entire week we're back to the end of July. Okay, can I get your full name as it appears on the card, please?" He waved to Ian.

"Holy shit! Who's that from?" Ian flew into the office. On the edge of the front desk was a gargantuan floral arrangement.

Alex held up his finger, indicating he'd be a minute. "Your card number, please? Let me repeat that back to you."

The morning was out of control. This was the fourth reservation he'd taken, and it wasn't even nine yet. Was it all because of the article? An earlier caller had mentioned a glowing review in the travel section of a Twin Cities magazine. The caller had offered to send it to him via e-mail. He'd tell Ian about it when he got off the phone.

"Okay, well, that's all I need. We'll look for you on the twenty-seventh. If you have any questions, give us a call. Thanks again for choosing the Palisade Beach Cabins."

"You sound great on the phone, Alex. Keep up the good work. This, this is one of the most incredible arrangements I've ever seen. Oh wait, I missed the card."

"It's from Andy and Emmett. Someone woke me up this morning with it." Alex stapled a receipt to a piece of paper from the printer. "They're friends of Andy's who are headed up the shore for a few days. It's so cool. The guy told me Emmett made it. He's been selling them at the garden center."

"Who were they? Did they say?"

"Yeah, but I forgot. Sorry, it's been crazy here."

"Dear Ian, Harper, and Alex," Ian read aloud. "Sorry Em and I can't be there with you knuckleheads on this very important weekend. We wish you the greatest success, and as soon as the season slows down, we'll be back up to see you. All our love, Em and Andy." Ian replaced the card in the arrangement. "Looks like Emmett has a real talent for arranging. Wow!"

"Ian, come here and look at this. It's an article on the cabins. A lady told me about it this morning when I made her reservation. She e-mailed it to us. Take a look at the guy in the picture."

Ian walked behind the desk and looked over Alex's shoulder. "It's the older guy we put in Cabin 4, the week we soft opened. He's a travel writer." Alex moved over to the side so Ian could see the entire article.

"It *is* that guy. Did you read what he wrote?"

"Not all of it. I've been on the phone nonstop."

> *You can imagine my surprise when I turned off the busy highway and drove toward the lake. Nestled right up against the dramatic backdrop of the palisade on the North Shore of Lake Superior, you'll find the Palisade Beach Cabins. Nothing too out of the ordinary here, the cabins are updated, comfortable, and spotless. What's so wonderfully magical about this place is the gardens, speckled in and amongst the towering pines and birch. Co-owner Ian Burke, of Burke Landscaping, is the culprit. He and his partner, Harper Callahan (yes, he's that attorney), have restored these little gems that date back to the 50s in marvelous fashion. If you're looking to get out of the city this summer, I strongly encourage you to check this place out. Burke, Callahan, and their friendly staff will ensure your visit is perfect in every way. PS: Make sure you ask for the complimentary s'more kits. A sweet treat to compliment a sweet stay.*

Ian stepped away from the computer. "Who knew? That's awesome! What's his name... Leonard Milling. Leonard is our new best friend. I can't wait to tell Harper. Where is he, by the way?"

"He stopped in earlier for a second, but I was on the—" Alex smiled over at the ringing phone. "Palisade Beach Cabins, can I help you? Oh hi, Audrey. Hmm, not sure. Ian's right here, let me ask him. Now that the rain is out of the forecast, Audrey wants to know if we still want Bud to drop off the tent."

"Tell her yes, if it's not too much trouble. I'm sure we'll find a use for it somewhere." Ian was back to admiring Em's floral work.

"He said yes, if it's not too much trouble. Okay, yep. Yep, sure. Thanks, Audrey. We'll see you then. Bye." Alex made a note on the legal pad he had parked by the phone. "She's having Bud drop the tent by now, and she said she'd be over tomorrow about eleven with the pies."

"That's so nice of her. Hey, Harper told me all the cabins are rented through the weekend. That's pretty cool. Oh man, I never thought of this, but Saturday is going to be a madhouse around here. Are you ready?"

"We have a few parties coming in tonight, so that should help spread it out. But yeah, most of the cabins are rented Saturday through Monday. You know Brent, Harper's assistant, right? Harper has him in Cabin 3 beginning tomorrow."

"Oh great, it will be nice to have him around."

"Can you cover for me a minute? I have to pee."

"Go pee. I have to get back to my own projects. Alex, plan on being up at the house for dinner tonight. We'll put the sign out on the desk. Harper and I want to have a little kickoff meeting before the weekend gets nuts. Spencer and Allison will be here."

"THE arrangement, can we talk about how spectacular that is? I loved how Emmett used herbs and actual plants instead of flowers. The best part, it fits exactly with the setting up here." Allison expertly twisted a wad of pasta around her fork.

"He's such a little sweetheart," Harper added. "He and Andy make a great pair."

"I'm kind of freaked, to be honest with you." Ian stabbed a leaf of lettuce. "I've never seen Andy fall this hard. The man's out of control."

"They're soul mates, like a few others I know." Allison helped herself to seconds. "Harper, this pasta is wunderbar."

"Thanks. I was watching the cooking channel the other night, and they tried something like this. It's super easy. I think I'll have a little more too."

Spencer took the bowl of shrimp linguini from his wife and passed it across the table. "Last week when I stopped by Jungle Gems to see Andy, Emmett had a few arrangements on display. Both were really different, and talk about sticker shock, they were priced over a hundred bucks each. I grabbed Andy and asked what was up with that. He told me they were priced low compared to what some of the florists charged for pieces half as nice. He said he could probably double the price and they'd still go out the door."

"Amazing. Anyone for more bread?" Ian held up the basket after taking a piece for himself.

"Me." Alex took the basket off Ian's hands.

"Have you guys met Alex, the bottomless pit?" Harper socked his young friend in the arm. "You should've seen the size of the steak this dude inhaled. Seriously, it was impressive."

Alex blushed, shaking his head innocently.

"Before we get too relaxed, let's talk about tomorrow. Hang on." Harper got up from the table for a minute, returning with his clipboard.

"Ah, the clipboard." Ian snickered. "I'm going to talk to Dr. Monroe about having it surgically removed."

"I'm choosing to ignore that. Okay, so here's how tomorrow is staffed. Alex and I will be taking turns in the office. When we're not there, we'll be helping with the food and stuff."

"Oh, that sucks. I'll sit in the office if you guys want to be outside." Allison looked over to Alex and frowned. "It's supposed to be so nice tomorrow."

"Nope. It's fine. I have you and Spencer greeting people in front of the office. We plan to have sodas and bottled water you can hand out. The food will be available down toward the lake. The barbecue outfit will be here early in the morning to start cooking and setting up."

"It's going to be yummy. Pulled pork and beef brisket sandwiches." Ian reached for the wine. "Audrey's bringing over a slew of her pies. Oh, that's one thing we have to make sure to do. The world needs to know the pies come from the Lip Smacker. Even if people don't ask, tell them that. There'll be little Smacker menus on the food table. Try to hand those out too whenever you get a chance. Sorry, that wasn't on the clipboard, was it?" Ian looked over with a bucketload of sass.

"No, it certainly wasn't. But it was an appropriate addition, and the table thanks you for your contribution." Harper took a minute to write down Ian's point.

"Geesh!" Allison grabbed the wine from in front of Ian and filled her glass. "Wake me when this is over."

"Ian and I are in charge of breakfast tomorrow morning. Alex, you're invited to help if you feel yourself so inclined."

"Got it." Alex laughed at Harper.

"Wait, how come Ian doesn't have a special task?" Spencer, who up to then had been quietly annoying his wife with pokes and inappropriate hand gestures, sat up in his chair. "Sounds like after breakfast, he's free to fuck off."

"I'll be at the casino. Smoking and spending money we don't have. I'll check back with you guys on Sunday to see how it all went. We need more wine." Ian got up and left the table.

"See? What did I tell ya?" Spencer crossed his arms and rolled his eyes.

"Ian will be giving garden tours. Why, you might ask?" Harper paused until his partner had returned to the table.

"Yeah, why is that?" Ian filled Spencer's glass before sitting back down.

"It's simple. You're the only one here that knows what any of that shit is."

"Oh, okay."

"So there you have it. Does anyone have any questions?" Harper looked around for a response. "Very well then, meeting adjourned."

"Wait," Ian protested. "You forgot the most important thing of all."

"He's right, I did. Damn it. Does everyone have a full glass? Alex, how's the Dew? You in good shape?"

"I'm good, thanks."

"Okay, firstly, I'd like to thank our dear friends, Allison and Spencer, and even though they aren't here right now, Andy and Emmett, for everything you've done to make tomorrow a reality. You're better friends than I deserve, I know that. Ian?" Harper paused and sipped his wine.

"They're lucky to have me."

"There you have it. Thank you, Ian, for your heartfelt sincerity. Anyway, from the bottom of our hearts, please know how much we love and appreciate you in our lives. Okay, next up, lady and gentlemen, friends and country folk... and Ian, I'd like to introduce Burke Callahan's first full-time employee. We are very pleased to announce to you that Mr. Alex Stevens has accepted the full-time position of office manager, which includes benefits and a substantial retirement package, I might add. Please give him a warm round of applause."

"Harper, you blew it again." Ian stood and raised his glass.

"What'd I blow?"

"At least he didn't say *who'd* I blow," Spencer added smugly.

"He didn't have to, honey, because he knew you'd say it for him. Go on, Ian." Allison waved her hand for Ian to continue.

"Alex, as the newest employee of Burke Callahan, is there anything you'd like to say?"

All eyes were on Alex. Harper sat poised for a rescue. This was a pretty intimidating group to have been thrust into. After all, who would know better than himself? Harper watched carefully for any cracks in Alex's surface. Alex was visibly surprised to have the evening's focus turned in his direction, but he was doing admirably.

"Wow! I suppose I should say something." Alex began to fidget.

"Or not," Spencer added. He'd also begun to fidget.

Harper couldn't stand watching him suffer. "Alex, sorry to put you on the spot like this. But we love ya, dude, and want you to hang around here for a long time. Whattaya say?"

"How many vacation days do I get?"

Harper tried to look appalled while everyone else at the table exploded in laughter. "See? He's a perfect match!"

ARMED with a can of Dew, Alex headed back up the trail to the main house. He'd thought about smoking some of the weed Colin had left him but decided he didn't need it. He was on a natural high tonight, and he wanted to be fresh for tomorrow. Before reaching the house, he exited onto a side trail leading down to the lake. The almost full moon was bright enough to help lead the way. When he'd almost reached his destination, a pair of Adirondack chairs Ian and Harper had placed in a spot giving themselves a prime view of the lake and the palisade, he stopped. Voices from the house weaved their way through the trees and shrubs. "Anyone here?" he asked. Only the waves crashing up onto the rocks answered back. *Ah great! I've got the place to myself.* He continued a few more feet until he came upon a clearing. Brushing off one of the chairs, he sat.

The reflection of the moon, positioned directly behind him, shimmered on the water. It was the only source of light visible from where he sat, and it took several minutes for his vision to acclimate to his surroundings. A cool, gentle breeze blew off the lake, rustling the early spring leaves on the bushes and trees. He was glad he'd put on a coat.

Never in a million years would he have guessed he'd be working for two gay dudes right here, where he grew up. *Amazing.* It had changed him. Plans to head west had mysteriously disappeared. *Where did they go? It was all I thought about for so long.* Those dreams seemed so distant. They had been replaced with new friendships, a reservation system, office duties, and a million other new distractions.

Sipping his soda, he looked up to the sky. A bank of clouds moved like a starship above him. The sound of a boat motor brought his focus back to the lake. It took him a few seconds to locate the source of the dim buzzing, and then he had it. A tiny white light skipped across the water toward Duluth. *I wonder where they're coming from?* Someday, if things worked out like he'd planned, that would be him. He'd be on the boat with a bunch of his friends coming back from one of the Apostle Islands where they'd spent the day relaxing and soaking in the warm summer sun. Yep, and with the way things were going here, that dream didn't seem too far off. He was a good saver.

Tilting his head back to enjoy some star watching, he was surprised to see the beginnings of Northern Lights. The bank of clouds he'd noticed earlier had moved out onto the water. In its place he watched eerie, supernatural pools of fluorescent green light pulsate in columns toward the water. The light twisted and danced, intensifying with each passing minute.

Alex thought for a second about running up to the house and informing the others so they could enjoy them too, but a burst of laughter from the house changed his mind. They were having a great time, and there would be plenty of opportunities in the future. The exotic light show made frequent visits to the North Shore. Most often they appeared, like tonight, in shades of green. Rarer were the instances when the display included brilliant reds, blues, and purples. *I'll definitely go get the others if I see some other colors.*

Downing the last of his soda, he brought his feet up onto the edge of the chair and hugged his knees. What was the summer going to be like? he wondered. Would he tire of it? *Probably not.* It will be fun to meet all the people who spend time here. He laughed out loud at the thought of a handsome dude, maybe someone like Mike, staying in the cabins. It would be fun to flirt, knowing that at least here, he could be himself. Nobody would hassle him for being gay, and if they did, they'd sure as hell wish they hadn't if he made it known to Ian or Harper.

A huge yawn caught him by surprise. It was hard to say goodnight to the sky, but it had been a full day. Picking up his empty can, he got up and started for home. As he neared the house, he could hear Allison shriek. Alex giggled. Everyone was so cool.

Reaching the end of the path, he spotted a figure open the office door and walk in. There hadn't been much time to catch a glimpse, but he was pretty sure it was a man. Brent? A few couples had checked in. Maybe someone needed ice. That reminded him to talk to the guys about putting a small freezer somewhere where guests could grab ice whenever they needed it. For now, he had to go back into his apartment and grab a bag for them. No big deal.

When he reached the office, he threw his soda can in the trash bin located on the side of the building. Stepping through the door, he was stopped in his tracks.

"Alex."

"What are you doing here?" Alex wasn't sure what to do. This was the first time he'd seen his dad since the bastard had stolen his savings.

"I wanted to come by earlier, but I thought I'd better go to my meeting. Getting off the juice isn't as easy as I thought it would be. I've had a few setbacks, but for the most part, I'm stayin' off it pretty good."

Alex waited until his dad had moved away from the desk to make his move. He made a beeline to behind it before he lost the opportunity. He'd always envisioned going off on the old man if they crossed paths. With the opportunity staring him in the face, he was surprised not to feel anger. On some level, the guy still scared him. He couldn't be trusted, and that made Alex feel uncomfortable. Standing behind the desk felt safer.

"You look good, boy. I ran into that dishwasher you worked with at the Lip Smacker, and he told me you were working here. I can't remember his name."

"Louie." *That dumbass.*

"Yeah, Louie, that's right. Anyway, he didn't know what you did. Just that you worked here. What do you do here, anyway? You mind if I take a load off?" His old man pointed to the chair.

"I'm supposed to shut down the office in a few minutes," Alex lied.

"Well, I don't want to get you into trouble."

"There's no money here. It's in the bank," Alex lied again.

"Hey, that was the booze that made me do that. As soon as I get back to work, I'm going to pay you back. I promise." His dad took a step forward.

"I don't want your money. You should leave." Alex pretended he had work to do, shifting through some papers.

"You know, your mom and I stayed here one time. Jesus, I haven't thought about that for years."

Alex stared down at the desk. He didn't want to hear this. He didn't want this asshole talking about his mother. To his horror, his dad stepped up to the desk and leaned in.

"It was our anniversary. We'd been up to the Temperance River for the day. Had a picnic up there. Your mom was so pretty. I remember she had on this red and white checked dress. Her hair, it was all done up so nice. I was really proud. Anyway, instead of going home, we stopped here. Doesn't look the same though. I remember this being a store too. Ah hell, I don't know what I remember anymore. Mind's about gone."

Growing impatient and unwilling to listen to any more of these awful memories, Alex found his voice. "If you don't need money, I'm not sure why you came here. I want you to leave. I never want you to come by here again. Never."

His dad stepped away from the desk. "Look, boy, you have every right to be angry with me. To hate me a little. But I'm working my way back. I'm going to make it up to you, I promise."

"It's too late for that. I don't want you in my life. I don't love you. You should leave." Alex folded his arms across his chest.

"I'd like a second chance, if you could see clear to give it to me." His dad walked to the door.

Alex thought of a million things he could say but chose none of them. Even sober, the figure standing by the door was a pitiful excuse for a man. He could spend a lifetime trying to make up for being a bad dad, but it wouldn't be enough. It wouldn't even come close. Looking at him was like looking at an alien. "Leave or I'll call the police."

He watched as his dad looked over at him, as if taking in one last look. Then he turned, shook his head, and walked out.

His heart was pounding in his chest. Looking down, he wiped his sweaty hands on his jeans. His body remained tense until he heard the sound of a car starting. Coming around the side of the desk, Alex watched through the small office window until the car carrying his father was lost behind the trees.

SATURDAY, the first morning of the long Memorial Day weekend, was picture perfect. Spencer and Allison were up and moving around as soon as he and Harper hit the kitchen. Together they sipped coffee and speculated on how the day would unfold. Ian hated to admit it, but he was nervous. He wasn't sure why he felt the way he did. Maybe it was the uncertainty, having never co-hosted the opening of a resort before. *You think? I wonder how Harper feels this morning.*

Alex joined them for breakfast, and after a quick review of everyone's tasks, they dispersed to their assigned areas. Though planted, the gardens weren't too showy. It was still early in the season. It would take several weeks of warm weather before the annuals would kick into high gear. Still, the designs were clever, and the hostas and ferns gave off a feeling of tranquility. Exactly what he hoped their guests would find appealing.

It was before nine, and already he detected a tantalizing aroma emanating from the grills. The caterers had arrived to start cooking before they'd finished breakfast. By eleven, Audrey had stopped by and unloaded a dozen of her delectable pies. Confident all was going as planned, Ian headed for the office.

"Hey, let's get this party started," Ian shouted as he blasted into the office. Harper and Alex were giving the office a once-over with Windex and paper towels. "I'm going crazy waiting around."

"Ian, don't run away." Alex was sporting a megawatt smile. "I have something for you and Harper. Be right back."

They exchanged glances while Alex left the office to go back into his apartment. He returned carrying a large flat object wrapped in brown grocery bag paper.

"Sorry about the crappy wrapping paper, it's all I had. This is for you guys."

"What's this all about?" Harper came around to the front of the counter to stand next to his partner.

"Alex, what did you go and do?" *It's a picture of some kind. Oh man, I hope this isn't bad.* Ian gestured for Harper to take the lead. "Go ahead, hon, open it up."

"Okay...."

Ian sensed Harper had the same worry. *What if it sucks?* The chances were high. Not because Alex had bad taste... well yeah, that was most of it.

"You guys have been so cool. My life sucked the big one until you came around." Alex giggled, catching the naughty innuendo in his comment.

Ian and Harper giggled too. Nerves were on high alert for this one.

"Anyway, it's not much." Alex couldn't stand still. "Go ahead, open it."

Harper carefully peeled off the paper, uncovering the back of a picture of some kind. There was a strand of wire making it ready for hanging.

"I was right, it's a picture. Ready?" Harper looked over and winked.

"Yes, I'm dying to see it." *Oh please don't let this suck.*

Harper turned the picture around, holding it in his hands. "Wow!"

"Wow is right. It's gorgeous." Ian took it out of Harper's hands. "If I'm not mistaken, the artist had to be standing almost directly in front of Cabin 10 when they painted this." The painting had an edgy quality to it. It captured for Ian one of those moody days in the middle of winter when the sky is steely gray and the water almost black, on the verge of freezing. The palisade was majestic and cold, adorned with long, cascading streams of frozen ice tinted naturally by the minerals it had encountered on its journey to the lake. "This is a fabulous watercolor, Alex. It must have cost you a fortune. I love it."

"I love it too. It's fantastic." Harper took the painting back and placed it on the counter so they both could have a better look. "I feel bad you spent money on us. But not too bad, because I really like this a lot. It's something I would buy if I saw it hanging in a gallery. I really mean it."

"Is the artist local?" *This had to cost him a few dollars. Bless his heart.* "Maybe we can acquire more of their work to hang in the office. You know, to start a little gallery of our own."

"Alex... your face, it's so damn red." Harper chuckled. "Ian, check it out."

Alex's face was lipstick red. "Dude, you embarrassed or something? Relax, this is an awesome gift."

"I'm the artist. I painted it early this spring."

"Shut the fuck up!" Harper appeared dumbfounded.

"Yeah, shut the fuck up." Ian looked over to Alex to see if he was kidding.

"You guys shut the fuck up. I didn't have a computer all winter. You can only watch so much television. My art teacher in school taught watercolor. I got into it. He said I should pursue art."

Their reaction to his picture was obviously what Alex had hoped for. He was proud, there was no mistake about it, and most likely relieved his painting had been so well received. His face toned down quickly about the same time he'd regained the ability to stay in one spot for longer than a second.

"You have a hammer and a nail around here, Alex?"

"Yeah, hang on."

"He's fantastic," Harper mouthed when the artist had left the office.

"Where do you think it should go?" Alex asked, returning with hammer in hand.

"No-brainer." Ian looked over to Harper.

"Yep. How about behind the desk? It will be the first thing our guests will see when they walk in. What a great way to greet them." A car door slammed.

"Speaking of...."

"Is this where we check in?" A woman peered through the screen and then opened the door and stepped into the office, her frizzy brown-gray hair pulled casually back into a ponytail. She wore khaki pleated shorts, a "Marriage Equality Now—Damn it!" T-shirt, and hiking boots appropriate for hiking in the Himalayas. A shorter, rounder, softer woman dressed almost identically followed her in.

"Is Alex here?" the first woman asked.

"I'm Alex. Welcome to the Palisade Beach Cabins."

A FEW minor computer glitches during the busy late-morning, early-afternoon check-in rush was the only thing so far that hadn't gone as planned. Harper looked on with confidence as Alex, undaunted by the intimidating owner's manual, identified the problem, and the two guest parties affected were only momentarily inconvenienced.

By midafternoon, the celebration was in full swing. Curious locals, the majority of those attending, swarmed the property. Everyone seemed surprised by the transformation. In many cases, it had been years since some of them had been down to the cabins. A few had never set foot on the property.

When Colin showed up unexpectedly, Harper manned the office for an hour so Alex could spend some time with his friend. After Alex returned, Harper walked the grounds, schmoozing and introducing himself. One of the first people he ran into was their realtor, Tiffany.

"Hey, Harper. Wow, is all I can say. You and Ian have really turned this place into a paradise. Nice work."

"Oh thanks, Tiffany. It's nice to see you."

"It almost looks like a theme park. Hey, I'd like to introduce you to a few of my friends. They're in the travel biz, so I thought it might be good for them to see what you've got going on here."

Tiffany introduced her gal pals. Harper made sure they had found the tap beer before moving on. The next surprise was running into the previous owner of the cabins, Floyd Hutchins. Decked out in jeans and his signature rainbow suspenders, he came down for a peek with his daughter, Judy.

"Rosie's up there proud as can be. I can tell you that. She had the gardening touch too. Used to keep a vegetable plot right outside the office. I don't know how many tomatoes she sent home with people over the years. Looks like you guys have her green thumb too!" Floyd was having a good day.

Harper wanted to show Floyd the new house but decided against it. The last thing he wanted to do was take away anything from Floyd's beloved Rosie. When the Dixieland combo from the college started up, Harper made sure Floyd and his daughter, with plates of Audrey's delicious cherry pie in hand, had a front row seat.

"If Rosie were here now, she'd be out there dancing. I can tell you that much."

"Enjoy the day, Floyd. Nice meeting you, Judy."

Grabbing a pulled pork sandwich from the food tent, he turned to see Audrey and her husband, Bud, coming down the incline.

"There she is! Bud, right? I'm Harper Callahan. You're one lucky man, I've got to tell you that. Ian and I love this woman." After shaking Bud's hand, Harper took Audrey into his arms and gave her a huge hug.

"Well, the feeling's mutual. I was telling Bud on the way over how lucky we are that you and Ian moved into the area. Darn it if we didn't need some new blood around here."

"Audrey, you outdid yourself. The pies are wonderful, and as you can see, disappearing at a good clip. Can I grab you a beer or anything?" Harper pointed toward the beer tent.

"You run along. We can take care of ourselves. I'm going to want to see that house you had moved in before we go, though. Alex tells me it's really something."

"If I don't get to you first, make sure to grab me. I'll give you the full tour. But Ian and I are hoping you'll come by one night soon for dinner. We really owe you our thanks."

"Did you hear that, Bud? Somebody's actually going to cook *me* a dinner for a change. Let us know, Harper. We'll be there... a day early!"

He walked down the path toward the cabins. Ian's garden tour was parked outside Cabin 4, where he'd put in a kidney-shaped shade garden. Brent was amongst the group of mainly women, admiring Ian's garden skills.

"Actually, you don't want to get rid of worms in your garden," he heard Ian explain when he'd gotten close enough. "They have a special job. They crawl throughout the soil and loosen it so the plant's roots can grow and spread out easier. Hi, Harper."

"Hey, everyone! Brentster! Come here and give me a hug, buddy."

"Hey, Harper. Wow, this is really amazing. I'm so impressed."

"Oh, thanks. You look great. So glad you could come up this weekend. Everything going okay?" Harper and Brent held back while the tour moved over to a patch of perennial hibiscus.

"Yeah. It's different not working with you, but all in all, it could be worse, I guess."

"I have to be honest. You're the only thing I miss about not being there. Have you been up to see the house yet?"

"No, I'm dying to see it."

"Great! You hungry? There's some tasty barbecue on the way over. Come on."

Spencer intercepted them on the way to the house. "Hey, looks like the Coast Guard heard about the free BBQ. Have you guys noticed them? They've got their boats below the palisade."

"Let's give Brent a chance to grab a sandwich, and then we can walk down and take a look."

"Cool. I'm going for another piece of pie. Don't tell Allison."

"Where is she, by the way? I haven't seen her all afternoon." He looked into the crowd assembled down by the band.

"She's been hanging around the office. Alex is getting a pretty good workout up there. He's doing a terrific job." Spencer trotted off in search of more pie.

"Who's Alex?" Brent asked, returning with a heaping plate of brisket and some potato salad.

"He's a local guy we hired. Technically he's our office manager. But like Ian and I, he's on toilet scrubbing and bed changing detail until we can afford to take on another employee. Great kid. I'll introduce you later."

Harper led them down the cabin pathway toward the palisade. They stopped for a minute to plug back into Ian's tour.

"I've never heard that the number of blue jays in your yard is a sign that rain is on the way. Interesting." Ian fake smiled as they walked past.

"Poor dude. This has got to be hell for him." Harper chuckled.

"Trust me, he deserves it." Spencer gave Ian the thumbs-up as they passed the group.

Nearing the end of the cabins, they could clearly see the Coast Guard. Two boats were hovering in the area, and an inflatable was pulled up onto the rocks.

"You think this is an exercise?" Brent carefully stepped over the large rocks for a better look.

"Not sure. I suppose it could be. I've never seen them near our shore before." Harper followed Brent, eager to solve the mystery.

"Hey, guys, I don't think this is a drill. Check it out." Spencer pointed into the distance to a police boat with its light flashing, speeding toward the flotilla.

The police arrived in an inflatable similar to the Coast Guard's. Two officers jumped off and pulled the boat up onto the rocks. When they left the boat, they were immediately hidden by large rocks at the bottom of the palisade.

"Maybe they found something. God, I hope it's not a person. Someone could have drowned and washed up on shore there. That's kind of freaky." Spencer looked over their shoulders. "What were you telling us last night, Harp? A person can only survive for about forty-five minutes in the water before they die from hypothermia? Crazy!"

"Yeah, the lake is still pretty damn cold this time of year. And I guess in the big part, it doesn't warm up that much all summer."

"Hey, look." Brent pointed toward the action. "They've come back. I think something's up for sure."

"I bet somebody fell off a boat." Harper took a tentative step forward. "Look, they're going back with cameras. That can't be good."

"Nope. I'd say we have a problem. A dead body problem. Sorry." Spencer took a step back, realizing on his own he was breathing heavily on Brent's neck.

"There're some *really* big waves out there. A few weeks ago, Ian and I took beers down here, and you wouldn't believe the monsters that were crashing up against the rocks. You couldn't stand where we are now. You'd be drenched."

"Supposedly, Lake Superior is the largest lake in the world." Brent looked down to make sure the rock he was standing on was secure.

"Oh God...."

Two of the Coast Guard guys came up from behind the rock carrying a body bag. One of the policemen hopped back in the boat to help lift it on board.

"That's creepy. Really creepy." Brent turned but couldn't go anywhere because Spencer was in his way.

"Yeah, I'm with you, Brent." Harper motioned for Spencer to turn around. "I've seen enough. I'm sure there'll be talking at the Smacker tomorrow morning. Somebody will know the whole story."

Back on the grass, they watched the boats speed off.

"I'm thinking beer. How about you guys?" Spencer was off.

"Oh yeah. Let's go." Harper gave Brent a playful punch on the shoulder. "You guys go on, I'll meet you there in a minute. I need to check in with Alex. Wait! Brent, come on along and meet Alex."

"Fine, be that way." Spencer trudged toward the beer tent.

"Hey, guys." Alex smiled from behind the desk. Colin stood close by. "How's the party? A bunch of people have stopped in to say thanks. Sounds like it's going great."

"Yeah, everyone seems to be having a good time. Alex, I'd like you to meet Brent. We worked together at the firm."

"Oh hey, nice to meet you." Alex reached over and offered his hand.

"Hey, Alex. Good to meet you too." Brent shook hands.

"Alex, when's the last time you had a breather from all of this? Why don't you take a break. I'll hold down the fort." Harper walked around to the other side of the counter.

"It's not that bad. Are you sure?" Alex was being professional, but Harper could tell his young employee was eager to get out and inspect the festivities.

"Yeah, go enjoy yourself for a while. You've earned it. Just don't leave me here all night."

"Thanks, Harper. I'll be back in a few. Brent, have you eaten? There's a ton of food down by the lake." Alex held the door open for Brent and Colin.

"Thanks, I had some brisket." Alex and Brent's conversation trailed off. *I have to pee.* Harper walked back to the bathroom. *Damn, the kid even makes his bed. I need Ian to hang around him more.* When Harper returned to the counter, Allison was sitting at the table. "Hey, stranger. Everyone having a good time?"

"Oh Harper, it's lovely. I've met some of the nicest people in the world. Here." Allison held up a glass of beer. "Spencer thought you might be ready for this."

"Oh yeah, perfect."

"You know, it was kind of cute. I had several people make it a point to tell me that they were happy you and Ian were running the place. You know, the subtext was they were okay with a couple horny gay guys movin' into town."

"Really? That's good to hear. Did they really say the horny thing?"

"Yeah. And then they'd giggle afterward and touch their 'special' place. God, you're such a dork."

"Did you meet Floyd? The guy who used to own the place? What a character."

"The dude with the rainbow suspenders dating the younger plain girl?"

"That's his daughter." Harper laughed.

"Yep."

"He really misses his wife…." Harper was interrupted by a police officer who walked past the window. "Did a cop just walk by?"

Before Allison had a chance to answer, the screen door opened and a cop entered the office.

"Hello, can I help you?" Harper and Allison stood at the same time.

"I'm Officer Doogan from Two Harbors. Does Alex Stevens work here? Is he around?"

"He was just here a minute ago. Is there a problem? I'm Harper Callahan, one of the owners."

"If he's still around, would you mind bringing him back here? He's not in any trouble. I have some information for him." The radio on Doogan's belt kicked in, but he ignored it.

Allison headed for the door. "I'll get him."

Harper spent a few uncomfortable minutes bringing the officer up to date on the grand opening before Alex, with Colin and Allison in tow, strolled into the office.

"Which one of you is Alex Stevens?" The officer assumed a softer tone.

"I'm Alex. Is there something wrong?"

"Do you all mind if I have a word with Alex in private?"

"Oh, not at all." Harper led the group out.

"What's that all about? You know anything, Colin?" Harper hoped that if there was some kind of problem and Colin knew about it, he'd have the good sense to tell Harper.

"I don't have a clue. I've seen the officer around town. He's fairly new." Colin shuffled his feet and jabbed his hands into his pockets. Harper knew he was worried.

After a few minutes, the officer stepped out of the office. "Very nice place you have here. Good luck."

"You guys wait out here for a minute." Stepping into the empty office, Harper called out, "Alex, is everything okay?"

A second later Alex emerged from the apartment holding a Dew. Harper tried to read the young man, but if what Alex had just been told was anything serious, he had chosen to act as if it were nothing. No matter what, his attitude was too nonchalant, a strange display of overcompensation, Harper thought.

"My dad decided to take a leap off of the palisade. Crazy fucker." Alex sipped his soda and stared at the computer screen.

"Oh my God, I'm so sorry." Harper couldn't believe what he'd just heard. "When did it happen?"

"This morning, they think. A fishing boat spotted his body and reported it to the Coast Guard. What a stupid fuck."

Allison tapped the screen. "Is everything okay?"

Harper motioned for her to come in. "His father fell from the palisade."

"Oh God!" She and Colin stood with their mouths open.

"He didn't fall, he fucking jumped." Alex glared at them from behind the desk. "He didn't fall."

"I was just telling them…."

"He fucking knew today was important to me," Alex snapped back, his face scrunched up with emotion. "It was the only thing, the last thing he could do to screw me over. What a prick! I'm so glad he's dead. I hate him."

"We're all so sorry, Alex." Allison turned to go behind the desk but was stopped in her tracks.

"Don't look at me like that! Do not look at me like that," Alex screamed and then checked himself. "I'm fine. I'm happy. Relieved, okay? I'm… I'm sure that's hard for you guys to understand…. I don't want him to ruin another minute of my life. It's not fair. It's not…."

Alex shook. Tears rolled down his cheeks. He attempted to speak, but when he realized he was too far gone, he turned and fled into his apartment.

Harper, reaching for Colin's arm to hold him back, moved around Allison and headed after Alex. "Guys, I've got this."

Walking around the desk, Harper peered into the apartment. "Alex, I'm coming in." Crossing through the living room into the kitchen, Harper could hear Alex sobbing in the bedroom. Sitting at the edge of the bed, he was hunched over, his head in his hands. Harper sat next to him. *God almighty, will this kid ever get a fucking break?*

"He was here...," Alex cried out before huge, powerful sobs robbed him of words.

Harper took him into his arms and held him tight to his chest. Alex wailed. Harper stroked his head, hoping to calm him. Several minutes passed. Years of frustration and hurt poured out of the young man. "Let it go, Alex. Let it go."

Harper rocked him in his arms as he cried. Eventually, Alex got to the point where he'd cried himself out. Harper continued to rock him.

"I didn't want to tell anyone." Alex sat up and reached for his pillow, wiping his face on it. "My dad came here last night. He wanted to make up...." Alex struggled to manage his emotions. "I told him to leave. I told him I didn't love him and he should never come back here."

Harper's heart ached. Somehow he needed to let Alex know he wasn't to blame for his father's death. "I would have said the same thing to him, Alex." Harper allowed his comment to float around for a few moments before he continued. "He might have been your father by blood, but we both know he wasn't that to you. He was a very troubled man. There's a very real possibility that even if you had accepted him back, well, it's entirely possible the outcome would have been the same."

Alex stared ahead at the wall. He was spent, unable to sort through the emotions and images that were most likely flooding his mind. Harper thought for a minute and then had it. He wanted Alex to hear one last thing before he left him. "I have a feeling you may already know this, but if you don't, now's a really good time, I think, for you to hear what I have to say."

Harper stood and walked to the door of the bedroom. "If Ian's taught me one thing in the short time we've been together, it's the importance of friendship. Those of us who don't have close, conventional family situations, you know, like you and I, well, we always have our friends. Ian and I, Colin, Audrey, we're your family too. You're family to us. Please don't forget that, okay?"

Alex wiped his face and nodded. "I won't."

"Promise you'll come to me if you're ever hurting or you need to work something out. I'll never be too busy for that, understand? I'll be there for you. Ian too, I know he would want me to tell you that."

"Thanks. I love you." Alex stood up and then sat back down. "I don't know what I'm doing." He shook his head and chuckled.

"We've got you covered. Stay here for a while and put yourself back together. When it feels right, jump back in. Okay?" Harper winked.

"Yeah… I'll hang here for a while."

"Love ya, dude." Feeling like he'd said everything that mattered, Harper left Alex to his thoughts.

"WHAT do you call these things?" Ian zipped up his jacket. The cold wind blowing off the lake was starting to get to him.

"Booze chairs." Harper sipped his beer and chuckled. "We had booze chairs on our porch at the frat. We used to sit there after class in the afternoons drinking beer and making stupid comments about everyone who walked by."

"Booze chairs. You never told me you were in a frat. How'd *that* work out for you?" Ian stared out at the lake. It was getting dark enough to see the bright lights on a tanker slowly heading into the Port of Duluth.

"Well, it wasn't a social frat, but it was still hell. I had, like, seventeen crushes on guys at the same time. I can't believe I still managed to get the grades I did. It was like a wet dream that never ended."

"Binky was very frustrated, I'll bet." Ian shook his head sadly.

"Oh man, Binky was rubbed so raw, he almost fell off." They both laughed.

Ian reached over for Harper's hand. "You think Alex is going to be all right?"

"Yeah. He's so angry. I believe him when he says he's happy his old man is gone. He's tired of being humiliated. Think about it, having to go home to that loser all the time. Shouldering the burden your dad's a drunk while all the other kids went home to what Alex imagined were normal, healthy parents, even though half of them probably weren't. He couldn't have known that."

"That's true." Even though it was hard to comprehend, Ian understood how Alex could feel the way he did.

"I remember a good friend of mine in law school was having issues with depression. Anyway, after talking it out with a therapist, it was determined the guy had a ton of guilt associated with the fact he hated his family. Not only were they madly dysfunctional, they were cruel. His parents used to ground him for weeks at a time, making him sleep on the floor of his room instead of on his bed. I mean, we're talking wicked folk here."

"Stuff like that makes me sick. I wonder how people who are cruel like that can live with themselves. I'm so lucky to have the family I have. You too, Harper." Ian squeezed his hand.

"Anyway, this guy obviously knew early on something about them wasn't good. He kept fighting his true feelings." Harper sipped his beer. "The therapist basically told him he was dealt a bad hand. It happened. He pointed out to my friend how many people move away from their families because they can't deal with them. My friend didn't do this. He tried to stick it out and make it work. The therapist advised him to kick them to the curb and move on. Funny, that little bit of advice was all it took. Hey." Harper looked at his watch. "We should go back and see if Allison and Spencer are still up. I highly doubt it, though. We ran their asses off today."

"I'm really glad Alex found his way into our lives. I hope he sticks around here for a while. This is kind of weird...." Ian searched for the perfect way to communicate his feelings.

"What's weird?" Harper picked up his beer and stood.

"I can see Alex being a part of us, growing old with us. I think he's good for us." Ian drained the last of his beer and got up out of his chair.

"Like family, you mean?"

"Yeah, that's what I meant." Ian planted a smooch on Harper's cheek. "Come on, Bink. I need to check you for ticks."

Epilogue

"WHOA, sugar, aren't you just about the cutest little thing I've ever seen? Check this boy out, Pearl, he's like *sugar*. Honey, let me have a little teeny tiny touch, okayyyy?"

Colin smiled from ear to ear while a towering drag queen dragged her fingertip over his underwear-clad butt to the small of his naked back.

"Move over, Sasha. Let *me* have a little slice of pie," Pearl begged.

Harper and Ian roared while Colin graciously allowed a small pudgy queen to trace a circle around each of his nipples.

"Pride can end right now, Sasha." Pearl licked the fingers she'd used to stroke Colin. "I feel like I've died and gone to heaven. Baby, you are one… fine… sugarrrrrr-coated nugget."

"Girl, I have to get you to our float before you melt like the ugly old witch you are. We can't let down all the happy homos from Rochester." Sasha grabbed Pearl by the arm and hauled her away. "Have a fantastic Pride, dumplin'! Thanks for the freebies."

"Happy Pride," Colin and everyone on the float cheered as they watched the sequined queens saunter away in their mile-high heels.

"Colin, you're one hell of a good sport. Alex, how you ever talked your best… your *straight* best friend into marching in the Pride Parade is beyond me." Allison laughed.

"He loves to have his butt played with. Doesn't care who does it." Alex punched Colin in the arm before retreating behind Ian, who was busy adding the last few stems of plastic flowers to the "Palisade Beach Cabins Sponsored by Jungle Gems" Pride float.

"Hey, guys, happy Pride!" Brent rounded the back corner of the float.

"Brent, you made it. Happy Pride, dude." Harper jumped to the ground for a hug.

"Hey, what gives?" Alex slid in under Harper, giving Brent a hug. "I thought we had a deal."

"Hold on to your horses, stud boy." Brent stepped back and peeled off his shirt.

"Yes! Yes! Yes!" Alex chanted.

Next he undid his belt and dropped his cargos, revealing a pair of skimpy white underwear identical to those worn by Alex and Colin.

"Woohoo!" a few onlookers cheered, clapping their appreciation at the impromptu striptease.

"Okay, before we get going, I want you guys to line up next to our float. We need some beefcake footage for posterity." Spencer positioned Alex and Colin, with Brent, the shorter of the three, in the center. "If this video somehow finds its way onto the Internet and I show up driving a brand new Lexus, I had nothing to do with it."

"Woohoo!" The onlookers cheered while the three nearly naked twinks preened and posed for the camera. Alex stuck a rose stem down the front of his shorts, mugging for more cheers from the crowd.

Ian looked up to the sky and smiled. *What a perfect day.* He'd never imagined feeling this good. *You're one lucky man, Ian Burke.* Reaching over, he kissed Harper on the cheek.

"What was that for?" Harper kissed him back.

"Just a little pre-parade kiss."

"And to think we get to do it all over again this fall for Duluth Superior Pride."

Ian watched the three young men work the crowd in their tighty whities. "Wow, is there something going on between Brent and Alex?"

"I was wondering about that too, but I don't think so." Harper leaned over and planted a kiss on Ian. "He'd probably never admit it, but Alex is too damned independent to settle for one guy. He's got the world to explore. I have a feeling we're going to have our hands full with him. And Brent, well, he's kind of like that too. Fuck buddies, maybe?"

"Fuck buddies. Yep, I can see that. What's that?" Ian looked around, trying to determine the location of the muffled music.

"It's my phone." Harper pulled it out of his pocket and stared at the screen. "Oh no."

"What do you mean, oh no? It's Andy, right?" Ian was sure it was Andy calling to tell them they'd be late.

"I wish. It's Audrey."

"Oh no." Ian watched as Harper answered the call.

"Hello, this is Harper. Hi, Audrey, what's up?" Harper bit his lip with a look of worry while he listened. After a few seconds, his face relaxed. "That's so sweet. Ian and I sure appreciate you stepping in for us so we can be here. We owe you one, big-time. No, absolutely not. We'll be back around six, I would think." Harper covered his phone. "She wants us to stay down here tonight if we want."

"Nope." Ian shook his head.

"Thanks heaps for offering, but we'll be back to take over by six at the latest. Okay, hang on." Harper covered the phone again. "Alex, get your hot little butt cheeks over here."

"What's up, boss?" Alex hopped up on the float.

"Talk to your mother." Harper handed over his phone.

"Oh." Alex giggled. "Hi, Audrey. It's amazing. I wish you could see it. There are drag queens and rainbows... everywhere. I'll be safe. I love you too. Bye!"

"Hey, they're starting to move up ahead." Ian checked his watch. *Dammit, Andy! Where the hell are you and Emmett?*

"Where's Andy and Emmett? It's showtime." Allison tossed a piece of candy at him.

"I don't know. But I'm starting to get pissed off. How could they be late for *this*? And they're supposed to be bringing T-shirts to throw out. Harper, can you try Andy again and see if he picks up? The parade's starting."

"Sure."

"I'll kill those two if they miss this." Ian forced the last of his plastic flowers into the floral archway in the center of the float.

"He's not—" Harper stopped midsentence.

"What's the matter? Did you... oh... my... God." Ian felt his mouth drop open.

"Happy Pride, everyone!" Andy, dressed in black leather chaps, matching vest, and a leather biker's cap, gave a hearty tug on a leash he was holding. Emmett, dressed in skimpy leather shorts and nothing else but a studded collar attached to the other end of the leash, came flying around the corner of the float holding a box of T-shirts.

"Sorry we're so late. We met some people for the Bears and Cubs breakfast this morning, and it ran a little late."

"Here." Emmett, all smiles, presented the box to Ian.

"Bears and Cubs breakfast?" Ian, clueless, looked over to Harper. "Did you know anything about this?"

"Let's just say I stumbled onto a clue awhile back. I'll tell you later." Harper jumped down and hugged both the men. Ian followed.

"You guys did a great job finishing up the float. By far the best one we've seen so far." Andy tugged on the leash. "Doesn't it look fabulous, Em?"

"Yeah." Emmett giggled.

"Yeah?" Andy fired off a quick swat to Emmett's behind.

"Sorry." Emmett blushed. "I mean, *yes, Sir!*"

"That's my boy."

"Ian?"

"Yeah... sorry, but damn that was funny." Ian laughed so hard tears rolled down his cheeks.

"Well, come on, say it. What do you think?" Andy beamed as he looked down on Emmett.

"I...." Ian thought for moment. "I think you guys look totally awesome. You want to walk or ride the parade?"

"If you don't mind, Em and I would like to march with the Leather Knights. We've been spending a lot of time with them lately."

Andy and Emmett looked so happy. "Come here, you loveable numbskulls." Ian hugged them as hard as he could. "You guys do your thing. We'll catch up with you after the parade."

"Okay." Andy gave the leash a jerk. "Come on, boy."

"Yes, Sir!"

"Have a great Pride!" Andy and Emmett waved, disappearing into the crowd.

"We're up! Everyone ready?" Spencer hollered from the cab of his truck with Allison at his side.

Ian and Harper jumped up on the float. "Ready," they shouted.

"Palisadettes? You boys ready?" Allison shouted out her window.

"Ready," Alex, Colin, and Brent hollered back.

"Ride 'em wet and ride 'em hard!" Spencer gave the horn a few quick blasts, and they were off.

"Feelin' proud, Mr. Callahan?" Ian threw his arm around his handsome partner, pecking him on the cheek.

"Proud and blessed, Mr. Burke!"

JOEL SKELTON lives with his partner in the thriving Minnesota arts community commonly referred to as the Twin Cities. Writing is the latest destination in the author's tour of the arts. When he's not writing, scamming on a character, creating a chapter outline, or editing a portion of his manuscript on the bus in and out of the city, he's playing law firm—a whacky, highly entertaining way to put food on the table.

Visit his web site at http://www.joelskelton.com.

Also from JOEL SKELTON

http://www.dreamspinnerpress.com

www.ingramcontent.com/pod-product-compliance
Lightning Source LLC
Chambersburg PA
CBHW070056030726
47506CB00002B/487